I0760638

OF AIR AND MEN

a novel by

Damien Lay

OF AIR AND MEN

The author has tried to recreate events, locales, and conversations from their memories of them, and in other instances has interpreted historical events in a fictitious manner. In order to maintain their anonymity in some instances, the author has changed the names of individuals and places, and may have changed some identifying characteristics and details such as physical properties, occupations, and places of residence.

Published in Australia by Busybird Publishing

Distributed in Australia by Busybird Publishing

ISBN-13: 978-1-923501-59-1

First edition 2025

dedicated to

John 'Jack' Hodder and Edward 'Ted' Wixted

and

to all those who supported them

and

to those who continue

CHAPTER 1

Gulf of Martaban
Burma. 1935.

It was a beautiful night to die. Unlike the many they had seen before, it would be on this night—on this ship—when the still calm of the glassy sea beneath them, dancing with the reflection of a moon surrounded by a million stars, would call their name.

'Charles!' Tommy screamed, his voice slicing through the thick tropical heat clinging to the early morning air. Exhaust and smoke—heavy with the sharp taste of burning oil—blasted through the shattered protection where a windshield once was. The open cockpit canopies did little to vent the smoke-laden acrid stench penetrating the firewall. Their eyes stung. Their airways tightened.

They knew.

The ship's engine—once powerful and strong—now roared like a wounded beast, tortured and dying, thrashing in the throes of its final breath. The vast wastelands of the oceans over which she had soared, proud and steadfast, stretched before them no more.

'I have control!' Charles yelled over the noise, his voice calm amid the chaos rapidly closing in.

They knew.

Her propeller vibrated recklessly, furiously inflicting gaping wounds upon her. The sound of tearing metal and cracking timber filled their ears—deafening—as she was shredded from within. Flesh torn from her hull, flung violently into the sky, left a trail of agony in her wake.

They knew.

They had passed that point.

'Call it!' Charles yelled again—loud, steady, unwavering. His hands moved with precision, finessing the controls with a tender pressure born of instinct. He breathed deep, slow, measured breaths. Sweat trickled from his brow, but his focus remained sharp.

'Fifty!' Tommy called. His eyes, blurred from tears, flicked from instrument to instrument in a dance of calculation. The control panel flared with urgency—every gauge screaming fate, every needle sealing it.

'Twenty!'

Charles had met death many times before—shaken its hand and walked away.

We have a deal, he reminded himself, the words echoing defiantly through the chambers of his mind.

'Ten!'

Against the fury of the failing ship, he pressed back—guiding her down gently, deliberately—taming her wrath, soothing her torment.

'Five!'

They breathed. Braced.

Impact.

She hit hard—instantly spinning, twisting, then upturning violently before plunging nose-first. The force ripped her heart from her chest.

They slammed into the controls, bodies thrown forward, brutally, in the surreal silence of semi-consciousness. Ears ringing. Blind in the darkness, rapidly swallowing them.

On a shallow lungful of air, Charles clambered, searching for a handhold, his mind battling the pressure, the weight of the water crushing his chest. His heart pounded, clawing for escape. His lungs screamed.

Seconds passed.

Charles broke the surface, gasping, the saltwater stinging deep into his lungs. He breathed hard amid the hiss of steam and air rising turbulently from below—like the ghostly whisper of a thousand drowning souls in the emptiness of night.

'Tommy!' he yelled, voice raw and desperate. No reply.

'Tommy!' Again. Again.

The realization set in—dark, gnawing. Tommy was still inside.

'Tommy!'

He refilled his lungs—large, long, deep. Chest heaving. Charles dove toward the stern as it began to rise perilously, the water pressing in from all sides, the darkness swallowing him whole.

'No, no, no!' he breathed. Painfully. Lungs expanding to capacity.

He dived beneath the ship's sinking mass, the water closing over him like a shroud.

Seconds stretched into eternity.

Below, he grappled, feeling for Tommy in the black water, wrestling against time to free him from the confines of the cockpit. His lungs ballooned under the pressure. The need for air became sharp, insistent, stabbing pain.

He could not see. The darkness disoriented every move as he pulled Tommy this way and that, desperate to free him.

Time passed—seconds into minutes, more than should be possible.

Above, a silent calm crept back in—

—until suddenly Charles broke the surface, Tommy blue in his arms.

'Tommy!' he screamed amid gasping breath. 'Tommy! Look at me!' He clutched Tommy's chin, desperate to find life in him.

'No, no! Don't you—Tommy, no! Come on, Tommy!' He begged. But there was no reply.

Tommy's eyes were closed. His face, blue.

'No, Tommy! No!' Charles screamed, shaking him, denying the stillness in his arms.

A low whimper—not from Tommy, but from the ship—before it slipped quietly away into the depths beneath them.

Flailing in the isolation, left behind, Charles held on. Defiant. Not letting go.

Straining against the weight of his bearskin suit, his gloves were heavy, his boots were full, water consumed the fabric tightening around him, restricting every movement—he clung to hope, to Tommy, to life.

'Tommy, come on!' he pleaded, the water lapping at his nostrils, the taste of salt bitter on his lips.

'Tommy, you got to help me!'

Scraping. Kicking. Clawing. Fighting for every inch toward survival.

'We ain't goin' out like this.'

Determined.

'We can make it.'

The shoreline rose and sank before him. Close. Yet far.

He reached for it—dragging, pulling, gasping—

His breaths, narrowing.

His muscles, burning.

'We can make it, Tommy!'

Desperate was the prayer.

'I got you, Tommy. We can make it.'

His voice willed belief into the impossibility of a body failing him—muscles cramped, his heart pounded against the current, strong, too strong.

'We're gonna make it, Tommy!' he gasped again and again, chest collapsing.

'We are going to make it.'

Straining.

'Tommy.'

Fading.

'Tommy.'

Exhausted.

He drew Tommy close—his final strength spent—whispering with heartbreaking sadness, 'We are gonna make it.'

Softly.

'We are gonna make it.'

His plea faded, as together, they were absorbed into the restored tranquility of the glassy sea above them, dancing in the reflection of a moon surrounded by a million stars.

CHAPTER 2

Gulf of Martaban
Burma. 2012.

Eerie was the silence that lingered over their fate—unknown, a mystery unsolved. The many left behind were left to wonder, to grieve, to live with loss.

The years would come—and come to pass. Their memory would fade, forgotten by the many, remembered by the few, vanquished into the quiet of history, legend, and mystery, as the slow march of time moved onward from the era in which they roamed— An era where men, untrammeled by earthly things, could look far into a new horizon and be free.

The ocean would keep its secrets, as it does—

Holding them beneath the dark veil of its depths, offering no hope, no comfort, no closure.

For years, the rich change of seasons would stir. The once smooth, silky waters would be rippled by the tender teardrops of pounding monsoonal rain. Dark clouds—heavy, bursting with electric thunder—would fill the skies. The once gentle breeze would swell into cyclonic winds, churning the sea into a ferocious whitewash of rampant carnage.

Whispering—

To those willing to listen.

It would call *my* name, as it had called the names of those who had gone before.

'Damien!' Aung Kyaw yelled, his voice cutting through the storm. The bow of the small timber fishing boat split each sickening wave, puncturing forward with each surge. Its single-cylinder engine thumped hard, straining against the relentless onslaught of the unforgiving ocean.

'Damien!' Aung Kyaw called again, standing perilously on the foredeck, his body braced against the fury of the sea, his voice lost to the wind. He paused between cries, his hawkish eyes scanning the darkness.

'Damien!' he called once more, the name swallowed into the tempest.

The boat pitched and rolled violently. Each impact sent a shudder through the timbers from bow to stern. Salt water and driving rain drenched everything and everyone aboard. Mark struggled to stay upright on a deck slick with oil and diesel, wrestling with four unsecured oxygen bottles slamming into each other.

'Come on!' he gritted through clenched teeth, straining to free the ratchet strap holding them.

The boat groaned and twisted beneath them, its timbers exhausted. The coir caulking barely held back the sea, which seeped through like a slow, thousand-cut death.

The air reeked of failing damp wood and the acrid burn of black diesel, the engine thumping with an ear splitting tone.

Rain hammered the deck, heavy droplets pelting down like stones, bouncing into mist. Tattered tarpaulins snapped with whip-cracking sharp

Below, two army soldiers braced in a corner of the lower deck, indifferent. Their focus was on their rifles, shielding them from the downpour, uniforms soaked and clinging to their bodies. They looked more at home in a jungle than on this heaving, groaning deck.

Mark checked his watch, then left the gear. His expression said enough as he shouted to Aung Kyaw.

'That's twenty, A. K. He should've been up by now.'

'I not see him. Nowhere. Min nah goh thet nay talla!' Aung Kyaw shouted back.

'What?'

'You try to kill onto him again, Mark! You know he pay za bill, right? Right?' A. K. laughed, waving wildly. 'Swel! Swel! Faster!' he yelled to the boatmen, their teeth stained red from betel nut, the intoxicant dulling hunger and pain.

Crude flashlights swept over the black water. Their beams flickered uselessly in the rain, barely piercing the night.

'Ho mhar! Ho mhar! Myan myan!' one boatman shouted, and the other spun the vessel.

'Mark! He there, he there!' Aung Kyaw cried.

His body tumbled helplessly in the wash, rising and vanishing with each wave.

Mark and Aung Kyaw clambered quickly to the right to starboard.

'He ain't responding, A. K.!' Mark screamed.

'Twar mei! Twar! Twar!'—commands fired rapidly among the crew as they closed in.

A wave lifted the bow, then slammed the diver hard against the hull. Arms stretched over the gunnel, reaching.

'Closer!' Mark yelled.

'Bel! Bel!' Aung Kyaw echoed, as another wave smashed the vessel down.

'Now!' Mark shouted. They leaned hard, braced at the hips, grasping for anything.

Frantic and uncoordinated, the boatmen scrambled, finally hooking and dragging the diver's waterlogged body aboard. Their hands were raw, bleeding from the rough timber. Splinters dug deep, but they kept working—driven by instinct and duty.

It was a contrast of urgency and apathy. Shouts, roaring sea, and blank-faced soldiers. A night of violence and survival.

'Ma ma! Ma!' the boatmen cried as Damien hit the deck hard; the thud echoed through the hull, knocking the wind back into him as he gasped, then coughed, water and blood expelled from his lungs. He coughed, choked—then grinned through blood-filled gums.

'Man. That ain't good,' he rasped, voice thin but laced with that perverse humor.

Mark stepped in quickly as the boatmen stripped off Damien's tank and dive gear. The wet suit clung to his body, clammy and suffocating.

'Aung Kyaw—water!' Mark demanded, checking the dive cylinder gauge.

He tapped it twice, scowling.

'You're empty.'

Damien coughed more through a bloody laugh.

'Again? You gotta start putting more air in these things.' He spat blood, tasting iron.

'You were down for twenty-two minutes. Any longer, you'd be bent.'

'I am already bent Mark,' Damien laughed, wincing as pain lanced his side. 'Ah man, think I burst a lung,' he moaned.

Aung Kyaw returned with a half-full bottle of Grand Royal whiskey.

'A. K., I said water.'

'No water. This better,' Aung Kyaw said earnestly.

Damien downed a fifth, it wasn't just whiskey, it was the kind of whiskey run through lead pipes, good whiskey that rotted your brain cells and sent you mad. The burn cleansed the blood and salt from his smile as he probed a cracked tooth with his tongue.

'Damn it.' He coughed again, accepting a lit cigarette from Aung Kyaw.

'Thanks, brother.'

'You don't give a damn, do you?' Mark muttered, frustrated.

Damien drew deep on the cigarette, exhaling into the storm.

'Sooner or later.' His voice was calm now, too calm. His eyes still burned.

Mark shook his head.

'What am I meant to do with your body if you die out here?'

The question hung like a weight in the wind.

'Don't stress, Mark. Just throw it in the icebox. FedEx it back to Australia.'

Aung Kyaw chuckled.

'We have only DHL now. Same same.'

'So, if anything happens, I get posted home?'

'Yeah.' Damien grinned.

'Don't worry, mate. I'll be sure to put plenty of fragile stickers on the box.'

Aung Kyaw laughed.

'Stop your worry Mark, Damien worry on you, Mark. He like the brother. He worry when you dive, all time worry worry worry,' Aung Kyaw said in Burmese, voice softer now.

'What did he say?' Mark asked.

'He said we're running out of time. Get your gear on,' Damien lied, eyes sharp.

'This is insane. I'm not diving in this, man.'

'It's just rain, Mark. Stop moaning and get in the water.'

'I'm not moaning!'

'Mark. You're moaning,' Damien insisted, nodding to Aung Kyaw.

'Stops squealin' likesss zaa pig boy,' Aung Kyaw recited, grinning.

'What? Did you teach him that?' Mark asked as Damien simply responded with a laugh.

'You're insane.' Mark furthered.

'I know,' Damien confirmed as Aung Kyaw and the boatmen slowly assisted him to his feet.

'This is insane,' Mark affirmed. 'You found the thing four years ago. No one cares. No one cares about this, cares about you, me or what we are doing, I am pretty sure by now that would be pretty damn obvious to you,' Mark blasted, the frustration and stupidity realized.

'I need more,' Damien replied, refusing the truth.

'How more do you want?'

'More.'

'I'm not dying for this, Damien. Neither are you,' he replied.

Through Mark's protest Damien casually picked a rifle left unattended in the chaos and calmly chambered a round. The soldiers, quick to notice, yelled, raising their rifles toward him.

'Mark, you can die up here, or you can die down there,' Damien said evenly.

Mark froze, calculating as he shook his head in dismay.

Then—'Aung Kyaw, hand me my mask.'

Laughing, Aung Kyaw shoved the gear into his chest.

'You be okay. No problem.'

Damien lowered the rifle, handing it over as the soldiers lowered their aim.

'Last one, Mark.'

'You said that last time.' Mark replied.

'You'll be right. Just watch for crocs.'

Aung Kyaw walked away, muttering:

'Stops squeeealin' likes zaa pig boyyy.'

'Yeah. Like I'm gonna see 'em.'

'Don't stress, Mark. We've got plenty of ice.'

'You're insane.'

'I know.' Damien took another shot of whiskey and turned away, leaving the pair.

'You know he joking, right?' Aung Kyaw explained with a smile.

'What?'

'Ya ya. He not make you dive. It like the test.'

'Thanks, mate!' Mark yelled upon the realization.

Damien smiled.

'I'm gonna kill him, A. K.,' Mark continued.

'Not if he kill onto you first,' Aung Kyaw laughed. 'You both like the crazy. Damien nearly die seven time. You only three. He beat you!' Aung Kyaw laughed outrageously.

The night was long. The storm had departed to the east with the same speed it had arrived, clearing the skies and calming the sea. Now, the only sound was the faint dripping of water, each drop echoing in the stillness.

Damien smoked, waiting for sunrise and the new day. He hadn't slept, watching as a million stars emerged from cover.

As he looked south, down the long stretch of coastline, something unfamiliar caught his eye—something he had never seen from this location before. It was a sign. The Southern Cross lay on her side, low on the horizon. His eyes checked, then checked again. There she was.

'Ha,' he murmured in awe. Visible only in the Southern Hemisphere, she had risen—this time—for him. As if only to remind.

Beneath the velvet canopy of the southern sky, where midnight blue merged seamlessly with the void, she rested.

Damien breathed her in.

Known to astronomers as Crux, the Southern Cross held a near-mystical significance for those who knew her. She was a celestial compass, guiding explorers and adventurers for centuries across the treacherous waters of the Southern Hemisphere.

Each of her five stars carried its own tale, but together they formed a cruciform beacon of light. Alpha Crucis, the brightest, shimmered like a diamond, anchoring the constellation in the firmament—a symbol of constancy, unwavering through the ages.

To her left, Beta Crucis gleamed with cool, sapphire brilliance, evoking the deep, uncharted ocean below.

Gamma Crucis, tinged in ruby red, burned like a fierce southern heart—a beacon of passion and defiance, a reminder that beneath the still surface of the sea, tremendous currents stirred.

Delta Crucis and Epsilon Crucis, though less radiant, completed the form—embodying the symmetry and quiet strength that bound the constellation together.

To those who traveled under her light, she was more than a pattern in the sky. She was a guidepost. A symbol of direction and hope. A reminder that even in the darkest night, there are beacons to follow.

Damien watched as she faded into the pale blue of early dawn.

The sun of Burma rose slowly, casting a gentle pink hue across the horizon, shrouded in the silk of morning mist. Its light spilled softly across the small island of Aye to the west, illuminating the dense jungle in rich, wet green. As it climbed, the sun brushed the summit that loomed over the anchored vessel, leaving the crew nestled deep in its shadow.

The calm, mud-brown sea lapped gently against the granite boulders along the island's rocky shore. It stood there—monolithic, stoic—untouched by time. Pristine. As if the past had not passed. As if the events that had occurred still lingered, echoing in the stone.

To the east, the formidable Palen Mountains stretched across the mainland—a natural fortress of impenetrable jungle and ancient stone. They concealed what watched from within. By night, the People's Army lit their fires in the high ridgelines, a reminder to Damien they were there. By day, they remained silent—hidden behind scratched lenses—they watched the operation from deep within.

Once a friend—security—they were now the pursuant. Across the many expeditions over the past years, the political landscape had shifted. What was once cooperation had turned to quiet conflict. The militia was now at war with the government, and Damien had become a target of value.

Though the militia posed a distant threat on land, their rifles well out of range, at sea the real danger lay further north—pirates. Frequent reports of their presence and the looming threat of raids made every passage perilous, casting a constant shadow of concern over the crew.

The nights were the worst—long and exposed, when they were most vulnerable to attack. Darkness provided perfect cover. Someone was always on watch.

Damien sat heavily at the stern of the vessel, penning a letter, lost in the solitude of thought as he waited for the tide to turn.

The sticky morning air clung to his skin as he smoked his breakfast—the cool, smooth taste of Marlboro mingling with the bitter remnants of the long night. He exhaled slowly, his mind adrift in the haze of memory.

Below deck, the boatmen slept soundly in makeshift hammocks swaying gently beneath the beams—five-star luxury compared to the soldiers, who spooned their rifles on what little bamboo deck remained.

The lingering damp brought no comfort, but it helped keep the mosquitoes at bay.

Aung Kyaw lay curled awkwardly among the dive gear, a rolled-up wet suit serving as a mattress. He snored like a baby, undisturbed.

The peaceful quiet was broken only by the soft cries of two sea eagles overhead, circling in the morning updrafts as they dried their wings. Damien watched them descend with grace, talons gripping fresh catch still twitching—plucked from the ocean just moments before.

They nested in two dead trees perched high on the island's eastern headland. Long since lifeless, only the soft gray bones of their trunks remained. Like cathedral spires, they rose above the dense green canopy sprawling beneath them—monuments standing tall over history.

Damien folded the letter carefully, placing it into the breast pocket of his tattered, war-worn expedition shirt. The embroidered sponsor logos that once gleamed with pride had long since faded.

He looked slowly around the deck. All was quiet. Mark was asleep, slumped against a dive cylinder for support, his head resting uncomfortably on a crumpled tarp. He looked peaceful—until an empty baked bean tin sailed through the air and struck him in the shoulder.

The impact stirred him.

'What?' Mark groaned, unappreciative of the early wake-up call. He didn't need to check to know who had thrown it.

'You alright?' Damien asked softly.

'I was.'

'Get up,' Damien whispered.

Mark looked at his watch.

'It's five in the morning,' he moaned.

'Get up.'

With a sigh, Mark dragged himself over beside Damien, still half asleep.

'Give me a cigarette.'

He lit it in silence, inhaled deeply, then exhaled with the weight of it all.

'I can't do this anymore,' he confessed, weary-eyed, the sleepless night still etched across his face.

'I'm surprised you lasted this long,' Damien replied.

'Lasted longer than the others.'

'Ha. True.'

'You're just tired. What's this? Your sixth or seventh?'

'Seventh, I think. Yeah,' Mark said, not entirely sure. The expeditions had long since blurred into one long, waking nightmare.

'Most of them didn't even make it through the first.'

'No.'

'You know this is impossible, right?' Mark said quietly.

'So they keep telling me.'

'Damien, no one is interested. This is impossible. You're not going to find what you're looking for.'

Damien nodded, smiling as he lit another cigarette.

'Yeah.'

He looked up, directing Mark's gaze toward the eagles perched in their nest.

'See those guys up there?'

'What?' Mark asked, squinting.

'The one on the left—that's Aaungpwel. The one on the right, Bhay-andayel.'

'Huh?'

'Yeah. Triumph and Disaster. Rudyard Kipling, the two imposters.' Damien paused.

'They've been with us on every expedition.'

Mark stared at him blankly.

'Mark, nothing is impossible.'

Damien looked cautiously over the deck, making sure no eyes were on him. From inside his shirt, he pulled a small, balled-up cloth. Unfolding it with care, he revealed a tiny piece of wreckage—no larger than the palm of his hand. Encrusted in thick marine growth, it was almost unrecognizable as a relic.

'What's that?' Mark asked.

Damien handed it over.

'That,' he said with quiet pride, 'is what I've been looking for.'

Mark turned the object over in his hands, studying it carefully. His tired eyes flickered with something else—understanding.

He smiled.

'Great. Can I go home now?'

'What for? I thought you were having a great time,' Damien said, grinning.

His laugh wasn't exactly an answer.

CHAPTER 3

Yangon, Burma. 2012.

The thick, humid air of the bustling third-world city choked with pollution, heavy traffic, and the incessant noise of a never-ending sea of people.

'Aung Kyaw, you're killing me. How much further?' Damien groaned, melting in the furnace-like interior of the idle taxi, caught in peak-time gridlock.

'Ha, ha! Ney nago thet nee dhalla! I trying to kill on you,' Aung replied with a playful laugh.

'This not so far. It took me three whole days to find this dentist!' he added, clearly feeling under-appreciated. 'There are no dentists in Myanmar—this is what I try to explain to you. This is why no one here has the teeth! You see this. You know this. Why you not listen to me?' Aung Kyaw pushed back.

His complaint was cut short by the shrill ring of his phone. 'Hang tight. Mingalabah!' Aung Kyaw answered quickly.

The driver watched them closely in the rearview mirror, his eyes filled with suspicious curiosity as he listened to Aung Kyaw's cautious tone. Damien shifted uneasily, avoiding the driver's gaze, assuming it was simply the rare sight of a westerner sweating through his clothes in an unairconditioned cab that drew the man's attention.

But Aung Kyaw's tone was different—tense. Serious. Damien, though he couldn't decipher the language, felt every syllable tighten in his chest. Aung Kyaw kept repeating a phrase that stood out.

'Hote kelt bar,' he said. Again and again.

Damien recognized it: Burmese for 'I understand' or 'Do you understand?'

'Hote kelt bar.' Aung Kyaw hung up.

'All good?' Damien asked, sweat clinging to him, thick with both heat and dread.

Aung Kyaw didn't answer right away. He reached out, hand trembling slightly.

'Give me a cigarette, Damien. Please.'

Damien handed one over. Aung Kyaw lit it with a shaky breath.

'Hote kelt. Here is the situation.' He inhaled, buying time.

'That was the Ministry of Information. Mr. Kyaw. He call to you with . . . not-so-good news. Mr. Kyaw knows you recovered some wreckage.'

'The hell, Aung Kyaw!' Damien snapped, panic spiking.

'I know, I know! I don't know how this is possible. Maybe he's guessing on this situation—'

'How the hell, Aung Kyaw?' Damien shouted, fist clenched he slammed the headrest in front of him.

'This is the Ministry of Information. The MOI, Damien—they know everything. All the time.'

Damien shook his head; the frustration was clearly evident.

'Maybe they have the spy somewhere,' Aung Kyaw offered. 'I don't understand it either.'

'Damn it, Aung Kyaw!'

'Damien!' Aung Kyaw snapped, defensive now. 'I am just the messenger—clam down!'

'Don't tell me to clam down, Aung Kyaw!'

'Damien, you need to clam down! Let me finish. *Hote kelt bar.* This is not a good situation for you. *Hote kelt bar.*'

'No shit, Aung Kyaw,' Damien muttered, catching the nervous glances from the driver, who clearly didn't understand the context but definitely understood the tone.

'They want your report on the discovery.'

'When?'

'Today.'

'Damn!' Damien growled, checking his watch.

'I told them everything is at my home.'

'The monastery?'

'Yes. Everything, I am holding there. They're okay with this—for now.'

Damien leaned forward, urgency in his voice. 'MOI doesn't know what we found, right?'

'Exactly this,' Aung Kyaw reassured him as the traffic finally began to crawl forward.

'But MOI swore on to me—you not take the discovery with you when you leave from Myanmar. I have no suggestion for you, Damien. I don't know on this.'

Damien ran both hands down his face, the weight of it all crashing in.

'Aung Kyaw, after all this. . . .'

The anguish clung to his voice like the heat to his skin.

Stepping into the surgery raised immediate concern. Aung Kyaw, noticing the expression of concern fall over Damien's face, slapped him on the shoulder and laughed.

'This it. This all I can find.'

The interior presented a stark, unsettling scene. Once-white walls had yellowed and peeled, patches of mold and grime clinging to the corners. The air was thick with a musty odor, layered with the sharp, metallic scent of rusting equipment. The chaos of the city faded behind them, replaced by an eerie quiet, broken only by the occasional honk and the distant murmur of street vendors outside.

The dental chair—once a symbol of modern care—was cracked and worn. Its leather upholstery was torn and stained. The metal frame was speckled with rust, the foot pedals caked in dirt.

Outdated, corroded dental tools lay scattered across dusty countertops. Once-gleaming instruments were dulled and tarnished, some still bearing faint traces of blood and other residues.

Cabinet doors hung ajar, revealing a chaotic tangle of old supplies: faded boxes of rubber gloves, brittle gauze, and discolored syringes. Glass jars filled with unknown liquids sat forgotten, their labels curling at the edges.

The sink, intended for sterilization, was stained and clogged, with a leaky tap dripping steadily into a grimy basin. The floor was a mosaic of cracked tiles—some missing altogether—exposing dirt-streaked concrete beneath. Cobwebs clung to the ceiling corners.

A single flickering overhead bulb provided the only light, casting warped shadows across the room. It felt less like a surgery and more like a relic—abandoned, haunted by the ghosts of patients and practitioners long gone. A place frozen in time, slowly being consumed by it.

Masks on, the dentist entered, trailed by a nurse. He was barely five feet tall.

Damien looked at the instruments laid out beside the chair—rust, dust, mystery stains. Still, he slid wearily into the seat. Aung Kyaw grinned wide, proudly.

'They fix your tooth. Only five dollars US. Cheap!' He laughed, delighted.

'Aung Kyaw, it's been like an hour, we need to stop. I need to go for a smoke,' Damien mumbled mid-procedure, his jaw aching.

'No, no,' Aung Kyaw replied, lighting a cigarette and handing it to the nurse. She carefully placed it between Damien's lips, letting him draw before applying suction so the dentist could continue.

'Aung Kyaw! This is the best dentist ever!' Damien managed through a mouthful of spit and blood, taking another drag as the suction resumed.

'See? This is why you should trust on me.' Aung Kyaw beamed.

The pain was gone now, though Damien could still feel the uneven edge of the filling when he bit down.

He sat up, groggy, and nodded his thanks to the dentist. 'Mingalabah.'

'Mingalabah,' the dentist replied politely as he lowered his mask, Damien, confused by his youthful features, queried Aung Kyaw with his eyes, as he paid cash.

Outside, the noise of the city returned all at once—the blaring horns, the chatter of vendors, the constant buzz of motorbikes weaving through chaos. Damien and Aung Kyaw lit cigarettes as they stood on the roadside of relentless activity.

'Aung Kyaw. . . how old was that guy?' Damien asked with trepidation.

Aung Kyaw hesitated, then grinned.

'Thirteen.'

'Thirteen! The hell, are you serious Aung Kyaw?'

'No, no, this okay. He learn from his father!' Aung Kyaw laughed. Damien shook his head, bemused.

'Get us a taxi.'

'Where to?' Aung Kyaw asked.

'DHL,' Damien replied, his tone serious.

Aung Kyaw's face lit up with sudden understanding.

'Ohhh, this brilliant idea, Damien!' he said excitedly. 'Do we need ice?'

'Ha!' Damien laughed, 'No ice.'

CHAPTER 4

Montana, United States. 2012.

Nestled among the rolling hills of Montana, the farmhouse radiated a rustic, storybook charm. Its weathered white siding stood in gentle contrast to the sweeping emerald fields stretching to the horizon. A wraparound porch, framed by hanging flower pots and a swaying wooden swing, seemed to beckon passersby to pause and breathe in the beauty of a quieter world.

The surrounding landscape was nothing short of idyllic. Distant mountains loomed like silent guardians, their sunlit peaks casting a golden hue over the valley below. Overhead, the sky unfurled in a vast expanse of cobalt, brushed with cotton-white clouds. A narrow dirt path, lined with blooming wildflowers, wound from the farmhouse to a shimmering lake, where the water mirrored the sky and the whispering trees along its shore.

Birdsong laced the air, joined by the soft rustle of leaves in the breeze. Here, time moved at its own pace. The farmhouse offered more than shelter—it offered solace, a return to simpler pleasures.

In the heart of the home, the kettle shrieked atop the old stove, steam curling into the air. The kitchen smelled of bread and baked goods, warm nostalgia baked into every corner. Vintage sunflower wallpaper clung to the walls—faded, but familiar. Wooden cabinets, polished smooth by decades of care, held mismatched dishes and well-loved utensils. Sunlight filtered through lace curtains, casting soft patterns of light and shadow across the checkered linoleum floor.

At the center of it all stood a broad oak table, scarred and stained by time. It had borne witness to celebrations, scraped knees, whispered confessions, and laughter that echoed into memory. The refrigerator door, a patchwork of magnets and photographs, opened and closed like a chapter turning—each image a moment, a story, a reminder of the life lived within these walls.

Mary lifted the kettle from the stove, her gaze drawn to the picturesque landscape beyond the window. She wore her age with grace and quiet confidence. Time had not diminished her elegance—only softened it. Her silver hair, cut into a chic bob, caught the sunlight and framed her face with a subtle glow. High cheekbones, smooth skin, and the lightest touch of makeup spoke not of vanity but of self-respect. Her eyes, a deep, knowing blue, held the richness of a life fully lived.

Mary tied a floral apron over her dress. Her movements were assured and fluid, the result of years spent navigating this space. She eased the kettle off the stove and began assembling a sandwich—simple white bread, butter, and one key ingredient she knew Charles would appreciate. The scent of blooming gardenias drifted in through the open window, mingling with the warmth of the oven.

She paused, glancing into the backyard, its vibrant colors momentarily holding her attention.

'Charles Arthur, how many times have I asked you not to use the kitchen table as a workbench?' she said, not sharply, but with a bemused lilt.

Seated at the table, Charles worked with steady hands on a small aircraft component. His glasses bridged his identifiable nose, aiding his vision, yet he still maintained the focus and resolve of a man who had lived with purpose. His once-light hair had turned silver, combed back neatly to compliment his well-rounded worn features. His sharp blue eyes—still keen, still full of mischief—were fixed on the intricate piece before him.

'Well, remind me who you are again?' he asked, feigning forgetfulness—a familiar game.

'Mary. Your wife. For the last fifty-two years,' she replied, lips quivering into a smile. 'You do have a hangar full of tools, Charles. Why insist on taking over my kitchen?'

'If I stayed in the hangar all day,' he said, setting down his screwdriver, 'I'd miss the pleasure of your company. This is quality time, darling.

She sighed, though the affection in her eyes betrayed her surrender.

'Time may have stolen your looks, Charles, but it hasn't taken your charm.'

'Stolen? I like to think I've aged like fine wine,' he grinned.

'You certainly require decanting.'

She leaned in, kissed his cheek, and admired the completed component. He wiped his hands on a rag, looking proud.

'There we go. Should hold for another decade.'

'Well done. Now, if you're feeling so productive, there's a dishwasher that needs your attention.' She placed the sandwich beside him. 'Here. Your favorite.'

'Vegemite?' he asked, mock surprised. 'To what do I owe the honor?'

'It's your eightieth birthday, Charles. Or has that slipped your mind too?'

'Eighty already? How time flies.' He leaned back, his gaze drifting across the kitchen. Memory softened his features. 'Hard to believe.'

Mary wrinkled her nose. 'I still don't know how you eat that ghastly stuff.'

'Mary! Vegemite is sacred. It's the Australian version of caviar! We all love it. Puts a rose in every cheek,' he sang, mimicking the old jingle.

'If it weren't for Vegemite,' he added with a grin, 'I might not have made it to eighty.'

'If you scratch this table, you might not make it to eighty-one,' she teased.

Laughing, he pulled the sandwich closer and pressed it flat with both hands, leaving faint grease marks on the bread.

'Perfect,' he declared.

'I will never understand why you insist on ruining a perfectly good sandwich.'

'It's a tradition. Every Aussie schoolboy knows.'

'Is that so?'

'Oh yes. Every morning, Mum made my lunch—Vegemite sandwiches—tucked them in a brown paper bag with a note like 'Don't trade with Jack today.' Into the satchel it went with my homework and footy. By midday, after we'd run, wrestled, and kicked our bags around, the sandwiches were as flat as your blueberry pancakes.'

'I see,' Mary said, already picturing it.

'We thought that's how mums made them. Squashed. Tradition.'

He chuckled, then took a bite, closing his eyes in bliss. 'Ah, takes me back.'

'You've told me that story before,' Mary said softly.

'I know. But I like the way you look at me when I tell it.'

She smiled and brushed a hand across his shoulder. 'And I like the look in your eyes when you do.'

He chewed contentedly, then reached for the mail. 'Is this today's?'

'Yes,' she replied. 'There's a letter—from Burma. Looks like it's taken a while to arrive.'

Charles froze mid-motion. The joy in his face dimmed. He set the bundle down, sliding his plate aside.

'I think I'm done here, Mary,' he said quietly, rising from the table.

'You barely touched your sandwich,' she said, a small amount of concern entering her voice.

'I'll save some room for later,' he replied, already walking away.

'The family will be here at six,' she called gently, watching him go.

The door closed behind him with a soft click.

'Oh, Charles,' she murmured, tidying the mail and smoothing the unopened letter with careful hands. 'You're going to have to open them one day.'

Charles busied himself with small, mindless tasks in the hangar, trying to outrun the memories steadily catching up to him. Though not cluttered, the space had grown weary with time. Shelves sagged under the weight of tins, containers, and years of dust. Aviation memorabilia crowded the walls—parts manuals, faded newspaper clippings, sepia-toned photographs of men beside machines, and fragments of history tacked above the workbench like old dreams preserved.

The scent of aged oil and sawdust lingered, mingling with the sharp tang of cleaning solvent in which a drum of paint brushes soaked. A dim, yellowed lamp cast long shadows across the room, deepening the sense of solitude that had settled over the years like a second skin.

Charles knocked the drum accidentally. A swirl of color spilled across the bench, bleeding into a stack of old invoices and forgotten papers. He moved quickly, trying to rescue what he could. Among the mess, several unopened letters slipped loose—letters in handwriting he recognized too well, mirroring the one that had arrived that morning. He froze.

Gently, he wiped each envelope clean, the smudged ink failing to obscure the weight of what was written inside. As he unfolded one, his eyes scanned the lines slowly, cautiously, as if the words might leap off the page and pull him under. His breath caught, the past pressing in from all sides.

A sharp buzz rattled the makeshift intercom connecting house and workshop. Mary's voice crackled through.

'Charles, come wash up. The kids are here.'

He pressed the reply button, leaving a streak of paint behind.

'I'll be up shortly.'

He clipped the damp letters to a wire above his bench, watching them sway like ghosts in the low light. Before he could turn away, the buzzer crackled again.

'Granddad, where are you? Granddad.'

Genevieve's small voice, aided by her father, Stephen, chirped through the static.

'Say happy birthday, Granddad,' Stephen coaxed.

'Happy birthday, Granddad?' she echoed sweetly.

Charles exhaled deeply, a smile forming. He stared at the drying letters, the weight of their contents settling slowly over him.

'You know, Charles . . . maybe it is time,' he whispered to himself.

As the day faded into dusk, a gentle breeze teased the curtains in the bedroom. Mary sat at her vanity, running a brush through her hair with a steady, familiar rhythm. Her reflection, framed in warm lamplight, softened her features and restored a whisper of youth.

'It was nice to see the kids,' she said, her tone content, but thoughtful.

'It was,' Charles replied from the edge of the bed, dressed for sleep, a letter still in hand. The one from Damien. It hadn't left his side all evening.

'I spilled paint down in the workshop—covered these letters,' he said, holding it up. Mary saw the reflection of it in the vanity mirror.

'Oh no. Are they alright?'

'Yes, I saved them.'

'Good.'

'I read them. Some of them, anyway.'

'Do you want to talk about it?' she asked gently.

Charles hesitated, eyes fixed on the page. 'He's . . . determined.' He gave a small, unsure nod. 'I don't know.'

'Maybe you should write back.'

He looked at her, almost apologetic. 'He wants to visit.'

Mary said nothing at first, allowing him space to think. She returned her brush to the vanity and crossed to the closet, exchanging her gown for a house robe.

'It's not a place I want to revisit,' Charles said quietly, placing the letter on the nightstand. His eyes found a framed black-and-white photo—a boy on his father's knee. A different life. A different world.

'It's been so long, Mary.'

She came to sit beside him, hands folded in her lap. 'Charles, you can't live inside the past forever. Maybe it's not about revisiting it—but moving through it.'

He shook his head slowly, as if trying to dislodge the weight of doubt. 'I'm not sure what he's looking for . . . or what I can give him.'

'Maybe it's not about having answers,' Mary said softly. 'Maybe it's just about being there. Listening. Understanding.'

He let her words hang in the air, quietly mulling them over.

'Maybe it is time to stop looking behind and start looking ahead?' she offered gently.

Charles managed a small smile. 'The Lord did put eyes in the front of our head for a reason.' He looked at her now, really looked. 'And He does know best.'

Mary reached down and pulled a wrapped parcel from beneath the nightstand.

'Here, I saved this one for you.'

Charles laughed, his mood lightening. 'Where were you hiding that?'

'In the cleaning closet. The one place I knew you would never look.'

'Smart and beautiful,' he said, smiling fondly. 'I really did get lucky when I found you.'

'You don't turn eighty every day,' she replied, placing it in his hands.

'You and the kids have already done too much.'

'Open it.'

He handled it carefully, sensing its shape. 'Feels like a book.' He peeled back the wrapping. 'Oh . . .' His voice softened.

The cover read: *Sir Charles Kingsford Smith*.

'This is the latest one,' Mary said. 'I know it's hard, but I thought . . . maybe you'd be interested.'

'I haven't seen this one.'

'It hasn't been released yet. Look inside.'

He opened the cover.

'Signed by the author.' He smiled in disbelief. 'That's . . . quite special.'

'Happy birthday, Charles.' She leaned in and kissed his cheek.

'Thank you, Mary.'

As Mary pulled the covers back and climbed in, she patted the bedside next to her tenderly.

'Come. We can read it together.' She smiled.

CHAPTER 5

State Library
Sydney, New South Wales, Australia. 2012.

High society gathered beneath the enormous geometric glass ceiling of the prominent atrium. The daytime event was about to begin as guests—dressed in casual formal attire—mingled and gradually made their way into the auditorium. They moved with practiced grace, sipping sparkling white wine and savoring gourmet hors d'oeuvres. The air was alive with the clink of crystal glasses, the murmur of cultivated conversation, and the mingled aromas of expensive perfume, smoked salmon canapés, and truffle-infused delicacies.

Backstage, Richard Mack Simmons—celebrated, ego-prone, and unapologetically theatrical—prepared for his moment in the spotlight. His silver hair was slicked immaculately back, his tailored suit carefully designed to complement his slightly portly frame. He radiated self-importance, his sharp, calculating gaze sweeping the room.

'Do you know if he came?' he asked curtly.

'I haven't seen him,' an assistant replied.

Richard's frown deepened, his thin lips pressing into a narrow line of disapproval.

'You're on in about three minutes,' someone warned.

Turning to the mirror, he inspected himself with meticulous precision. Adjusted his bow tie. Smoothed his hair. Checked his teeth. The glint of his signet ring caught the light as he flipped through his notes one final time. A deep breath. A steady sip of water. He was ready.

Onstage, the master of ceremonies—resplendent in a flowing peach gown—stepped to the podium as the room gradually hushed.

'Ladies and gentlemen, distinguished guests . . .'

Large poster-sized covers of Sir Charles Kingsford Smith, Simmons's latest release, flanked the stage. Their bold design and dramatic typography commanded attention, promising revelation and controversy.

As Richard stepped into the spotlight to polite applause, a man dressed entirely in black shifted near the back of the room. Damien—unassuming, yet sharply present—stood just beyond the reach of the stage's glow. He held a glass of whiskey, neat, his expression unreadable. Watching with quiet intensity, he said nothing.

Richard adjusted the microphone, his voice deep and deliberate.

'My new book dismantles history, uncovers the truth, and exposes Sir Charles Kingsford Smith for the man he truly was.'

A hush fell over the crowd. Critics, aviation historians, authors, and socialites leaned forward as one. Damien remained still, though his gaze sharpened.

'As a pilot, he had no equal. But the man on the ground was far removed from the one in the air.'

A flicker passed across Damien's face—a subtle lift of the brow.

'At the age of seven, young Smithy was pulled from the surf at Bondi Beach, nearly drowned. That trauma, buried deep, evolved into aquaphobia—a lifelong fear of water. It shaped his behavior, driving him toward recklessness, denial, and increasingly dangerous practices in the air.'

Damien's jaw shifted slightly. Not in disbelief—but recognition. Like hearing a truth echoed in a stranger's voice.

'He was widely known as an alcoholic. Addicted to fear. Drawn to risk. Lured by the hollow promises of fame and fortune. And though married, his appetite for women was legendary. If sex were a sport, he'd have been a national champion.'

The crowd erupted in laughter—some startled, others amused. Damien didn't move. His grip on the glass tightened. A faint crease formed between his brows.

Richard lifted a hand to silence the room.

'Behind the glamour of the 1930s stood a failing businessman. Even with immense support from the Australian government, he could not compete as the age of commercial aviation dawned. Unwilling to face failure, he fled the country—and never returned.'

Damien's eyes darkened. He remained silent, yet the energy around him shifted—like pressure building beneath still water.

'In his desperation, he gambled everything. And lost. Taking the life of his young passenger—'Tommy'—a boy woefully unprepared to fly.'

Still no visible reaction, but his posture stiffened. The space around him seemed to subtly widen, as if the crowd instinctively granted him distance without knowing why.

'High above the Indian Ocean, aboard a poorly designed American aircraft, they suffered catastrophic mechanical failure. The plane ignited, exploded mid-flight, and plunged into the sea.'

The crowd fell deathly silent, holding their breath.

'Despite searches in the late thirties, the eighties, and most recently by Damien Lay—all in the wrong location, I might add—the wreckage was never recovered. Their final moments—harrowing, terrifying—remain one of the great unsolved aviation mysteries in the world.'

A pause.

Then Richard lifted his book, holding it aloft like a verdict passed down.

'Until now.' 'Thank you.'

Applause thundered through the atrium. The audience rose to their feet, swept up in the drama and flair of the moment. Murmurs of admiration spread in waves. Cameras flashed. Reviewers exchanged excited glances.

Only Damien remained unmoved. He watched Richard with calm detachment, his expression unreadable. Where others saw revelation, he saw something else—something heavier. Something incomplete.

Then, without a word, he tipped back the rest of the whiskey in a single, quiet motion. Exhaling slowly through his nose, he turned and disappeared into the crowd.

Unseen by most. But not unnoticed.

Damien stepped into the hot sun, pausing on the sandstone steps outside the atrium. Across the road, the Royal Botanic Gardens shimmered under the midday glare. He removed his jacket, folded it neatly over one arm, and reached into his pocket for a cigarette. With a flick of his thumb, he lit it, drew in deeply, and stood smoking in silence—unmoved by the revelations he'd just heard.

His phone rang.

He glanced down. Unknown number. Normally, he'd ignore it. Not today. He swiped to answer. 'Hello?'

A man's voice came through—cautious, uncertain. 'Is that Damien Lay?'

'It is.'

'This is Officer John Savage, Australian Customs and Border Patrol.'

Damien smiled to himself. He'd been expecting this.

'We've got a package here—from Burma. It looks like you . . . ah, sent to yourself. That sound right?'

'Yeah,' Damien said, calmly. 'I sent that months ago.'

'Right. Well, we've had this one here for quite a while, been trying to figure out what to, ah, do with it.'

There was a pause on the line. Damien remained silent. Paper rustled. The voice grew even more unsure.

'Ah, the customs form says it contains . . . ah, 'wreckage and remains of Sir Charles Kingsford Smith's aircraft.' Is that . . . is that correct?'

Damien took another slow drag. 'Yeah,' he said simply, a wry smile tugging at the corner of his mouth.

'Umm. Right. Okay. Well . . . I'm going to have to get back to you on this.'

'No worries,' Damien replied, as the conversation ended.

He stood for a moment, cigarette burning between his fingers, letting the dry heat settle on his skin. Then a chuckle escaped—quiet and amused—as he exhaled.

'Shit!'

Chapter 6

Montana, United States of America. 2012.

In the faded phone booth of a lonely gas station tucked deep in the backcountry, Damien dropped several quarters into the slot and dialed. The long ringtone echoed in his ear as he rested one hand lightly on a small, plain box atop the phone. Wrapped in brown paper—no bow, no ribbon. Just simple. Just enough.

Finally, someone answered.

A woman's voice—clipped and cold. 'Hello.'

'Yeah, it's me.'

'Oh.' Her tone tightened. 'Hang on, I'll get her.'

Damien stood in silence, gripping the receiver. His thumb traced the folded edge of the gift, as if the paper itself could remind him why he was there. Outside the booth, through scratched, milky plexiglass, the world waited in stillness—a sagging awning, rusted pumps, a wheezing windmill creaking beneath a sky that didn't care.

The kind of place that lived in the pause between two moments.

A light static buzzed in the receiver, until a small, bright voice broke through.

'Hello?'

'Hello my little angel.'

'Daddy!' Joy spilled into the line. 'You missed Santa.'

Damien closed his eyes. A breath swelled in his chest and drifted out slowly.

'I know,' he said, barely audible.

His voice bore the weight of too many missed mornings, too many empty chairs at breakfast. The ache of a father who lived in the wrong time zone, on the wrong side of a promise.

There was a pause. The woman's voice background hurrying Maddy along.

'Will you be home for my birthday?'

Damien swallowed. A crow called somewhere overhead—flat, final.

Behind him, a truck horn sounded—short, sharp, impatient.

He raised a hand toward the waiting pickup. Soon. Just a minute.

'Maddy,' he said, the name tender on his tongue. 'Dad has to go now, okay?'

Her reply came quickly, certain.

'Okay. I love you.'

Then—a click.

Silence.

The coins dropped heavily from the slot, crashing down like punctuation. Damien checked the return with his fingers. Empty. The dull hum of the disconnected line filled his ear.

'I love you too,' he whispered, the words slipping into the dust. Another horn blast—longer this time. Urging. Breaking the moment.

Damien snatched the gift and shoved open the booth's door. His boots crunched on the gravel as he jogged toward the idling truck. He climbed into the bed just as it rolled forward, tires stirring a pale veil of dust that curled and danced in the rearview silence.

The road stretched out ahead—a long, winding ribbon of gravel flanked by golden wheat and weather-worn fence posts. On either side, only sky.

Damien dropped into a seated position in the truck bed, the parcel at his side. He lit a cigarette and drew from it slowly. The wind tore at his coat, flicking the edges of the copy of Sir Charles Kingsford Smith he pulled from his satchel. He flipped toward the back, the pages fluttering wildly before settling beneath his fingers. He tried to read. The words were there. But they wouldn't hold.

The roar of an engine built slowly from a distance. Damien looked up, squinting into the sky. A low-flying crop duster tore overhead, engine growling, slicing across the blue. It banked low over the field beside the road before dive-bombing the truck in a showy, tight pass.

Damien followed its arc, his eyes tracing the climb as the plane disappeared over the ridge. A breath later, the stirred air rushed over him, flapping the edges of his jacket.

He lit another cigarette. Closed the book. Smoke curled from his lips and vanished into the wind. In the stillness of the countryside, Montana reclaimed the moment—the buzz of insects, the distant rustle of grass, the far-off bark of a dog, fading into the long silence of open country.

As the truck dwindled to a dusty line behind him, Charles turned his gaze forward, hands resting lightly on the controls. He flew low over the fields, perfectly at ease.

The engine's steady drone mingled with the wind rushing over the wings. Below, the crops rippled in green and gold waves. Above, nothing but open sky. The cool morning air filled his lungs with life.

It was freedom. Precision. The quiet exhilaration of flight—where danger met peace and man became machine and in that moment, he flew as if the world beneath him disappeared.

The porch groaned softly beneath Damien's weight as he stood alone, the wooden boards creaking in quiet protest. A cigarette smoldered between his fingers, its smoke curling lazily into the crisp air. His gaze stretched out over the familiar landscape, a tapestry of memories and time.

Inside, Mary moved with practiced grace in the kitchen, her hands laying out sandwiches—white bread spread with Vegemite, a simple comfort. Through the open window, she caught sight of Damien's silhouette against the morning light.

'It must have been a long trip; you must be exhausted,' she called out, her voice gentle yet carrying.

Damien took a slow drag, the ember glowing briefly. 'It's a lot easier these days,' he replied, exhaling a plume of smoke that dissipated into the ether.

'True,' Mary replied, stepping out onto the porch, the screen door protesting with a squeak. She placed the plate of sandwiches on the small table between them. 'I thought you might like these—Charles's favorite,' she offered with a warm smile.

'Thank you, Mary,' Damien said, his lips curling into a faint smile.

'It's been a long time for Charles,' she said softly, a concerned warning. Damien nodded, the weight of unspoken thoughts passing between them.

As Mary retreated inside, Charles emerged, his presence filling the space with a quiet energy. He and Mary exchanged a brief, affectionate smile as they passed each other.

'You know those things will kill you,' Charles remarked, nodding toward the cigarette. 'The cigarettes, not Mary's sandwiches,' he added with a grin.

'I can hear you in here, Charles!' Mary's voice rang out from the kitchen, laced with amusement.

Charles chuckled, holding out an old black-and-white photograph, its edges colored with time. 'Given your keen interest in my history, I thought you might appreciate this. It's never been seen outside the family. I'm not sure when it was taken, but it's the only one I have of us together.'

Damien accepted the photograph, his eyes tracing the faded image.

'I was certainly a lot younger then,' Charles mused.

'You don't know when this was taken?' Damien inquired.

'I remember very little from that time. Not that I could be expected to, I guess, after so many years.'

'It's a beautiful photograph, Charles,' Damien said, placing it gently on the table beside the sandwiches.

'Please,' Charles gestured toward the plate.

'Thank you, Charles,' Damien replied, taking a sandwich and pressing it flat with his palm—a familiar ritual. Charles watched, a smile tugging at his lips, the shared culture bridging the years.

'From your letters, it would appear that you've been on quite the crusade,' Charles observed.

'It has been an adventure, one could say,' Damien responded, their conversation dipping into reflective silence.

'Have you read the latest book?' Charles asked, breaking the quiet.

'I have, yeah, in part,' Damien admitted.

'The parts that talk about you?' Charles teased, a hint of sarcasm in his tone.

'Yeah,' Damien replied, a knowing smile playing on his lips.

'Not to worry, I do the same,' Charles said, easing the moment with a chuckle.

'It's a good book. Just no great revelations, I guess—just the same history repackaged.'

'Hm, true,' Charles agreed. 'I guess when there's nothing new to offer, all that's left to do is sensationalize the shreds of history that are left.' He laughed softly. 'It did focus on the said 'popularity with the ladies' quite heavily.'

A deliberate cough echoed from the kitchen. Charles glanced over his shoulder, a sheepish grin on his face.

'I know you don't know, I know no one could know, Charles,' Damien said, his tone shifting.

'I only know what I've read, Damien,' Charles replied curtly, a defensive edge creeping in.

'What you've read is wrong, Charles.'

'Right wrong, Damien; it doesn't change anything, it certainly does not change the past,' Charles retorted, his voice firm.

The conversation stalled, the silence between them stretching taut.

'I often think about Tommy. His family—do you talk with his family?' Charles asked, his voice softening, shifting direction.

'I do,' Damien answered.

'I assume they want to know?' Charles asked tentatively.

'They do.'

Charles swallowed hard, his eyes locking with Damien's in a moment of shared pain and understanding.

'The question is, Charles, do you?'

Chapter 7

Wyndham, Western Australia, Australia. 1933.

The distant rumble of an engine grew steadily louder, rolling across the scorched expanse of the desert. Sprawled atop a dead tree stump, nestled among a dispersion of flowering bush scrub and natural baked red rockeries, a frill-necked lizard absorbed the searing heat of a relentless sun. Its leathery body, perfectly adapted to the harsh environment, remained motionless as it absorbed the warmth. Narrowed eyes, half-closed to conserve moisture and shield against the blinding glare, remained ever watchful, attuned to the slightest hint of danger.

The rumble broke the crackling silence, growing into a thunderous roar that shattered the desert's serenity. A fleeting shadow swept over the parched ground, disrupting the stillness. Instantly, the lizard reacted. In a sharp, snapping movement, its frill flared outward—an electrifying explosion of vibrant color. Sunburst yellows, fiery oranges, and stark blacks radiated in defiance, a bold display of survival against the encroaching threat.

The aircraft, Miss Southern Cross, soared low, her gleaming white fuselage catching the sunlight as it sparkled like a diamond against the rich, deep blue expanse of the endless sky she so effortlessly traversed.

The heat inside the cockpit was stifling, intensified by the greenhouse effect as the unfiltered sun streamed through the glass canopy, meeting the rising heat reflecting off the sands below. The pilot felt it, as did the aircraft—a slight shudder, followed by a misfire, rattled the frame. His hands tightened on the controls, his eyes moving methodically across the instrument panel. The engine sputtered again, the sound unsettling, as the temperature gauge slowly climbed upward, needling toward the red.

The engine whined in protest, its struggle to maintain steady revolutions becoming a growing concern as the pilot calmly evaluated the situation. He throttled back, reducing airspeed and the strain on the engine as the revolutions per minute dropped, then lowered the flaps to half, initiating a slow descent.

The aircraft settled slightly, momentarily calming itself. It wasn't enough. Bang! The aircraft lurched violently, the jolt throwing him against the straps of his harness. Behind him, the jury-rigged makeshift fuel tank—a forty-four-gallon drum installed specifically to increase the aircraft's range for this flight—broke loose from its mount, instantly shifting the centre of gravity, forcing the aircraft into a potential spin.

Smoke burst from the nose of the aircraft, erupting through the engine cowl and clouding his forward view, adding yet a further issue to the increasing list of potential problems, any one of which could amount to a disaster. The smoke could have been from a ruptured oil line, an overheated engine, a broken exhaust pipe spewing hot exhaust like a blowtorch on the fragile structure; his mind processed all of this quickly, then he dared a quick glance at the fuel gauge, where the needle bounced on empty. The engine sputtered and coughed, starved of that essential liquid and gasping for breath.

Instinctively he reacted, no hesitation—chopped the power, centered the ailerons, and with brute strength, pushed his foot down hard on the rudder pedal, pulling the aircraft out of its desire to uncontrollably spin, while he finessed the control stick forward, breaking the stall, recovering control.

Calmly, without a hint of panic, the pilot voiced his analysis aloud. 'We have lost the engine.' His eyes moved to the temperature gauge, still in the red. 'We have lost oil.' His tone was measured as he thoughtfully assessed the situation, thinking. He checked again as he systematically worked through the situation. Carefully, leaning his chest as far forward as the confines of the cockpit allowed, he suddenly slammed the entire weight of his body backward, hard against the seat, the force driving the fuel tank back onto its mounts and into position.

The engine sputtered, coughed again, then roared back to life before settling into a steady, albeit labored, rhythm. His eyes darted back to the instrument panel, watching as the fuel gauge flickered, then slowly began its climb. 'One down!' he acknowledged to himself, gently feathering the controls, as he nursed the aircraft carefully. The steam pouring from the cowling gradually abated, improving his visibility, but no smoke meant no oil, he knew. The engine would stop.

His eyes turned to the temperature gauge, still in the red. Sweat trickled unnoticed down his temple, his focus entirely elsewhere as he began to methodically scan the surroundings for somewhere—anywhere—to safely set the ship down.

As he descended slowly, the desert below revealed a dry, dusty flat strip of prehistoric riverbed. Gently, he circled the area, carefully inspecting the surface for its suitability to land before making his decision. 'It's a little short, Charles, but I think we can make it work,' he confidently assured himself, aloud. With steady hands, he turned into a final descent.

The wheels glided gracefully over ground, before touching down deep into the soft rutted, sandy surface with a jarring thud. The aircraft shuddered violently on impact, the vibrations rattling through its frame as plumes of dust shrouded the aircraft in a display of aerodynamic turbulence, rolling a short distance before coming to a gentle stop.

Dust swirled lazily around the cockpit as he methodically shut the aircraft and engine down, his movements deliberate and precise. He leaned back in his seat, taking a long, deep well-deserved breath. A grin broke across his face. 'Any landing you can walk away from, Charles, is a good one!'

As the dust settled, the aircraft sat idle, resting in the desolate isolation of nowhere. Charles slowly unlatched the canopy, the faint metallic click echoing in the stillness before he pushed it open. The hot air outside surged in like the blast of an open furnace, offering no relief, only further discomfort.

Reaching for his logs and maps, he spread them across his lap, their edges frayed and soft from repeated use. Carefully, he noted the duration of airtime, penciling a bold entry into the log: six hours thirty minutes from his last departure point in Koepang, East Timor. Satisfied, he tore a small blank section from the corner of the page, jotted down a concise but detailed message, folded it meticulously, and stuffed it firmly into his jacket pocket. His eyes scanned the horizon briefly before he turned back to the map, unfolding it with care.

Tracing his finger over the worn chart, he adjusted his calculations, measuring distance and landmarks to pinpoint his position. A small smile crept across his face as he whispered to no one, 'Almost, almost!' He chuckled softly, a sound that broke the oppressive silence, quietly proud of what only he could fully understand—what he had just achieved.

Stowing the log and map back within the cockpit, Charles braced himself against the canopy, pulling his weight upward. The groan of a man escaped his lips, unbidden but obligatory, as his stiff legs stretched for the first time since the flight began. The numbness clung stubbornly, and he gave himself a moment, standing half out of the cockpit as blood returned to his limbs.

When he finally stepped out, the stark reality of his surroundings struck him anew. The landscape stretched endlessly in all directions, a harsh and barren canvas of earth and an unbroken expanse of sky. Any fleeting notion that the world might have shifted, that something might have changed since landing, was dismissed almost instantly. The desolate, unforgiving emptiness seemed even more profound from the ground.

Climbing down cautiously from the cockpit, Charles steadied himself as his boots sunk into the soft, shifting sand. Each step assisted in the recovery of his legs as he made his way toward the engine, its metallic surface radiating heat that shimmered in the dry air. He reached for the cowling but quickly retracted his hand, the searing metal too hot to handle directly. With more care, he fumbled it open, mindful as to avoid injury.

Even in the bright daylight, the faint, reddish-white glow of the overheated exhaust was unmistakable. The engine hissing and ticking vents. Charles, realizing that only the cool air of the night would temper its fever, cast a glance over each shoulder, scanning the barren horizon in the faint hope of seeing another human figure, a vehicle, a sign of life—anything. There was nothing, just the unbroken desert. 'We are not doing this again Charles!' he said aloud with a chuckle of reminiscence. Resigned, Charles turned away from the engine, took a deep breath, removing his long leather flying coat and slinging it neatly over his forearm as he began to walk in the knowledge there was no other alternative.

Sequestered in the deep shadow of the corrugated iron awning draped over the Wyndham Hotel, Jack and Henry squared off, their breath thick with whiskey and unresolved history. Two mates turned rivals, their bond stretched taut and fraying under the weight of old grudges and too many empty beer glasses scattered around them like discarded tokens of better times.

The world around them seemed to fall away, leaving only the stretch of red dirt beneath their boots and the oppressive heat pressing down from the iron roof above. The faint hum of flies hovered in the still air, their lazy movements mocking the storm brewing between the two men. No voices cheered them on, no hands tossed coins; there was only the silence of an unspoken reckoning.

Jack's eyes fixed on Henry, his expression unreadable save for the tautness in his jaw and the faint twitch of his fingers. An Aboriginal stockman hardened by decades in the punishing outback, Jack stood like a figure carved from the very land itself. His dark, weathered skin gleamed with sweat, the sheen highlighting scars that traced a map of his battles—against beasts, against nature, and, perhaps, against himself. Flies clung stubbornly to his shoulders and forehead, but he didn't flinch. His bloodshot eyes, sharp as flint, bore into Henry's with the force of a man who had endured the worst the world could throw at him and refused to yield.

Henry stood steady, broad-shouldered and deliberate in his stillness, his hands loose but ready at his sides. His sweat-streaked skin glistened, each droplet carving a slow path through the dirt and grit etched into him by a lifetime of labor. His chest rose and fell in measured rhythm, but his dark eyes betrayed nothing, meeting Jack's unwavering gaze with a weight that spoke of years—decades—of shared toil, triumph, and hardship. Together, they had carved out lives in a world that demanded everything and gave nothing. Yet now, they stood opposed, the weight of betrayal heavier than the miles they had ridden together.

The silence pressed down on them like the heat, thick and inescapable. Jack's boots shifted slightly in the dirt, the crunch of dry earth beneath his weight the only sound. His eyes flicked downward—Henry's feet, his fists—before snapping back up, his focus razor-sharp. The movement wasn't hesitation; it was calculation, the same instinct he'd honed through years of staring down bulls, storms, and death itself.

Henry exhaled slowly, his nostrils flaring as he drew the still air deep into his lungs. His fingers curled into fists now, the veins in his forearms standing out like rivers on a map. He said nothing, the silence between them louder than words could ever be. The past hung thick between them—decades of trust, betrayal, and the unbearable weight of what had been lost.

For a moment, the world seemed to pause, the air charged with the inevitability of what was to come. Jack's jaw tightened, his muscles coiled, every line of his body taut with purpose.

And then, Jack moved.

'Checkmate!' he proclaimed, leaning back with satisfaction as Henry studied the board, doubt flickering in his eyes.

'Nah, check,' Henry replied, his tone sharp, refusing the claim.

'That's what I said. Check! Mate,' Jack insisted, gesturing pointedly at the board.

'Nah, it's check,' Henry repeated, raising his voice, his frustration evident.

'Mate, I'm telling you. Check. Mate,' Jack declared louder, his conviction unshakable.

Henry shook his head and turned away, muttering under his breath as he squinted into the shimmering haze above the horizon. His eyes narrowed further, catching movement—a lone figure emerging from the blur of heat. For a moment, he watched in silence, then tilted his head, curiosity cutting through his annoyance. 'Get a load of this bloke's swag, will you,' he muttered, tapping Jack's arm to draw his attention. Jack followed Henry's gaze, and his face split into a wide grin.

The man approaching them was dressed in sharp, polished attire, his neat appearance a stark contrast to the rugged, dusty surroundings. His shirt was crisp and white, his trousers perfectly pressed, and his jacket slung casually over one shoulder. Each step stirred up puffs of red dirt mucking the polish, but his nonchalance suggested he was utterly unfazed by the setting.

Jack, never one to miss an opportunity, cupped his hands around his mouth and called out, 'Didn't anyone tell you? Ladies' night's not 'til Thursday!' He and Henry erupted into deep, self-congratulatory laughter, reveling in their own wit, their mirth echoing across the quiet expanse.

The figure—a man they both immediately recognized—didn't falter in his stride. Charles carried himself with an air of quiet confidence, the faintest smirk tugging at the corner of his lips as he approached. His movements were deliberate, his demeanor laced with an easy knowingness that seemed to draw the moment into his orbit. As he reached them, he offered a nod of acknowledgment, his gaze steady. 'Jack. Henry.' His voice, calm and familiar, broke the silence.

Pausing at the entrance, Charles turned back, his expression light but teasing. 'I'm surprised you two aren't covered in cobwebs,' he quipped, a gentle laugh escaping as he pushed open the door and stepped inside.

The hotel itself was modest, a simple bar with a handful of rooms attached. Yet it carried a quiet charm, a refuge for the weary. Its scuffed wooden floors and heavy, timeworn furniture exuded a rugged hospitality, while the cool shade offered respite from the unrelenting Kimberley heat. The air carried a heady blend of tobacco smoke, spilled beer, and the faint tang of red dust, a scent that clung to the walls like a memory.

The Wyndham Hotel wasn't just a resting place; it was a haven for those braving the Kimberley wilderness, a space where the untamed spirit of the land found shelter within its sturdy walls. Those walls had seen many adventures, yet far fewer adventurers, their stories lingering like whispers in the grain of the wood.

Charles stood in silhouette as the door eased shut behind him, his eyes adjusting to the dim, cool interior. From the inside breast pocket of his jacket, he removed a small slip of paper, then hung the coat neatly on the familiar hook by the door. Across the room, Reg, an elderly bushman, sat nursing a beer that had seen better days, swatting lazily at the relentless flies. His battered hat perched askew on his head, and his clothes, coated in a fine layer of road dust, clung to him like a second skin.

Bill, the local postmaster and publican, leaned heavily on his elbows behind the bar, his focus buried in the crinkling pages of the newspaper spread before him. The slow, rhythmic squeak of the ceiling fan overhead mingled with faint, crackling tunes from the old radio behind the bar. The air felt thick and unhurried, a place where time itself seemed to take its leisure.

The lines on Bill's weathered face deepened as he looked up, his eyes widening in surprise. 'Christ, Smithy! I haven't seen a man in a suit and tie walk through that door since old man Clary died.' His voice boomed, a mix of astonishment and amusement. 'Hey, Reg! How long's it been since old Clary kicked it?'

From his corner, Reg didn't miss a beat. Chuckling, he shot back, 'I don't know mate, but I'm sure he kicked the bucket waiting for a beer around here. I don't want to be next!'

Reg sinisterly laughed, the crack drawing Beverly's sharp ear as she entered, balancing a tray of empty glasses with an air of authority and ownership. Her tone, stern and measured, cut through Reg's laughter like a blade. 'That's enough out of you, Reg,' she scolded, silencing him on the spot. Then, turning to Charles with a warm smile, her demeanor softening, 'G'day, Smithy. Where'd you blow in from?'

'London,' Charles replied. The single word carried the weight of the distance with it.

'London, ay?' Beverly echoed, her tone tinged with dry humor. 'Well, we'd better get you a real beer then, aye love?'

Reg chuckled again, a grin pulling at his dusty face, while Charles returned a knowing smile. From his coat pocket, Charles produced a folded note and handed it to Bill. 'Wire this for me, will ya?' he asked politely. Bill unfolded it, his eyes scanning the contents once, then widening as he read it again. 'Christ, Smithy! What'd you do, go the long way?' he said, shaking his head in mock amazement. Charles smirked. 'I would've been here sooner, but I had to walk the last few miles.'

Bill snorted, still turning the note over as though it might change on a second inspection. 'Look at this, Bev,' he said, showing it to her. Beverly leaned in, her eyebrows lifting in surprise before she broke into a grin. 'Well, I'll put this one on the house, Smithy, but the rest you'll have to pay for,' she teased, her voice firm but kind. Charles smiled back, the broken calm in the room evaporating into an easy, familiar rhythm—flies buzzing, fans turning, and Reg, always ready with another quip, still waiting for his beer.

Chapter 8

House of Lords
London, England. 1933.

Collins walked with a determined pace through the corridors, his steps measured and deliberate. In his wiry hand, he carried a letter, its weight far greater than the paper it was written on. He cut a distinctly stuffy and snobby figure, his meticulously tailored suit—dark and somber—clinging to his thin frame with a precision that spoke of both wealth and an aversion to any hint of disorder. A crisp white shirt peeked from beneath the high collar of his jacket, its edges sharp as if they too shared his disdain for informality. The knot of his tie, perfectly symmetrical, seemed almost too tight, as though it choked out any semblance of warmth or spontaneity.

The undersecretary to Lord Liard, the Minister for Air, moved briskly, his steps muffled by the plush carpets that lined the corridors. The ornate fixtures of the House of Commons—gilded sconces and heavy drapes—framed his progress, each detail a reminder of the gravity and tradition of the institution he served.

Upon reaching the door to Lord Liard's office, Collins paused for the briefest of moments. He knocked once, sharp and precise, before entering. The room was cavernous and richly appointed, its towering bookshelves and grand windows suggesting both wealth and authority. Light spilled through the tall panes, casting sharp shadows over the dark, patterned rug that stretched across the floor. The scent of leather and faint traces of old pipe smoke lingered in the air, mingling with the subdued hum of activity in the distant corridors.

Lord Liard sat resolutely in his grand chair, his gaze fixed on the world beyond the ornate windows. An imposing figure, he commanded both attention and unease through his demeanor alone. Though short and robust—a build forged more by privilege than exertion—he carried himself with the unshakable confidence of someone accustomed to obedience. His impeccably tailored dark suit seemed to absorb the light, while his puffy, well-rounded face appeared stark and pale in contrast.

'Hah hmm,' Collins cleared his throat gently, a sound that seemed faint against the imposing silence of the room.

'Yes, Collins?' Lord Liard responded, his gaze remaining firmly on his view across the River Thames outside.

'Begging your pardon, my lord, I do apologize for the interruption. An urgent communication from Australia has been received, my lord.'

'Yes, yes?' he replied, the impatience in his tone unmistakable.

Collins stepped forward, holding out the letter with careful precision. 'Sir Charles Kingsford Smith has reduced Scott's record from England to Australia by one day and sixteen hours.'

At this, Lord Liard turned slowly in his wing-backed chair, the leather creaking faintly with the movement. He extended a long, pale hand, taking the letter from Collins without a word. For a moment, he studied the undersecretary's words, the silence between them stretching like a taut wire.

Parliament House
Canberra, Australian Capital Territory, Australia. 1933.

The halls echoed with the sharp, purposeful cadence of Shephard's footsteps, each one reverberating like the sound of indignation itself. The Secretary to the Minister of Air strode with vigor, his lean frame cutting a precise figure against the austere backdrop of the corridor. His crisp dark suit, tailored to perfection, carried an air of authority, while his neatly combed salt-and-pepper hair framed thin, angular features that accentuated his gaunt presence. A faint furrow marred his brow, a silent testament to the weight of his errand.

Reaching the heavy oak door of Sir Duddevin's office, Shephard paused briefly, his hand hovering over the polished brass handle. With a quiet but deliberate knock, he entered, stepping into a room where authority seemed to linger in the very air.

Sir Duddevin sat slouched over his vast mahogany desk, its surface a battlefield of papers and correspondence. His broad shoulders were hunched, his hands occasionally brushing aside errant sheets as if trying to make sense of the chaos before him. The sunlight streaming through the tall, narrow windows pierced through the heavy drapes, throwing jagged beams across the polished wooden floor and gilding the edges of the room in stark light.

The office carried an air of austere grandeur. Dark wood paneling climbed the walls, interrupted only by the solemn faces of past statesmen whose portraits seemed to oversee the proceedings with a mix of judgment and expectation.

Sir Duddevin's appearance betrayed none of the fatigue his posture suggested. His navy suit, subtly patterned with pinstripes, was impeccably tailored to accentuate his broad frame, tapering neatly to the polished black leather shoes that rested flat against the floor. A maroon tie, adorned with understated geometric patterns, added the barest whisper of color to his otherwise conservative attire. His dark hair, tinged with the faintest streaks of silver, was slicked back with precision, framing a face marked by sharp, commanding features.

As Shephard stepped closer, the sound of his approach caused Sir Duddevin to glance up briefly, his eyes sternly narrowed in acknowledgment before returning to the chaos of his desk.

'Yes, Shephard?' Sir Duddevin asked, his voice low and steady, never breaking the rhythm of his work.

'He did it in seven days, four hours, and forty-seven minutes, sir,' Shephard replied, his tone clipped but carrying the weight of the news, as he handed the communication to Sir Duddevin.

Sir Duddevin's hand froze mid-motion. He read slowly, leaning back in his chair and taking a deep breath. His expression shifted as his eyes slowly crept upward, back to Shephard.

MacRobertson Steam Confectionery Works, Melbourne, Victoria, Australia. 1933.

The offices loomed large within the industrial outskirts of the city. The imposing factory and its attached office buildings stood as monuments to the ambition and success of their founder. Above it all, towering smokestacks exhaled steady plumes of steam, twenty-four hours a day, a ceaseless proclamation of the factory's vitality. Shift workers, fortunate to have employment in these difficult times, meandered in and out to the call of the shift whistle's scream. The large clock adorning the facade ticked methodically, an ever watchful reminder of the industrial progress.

Inside, Sir Macpherson Robertson addressed the board members seated in attentive silence. The boardroom exuded an air of refinement and authority, a space designed to inspire deference. Polished wood paneling lined the walls, their rich, dark tones glowing faintly under the golden light of early art deco light fixtures hung grandly above the long mahogany table. Gleaming brass fixtures caught the light, adding subtle warmth to the otherwise deep, dark atmosphere. The air was thick with the scent of cigars, their smoke curling in languid tendrils from ashtrays, forming a haze that hung low over fine crystal glasses of gentlemanly whiskey, imported.

The assembly of sharp suits and sharper minds sat in a tense, watchful stillness. Their collective focus was fixed unwaveringly on Sir Macpherson, who stood at the head of the table. His tall frame, clad in a perfectly tailored three-piece suit, leaned heavily forward, his hands splayed on the table's glossy surface—a posture of authority and conviction.

Sir Macpherson's hair, once a rich chestnut, was streaked with the dignified silver of age. His mustache, neatly trimmed and meticulously combed, added to his aura of precision.

Below thick, bushy brows, his deep blue eyes scanned the room with a sharp, unwavering focus and a no-nonsense intelligence that tolerated neither mediocrity nor hesitation.

'Gentlemen,' Sir Macpherson said, his voice resonant and commanding, 'the world is shrinking. I see this as a great opportunity.'

Lord Liard absorbed the news with measured forethought, his demeanor betraying no immediate reaction. His pale fingers tapped lightly against the armrest of his chair, the silence stretching as he weighed the implications. There was no hint of congratulations, only a cold, calculating concern.

'When will Scott make his next attempt for the record?' he asked, his tone sharp and deliberate.

'He is planning his next attempt for March, my lord,' Collins responded, his voice steady, though the weight of the question pressed on him.

'Great Britain cannot be seen to be second to its colonies.' Lord Liard paused, his eyes narrowing as though addressing the very fabric of the room. 'See to it that Scott has everything he needs.'

'Yes, my lord,' Collins replied, the gravity of the directive, clearly evident in his tone.

A tenuous furor burned within Sir Duddevin as he stood abruptly, the motion sending his chair skidding slightly back against the polished floor. Shephard instinctively took a half step backward, in a slightly nervous retreat.

'Why were we not informed of this?' Sir Duddevin demanded, his voice laced with spite.

'I do not know, sir,' Shephard replied, his words squeaking under the intensity of the glare directed at him.

'This is an embarrassment to this office and to the Government of Australia,' Sir Duddevin continued, his voice rising with indignation.

'What action would you wish to take, sir?'

Sir Macpherson's voice filled the boardroom, his spirit growing as his thoughts took shape.

'I want to organize an air race,' he declared, his voice beaming with ambition. He paused, letting the idea settle in the room, his gaze sweeping across the gathered faces. 'Yes! An air race from England to Australia to mark the centenary of Melbourne.'

Calculating the situation with precision, Sir Duddevin leaned back into his chair, his manner calming, yet resolute. His voice dropped to a more measured, deliberate tone as he addressed Shephard.

'Collins, ensure that this does not happen again and in future make certain that we are seen to be . . . how should I say it . . . involved next time.'

'Yes, sir,' Shephard responded, the understanding clear in his voice.

The boardroom erupted into chaos. Members shuffled in their seats, murmurs rising into louder protests.

'Sir Macpherson, this is preposterous!' a board member shouted, his voice laden with skepticism.

'Impossible sir! We are not in the business of aircraft!' another protested, his tone incredulous.

'An air race, Sir Macpherson! For what purpose?' questioned another.

Sir Macpherson, unperturbed by the objections, raised his voice above the clamor, his tone sharp and commanding.

'To sell chocolate, of course!' he bellowed, silencing the room.

Sir Duddevin elevated his voice to a thick, authoritative seriousness, his words cutting through the room with finality.

'Collins,' he said, his tone unwavering, 'the pride of the Empire is at stake.'

'Yes, my lord,' Collins replied, the weight of the statement reverberating in the silence that followed.

Chapter 9

Melbourne, Victoria, Australia. 1933.

The propeller of the *Miss Southern Cross* slowed to a halt, its final rotations faltering before stopping completely. The day was bright and clear—a beautiful day, unusually warm for the southern city's climate. The sleek, silver Percival Gull glistened under the sun, its silver fabric covering contrasting the vivid blue of the sky. A marvel of craftsmanship, the aircraft stood apart with its elegant design—its tapered wings flowing seamlessly into a streamlined fuselage, every curve a testament to precision and beauty. The jewel-like cockpit canopy, its glass catching the light like facets of a gemstone, crowned the slender form, adding a touch of sophistication uncommon in typical British design.

Inside the cockpit, Charles remained seated, the exhaustion finally catching up with him. The hum of the engine's final vibrations had faded, leaving a profound silence that enveloped him within the resting calm. Though the flight had been uneventful, its length had taken its toll, leaving every muscle in his body weighted with fatigue. He lingered in the quiet momentarily, his hands still resting on the controls, as if letting go would signal the true end of another survived journey.

He drew a deep, steadying breath, the smell of fuel, still strong, mingled with the distant smell of fresh-cut grass from the airstrip. The weariness in his soul was tempered by a flicker of pride—pride in the aircraft that had carried him, pride in the journey he had completed. Collecting his thoughts and composure, he reached for the canopy latch. With deliberate care, he unlatched the canopy.

As he pushed it open, the faint murmur of a crowd filtered into the cockpit, growing steadily louder. By the time he stood, the sound had risen into a deafening roar. Over one hundred thousand people had gathered on the makeshift grass airstrip in Central Park, their jubilation pouring forth in waves of cheers and applause. They swarmed from all directions toward the aircraft like a living tide, men, women, boys, girls. This achievement was theirs, yet something about this return felt different.

The throng was electric, tossing hats into the air and waving shawls with unrestrained joy. Charles rose to his feet, a tired but genuine smile spreading across his face as he took in the spectacle. Raising a hand in acknowledgment, he greeted the crowd with quiet gratitude, their fervent energy seeming to lift the weight of the journey from his shoulders.

Suddenly, with an agility that stood out amid the chaos, a young man leaped up onto the wing. His sharp suit and tightly groomed hair reflected the sunlight, and his face, a picture of unrestrained pride and joy, caught Charles's eye.

'Tommy!' Charles exclaimed, his voice filled with relief and happiness as his smile grew larger than life, radiating pure elation in seeing his friend emerge from the sea of strangers.

'You bloody beauty,' Tommy replied, his voice cracking with emotion. He grasped Charles's hand vigorously, then pulled him into a firm, congratulatory embrace. Their reunion was amplified by the crowd's overboiling excitement, cheers, and applause, which magnified the moment triumphantly. Any chance of sharing further words was lost, as the crowd surged forward, sweeping Charles off his feet. Hands hoisted him high, floating him triumphantly above their heads.

'Tommy, you need to look at the cooling system!' Charles yelled over the din, his thoughts momentarily slipping back to business. His legs and arms flailed about, but his face beamed with exhilaration. Like a winning jockey, he rode through the crowd, reaching out to shake the many hands stretching toward him. His joy mingled with the unrestrained energy of the celebration.

As the crowd tossed him like a hero, his gaze caught on something—or someone—amid the chaos. A young woman stood apart from the frenzy, her presence striking in its stillness. The sunlight caught her deep brown hair, while the faint flush on her porcelain skin lent her an almost ethereal beauty. Her eyes, bright and sharp like polished emeralds, locked onto his with an intensity that pierced through the jubilant haze. The curve of her lips held an enigmatic mix of relief and reproach, her serene composure belying the emotions simmering beneath. Her folded arms and unimpressed look of disapproval shadowed her expression; however, her eyes told a different story, their depths carrying an unspoken question that lingered between them, as if daring him to explain.

Charles wrestled himself free from the shoulders of the men carrying him, landing heavily on his feet. As he reached the ground in front of her, the noise seemed to fade, leaving only the weight of her gaze. They stood there for a moment, the world around them a blur.

'Well, well. Sir Charles Kingsford Smith.' Her tone, cool, calm.

'Mary,' Charles stoically replied.

'What took you so long?' she asked, demanding an explanation.

For a split second, Charles hesitated, meeting her expressionlessness with his own, until Mary suddenly cracked a smile that enveloped her even as Charles's face lit up to match hers. Then, with a passionate surge of emotion, he swept Mary off her feet, spinning her around in a whirlwind of smiling happiness. The crowd around them erupted in cheers, egging on their public display of affection as they kissed briefly with a longing of love.

'I missed you,' he whispered, his voice raw with sincerity, his face inches from hers.

Mary's expression softened, though her sharp eyes still searched his. 'Do we have a deal, still?' she asked, her voice steady.

'We do!' Charles replied, his answer swift and resolute.

'Good,' Mary said, a pleased smile curling her lips. Her tone grew warm as she added, 'Now, I do believe there is a little boy waiting to meet you.'

Charles's smile faltered for only an instant, his expression softening into something deeper—a mixture of awe and anticipation. A boy. His son. The reality of the life waiting for him on the ground, so different from the life in the sky, was both daunting and exhilarating.

Through the crowd, a gentleman approached with deliberate intent, his polished demeanor cutting through the chaos like a knife.

'Sir Charles! Sir Charles!' he called, his tone respectful yet firm enough to draw their attention. Both Charles and Mary turned toward him, curiosity sparking in their expressions. The man tipped his hat, his posture impeccable, before continuing.

'Sir Charles, the mayor of our fine city of Melbourne has graciously sent his private car for your arrival,' he announced with a formal air, his voice carrying above the murmurs of the surrounding crowd. 'If you would follow me, please—this way, if you will.' He extended an arm in a sweeping gesture, beckoning them to follow.

Charles glanced at Mary, their eyes meeting briefly. A shrug passed between them—an unspoken exchange of bemused agreement.

'Well, I wasn't expecting this,' Charles murmured with a faint smile, his tone light but appreciative.

'I suppose we should not keep the mayor waiting,' Mary replied with an impressed raise of the eyebrow, her lips curling into a knowing smile.

With gracious steps, arm in arm, Charles shielding her from the clambering crowd, they accepted the unexpected offer, weaving their way through the throng as the gentleman led them toward their awaiting transport. The crowd parted reluctantly, their cheers and applause lingering in the air like an electric charge, a reminder of the shared triumph still reverberating through the moment.

The crowd showed no signs of thinning as the motorcar rolled forward. The city streets were packed four and five people deep, a sea of jubilant faces cheering, waving, and applauding. Charles and Mary sat comfortably in the back seat of the fancy open-top vehicle, and they could feel the energy of the celebration as they were paraded. Streamers floated down from the windows above, twisting gracefully among the volumes of ticker tape fluttering through the air. Mary, momentarily overwhelmed by the grandeur of the moment, smiled proudly at her husband as he returned waves and nods of gratitude to the adoring crowd.

Children chased after the car, their laughter rising high above the rhythmic roar of applause. Their small hands reached out to grab at ribbons and streamers, their movements full of uncontained joy. One boy, quicker than the rest, darted ahead. His little straight legs and knobby knees pumped, his socks, low and loose, fell to his ankles, dangling over his scuffed leather shoes. His cap sat tilted precariously on a head of unruly brown hair, and his freckled face, mucked with dirt from a previous adventure, shone with excitement. Determined, he sprinted alongside the vehicle, gripping the side with surprising agility.

'Smithy! Smithy!' he called, his voice piercing through the commotion. Charles turned, catching sight of the spirited boy, and grinned. 'Smithy!' he yelled again. Then the boy, undeterred, leapt onto the running board, his elbows hooked securely over the car door.

'Hey Smithy! Hats off to ya!' he exclaimed, sweeping off his cap in an exaggerated salute.

'We sure gave it to those poms, didn't we?'

Charles smiled proudly, reaching out to tousle the boy's hair. 'That we did, kid, that we did.'

Before the moment could stretch further, a police officer, noticing him hanging precariously, caught the boy by the scruff, yanking him from the car with a swift tug. The boy kicked and wriggled, protesting with the righteous indignation of youth, but his efforts were in vain. Charles and Mary turned to watch as the officer hauled him back into the crowd with a swift boot to the backside. The boy, undaunted, waved his cap one last time before disappearing into the sea of onlookers, as his figure was slowly engulfed into obscurity.

Mary, her eyes sparkling with amusement, covered her mouth with her hand to stifle a laugh. Charles shook his head, the laughter rumbling deep in his chest as he turned back to face her.

'You are going to make a great father!' Mary said, her smile softening as she placed her hand over his and clasped it with affection. 'If he is anything like you though, you have it all ahead of you,' Mary quipped.

Charles smirked, his gaze twinkling with mischief. 'I was a lot worse at his age.'

Mary cupped his face gently, a playful sigh escaping her lips. 'I am going to have to raise two of you, aren't I?'

Charles chuckled, capturing her hand in his and pressing a kiss to her knuckles. 'If anyone can do it Mary,' he replied, believing in her, 'you can.'

Charles stood by a small porcelain basin filled with warm water, gently bathing his three-month-old son, Charles Jr. The baby's soft coos blended with the rhythmic splashing, creating a melody that seemed to soothe the weight in his chest, if only for a moment.

The room around them was modest but elegant, a hallmark of 1930s practicality blended with art deco charm. The walls were painted a soft cream, adorned with a geometric-patterned wallpaper that caught the dim glow of a brass table lamp. A sturdy oak dresser stood against the wall, its surface neatly arranged with a silver brush set and a single photograph in a wooden frame. Heavy drapes hung over the window, their deep burgundy fabric muffling the city sounds outside, while the plush carpet beneath their feet absorbed every step, lending the room a hushed intimacy.

Behind him, Mary entered, brushing her hair. Her footsteps were light on the carpet, but her presence carried the quiet strength of someone accustomed to holding the family together. She paused, watching her husband with a mixture of tenderness and worry before stepping closer and wrapping her arms around his shoulders. Resting her chin lightly on him, she felt his tension beneath the surface.

'He has my nose,' Charles said, a touch of pride in his voice, the words of a first-time father.

'Charles Arthur Kingsford Smith.' He whispered further.

'You gave away the Lord Mayor's fund,' Mary murmured, her voice a quiet thread of awe and reproach. It wasn't an accusation, just an acknowledgment of the selflessness that defined Charles—and the burdens it often brought.

Charles didn't look up. He kept his focus on his son, his hands moving with practiced care. 'He looks like a little cherub,' he said softly, as though louder words might shatter the fragile peace of the moment.

Mary smiled faintly. 'I am surprised he was not born with wings,' she teased, though her words carried an edge of concern.

Charles chuckled gently but then glanced her way, his smile faltering. 'I cannot keep doing this, Mare.' His voice was quiet but heavy, as if each word carried the weight of his exhaustion and doubts.

Mary's arms tightened around him. She kissed the side of his head, and spoke with quiet determination. 'That is just the tired talking. You have given so much, Charles. More than most could. But you do not need to carry all this on your own.'

He exhaled slowly, his gaze dropping back to the basin. The water rippled faintly as if echoing his unrest.

Mary gently lifted their son from his arms. Charles Jr. yawned, his tiny face scrunching in a way that made her heart ache with love. 'Let us get this little pilot into bed, shall we?' she said softly, cradling him close.

'Tomorrow will come soon enough, and you will face it, just like you always do. But tonight, let it be enough.'

Charles watched them, the image of his wife and child filling him with equal parts love and sadness. He ran a hand through his hair, feeling the crushing weight of what lay ahead: the expectations, the sacrifices, the uncertain future.

Mary, sensing his turmoil, met his gaze with a steadiness that made him feel seen, understood. 'We will get through this,' she said, her voice a quiet promise.

Charles nodded. He knew she was right, though the doubts in his heart still clawed for space. 'Thank you,' he murmured, his voice raw with gratitude.

Mary smiled, brushing a strand of hair from her face. 'Always,' she replied.

Placing Charles Jr. in his crib, she smoothed a cloth over his tiny form, drying the water from his supple skin. Charles Jr. stirred, one small hand reaching up toward the faint light of the room. Mary lingered, watching him. 'He looks like he is reaching for the skies,' she murmured softly.

Turning back to Charles, she extended her hand. 'Come on. I will help get you ready.'

He took her hand, standing, the weariness in his body lessened slightly by her touch. Together they moved toward the dresser, where the rest of his suit lay neatly folded. Mary gently tied his black bow tie, then tidied and straightened his crisp white shirt with unspoken tenderness. 'Well, you do look quite handsome, Sir Charles, I must admit.'

As they stood there, he leaned in, his forehead resting against hers, finding solace in the quiet moment they shared.

'Promise you will behave,' she teased.

'I do not know what I would do without you,' he admitted.

'You won't have to find out,' she said, her voice firm but warm. 'We are in this together.'

The baby let out a small sigh in his sleep, the sound filling the room with an almost magical stillness. Charles glanced back at the crib one last time, his heart swelling with both love and determination.

Mary helped him with his jacket, straightening the shoulders and pinching a small piece of lint from the breast. 'Now, not too late tonight, young man,' she said playfully.

'Are you going to be alright?' he asked, hesitating slightly.

"I will be just fine,' she assured him as she gently kissed his cheek.

Charles gazed into her eyes. 'I have this little aviator to keep me company. Besides, with all the excitement, I think I am more exhausted than you.'

Mary smiled, her hands resting lightly on his chest. He took a deep breath, mustering his strength, both physically and mentally.

'I won't be late,' he promised.

'Promise?' Mary raised an eyebrow, a playful yet questioning tone in her voice.

'Well . . .' Charles replied with an air of maybe, earning a soft laugh from her.

'Go on, or you will be late,' she said, gesturing toward the door. As he turned to leave, she added softly, 'be you.'

Charles hesitated before closing the door behind him. Mary leaned back against it, exhaling as the strength she'd held so firmly seemed to seep away. Charles Jr. murmured for attention, pulling her back from her thoughts. Shaking off her concerns, she moved to him with renewed fortitude.

'So, little man, that is your father,' she whispered, her voice carrying both admiration and pride.

Chapter 10

Melbourne, Victoria, Australia. 1933.

Steam wafted from the locomotive below, curling like ghostly tendrils past the elegant red-and-yellow brick Edwardian facade of Flinders Street Station. Inside, the ballroom pulsed with the quiet rhythm of high society, where power danced as elegantly as the crystal chandeliers that hung above.

The coffered ceilings, heavy with intricate plasterwork, created an atmosphere of old-world grandeur. Each gilded detail seemed alive in the warm glow of the chandeliers, their crystal prisms scattering light like stardust. Deep mahogany paneling gleamed under the glow, while gold-leaf moldings and mirrors reflected every movement, doubling the room's brilliance. Velvet curtains in rich burgundy framed the tall arched windows, their golden tassels swaying faintly in the soft breeze from outside.

The tables were immaculate, draped in crisp white linen embroidered with gold. Centerpieces of fresh roses and lilies stood in crystal vases, their perfume mingling with the unmistakable scents of cigar smoke and aged whiskey. Flickering candles in elaborate candelabras cast long, dancing shadows over the silver cutlery and bone china rimmed with gold.

The guests, dressed to perfection for the black-tie occasion, moved gracefully through the room. The men wore impeccably tailored tuxedos, their bow ties crisply tied, with polished leather shoes gleaming under the chandelier's glow. The women exuded elegance in floor-length evening gowns, adorned with sequins, beads, and delicate embroidery, their jewels catching the light in dazzling flashes. Gloves of satin or lace adorned their hands, and their coiffed hair added a regal touch to the occasion.

A string quartet played softly from a corner of the room, their instruments producing lilting melodies that floated above the subdued conversations. The strains of a waltz filled the air, lending an enchanting rhythm to the scene as a few couples swayed gracefully in time to the music, their steps a quiet echo of timeless refinement.

As the quiet hum of conversation ebbed, the polite clink of silver against crystal began to gather like a signal—sharp, deliberate, a summons. Sir Macpherson Robertson rose slowly from his seat, the gleam of expectation catching in the crowd's eyes as he moved to the podium. His figure, tall and commanding, seemed to draw the room inward, each breath quieting in anticipation.

The air thickened, heavy with a mix of reverence and curiosity, as the audience prepared for the weight of his words to descend.

'Ladies and gentlemen, if I may,' Mac bellowed, his voice resonating across the grand hall and drawing all eyes to him. 'Thank you, my dear fellows, ladies and gentlemen. It is my great honor to have you join me tonight in this magnificent hall to celebrate Sir Charles Kingsford Smith's record-breaking flight from the motherland, England, to our homeland, Australia.'

Raising their glasses in unison, the room erupted into applause, cheers of 'hear, hear!' mingling with the melodic tinkling of crystal. A swell of admiration and pride filled the air, a heartfelt tribute to an achievement that seemed to touch every soul present. The applause resonated warmly, an almost physical manifestation of shared celebration.

'An astonishing flight of some ten thousand miles,' Mac continued, his tone a mix of reverence and delight. The guests, still riding the wave of enthusiastic praise, turned their admiration toward Charles, who accepted the attention with a beaming smile, unabashed in his enjoyment of the moment. 'A flight that affords Smithy the title and great honor of becoming the first man in history to traverse these two great nations of the Commonwealth in just seven days. The significance of which is underscored by this very fact.' Mac paused, his dramatic timing drawing the crowd in. 'On my last trip to the mother country by sea, it took so long that by the time I arrived, I had become a father of three.'

The room exploded with laughter, the rich sound trembling the very walls. Guests doubled over with mirth, their booming guffaws and delighted cheers a testament to Mac's perfectly executed jest. The clinking of glasses, the occasional pop of champagne corks, and the harmonious murmur of animated conversation added to the vibrant atmosphere.

Silverware tapped against fine china, blending with the festive hum as the guests indulged in a lavish meal, their spirits as high as the chandeliers overhead.

'Ladies and gentlemen, we stand witness—indeed, the nation stands witness—to an achievement once deemed impossible, an accomplishment that has forever altered the world in which we live.' Sir Macpherson took a deliberate breath, his words commanding the room's full attention. 'Ladies and gentlemen, again, we have beaten the British.'

The room erupted anew, this time with a thunderous ovation. Windows quivered, fine china rattled, and the chandeliers seemed to shiver under the force of stomping feet and raised glasses. The toast soared through the air, reverberating with a collective sense of triumph and national pride.

As the festivities continued unabated, the laughter and applause floated down the ornate staircase—a grand structure of intricately carved banisters and plush red carpeting, embodying the evening's opulence.

From below, the growing noise reached the ears of two men ascending the staircase. Beau Sheil, dressed in immaculate black-tie attire that contrasted sharply with the rugged lines of his well-worn features, cast a concerned glance at his companion. 'Well, we are certainly late Charlie,' he murmured, his tone heavy with the weight of the evening.

Charles Ulm, a tall and strikingly handsome figure of a man, equally well-dressed in formal evening wear, kept in step with Beau as they quickened their pace. They reached the top of the staircase, pausing at the grand entry to scan the room for their seats.

'Over there!' Charlie directed, his voice low but firm as he nodded toward their table. Without delay, the two men slinked their way between the tables, navigating the clusters of the attentive crowd in an effort to avoid disruption. As they approached their seats, they offered polite smiles and nods, exchanging brief acknowledgments with the other attendees before settling into their places with an understated air of confidence.

'Thank you, thank you,' Sir Macpherson continued, thoroughly enjoying himself as he reveled in his role, commanding the room with his natural charisma. 'It is only appropriate that we tonight acknowledge that this remarkable achievement be added to the long list of truly extraordinary accomplishments attributed to the great name of Sir Charles Kingsford Smith, our honoree this evening.'

Charlie and Beau exchanged a glance, their expressions warm with admiration, before joining in the applause that swept through the room like a tide.

'For those of you who may be unaware of Sir Charles's many achievements—or for those who may live on the moon, the only place Sir Charles has yet to fly,' Mac quipped, drawing a ripple of laughter from the guests, 'I have brought that list with me tonight.'

The laughter gave way to a quiet hum of anticipation, the room holding its collective breath as Elizabeth approached the dais. Her graceful steps carried her forward, her youth and beauty drawing appreciative glances from all corners of the room. With poise, she handed Mac a large scroll, its crimson ribbon glinting faintly in the light.

'Thank you, Elizabeth,' Mac said warmly, giving her a brief nod before fumbling in his coat pocket for his glasses. With deliberate precision, he perched them on his nose, their exaggerated placement earning a few light chuckles. He took the scroll with theatrical flair as Elizabeth stepped back, retreating slightly from the center of attention.

'Ha hmm!' Mac cleared his throat, his eyes twinkling with a mischievous sense of showmanship. With a slow, deliberate movement, he untied the ribbon, allowing the scroll to remain furled for just a beat longer, teasing the eager crowd. Then, with a grand flourish, he released it.

The scroll unfurled like a coiled spring, its length spilling across the stage and onto the floor, winding its way toward the audience. Guests erupted into laughter, the absurdity of its dramatic size filling the room with mirth.

Sir Macpherson smiled, basking in the laughter, and cleared his throat again. 'Ha hmm.' He raised his voice, beginning to read. 'Air Commodore, Sir Charles Kingsford Smith. Knight of the realm. Recipient of the Military Cross. The first man to circumnavigate the globe by air. The first man to fly the Pacific Ocean from the United States of America to Australia. The first man to fly the Atlantic Ocean from east to west. The first man to fly the Tasman Sea from Australia to New Zealand—in both directions, I might add.' Another ripple of laughter swept the crowd.

He paused, pulling at his collar with a mock expression of heat and awe. 'I need a drink,' he quipped, the room erupting in laughter again. Charles, visibly modest yet bemused, shook his head with a shy smile, his cheeks faintly flushed.

Mac continued, grinning. 'The first man to fly from Australia to England. And—need I go on?'

The crowd, exuberant and enthralled, shouted in unison, 'More! More!' Their cheers filled the hall, the air alive with jubilation and admiration, a celebration befitting the extraordinary legacy of the man at the center of it all.

Seated toward the front of the room at a table bearing significantly more prominence, Collins exuded a restrained air as he gauged the sentiment of the crowd. Applause thundered around him, the enthusiasm palpable, but his expression remained dour. Leaning subtly toward Sir Duddevin, he murmured in a low whisper.

'Minister, I think you would agree Sir Charles's popularity is becoming somewhat of a concern.'

Sir Duddevin's gaze swept the room, his eyes narrowing as they lingered on the jubilant faces of the crowd. With a tone laced in sinister undercurrents, he replied under his breath, 'Indeed, Minister. His continued elevation above the common man certainly poses implications.'

Sir Macpherson, ever the master showman, continued to rile the crowd, his voice booming over their applause. 'Ladies and Gentlemen, if I may indulge you for another moment of your time, I must confess that my motives for hosting this gala tonight have not been entirely forthcoming.' The crowd hushed, leaning in with eager anticipation. 'It is with this tremendous occasion that I am honored to announce the greatest aviation event in history: The Centennial Air Race—from England to Australia, marking the centenary of the great city of Melbourne! And to the winner, a prize of fifteen thousand pounds!'

With a dramatic snap, Sir Macpherson signaled, and the coverings concealing two freshly minted promotional posters fell away, unveiling his plan to all. The room erupted into gasping applause as the bold images came into view. A pilot clad in flight gear, goggles catching the sunlight, stared resolutely toward an unseen horizon. Above him, emblazoned in striking letters, were the words: World's Greatest Air Race. A sleek monoplane soared across an azure sky, evoking a sense of daring and adventure. The imagery was not merely an announcement; it was a rallying cry for dreamers and daredevils alike.

'And representing our great nation,' Mac declared, his voice swelling with pride, 'will be none other than the greatest aviator of all time—Ladies and gentlemen, the man of the hour, Sir Charles Kingsford Smith!'

Sir Macpherson began clapping, leading the crowd into a standing ovation. The applause filled the room, thunderous and unrelenting, as the crowd rose to its feet in unanimous admiration. Charles, caught off guard and uneasy, reluctantly stepped toward the podium, his movements hesitant. As he shook Mac's hand, his discomfort was evident. Leaning in close, Mac whispered firmly into his ear, 'We will talk in the morning.'

The dimly lit service alley offered a welcome reprieve from the clamor of the gala. Charles stood in solitude, the peacefulness of his cigarette enhanced by the smoky wisps curling into the cool, damp night air. The scents of burnt steam and grease from the nearby railway yards mixed with the rhythmic clatter of distant railway cars, creating a symphony of the city's nocturnal pulse.

The alley was framed by aged brick walls, steam pipes, and service vehicles, their utilitarian presence contrasting the grandeur of the event above. Nearby, a group of men huddled around a fire, the flames casting flickering shadows that danced along the walls.

The heavy wooden door behind Charles swung open abruptly, breaking the quiet. Charlie stepped into the alley, his presence instantly commanding. Charles, lost in his thoughts, barely reacted, his calm interrupted only by the familiarity of the voice.

'I thought I might find you out here,' Charlie said, his deep tone cutting through the stillness with friendly warmth..

Charles turned, his expression shifting from introspection to delight. 'Charlie?' A grin broke across his face as he straightened his posture. Stepping forward, he clasped Charlie's shoulder warmly. 'It is good to see you,' he said with genuine affection.

'You never did like these fancy do's, did you?' Charlie remarked, glancing upward at the glowing ballroom windows. The muffled sounds of laughter and music spilled softly into the alley.

'I did not know you were here,' Charles admitted, his surprise evident.

'We got in a little late. Beau is with me—free grog!' Charlie replied with a mischievous smile.

Charles chuckled. 'It is good to see you, Charlie.'

'Good to see you, Smithy.'

Taking one last puff of his cigarette, Charles stubbed it out against the pavement with a soft hiss, savoring the brief reprieve from the evening's demands.

'You catch the speech?' Charles asked, the formality of the gala still clinging to his voice.

'I did,' Charlie nodded with a grin. 'Still carrying the hopes and dreams of the entire nation on your shoulders, I see.' Charles raised an eyebrow, his bemusement breaking into a quiet laugh.

'Apparently! I remember when the only hopes and dreams we carried were our own. Look at us now—dressed like a couple of monkeys.' He tugged at his suit jacket.

Charlie chuckled. 'Yeah, well, now you just have to figure out if you're the organ or the grinder.' The two sharing a lingering laugh, their camaraderie a brief balm against the weight of the evening.

'It has been a long time, Charlie. It would be nice to do this one together,' Charles said, his voice tinged with nostalgia.

'The race?'

'Just like old times.'

Charlie hesitated, his expression softening. 'Oh, Charles . . . I have put those days behind me. We lost a lot of good flyers this year—Hinkler, Lancaster.'

'Good men,' Charles replied solemnly.

'Very good men. It's different now. The days of jumping into any old aircraft and just going—they are gone.'

Charlie glanced downward, his voice tinged with bittersweet reflection. 'John's thirteen now, Charles. I can't leave my son growing up without a father because I was off chasing some record, staring into an endless horizon.'

'The luck of the game, eh?' Charles murmured, his gaze drifting to the distant fire.

'It's not a game anymore,' Charlie replied firmly. 'It's big business now—government, airlines, corporate money. Aviation is everything we dreamed it would be . . . and everything we feared it might become.'

He lit a cigarette, the soft flare of his lighter illuminating his face. 'Besides, anyone standing next to you is just standing in your shadow.' He gestured toward the ballroom's glow. 'Smithy—the greatest flyer the world has ever seen.'

Charlie's grin widened as he added, 'And if you keep opening new flying routes the way you have been, there won't be a route left on the planet for the rest of us.' He chuckled, the jest drawing brief laughter from Charles, their camaraderie momentarily lightening the night.

The levity was interrupted as Elizabeth stepped gracefully into the alley, her presence immediately capturing the attention of both men. The soft glow of the ballroom's distant lights mingled with the flickering flames nearby, accentuating her elegance. Her figure-hugging, floor-length gown of shimmering emerald-green silk caught the light with every movement, complementing her porcelain skin and the cascade of dark curls framing her face.

A delicate string of pearls adorned her neckline, their understated beauty matching the refinement of her ensemble, while her deep red lips added a touch of bold sophistication. The rhythmic click of her heels against the cobblestones carried an almost hypnotic quality as she approached, each step exuding poise and purpose, yet innocently coupled with youthful naivety.

'I am terribly sorry to interrupt, Sir Charles. Sir Macpherson has requested your presence,' she said, her voice polite, yet laced with a gentle crackle of nervousness, underscoring her message.

Charlie turned back to Charles, resting a hand on his shoulder. 'Watch your back Charles,' he said warily. 'I will leave you to it—you would not want to keep the boss waiting.' Charlie smiled, the two shared a moment of understanding, a silent exchange that spoke of mutual respect. 'Good luck, Charles,' Charlie affirmed, extending his hand.

Charles clasped it firmly, their eyes locking for a brief, meaningful moment. 'Thank you, Charlie.'

As Charlie walked away, he paused and turned back with a parting thought. 'And Smithy, if you need a good man, P. G. Taylor is your guy.' Charles acknowledged his suggestion, watching him walk away before taking a deep breath of the cool night air. He stubbed out his cigarette against the cobblestones, savoring the fleeting tranquility, and let his gaze drift upward.

The Southern Cross shone brightly above, poised perfectly between the surrounding buildings. The squeal of railway cars breaking along the nearby tracks provided a rhythmic heartbeat. *Click clack, click clack.*

Elizabeth stepped closer, her eyes following his gaze. 'Is that the Southern Cross?' she asked softly, her melodic voice blending seamlessly in the reflection of the moment.

'It is,' Charles replied, his tone carrying the weight of reverent memories. They both stood in silence for a moment, the constellation's significance unspoken but deeply felt.

'Is it true that it cannot be seen in the northern skies?' Elizabeth inquired, her curiosity momentarily distracting her from her duties.

Charles nodded. 'It is,' he affirmed softly, pausing as his gaze lingered on the stars. Raising his hand, he pointed upward, guiding her eyes with gentle precision. 'The top star, Alpha Crucis,' he began, 'glows brightly, its bluish-white light piercing the darkness.'

'Below it, Beta Crucis,' he continued, 'slightly dimmer, anchors the vertical line of the cross.' He shifted his hand slightly. 'To the left, Gamma Crucis—a red giant—adds its own unique hue, its soft red glow standing out against the cooler light of the others. And there, at the bottom, is Delta Crucis, steady and unwavering.' His finger traced the final point. 'That small one just there? That's Epsilon Crucis, completing the constellation.'

Elizabeth's eyes followed his every gesture, her voice a soft whisper that seemed to blend seamlessly with the stillness of the night. 'You certainly know your stars, Sir Charles.'

Charles smiled faintly, his gaze never leaving the Southern Cross. 'It pays to Elizabeth, especially when they guide you home,' he said quietly, the appreciation in his tone revealing a deep connection to the constellation above.

'You certainly have an impressive repertoire of achievements, Sir Charles,' Elizabeth said, her admiration unmistakable.

Charles turned to her, his eyes meeting hers with a thoughtful intensity. 'I can only imagine the stories you could tell, the places you have seen,' she continued, her excitement bubbling over. A faint smile tugged at Charles's lips as he regarded her inquisitive enthusiasm.

'What is it like up there?' Elizabeth asked, her voice tinged with wonder. 'Do you get scared? It must be terrifying—and exhilarating all at once!'

Charles's smile widened slightly. Her energy was infectious, charming him in ways he couldn't quite articulate. 'It is both Eizabeth, but one cannot live in fear.' His tone, steady but warm. Elizabeth's eyes lit up, and before she could stop herself, she blurted, 'Oh, it must be wonderful to experience what it is like to fly. You must take me with you one day, Sir Charles.'

The words hung between them for a moment, her boldness surprising even herself. She quickly withdrew, clutching his arm impulsively before pulling back, her cheeks flushing with embarrassment. 'I am sorry, I do apologize, Sir Charles.'

Charles, bemused, took it in stride; he was not unaccustomed to such attention. Politely and gently, he replied to her fragility, 'We should go.'

He smiled affectionately, his calm demeanor softening her nerves. Elizabeth nodded, tilting her head with a gentle bow, her gaze lingering on his for a moment before flickering away.

'After you, Elizabeth,' Charles suggested, his voice warm and steady, as he gestured for her to lead the way.

With a final flicker of her gaze, Elizabeth turned, delicately lifting her dress from the ground. She stepped forward, her movements measured and graceful. Charles followed closely behind, the faint promise of the unspoken moment lingering between them.

As the evening wore on, the dim light of the hotel's pub barely illuminated the weary faces of the working-class men who occupied it. Their expressions, etched with the lines of exhaustion, depression, and stress, found brief reprieve in the simple pleasure of each mouthful of beer they consumed. With every sip, they momentarily escaped the hardships and the uncertainty of life, enduring their burdens alongside those who shared in the same struggle of the Great Depression.

The air was thick with smoke, and the pungent stench of stale liquor hung heavily beneath the tall, ornately plastered ceilings, yellowed by nicotine. The low murmur of conversation mingled with the sound of clinking glasses as the men sought solace from the rigors of their physical labor, the ache in their bones, and the relentless uncertainty of the times. Most, if not all, had suffered through the Great War, and still bore the physical scars of battle and the mental wounds of a brutal conflict. They carried with them memories of their friends, the ones who didn't return. Once heralded as heroes of an epic era, they were now fighting a different kind of war, a battle to survive. Despite their circumstances, they maintained their resilience and adaptability—a rugged determination they had forged together on the battlefields of Europe, now tested yet again on the home front. At a corner table, a group of men huddled together, their faces drawn and tired, yet united in camaraderie.

'We've been through worse,' one man remarked, his voice tinged with a mixture of resignation and hope.

'Yeah, better this than the bloody trenches,' another replied, his tone equally weary.

'You've got to wonder why they stick 'Great' in front of everything,' a third man scoffed. 'The Great War, the Great Depression—nothing bloody great about either of them.'

The others nodded and laughed sarcastically in agreement.

'They should just call 'em both hell,' he added.

'Feels like it,' another man agreed, and the conversation lapsed into its familiar rhythm, echoing the same sentiments they had expressed yesterday and the day before.

Behind the bar, the bartender slicked back his thinning hair in between polishing glasses, occasionally glancing at the patrons with a knowing look. He had seen countless men come and go, each with their own story to tell, most revealing it only through the look in their eyes.

'They're saying it can't last much longer,' one man offered, his voice laced with skepticism.

'They've been saying that for four bloody years,' another retorted, shaking his head.

The bartender interjected, setting down a fresh pint in front of one of the men. 'Aye, but we've got each other, lads. That's something they can't take away.'

'The pubs aren't suffering,' someone observed, prompting a ripple of laughter.

'The politicians can mess with everything else, but they know better than to mess with the beer,' a man joked, eliciting more laughter.

'If they did, it'd be the start of the next Great War,' another added.

'They better not mess with the bloody cricket, either,' someone quipped, and the men chuckled, momentarily finding humor in their shared plight.

Their laughter, though lighthearted, betrayed a deep longing for the better times of the past.

In a quieter corner, Mick sat alone, nursing his drink, his shoulders sagging under the crushing weight of recent news. His threadbare shirt, patched at the elbows, and trousers, held up by fraying suspenders, told the story of a man who, like so many others, had weathered too many storms. The scuffed leather of his worn-out boots, cracked and dusty, bore silent witness to work, while the flat cap resting on the table beside him was a relic of better days, now dulled by time and hardship.

'Bloody Mick over there. Poor bastard, he was in that four hundred that got laid off yesterday,' one man mentioned, bringing the conversation back to the harsh realities of their lives. A hush fell over the group as they glanced toward Mick with sympathetic eyes.

'We've got some room for the missus and kids if he needs it,' another offered sincerely.

'I'll let him know,' the first man replied, nodding gratefully.

Their attention shifted as the creaking entrance door announced a new arrival. Charles entered, overdressed and slightly disheveled, his bow tie hanging loose around his neck. Despite the formal attire, the lines on his face told the same stories as the men he greeted. His soles stuck to the beer-soaked carpet as conversations fell silent. Charles removed his jacket, undid his cuffs, and carefully rolled his sleeves halfway up his forearms. He stood tall amid their under breath whispers, taking a deep breath to steady himself.

'Any of you jokers got a beer?' he called loudly, a wide grin spreading across his face. The silence held firm for a moment before the room erupted in unison.

'Smithy! Smithy!' they cried, surrounding him with cheers.

'Well done, Smithy!' they called. 'You bloody beauty! Get this man a beer!' Another yelled. Amid the applause, a man stepped forward, blocking Charles's path with a display of mock aggression. He butted his chest against Charles's and firmly demanded, 'Not so fast, Smithy! You need to be hung, drawn, and quartered.' The room simmered with the building tension.

Drunkenly slurring his words, he spoke as he wobbled on his feet. 'Now that the pommy bastards know they can get here in seven days, they'll bloody swamp the place,' the man continued, 'Ya ya bastard!' before bursting into laughter. The room joined in again, the tension broken within the humor.

'Yeah! Do us all a favor, Smithy—give up bloody flying! You're going to ruin the place,' another man added, sparking another round of jostling and laughter.

Charles grinned, realizing he had averted what appeared to be a potential fist-filled altercation. Quickly, he slid an empty chair out from a nearby table and leaped up atop it to stand. He gratefully accepted a beer, raising it high above himself and the crowd in an informal salute to all who had gathered.

'Sorry, lads, but once you have tasted flight, you will walk the earth with your eyes forever skyward, for there you have been, and there you will long to return,' he declared to the birds.

Quickly came the response to the overly educated proclamation.

'Lookout the King has thus spoken,' one man yelled, mocking his impersonation.

'First you're a pilot, now you're a bloody poet,' another man quipped then laughed.

'That, gentlemen, is a quote from the inventor of flight himself—the great Leonardo da Vinci,' Charles explained, raising his beer higher.

Still laughing, a fellow patron climbed atop a chair next to Charles and stood, puffing his chest and pushing his stomach out before placing his thumbs into vest pockets, mocking the stereotypical pose of a fat, wealthy politician. 'No, no, no—quiet! What old Len meant to say was, once you've tasted the beer in this pub, it's here you've been and here you'll long to return,' he countered through a mouth full of marbles, earning a fresh wave of laughter. 'Yes! Yes! Gentlemen, a vote for me, the honorable Sir Drunk-a-Lot, is a vote for lower beer prices for my fellow man!' He laughed through a mouthful of half missing teeth.

'To the King!' Charles toasted, referring to the man next to him, having been outwitted.

'Hear! Hear!' The men replied as the barmaid approached, shaking her head at the spectacle, her hands firmly against hips in disapproval.

'Come on, you two—down from your bloody soapboxes. This is a pub, not Parliament,' she scolded as she waved them down from their makeshift soapboxes. 'Down, down you get before one you drunkards breaks your bloody neck.'

'A round on me!' Charles yelled in a final celebration, as he jumped down from his perch. The room erupted in cheers as the men eagerly stampeded the bar in lifted spirits, freeing the burden of their minds, for now.

'Gotcha!' Tommy muttered, finally wrestling free the stubborn engine component he'd been struggling with. His legs were awkwardly straddled over the engine of the Miss Southern Cross, grease streaking his overalls and smudging his cheek. With a final twist, the component popped loose, and he held it up to eye level, scrutinizing it with the precision of a surgeon.

The very late hours of the early morning afforded little light, but his makeshift lamp system cast a focused glow over the aircraft, illuminating the spot where he worked. The air hung thick with the pungent cocktail of oil, burnt rubber, and old fuel—a grounding, familiar stench that made Tommy feel at home.

Tracing the grooves of the component with his fingers, he shook his head, frustration and satisfaction mingling in his expression. 'Bloody poms,' he muttered. The clatter of a wrench echoed in the vast hangar as it slipped from his perch and hit the concrete below.

In the shadows behind him, Charles entered quietly, his footsteps soft, his silhouette blending with the gloom. He paused, watching Tommy in his element. For a moment, a flicker of pride crossed his face, though it was dulled by the haze of alcohol clinging to him like a second skin.

'Thought you could use a hand,' Charles said, breaking the stillness and startling Tommy.

Tommy glanced up, his grin broadening when he saw who it was. 'Oh! Hey, boss,' he said, wiping his hands on his already filthy overalls. 'Well, look what the cat dragged in, eh?' His tone was respectful, but the twinkle in his eye betrayed his teasing nature.

Charles managed a faint, weary smile. His shirt was crumpled, and his tie hung loose, the picture of a man worn down by the weight of the day—or perhaps something more.

'Guaranteed, if there's an aircraft nearby, Tommy will be in it, on it, or under it,' he replied, his voice slurring just enough for Tommy to notice.

Tommy chuckled, holding up the part. 'Your timing is perfect. I found the problem. The bore size on the radiator's a quarter of an inch too small. Look.' He thrust the piece forward, pointing out the issue with practiced authority. 'See here? It's supposed to increase flow rate, not choke it.'

'Yeah . . . throw me that screwdriver,' Charles interrupted, his tone casual but with an undertone Tommy couldn't quite place.

'This one?' Tommy asked, holding it up.

'Yeah. Thanks.'

Charles crouched under the wing, unscrewing an access panel. Tommy watched, his curiosity piqued. There was a deliberate nature to Charles's actions—a tension in his shoulders that belied his usual easy going demeanor.

'Normally cooling wouldn't be an issue,' Tommy continued, narrating as he worked, 'but when you came off the cool air over the ocean and hit the desert, it overloaded. I'm surprised you made it here at all.'

'Have Customs been through yet?' Charles asked, his tone casual as he worked, but with an edge that hinted at deeper concerns. One of the screws fell to the ground with a light ping, rolling away with a series of diminishing clicks.

'Yeah, they were here for hours, longer than usual. They went through everything,' Tommy replied, curiosity sparking in his eyes as Charles removed the panel and reached deep into the wing, his arm disappearing well past his elbow.

Charles grunted, his hand probing deliberately. 'Just making sure they didn't miss anything,' he said vaguely.

'Problem with the overheads?' Tommy asked, tilting his head.

'You could say that,' Charles muttered, his tone carrying a hint of amusement that didn't match the strain in his voice. Finally, he exhaled. 'There you are.' With a slow, deliberate motion, he withdrew his arm, clutching a neatly folded cloth. He paused, glancing at Tommy. 'Come down, have a look at this.'

Intrigued, Tommy climbed down from the engine, wiping his hands on his thighs. Charles unfolded the cloth with meticulous care, each layer revealing more of the object inside. As the final fold fell away, the dim light caught the unmistakable glitter of diamonds.

'Holy hell,' Tommy breathed, his eyes widening. 'Are they real?'

'Oh, they are real,' Charles replied, his voice low, almost reverent. Nestled in the cloth was a brooch—a dazzling, intricate recreation of the *Southern Cross* aircraft, glimmering with diamonds.

'That's the *Southern Cross*! Where the hell did you get that? It looks just like her.' Tommy's voice carried a mix of awe and disbelief.

Charles smiled faintly, but it didn't reach his eyes. 'Let's just say it's a long story.'

Tommy shook his head in amazement. 'That must be worth a fortune. Lucky Customs didn't find it.'

Charles nodded. 'Lucky Customs have no idea what they're looking for.'

Tommy smirked. 'Yeah.'

'The luck of the game, Tommy,' Charles replied, folding the brooch back into the cloth with the same care he'd unfolded it. He looked up at Tommy, his expression serious. 'Best you and I keep this between us, yeah? We would not want Mary to find out.'

Tommy met his gaze, his grin fading. 'You got it, boss.'

Charles straightened, sliding the cloth into his pocket. 'You're a good man, Tommy.' Charles paused momentarily. 'Are you sure you don't need a hand?'

'No I got it boss, I should have her ready in a couple of days.'

'Good lad, I will leave you to it,' Charles said, clapping Tommy on the shoulder. As he turned back toward the hangar's shadows, the faint scent of whisky and something above his pay grade lingered in the air.

Tommy stood there a moment longer, glancing at the wing where the brooch had been hidden. Slowly, he moved over, replacing the cover and screws with care. He laughed quietly to himself, shaking his head. 'Tommy, you do not want to know. You do not want to know.'

Chapter 11

Melbourne, Victoria, Australia. 1933.

Charles blinked a few times, the soft haze of sleep still lingering as the early morning light filtered gently through the curtains, painting the room in a golden glow. Outside, the melody of birdsong drifted in; he was tranquil in rest, his rise from weariness well earned.

Rolling toward Mary, he wrapped her in his arms, pulling her close. She stirred, her voice soft and tinged with curiosity.

'You got in late last night.'

Charles's heart skipped a beat, the remnants of drowsiness vanishing in an instant.

'I am late!' he exclaimed, springing to his feet. He moved with haste, searching for his clothes amid the chaos of the room.

Mary watched him, a bemused smile tugging at her lips. 'That is usually the girl's line?'

Charles froze mid-motion, her words cutting through his urgency. Turning to her, he studied her expression, a flicker of unease crossing his face.

'You are not—?'

Her smile widened, and she shook her head. 'No, I am not.'

Relief washed over him, though his hands still trembled as he buttoned his shirt.

'Here,' he said, crossing to the chair where his jacket lay. Reaching into an inside pocket, he withdrew a small cloth-wrapped bundle. 'I got you something.'

Mary tilted her head, curiosity gleaming in her eyes. 'What is it?'

'Open it,' he urged, fumbling with his boots as she unfolded the fabric.

Her breath caught. The brooch shimmered in the morning light, each detail of the Southern Cross captured in exquisite craftsmanship.

'My God, Charles. It is beautiful . . . is that the Southern Cross?'

'It is,' he said softly.

Tears welled in her eyes as she turned the piece in her hands. 'Charles, where did you—? This is stunning.'

'I love you,' he murmured, leaning in to kiss her gently.

Mary looked up, her voice trembling with emotion. 'Thank you. It is perfect. Oh Charles,' Mary said, in quiet disbelief.

A shadow flickered across his face as he straightened. 'Listen,' he said, his tone low and serious. 'If anyone asks where you got it, say it was a gift from your mother.'

Her brow furrowed. 'What? Why—?'

Charles was already moving, finishing his dressing with hurried efficiency. 'You are just going to have to trust me on this one,' he said, placing his hat firmly on his head. He paused at the door, his gaze softening as it lingered on her.

'I love you.'

'I love you too,' Mary whispered, watching him disappear through the doorway.

The brooch gleamed in her palm, a fragile spark of beauty amid the growing mystery. Warm affection filled her chest as she admired it, her fingers brushing over the delicate design.

She stood and moved to the dresser, holding the brooch against her heart. In the mirror, it glistened beautifully against the backdrop of her satin black negligee. Mary smiled, tilting her head to catch the reflection from different angles.

'It was a gift from my mother,' she repeated aloud with a curious smile. 'It better not be stolen,' she mused, her tone light, before setting the brooch gently on the dresser.

Still content with the love she felt, Mary turned her attention to Charles Jr., sound asleep in his cot. His tiny chest rose and fell, a soft snore escaping his lips.

'Just like your father,' she whispered warmly, adjusting his blanket.

Glancing around the slightly disheveled room, Mary sighed. The demands of life had left their mark, and she wondered where to begin. Her eyes landed on Charles's white shirt draped over the chair.

Grasping it, she held it to her nose and inhaled deeply, savoring his familiar scent. 'Hmm,' she murmured, smiling to herself.

Her smile faltered when she noticed a stain on the collar. She looked closer, her brow furrowing as her heart sank. The stain was dark, thick, and heavy—its smudged edges oddly reminiscent of mascara.

Mary stared at it, her mind racing with unwelcome thoughts. Her stomach twisted. No wife wanted to think this way, but the mark was hard to ignore.

Lifting the fabric to her nose, she hesitated before inhaling. Relief flooded her as a familiar scent hit her—grease. The pungent, oily tang was unmistakable.

Mary burst into a small, embarrassed laugh, shaking her head at her own imagination.

'Well, at least it is not lipstick,' she said aloud, her voice laced with amusement.

Folding the shirt neatly, she smiled, the silliness of her doubts fading away. The warmth of Charles's love and the glimmer of the brooch on the dresser reassured her that, for now, his love was true, and true to hers. Mary squealed a little squeal and gently and happily inhaled his scent.

The early morning light stretched long shadows through the streets of Melbourne, but the promising day quickly dimmed. Overhead, low-hanging clouds gathered, their weight pressing down on the city, and a biting wind snaked through the alleys and avenues, sharp enough to cut through even the thickest coat. Yesterday's warmth and sunshine felt like a distant memory.

Charles watched the city's slow awakening from the back seat of his taxi. The vehicle crept forward in heavy traffic, giving him an unhurried view of the street. His attention was drawn to a line of men standing silently along the sidewalk—a breadline that snaked down the block and disappeared around the corner. Their huddled figures, shrouded in threadbare coats, were etched with a grim resignation that seemed to seep into the air itself.

The sight pulled at him, a leaden weight settling in his chest. Charles exhaled slowly, his breath fogging the cold glass of the taxi window.

'I'll get out here,' he said to the driver, handing over the fare. 'Keep the change.'

The sharp chill hit him as he stepped from the cab, his polished shoes clicking against the pavement. The contrast between his tailored overcoat and the worn, patched clothing of the men in line could not have been starker. Their faces were gaunt and pale, their postures heavy with fatigue, as if they bore not just the chill of the wind but the weight of their collective hardship. Yet, as Charles walked past, quiet recognition flickered in their eyes. A few men tipped their hats, others nodded, their expressions softening as they acknowledged him. His name had been in the papers recently—a story of success that felt worlds away from the scene before him.

At the front of the line, an elderly man stood shivering in a coat so thin it seemed barely more than paper. His gnarled hands twisted a battered hat nervously as he waited. Beside him, a young mother cradled her baby, its face hidden beneath a tattered blanket. Her tired eyes, ringed with dark circles, darted toward the front of the line, silently counting the spaces until her turn. Nearby, a group of children huddled together, their clothes patched and oversized. A barefoot boy kicked at a stone, his cheeks raw from the cold.

Further back, a man in a frayed suit stood stiffly, his posture hinting at a past life of dignity, his vacant stare portraying thoughts of days long gone, when he might have commanded respect in a boardroom or shop. Beside him, a woman rested heavily on her cane humming softly to herself, clutching a shopping bag with fingers exposed through fingerless gloves. Her quiet melody, though barely audible, felt like a fragile defiance against the weight of despair.

Charles's steps slowed as he neared the end of the line, where a young man with hollow cheeks and a scruffy beard stood apart from the others. His darting eyes, hunched shoulders, and clenched fists spoke of a wariness that the others no longer carried, as if he still fought against the inevitable.

On the corner, a paperboy stood, small and shivering, his clothes a mismatched collection of patches and loose hems. His flat cap was too large, its brim fraying at the edges, and his shoes, worn nearly smooth, struggled to keep the cold at bay. His ink-stained fingers trembled as he fumbled with a stack of newspapers.

'I'll take a couple,' Charles said, fishing in his coat pocket for coins.

The boy's head shot up, his eyes lighting with recognition. 'Gee, thanks, Smithy!' he exclaimed, thrusting the papers forward with a grin. His voice rang out against the subdued background, a spark of cheer in an otherwise somber tableau.

As the boy turned and bolted down the street, calling for his mother in the uncontrollable excitement that he wished to share with her upon encountering the front page news in person, a faint smile tugged at Charles's lips. The sound of the boy's excitement lingered for a moment, a rare burst of life against the bleakness lining the street.

Charles unfolded the newspaper, his momentary warmth fading as quickly as it had come. The joy sparked by the paperboy's excitement gave way to a sharp shift in his expression. His eyes, bright with faint amusement only a moment ago, narrowed with unimpressed disdain as they scanned the headline. Whatever optimism the brief exchange had inspired was swiftly eclipsed by the weight of what he read, his brow furrowing in quiet displeasure.

'To Australia in seven days – His secret out – Kingsford Smith smashes record! An all-British triumph,' Sir Macpherson announced loudly, holding up the morning newspaper. His voice rang with both pride and purpose. The accompanying photograph showed Charles's triumphant arrival in Melbourne amid the sea of people who had welcomed him.

Pacing back and forth with deliberate strides, Sir Macpherson scanned the faces of the board members as he read aloud from the article. His thumb and forefinger pressed together, punctuating key phrases as he read further.

'When he left Lympne Airdrome at dawn a week ago, Kingsford Smith claimed his flight was not an official record-breaking attempt. Yet, as revealed here, Mr. Charles Scott—the aviator and previous record-holder—was privy to his true intentions. Kingsford Smith confided to Scott in London, saying, 'I am out to beat your record.' However, he had asked for silence until the attempt was complete.' Sir Macpherson's voice rose slightly with emphasis before slapping the paper down onto the table. The sound reverberated through the room, breaking the stillness and stirring the board members to subtle shifts in their chairs.

Seated among them, Shephard, Secretary to the Minister of Air, sat with an impassive demeanor belied by the sharpness of his gaze. Beside him, Sir Archibald, the Air Race Commissioner appointed by Sir Macpherson, leaned back in his chair as he meticulously clipped the end of his cigar. The room waited for Sir Macpherson to continue.

'Genius!' Sir Macpherson declared, his tone mingling admiration with recognition. 'If he fails, he was not making an attempt for the record. If he succeeds, it will be a great secret revealed.' Brilliance—sheer brilliance. Sir Charles should lead our marketing.' Sir Macpherson exclaimed, suggestively satirical.

The moment stretched, charged with unspoken agreement, until the creak of the door broke the tension. Elizabeth entered with quiet precision, her hands clasped in front of her.

'Excuse me, Sir. Sir Charles has arrived,' she announced, her voice soft but clear.

'Well, well, send him in!' Sir Macpherson's posture straightened, his commanding presence sharpened by a trace of excitement. 'Thank you, Elizabeth.'

Elizabeth nodded 'Yes sir.' and left the room, closing the door behind her with a soft click. Outside, Charles stood in the foyer, his gaze fixed on the vibrant Air Race poster that adorned the wall. Its bold lettering and dramatic imagery of soaring aircraft seemed to hold his attention. His expression was thoughtful, tinged with unease, as though weighing the gravity of what lay ahead.

Elizabeth's voice gently interrupted his reverie. 'Sir Charles, the board is ready for you now.'

Charles turned, offering her a polite smile. 'Thank you, Elizabeth,' he said, his tone warm. She stepped aside, her composed demeanor softening slightly as she watched him enter the room. Alone in the foyer, Elizabeth let out a quiet breath, her hand brushing briefly against her chest.

Inside the boardroom, Sir Macpherson moved to greet Charles with a firm handshake. 'Ah, Sir Charles! Splendid. Welcome.' He gestured toward the table. 'We've just been admiring your press.' Sir Macpherson gestured Charles's attention to two of the men in introduction, 'Mr. Shephard, Secretary to the Minister for Air and Sir Archibald, our esteemed Race Commissioner. Shephard and Sir Archibald are charged with the organization, rules, and regulations among other things. But first, I believe you will enjoy this small surprise we had put together.'

Sir Macpherson reached for a brightly colored box and handed it to Charles. Its lid bore the bold image of Charles himself, accompanied by the slogan: CHOCOLATE – FOR PIONEER AVIATORS.

Charles's eyebrows lifted slightly as he examined the box, a faint smile playing on his lips. 'Well, this is certainly unexpected.'

'Impressive, is it not? A symbol of your achievements, and a fine product to boot,' Sir Macpherson said with satisfaction. Then, his tone shifted, becoming deliberate. 'It is, of course, in my interest to ensure that the Air Race is won by an Australian. And I would like that Australian to be you, Sir Charles.'

Charles's expression tightened subtly, though his voice tentative. 'Mac, I have not made any—decision.'

'Sir Archibald,' Sir Macpherson interrupted smoothly, 'will make available ten thousand pounds to fund your acquisition of a suitable aircraft. I look forward to working with you, Sir Charles,' Sir Macpherson stated, slapping Charles on the shoulder and gripping him gently.

Charles hesitated, the weight of the moment pressing down. He nodded slowly, his voice quiet. 'Of course.'

'Sir Archibald, if you kindly accompany Sir Charles.'

Sir Archibald stood, his manner polite but firm as he gestured for Charles to follow him. As they moved toward the door, Sir Macpherson's voice rang out, heavy with authority. 'And Sir Charles, let me be clear: when I say a suitable aircraft, I do mean a British aircraft.'

Charles glanced back, his expression bore a disdain to the restraint being imposed. 'Understood,' he replied before stepping into the corridor, Sir Archibald leading the way as they closed the door behind them.

Shephard leaned back in his chair, his fingertips tapping lightly on the table. 'Whilst the minister respects your decision, Sir Macpherson, he is concerned that Sir Charles may not . . . conform to the ideals of the Commonwealth.'

Sir Macpherson, unyielding in his conviction, replied firmly, 'That may be true. However, you cannot deny his service to the Commonwealth and to the greater good of humanity. He has, after all, united the hemispheres, Shephard.' He paused, grooming his mustache with his fingers. 'Perhaps you could remind the minister his position only exists due to great men like Sir Charles.'

Shephard, persistent in his caution, continued, 'The Minister suggested that we seek a candidate more suitable to represent our interests,' he said, calmly, pushing back.

'There is no other pilot more suited or more capable of representing this great nation than Sir Charles, Shephard.' Sir Macpherson's eyes narrowed slightly, his voice taking on a tone of finality. 'Sir Charles is an international figure. During this time of Great Depression, he is seen as a symbol of light and hope by the very people you serve. I was a common man once, and I know what it is to have a hero. The people love him, and his loyalty to them is unquestionable. One should argue that he represents your interests very well.'

The silence was deathly. Sir Macpherson's words hung cold in the air. Shephard, stoic, expressed nothing as the two men glared.

'The decision has been made.' Sir Macpherson said, finishing the discussion.

Chapter 12

Sydney, New South Wales, Australia. 1934.

Nestled on the quiet outskirts of Sydney, Mascot Aerodrome sprawled along the picturesque ocean waters of Botany Bay. Once a lively racecourse, it had been transformed into a hive of aeronautical activity, its grassy runways and large expanse fit for aircraft of all shapes and all sizes.

Corrugated iron hangars dotted the fringes of the open space, some lined and stacked together, others smaller, further afield; some painted in white, some blue, some cream and others still in the raw silver tin in which they were manufactured. Their roofs creaked and cracked as the metal expanded and contracted under the sun, a shimmering heat haze danced atop each rooftop and rising into the dissipating sky above. The airfield carried an undercurrent of tranquility, a lazy stillness marking its role as a silent witness to this new era of flight.

Amid it all, the dark deep rumble of an engine grew in the thin air as it approached. The bright yellow Tiger Moth—two wings resting one above the other through a hatched cross-work of wires and struts, pilots seated one behind the other. The radial engine, bulbous, boldly powering the ship whilst the fixed undercarriage hung low beneath her, supporting the wheels for landing.

Descending, gently, gracefully, the ship grazed the ground, skipped once then touched down. It was a textbook landing. Smooth, slowly rolling safely into a controllable speed to make a turn toward her hangar, bouncing gently over the uneven grass as she approached. Its engine sputtered and missed, the propeller slowing down as it approached.

The silver-clad hangar, the largest among them, loomed iconically, not in belittlement of its competitors, but as an emergent leader in the field. Its barn-like design and pitched roof bore the huge, bold sign written in white lettering: KINGSFORD SMITH AIR SERVICES, unmissable and unmistakable from both the air and the ground.

Visible through the sliding hangar doors, a fleet of aircraft sat proudly, most notably front center sat the flagship Southern Cross; the large mono wing shone in bright silver, the fuselage painted a deep dark royal blue sat boldly against her large tri-motor configuration. Two large radial engines boasted polished timer propellers that hung below each wing on either side of the cockpit. The third protruded boldly in the center.

Stopping, Tommy leaped down from the rear cockpit. Nancy, in the forward cockpit, glowed with a mix of exhilaration and determination as she removed her flying helmet, revealing her dark shoulder-length hair, tied back neatly for practicality, her heart-shaped face beaming from the thrill. As she stood, then climbed down over the wing, her slender frame, wrapped in high-waisted trousers, was on full display as she excitedly jumped down over the wing, joining Tommy on the ground.

Nancy moved with a purposeful stride beside Tommy, reflecting the aura of a vibrant, spirited teenager, poised by her pioneering spirit and determination, her posture straight, shoulders back as they walked side by side, making their way toward the hangar.

'So, how did I do?' she asked, her voice bubbling with anticipation.

Tommy grinned. 'You're the best lady flier I've met.'

'Really?' Nancy's eyes sparkled with delight.

'Well,' Tommy laughed, 'the *only* lady flier I have met. But honestly, you did great. You are going to make a terrific pilot, Nancy. You even have the name for it. Nancy Byrd!'

'With a 'Y' not an 'I,'' Nancy replied with a gleeful cheer, as she jumped elegantly into the air, clicking her heels together and punching the air. 'Yes!'

Inside, the offices were cramped, tucked along one side of the hangar to maximize the space needed for aircraft storage and maintenance. The small rooms felt functional, almost claustrophobic, the windows letting in muted sunlight filtered through the thin, light curtains adorning the sides and offering a view of the airfield outside.

John Stannage leaned heavily against the wall, chewing his thumbnail in silent thought, one arm tucked neatly under the other. Broad-shouldered and sharply dressed, his ponderous expression and tense posture betrayed the weight of the decisions at hand.

Opposite him, Charles reclined casually in his chair, feet propped on the desk, hands clasped behind his head. His air of patience was deliberate, though it only highlighted the tension between the two men as he waited for John to speak.

Behind Charles, Tommy and Nancy approached from the outside, moving with an excited urgency. Stopping sharply at the glass, Tommy rapped loudly, pulling both John and Charles from their thoughts. Beside him, Nancy stood, grinning brightly, as Tommy gave a proud double thumbs-up—his silent declaration of Nancy's exceptional flight performance.

Charles turned and nodded, offering a small smile, acknowledging the gesture, but John barely blinked. His focus remained inward, fixed on the weight of their predicament. Finally, breaking the silence, he spoke.

'Charles, now is not the time for distractions,' John said firmly. 'Enrollments are down. Tommy is our only instructor. Taking him with you would gut what little income we have left.'

'Maybe we can take Nancy,' Charles joked, though his grin quickly faded under John's unamused stare.

'Charles, can we be serious?' John shot back, his tone sharp.

Charles sighed, rubbing his face as though trying to wipe away the reality of their situation. 'It is a lot of money, John.'

'It is only a lot of money if you win,' John replied, the words cutting. 'Whether you win or lose the race Charles, it is irrelevant, I don't see how this expands our services. This last flight and the purchase of the Gull nearly drained us. We would have benefited significantly from the thousand pounds of the Lord Mayor's fund, the business needed that money, Charles.'

Charles straightened, his voice defensive. 'So did those kids, John! That hospital could not build itself.' He paused. 'The Gull will make us money in time.'

John's expression didn't soften. 'We need to focus on finances, Charles. Not adventures.'

Charles dropped his feet to the floor and leaned forward, his elbows resting on his knees. 'So, what do you suggest?'

'Capital,' John said without hesitation. 'Cash flow. While you were away, the government called for tenders on the Singapore service. That's where our future lies. But we won't last three months if we don't get back to basics now.'

'Barnstorming?' Charles asked, the frustration clear in his voice.

'Barnstorming. Just a few joyrides, Charles.' John confirmed, crossing his arms.

'Three months?' Charles sighed.

'Just until we secure the tender; you opened that route Charles, it is ours.' John said. 'We will be fine after that,' he continued.

Charles exhaled sharply, shaking his head. 'Mary is not going to be happy about this, John.'

'I don't know what to tell you, Charles.' John's tone resigned as he moved toward the door.

Before he could leave, Charles stopped him. 'John!' John turned, raising an eyebrow.

'Do me a favor,' Charles said. 'Look into a pilot by the name of Taylor.'

John hesitated for a moment, then nodded. 'I will see what I can find.'

With that, he left, the door clicking shut behind him, leaving Charles alone with the ticking of the clock that hung on the wall over him.

The birds sang softly in the crisp air of a new country day as it dawned over the majestic *Southern Cross*. The aircraft sat idle in the field, its frame catching the early sunlight, casting long, sharp shadows over the dewy grass. The air was fresh and cool, tinged with the faint scent of wildflowers blooming thick among the greenery. Above, the sky was a masterpiece of pastel hues, streaks of pink and orange blending seamlessly into the fading indigo of the receding night.

Nearby, a line of cars and horse-drawn carriages had formed, the occupants making their way toward the rare and thrilling sight of the famous plane. A queue of passengers, bundled against the morning chill, awaited their chance to experience the marvel of flight. Children clung to their parents, their excitement barely contained as they bounced on their toes, while adults spoke in animated tones, their breath visible in the cool air.

Beyond the makeshift airfield, rolling green hills stretched endlessly, dotted with grazing cattle and shaded by gum trees. A distant farmhouse added a rustic charm, its chimney puffing soft wisps of smoke into the cool dawn. Somewhere in the distance, a rooster's crow echoed faintly, a herald of the day to come.

Ahead of the line stood Mrs. Jones, her frail form bundled in a warm mink coat draped over a long, dark green dress with a high lace collar. Her ensemble, though elegant, was mismatched by a slightly battered clutch purse—a detail forgivable in her elderly grace. Her hands trembled as she rifled through it, the motions betraying her anticipation. Charles stood before her, patient and smiling.

'I have never flown before. Is it safe?' she asked sternly, her voice quivering with a touch of doubt. Her wide, searching eyes met his, pleading for reassurance.

Charles, ever the charming aviator, bent down slightly to meet her gaze. 'Mrs. Jones, the old bus has never let me down. That will be one pound,' he reassured her with a warm smile that seems to melt away some of her fears.

'You certainly are more handsome in person than in the newspapers, Mr. Kingsford Smith,' Mrs. Jones stated with glowing affection, her wrinkled hand reaching up to gently pat Charles on the cheek. Her touch was light, but it sent a long-lost thrill through her, a reminder of youth and days gone by. 'Now, no loopy loops while I am up there in that ghastly contraption, Mr. Kingsford Smith. I would not want to lose my hat.'

Charles chuckled softly, his eyes twinkling with amusement. 'Madam, I have flown around the world in this fine aircraft. She is a fine aircraft, I promise you, you are in very, very good hands.'

'Good hands, Sir Charles? It has been rumored you are a man who has quite a way with the ladies. I suggest it best you do not apply your charms to me, albeit my being a widow of some years now,' Mrs. Jones said with a teasing smile, a sparkle of mischief in her eyes.

Charles held up his hands in mock surrender, still grinning. 'Now, now, Mrs. Jones, I assure you, madam, I am a happily married man.'

'Nonetheless, sir' Mrs. Jones replied with a gentle tap of her forefinger on the tip of his nose, a coy smile playing on her lips before diving back into her clutch. 'Ah, there we are, one pound. You may consider a discounted price for the elderly Sir Charles.'

'I will certainly look into that, Mrs. Jones,' Charles replied, slowly walking her over to Jessica, 'Mrs. Jones, this is Jessica, she will help you to your seat.'

Jessica approached, her emerald-green eyes catching the light as her auburn hair shimmered in the morning sun. Her slender frame moved gracefully as she offered Mrs. Jones a hand. 'This way, Mrs. Jones. Let me help you to your seat,' she said, her soft Irish accent lending warmth to her words.

'Ah! A foreigner, how lovely,' Mrs. Jones exclaimed. 'I dare say, you are quite the picture of beauty, you remind me of myself in my youth,' she continued as they made their way slowly toward the Southern Cross.

Charles lingered, bemused by the interaction. Behind him, a car came to a halt. Tommy burst from the driver's side, his urgency cutting through the tranquil morning as he raced toward Charles.

'Boss! Boss!' Tommy called, waving a folded piece of paper.

Charles glanced at him but kept walking toward the aircraft. 'Not now, Tommy. I have to get this lot up.'

'This came in last night—from London!' Tommy pressed, as he handed the telegram to Charles.

Charles stopped, his brow furrowing as he read the message. His jaw tightened, and his eyes darkened with frustration as he read . . .

"BE ADVISED STOP SCOTT TESTING NEW DE HAVILLAND COMET DH88 FOR AIR RACE STOP BIG BACKER STOP".

'Find out everything you can, Tommy,' Charles said, slapping the telegram against his palm, as he thought heavily.

'You got it, boss,' Tommy replied, his tone resolute. He turned to leave, but his gaze caught on Jessica, her glow; his eyes refused to lose sight of her as she assisted Mrs. Jones on the step leading into the aircraft. As she accidentally glanced his way, noticing him, their eyes locked. For a moment, the activity surrounding them fell away. Jessica smiled softly, brushing her hair back over her ear. Tommy replied with his own look, his eyes not leaving hers. Her smile deepened, and she returned to her passenger, gently slipping inside and out of view.

Inside, Jessica settled Mrs. Jones in her seat, helping her stow her purse safely back into her lap. 'There you are, Mrs. Jones. I will be right up here until you take off if you need anything.'

Mrs. Jones adjusted her glasses, her hands still gripping her handbag. 'Thank you, my dear.'

Charles climbed into the cockpit, his movements sharp with agitation as he strapped his helmet under his chin. Taylor, seated beside him, caught the tension immediately.

'Everything okay?' he asked, his voice low.

'We need to talk,' Charles responds curtly, handing him the telegram. 'Read this.'

Taylor's eyes scanned the telegram quickly, as his fingers brushed his neatly trimmed, classically tight mustache. He turned to Charles, raising an eyebrow of concern, their expressions mirroring one another in a shared unspoken understanding.

'Let's get her up,' Charles said curtly.

'All the passengers are seated.' Jessica let Charles know.

'Thanks Jess!' he replied as she exited and closed the door behind her.

Taylor nodded and began firing up the engines. As the propellers roared to life, Charles turned to address the cabin.

'Everyone alright back there?' he yelled.

A cheer went up among the passengers, except for Mrs. Jones. 'Mr. Kingsford Smith,' she called out, her voice trembling over the engines. 'I do hope you do not intend to send me to an early grave. I am not ready to meet the good Lord just yet!'

Charles chuckled, glancing back. 'Not to worry, Mrs. Jones. You did buy a return ticket, did you not?'

Her eyes widened. 'What?' she questioned, as she quickly opened her purse, removing her ticket and placing her glasses low on her nose to check.

Charles shot Taylor a playful grin as the engines roared to full power. 'What?' he asked innocently.

'You are a cheeky bloody bastard sometimes Smithy,' Taylor muttered, shaking his head with a grin as the aircraft moved slowly forward, building speed.

Tommy watched intently as the *Southern Cross* began its takeoff run, the Wright Whirlwind engines roared, sending vibrations through the cool morning air. The aircraft, majestic and determined, rolled steadily down the field before lifting gracefully into the sky, climbing sharply, the sunlight glinting off its wing as it banked low in a daring turn, passing over the gathered onlookers. Gasps and cheers erupted from the crowd, with several ducking instinctively beneath the swooping aerial display.

From inside the cabin, Mrs. Jones's piercing scream cut through even the roar of the engines, the sound faint but unmistakable. The noise faintly carried back to the crowd below, prompting a ripple of laughter among the gasping onlookers, perhaps rethinking the purchase of their ticket as they sensed her terror.

Tommy glanced sideways, catching Jessica moving toward him. Her emerald eyes sparkled with amusement as they both turned toward the *Southern Cross* now leveling out high above them.

'That did not sound good,' Jessica remarked, raising her eyebrows as she tilted her head toward the receding plane.

Tommy chuckled, folding his arms. 'I do not think that is a problem I can fix.'

Jessica laughed softly, her smile widening. 'I do not think anyone could.'

They stood there for a beat, the easy quiet between them punctuated by the fading hum of the aircraft engines. Tommy shifted slightly, his gaze lingering. 'I am Tommy.'

'Jessica,' she replied. Her voice was warm but tinged with shyness, as her cheeks flushed red. 'I have heard a lot about you. It is nice to meet you.'

For a moment, neither of them spoke. They stood side by side, both stealing glances at one another before their eyes drifted back toward the *Southern Cross*, now a speck in the vast morning sky. The silence was comfortable yet charged, the unspoken stretching between them.

Jessica snuck another glance at Tommy, her breath catching as she noticed the quiet confidence in his stance, the faint smirk playing on his lips. Overwhelmed by her own reaction, she turned her gaze quickly back to the sky.

But the thought lingered. *Wow.*

She mouthed the word silently, her lips curving into a private, almost involuntary smile.

Tommy, still watching the horizon, noticed her movement from the corner of his eye. His smirk softened into something gentler, and though neither of them said a word, the unspoken connection hung in the air, shimmering like the first light of day.

Chapter 13

Lympne Aerodrome
Kent, England. 1934.

Thick, dull gray skies hung low over Lympne Aerodrome, billowing ominously in the cold stillness of an early English morning. Winter clung to the air, heavy and unyielding, the weather a seemingly common fixture in the British landscape.

Under the somber blanket, the scarlet-red aircraft, emblazoned with the name Grosvenor House in bold, bright white lettering along her side, tore through the gloom, its twin engines thundering at full throttle. The roar of its exhaust rivaled nature's thunder as she flew low through the skies hard and straight like an arrow over the airfield.

The de Havilland Comet was a machine of dreams—a marvel of engineering and elegance. Its sleek, streamlined fuselage glinted faintly under the shrouded light, while its wings, gracefully arched and tapered to fine points, whispered promises of speed and agility. Her engines boasted two hundred and thirty horsepower each, through her Gipsy Six R air-cooled six-cylinder inline engines; tightly cowled and streamlined beneath the wings, they spoke of untamed speed, a ship built to race.

Completing a final run, the ship banked starboard sharply, descending as she reduced speed, her undercarriage lowered in a deliberate, fluid motion, locking into place as she lined up the grass runway marked with white-painted stones that provided a stark contrast against the rolling green countryside. She touched down with a gentle inevitability, and the aircraft landed, its grace belying the roar that had preceded it.

Lympne Aerodrome stood as a testament to history—a former military base where the echoes of Great War aces lingered, their courage and spirit honored in the rapid advancements of aviation technology. Rows of massive aircraft hangars lined the edges of the bustling field, and the tall control tower stood sentinel over the activity below.

As the Comet slowed to a stop near an enormous hangar, her engines whined to silence. Inside the sleek cockpit, pilot Charles Scott and copilot Campbell Black worked through their shutdown procedures with practiced ease.

'Magnetos off. Engine stop,' Scott instructed.

'Magnetos off. Engine stop,' Black confirmed, flipping the necessary switches.

'Fuel off. Controls locked.'

'Fuel off. Controls locked.'

They continued against the hum of the busy airfield, replacing the roar of the engines as they slid open the canopies above them.

'Good runs! Two fifteen!' Black commented on the speed, as they removed their leather flying helmets and stood.

'I think we can do better,' Scott replied, as they both removed their flight helmets. Scott climbed out, his boots hitting the ground as Black followed. Ground crew swarmed the aircraft, placing chocks on the wheels and climbing into the cockpit for postflight inspections.

Scott cast a critical eye over the Comet. 'I think we can get more out of her,' he muttered seriously.

Scott was a striking figure. His dark hair, slicked neatly back in the fashion of the day, gave him an air of meticulous precision. A neatly trimmed mustache framed his confident mouth, accentuating his strong jawline. His leather flight jacket bore the marks of countless flights, and beneath it, he wore a crisp dress shirt and tie, a nod to formality even in the rugged world of aviation. A silk scarf, practical yet stylish, often fluttered at his neck as he walked.

Beside him, Black mirrored Scott's aristocratic appearance—his tailored suit and polished boots lending him a sharp, almost villainous air. Their stride was confident, their conversation easy but tinged with purpose as together they turned, making their way toward the hangar.

'We are going to have to cut weight,' Scott remarked.

'From where, exactly? We have cut everything.'

Scott smirked. 'From your diet Black. You might have to give up the black pudding, old chap.' Scott was slapping him jestingly on the shoulder when their shared laughter was suddenly interrupted.

'Mr. Scott! Mr. Black!' a voice called out, cutting through their banter. Turning, they spotted a stout man hurrying toward them, his short legs pumping to close the distance.

'Alexander Allcot, Ministry of Transport,' he introduced himself, puffing slightly as he adjusted his round spectacles. His bow tie, a garish green, sat askew beneath a tweed jacket that seemed too large for his frame.

Scott and Black exchanged a brief, knowing look before Allcot continued. 'I am here to report to the government the various aspects of your performance and testing.' He paused, catching his breath momentarily.

'Is that so?' Scott replied, an element of suspicion in his voice, knowing they have sent someone to oversee.

'Um, right then, Mr. Scott, the government has requested I monitor your preparations in advance of the race. Would it be possible to receive a briefing on your current performance,' Allcot asked.

As Scott and Thomas continue to walk, Allcot continued. 'Ah yes, the government does want to ensure that you have everything you need Mr. Scott. Um. Do you have everything you need?'

'No,' Scott curtly replied, baffling Allcot somewhat.

'Um, um!' Unable to formulate an answer, Allcot stuttered over a nonverbal reply.

'I need more speed,' Scott answered, continuing to walk away from the bureaucratic intrusion.

'Yes, ah, how do I?' Allcott strolled along, keeping in step behind. Then Scott and Black abruptly stopped their crusade, pausing. Scott took a long deep breath. Black, amused, watched on as the interaction became seemingly frustrating.

'Mr. Allcot. I appreciate your interest in our performance, however this is truly not the best of times.'

'Right! Right!' Allcot replied, unsure as to how best to approach the situation, still catching his breath. Scott and Black turned again, continuing to walk away from Allcot, slowly leaving him the distance.

'If I could, perhaps, just collect your speed Mr. Scott?' he asked loudly.

'Two hundred,' Black yelled without looking back, leaving Allcot fading into the background as he feverishly scribbled into his clipboard, muttering to himself, 'Two hundred miles per hour.' Then he yelled, 'Thank you Mr. Scott, Mr. Black.'

Turning his head to Scott, 'Better to give them something,' Black said.

'We are not going to be able to keep it a secret forever that is certain,' Scott replied.

'Unfortunately we are going to have to report at some time,' replied Black.

Faintly, over Black's words, the low, mournful wail of an air raid siren began to build. Both Scott and Black froze, their conversation halting as they turned their eyes skyward. The siren's initial cry was hesitant, almost eerie, as if testing the stillness of the air. Within moments, the sound swelled into an unwavering howl, rolling over the landscape like an approaching storm. The mechanical voice warbled slightly as it climbed in pitch, trembling with urgency and dread.

Heads turned instinctively toward the skies, they saw the distinctive silhouette of a small biplane wavering unsteadily.

'There!' Scott yelled, pointing sharply.

Black followed his gesture, his eyes locking on the aircraft as it bounced, dipped, and dived erratically. The plane cut a jagged path through the air, lurching unevenly as the sputtering engine struggled, coughing violently before falling silent.

'Is that Williams?' Black asked, as he too sighted the aircraft, his voice tight with concern.

'He is in trouble,' Scott murmured, his sharp eyes narrowing as he tracked the aircraft's erratic descent.

The aircraft dipped dangerously, its nose dropping as the pilot wrestled with the controls. Banking low over the countryside, the biplane lost altitude rapidly, the deafening silence of the failed engine amplifying the tension.

Scott stepped forward, his voice low but urgent. 'Ease back. Nose up. Keep your glide steady!' he called out, willing the instructions to somehow reach the pilot. 'You can do this.'

The biplane hesitated, its nose lifting slightly as the pilot fought to stabilize the glide.

'Come on, man, you can make it,' Scott muttered, fists clenched as he willed the pilot on.

The altitude drained quickly, the aircraft wobbling unsteadily as it dropped lower and lower.

'Flaps down. Slow your speed,' Scott urged, his voice rising slightly.

'He is coming in way too slow,' Black warned, tension etched across his face.

'He is trying to stretch his glide, he is not maintaining airspeed, you are too slow, too slow! Oh no. He is going to stall!' Scott shouted desperately. Just then a wing dropped, and the plane banked with no altitude to recover.

'He is going to hit!' Black said.

As the realization hit, they both began running out toward the runway, keeping a close eye on the impending disaster as they made their way toward the field. Under a short burst of power, the pilot attempted to restart the engine, and the aircraft lifted slightly, climbing nose high in a futile attempt to level out and reach the airfield before expending every bit of energy. The ship took a steep nose dive, and the pilot managed to pull out slightly in an attempt to land. It was not enough; the ship slammed into the ground with devastating force. The wheels struck hard, the impact ripping the undercarriage clean from the fuselage. The left wing dug into the earth, snapping like a brittle twig, and the aircraft spun violently before coming to a jarring halt, flipping end over, upside down in a swirling cloud of dirt and torn grass and debris.

'Williams!' Black screamed, breaking into a faster sprint alongside Scott. The entire airfield swung into action and ground crews raced across the field to where the shattered aircraft lay motionless, its mangled frame a grim sight.

The pilot stirred weakly, his movements visible through the crumpled fuselage. As the men approached, flames erupted from the engine compartment, spreading rapidly through the fuel-soaked cloth covering of the wings and the timber airframe.

'Get him out of there!' Scott bellowed, his voice slicing through the chaos of the flames engulfing the pilot as he wrestled desperately to free himself. His blood-curdling screams pierced the air, cutting through the wail of the siren and the frantic shouts of the rescuers. Black froze, his face pale with horror as he watched helplessly.

'Williams!' he shouted again, his voice breaking.

The flames surged higher in a sudden burst, engulfing the cockpit as a fire crew arrived, its bell ringing out over the scene. As men hurried to form a bucket line, the pilot's cries stop abruptly, silenced as he faded away into the bright orange black smoke. The water could do little to quell the intensity of the inferno.

Every pilot's nightmare and fear crackled and burst before them through the billowing black smoke; the heat only intensified the horror.

Scott held Black back, gripping his shoulders tightly preventing him from running into the flames. 'He is gone Tom,' Scott confirmed, knowing there was no hope now.

Black's concern immediately turned to anger and he turned and stormed away, furious at his inability to save him. The searing heat hissed back toward the crews dowsing the flames.

Black stood silently, his eyes and thoughts cast out over the airfield, now silently still, as darkness slowly fell into night, Scott quietly approached, pulling a whiskey flask from his pocket and offering it to Black.

'Here.'

'Cheers.' Black took it, thanking him solemnly, as he removed the cap and took a large quick swig.

'He was gone before we could reach him,' Scott said quietly, his voice flat but heavy with grief.

Black gritted his teeth, exhaling the whiskey from his breath. 'I flew with him in the war, he was a good man. A good pilot.'

'The luck of the game,' Scott replied. Black shook his head in disbelief.

'Did you finish the reports?' Black asked quietly.

'I will have them sent over to Allcot tomorrow,' Scott replied.

Black took another hit from the flask and handed it back to Scott, who also took a deep mouthful. They stood in solemn silence momentarily.

'I will write to his family,' Scott said, quietly.

'Bloody shame.' Black was somber in his thoughts.

Chapter 14

Parliament House Canberra,
Australian Capital Territory, Australia. 1934.

Lazing comfortably in a large, plush wingback chair, Sir Duddevin exhaled a slow stream of smoke, the ash from his cigar drifting soundlessly to the carpet below. His eyes remained closed. The heavy curtains hung like drawn eyelids, starving the room of morning light and muffling the world outside.

The door creaked open.

Collins entered with careful grace, a silver tray of morning tea balanced between his hands. He placed it gently on the side table, the porcelain teacup rattling just faintly in its saucer, then moved quietly toward the windows.

'You know I do not wish to be disturbed this early, Collins,' Sir Duddevin grumbled, the cigar still between his fingers, its ember faint. He lifted it to his lips and drew a rigid breath. Smoke billowed again, reigniting its life.

'Yes, sir. I am sorry, sir.'

Collins pulled back the curtains. A cascade of sunlight burst into the room, golden and unforgiving. Dust motes rose like ghosts in the air.

'I have brought you tea, sir.'

'Tea?' Duddevin scoffed, not opening his eyes. 'Get me a whiskey, Collins. It is eleven in the morning, for God's sake.'

'Yes, sir.' Collins turned without pause, gliding to the cabinet where the decanters waited, dark and glistening.

'Collins.'

Collins returned and set the glass beside him, the clink of crystal against wood sharp in the stillness.

'If you look on my desk—there—what do you see?'

'Here?'

'Yes, where I'm pointing. There.' Sir Duddevin lazily raised his hand, fingers vague and smoke-tipped.

Collins followed the gesture, then leaned slightly over the desk. 'The tender for Kingsford Smith Air Service Limited.'

'Yes, yes. That one.' Duddevin's voice deepened, rich and faintly slurred, as he sank further into the chair and took a long sip from the glass. The amber liquid caught the morning light like fire.

'If you open it, Collins, what does it propose?'

Collins thumbed through the folder, the pages whispering secrets as they turned. 'Clearly, the proposed use of American aircraft within its filings.'

'That is correct, Collins. So one might ask why this proposal is still on my desk. I made my thoughts perfectly clear on the matter, and yet—it persists.'

'I will remove it immediately.'

'Thank you, Collins.'

A pause. The room hummed with the soft ticking of the mantel clock.

'I have confirmed your luncheon with Qantas Empire Airways at twelve, sir.'

'Hand me their submission.'

Collins retrieved the file without hesitation, crossing the room and placing it reverently in Sir Duddevin's outstretched hand. Finally, Duddevin opened his eyes—gray, bloodshot slits—then shifted his body upright with a creak of old leather.

He cracked open the tender. The first page stared back with clarity and conviction: an All-Red Route.

'What is on the menu for lunch, Collins?'

'Lamb, sir.'

'Mm. Thank you, Collins. That will be all.'

Sydney, New South Wales, Australia. 1934.

Afternoon sunlight bathed the lush green gardens, fringing the backyard in a warm, golden light as the sun slowly made its way lower in the sky. A gentle breeze rustled the leaves of the trees filtering dappled shadows across the lush green lawn, the smell of the end of summer's day hung in the air. A perfect day holding a promise of happiness-filled contentment.

Mary stood quietly on the patio, gently leaning her shoulder into the pergola, which supported a dense covering of brilliant purple wisteria. The birds chirped in a symphony around her, and a soft smile graced her lips as she admired the serene beauty of the moment.

Charles playfully swirled Charles Jr. through the air, whisking him up and down and around and around in circling flying motions, making loud aircraft engine noises—*Zoom! Vroom! Swoosh!* Charles Jr. happily giggled and laughed to the extent his little lungs could, his eyes alight with delight at the thrill, his soft curls whisping in the wind.

Mary turned her attention to the letter she held in her hand. She walked slowly over to her two men, her curiosity piqued. Charles smiled gently, slowing the ride as he embraced Charles Jr.. 'We are going to have to get him some goggles soon,' Charles said, a wide grin beaming with pride.

Mary smiled. 'Well, let us get him out of diapers first, shall we?' she said, raising her heels to give Charles a small tender kiss on the lips.

'Not like you to have business sent to the house, dear,' she remarked, her tone light yet inquisitive as she handed the letter over to him.

Charles's expression changed instantly as he exchanged the letter for Charles Jr., concern and frustration etched across his face as he read its contents. His brows furrowed, and his lips pressed into a thin line, the grin gone. His shoulders tensed, and he exhaled sharply through his nose, a clear sign of his mounting irritation. He scanned the lines of the letter rapidly, as if hoping that reading it again would change its contents.

'Charles?' Mary asked, her worry evident. She reached out, touching his arm gently, seeking to understand the contents contained within.

'Mary, I am . . .' Charles started to say, but the words caught in his throat. The sorrow in his eyes spoke volumes. His hand clenched around the letter, crumpling the paper in a physical manifesting of his frustration.

'I know, I know. Go,' Mary responded, her voice softly understanding, but with an evident undercurrent of disappointment. She understood without needing an explanation. It was one of those moments where unspoken words and shared glances conveyed more than any conversation could.

'I am sorry Mare,' he said, kissing her gently, then kissing Charles Jr. on his forehead before turning to leave; the reality of his impending departure set in. Charles Jr., sensing the change, started to wail, his tiny arms reaching out for his father. His cries only added to the tremendous difficulty of his leaving.

'I will call you as soon as I can,' Charles said, a promise through his strained voice, the frustration still lingering just beneath the surface.

Mary watched him go, holding their son close as the cries softened into sniffles. She kissed Charles Jr.'s cheek, bouncing him gently in her arms. 'Stay safe,' she said, watching as Charles walked away. Charles Jr.'s cries waned behind him, mingling with the fading light of the day, as Mary stood there, holding their son close,

'It will be okay, we will be okay,' she whispered, lifting him up in the air to restore his happiness.

'Maybe your father is right, I think you would look quite cute in goggles,' Mary added with a smile as Charles Jr. settled a little, bringing him down to her, rubbing her nose gently against his.

Melbourne, Victoria, Australia. 1934.

Charles stormed in, his eyes blazing with frustration, cutting through the orderly chaos of the office. Elizabeth hurried after him, her protests urgent yet futile. The workers paused momentarily, their gazes following the pair as they made their way to Sir Macpherson's private office. Charles's heavy footsteps echoed down the hall, Elizabeth's heels scurrying behind him.

'You can't go in there,' Elizabeth said, her voice rising. 'Sir Charles! Please!'

Ignoring her, Charles shoved open the heavy oak door to Sir Macpherson's office. The room was a world apart from the bustling exterior—spacious, richly appointed with dark mahogany furniture, a massive desk at its center. Shelves of leather-bound books lined the walls, and a towering globe stood in one corner, a quiet nod to the company's global reach. Above the desk behind him, Sir Macpherson's stern portrait watched over the room.

Sir Macpherson looked up, calm and composed, peering over the rim of his reading glasses. He removed them slowly as Charles paced into the room, his shoes sinking into the Persian rug.

'Mac, I cannot win this race,' Charles declared, slamming the letter onto the desk. His frustration simmered beneath his words.

'A race you have not entered?' Sir Macpherson replied, his eyebrow arching.

'De Havilland will not supply me with a Comet equivalent to that of Scott,' Charles said, pacing.

'Can not or will not?' Sir Macpherson asked, leaning back in his chair, his fingers steepled.

Charles's voice tightened with conviction. 'Without a Comet built to the same specifications, there is no point in entering.'

'Surely the advantage is not that significant,' Sir Macpherson suggested, his tone measured.

'The aircraft they have offered me would vest Scott with an advantage of one thousand miles over the distance. I need an American ship,' Charles insisted, his eyes narrowing in determination.

'I will not support the entry of an American aircraft in this race, Charles, I have made my position clear,' Sir Macpherson stated firmly. 'Charles, I understand and to some extent appreciate your position. Your views over the years have been well expressed, and as much as I desire for you to win, entering an American aircraft can only be perceived as anti-British.'

'Anti-British?' Charles shot back, incredulous.

'Charles, your efforts in promoting the use of American aircraft in this country have exceedingly attracted the attention of the government both here and at home. You are perceived and recognized as a protagonist on the matter, and this race is not a platform to be used by you in the promotion of your ideals. I will not diverge from the interest of the Commonwealth,' Sir Macpherson explained patiently.

'You are suggesting it is wrong for a pilot to demand the best aircraft for the conditions in which he flies, over an ideal?' Charles retorted, his passion undiminished.

'This is a race from England to Australia, Charles,' Sir Macpherson emphasized, his voice unyielding.

'We have lost too many good men, Mac. How many more? Who is next? Me? The Americans are building their aircraft for a distance and climate not dissimilar to our own; that in itself saves lives. The future of aviation does not lie in colonialist repertoire; it lies in the advancement of technology,' Charles argued passionately, his eyes blazing with conviction.

'Your pursuits are inherent with dangers that technicality does completely preclude, Charles,' Sir Macpherson countered.

'You are wrong Mac! It does not and nor should it matter which country builds the best, only that they are the best. Half of your candy, Mac, half of what you import is from the United States. Your best sellers come from America, and you sell more to the British than any other,' Charles pointed out.

'The Empire was not built on candy, Charles!' Sir Macpherson exclaimed, his voice filled with frustration. But then, he conceded. 'Contrarily, it is more than half.'

'And it is the best,' Charles replied with conviction, a small smile playing on his lips.

'Charles, you do raise a dilemma,' Sir Macpherson admitted, curling his mustache in deep thought. He considered the brinkmanship inherent within Charles's argument, breathing in a relaxed, measured approach. He stood walking over to his whiskey cabinet, and gently poured a short into a crystal glass.

'Whiskey?'

'No,' Charles replied.

'If I or the MacRobertson Company face censure over your decision, the financial obligations that go with it will be yours and yours alone. Are we clear, Charles?' Mac's tone was serious, his eyes locking onto Charles's as he sipped.

'Crystal,' Charles responded, his voice unwavering.

'If we have no further business Charles, I have a company to run and you have a race to enter, I suggest we waste no further time.'

Sir Macpherson had politely dismissed him. Charles turned and walked to the door, but as he opened to exit Sir Macpherson paused him.

'And Charles,' Sir Macpherson said, taking another sip of whiskey. 'If you do choose to enter an American aircraft, Charles, do me a favor—for your sake at least make sure she is fast,' Sir Macpherson advised, his tone softening slightly.

Charles nodded, a determined look in his eye as he left the office. Elizabeth, who had been waiting outside, stepped in. Sir Macpherson pondered the conversation, sipped his whiskey again, and looked over at the candy packaging featuring Charles.

'It is business, Elizabeth,' Sir Macpherson said, a faint smile playing on his lips. He waved her away with a flick of his hand. 'Well? Don't just stand there.

'Yes, sir,' she said, retreating from the room.

Sir Macpherson swirled the whiskey in his glass and took a deep breath, his eyes still drawn to the image of Charles as he threw back whiskey in one shot and slammed the glass down, hard.

The hotel foyer pulsed with life—guests lounged in plush chairs, bellboys navigated a maze of luggage, and muted conversations mingled with the distant chime of a piano from the bar. Inside a narrow pay phone booth, Charles stood stiffly, one hand gripping the glass frame as if to steady himself, the other clutching the receiver pressed hard against his ear.

'Who did it go to?' Charles asked, his voice strained, fighting to rise above the noise around him.

'Qantas Empire,' John replied, the words softened by static but clear enough to confirm Charles's worst fears.

The handset creaked under his tightening grip, his frustration building. Without warning, he slammed it against the cradle. The sharp clang rang out, cutting through the surrounding chatter. Heads turned—brief glances, curious but fleeting—before the hum of the foyer resumed. A bellboy froze mid-step, then hurried on his way.

'Charles? Charles?' John's voice crackled faintly from the receiver.

Charles grabbed the phone again, his knuckles pale against the black handset. 'I'm here.'

'I am sorry to add to it, Charles,' John continued, his tone low and uneasy, 'but from what I understand, our tender wasn't even considered.'

Charles's gaze fixed on the blurred figures beyond the glass booth. His reflection stared back at him, tense and unyielding. 'I pioneered that route, John. I opened it.'

John exhaled audibly, a sound barely louder than the faint hum of static. 'I do not know what to say, Charles.'

'That route was mine,' Charles said, his voice thick with disbelief. 'Everyone said it could not be done, and they just stole it from me.'

A siren wailed in the distance, its piercing cry fading into the steady rhythm of construction work outside. Charles's grip on the phone loosened for a moment, his fingers brushing the cool metal of the booth's edge.

'What do you want to do?' John asked, cautious now, each word deliberate.

Charles's jaw tightened, and he drew in a sharp breath. Beyond the thick glass, the bustling foyer blurred into a swirl of movement and sound. He straightened his posture, his reflection growing sharper, more focused.

'Take it back,' he said, his voice cold and resolute.

Sydney, New South Wales, Australia. 1934.

The crackled sounds of big band music drifted from the gramophone in another room, permeating the house with the smooth wail of a saxophone in a melodic arc. Sharp, staccato bursts from the brass section punctuated the rhythm, while muted piano chords blended seamlessly with the deep undertones of a double bass. The notes wrapped around the halls, a vibrant lifeline of sound cutting through the stillness.

Charles floated in blackness, the air fleeing his lungs. Behind his eyelids, illuminated sparks danced like dying stars, their brilliance ebbing as oxygen drained from his body. His heart pounded, its drumbeat distant but insistent, a metronome ticking against the silence in his mind. The crescendo of the music surged, colliding with the growing void within him. The final beat of the drum. Silence.

The needle scratched faintly over the Bakelite record as Charles broke the surface, gasping. The air seared his throat as he sucked it in, his desperate inhale echoing off the tiled walls. The bathroom was a picture of 1930s elegance: glossy white subway tiles climbed halfway up the walls, capped by a trim of black ceramic, while the floor displayed intricate hexagonal mosaics in black and white. A gleaming porcelain clawfoot tub stood at the center, its brass fixtures catching the low glow of a single art deco sconce.

'How long?' he croaked, his voice raspy.

Mary, perched delicately on the rim of the bath, dabbed at the water droplets on her cheek with a lace handkerchief. Her lips pressed into a thin line as she checked his wristwatch, its faint ticking marking seconds.

'Three minutes, forty-two seconds, Charles,' she said, her voice clipped.

'A new record.' Charles grinned, slicking his hair back, a glint of pride in his eyes. He was still catching his breath.

Mary sighed deeply, her exhale heavy with frustration. 'It scares me, Charles.'

'I am in a bathtub, Mary,' he replied, spreading his arms theatrically, water rippling outward.

'It is not the tub.' Her voice softened, trembling at the edges. 'It is the thought of it—of you.'

Charles met her gaze, his smile dimming as her words landed. He splashed her gently, his grin returning, a boyish charm masking his understanding.

'Hey!' Mary squealed, laughing despite herself. She quickly sobered, her amusement giving way to concern.

'You are going again?' Her voice quivered with worry.

'I have to.'

'You do not have to. It is just a race, Charles. I wish—'

'You wish you could hold your breath for as long as me,' he interrupted, his tone light, though the determination in his eyes was unyielding.

'No, I wish—'

Before she could finish, he tugged her into the tub. Her startled scream cut through the room as water splashed over the edges. The music continued, a slow, romantic rhythm filling the air. Mary's laughter bubbled up as she relaxed against him, her nightgown clinging to her skin, translucent from the water.

'Oh, why did I ever marry you?' she teased, resting her head against his chest. 'I should've listened to my mother.'

Charles chuckled, holding her close. 'Mary, do you know what keeps me going when I am up there? What focuses me?' His voice softened, barely audible over the gentle melody.

Mary's fingers tightened around his arms. 'What?'

'It is knowing that when I stare out into the distance, chasing the horizon, you are waiting for me beyond it.'

Her breath hitched, the weight of his words sinking in. For a moment, she said nothing, then burst into laughter, the sound light and joyful.

'You are such a sap,' she said, splashing him.

Charles laughed with her.

'Do you know what keeps me going when you are up there? Knowing that I am up there with you—and Swiss chocolate.'

Their laughter rang out, blending with the music. The levity subsided into a quiet intimacy as they held each other close, the water lapping softly around them.

'I love you, Lady Mary Kingsford Smith,' Charles murmured, his voice a caress.

'And I love you, Sir Charles Kingsford Smith,' she replied, her lips brushing his cheek.

They lingered in each other's arms, the world outside fading. Mary traced circles on his shoulder.

'When are you going to fly with me?' Charles asked softly.

'One day, I promise,' Mary replied.

'You are my compass, Mary. Without you, I would be lost.'

'And you are my wings, Charles. You give me the courage to soar,' Mary whispered, her breath warm against his skin, Charles tightened his embrace, leaning his lips slowly, tenderly toward hers, their eyes locked in one another's, as they touched; then, the cry.

It was Charles Jr., wailing as he woke, his screams echoing impatiently. Charles and Mary looked at each other, sharing the same thought—impeccable timing.

'Well, it looks like he will not be getting a little brother any time soon,' Mary whispered.

Chapter 15

Burbank Airport
Los Angeles, California, United States of America. 1934.

Robert Ellsworth Gross, the chief executive officer of Lockheed, stood alongside Charles in contemplative silence, taking in the expansive view from his second-floor office window. The room offered an ideal vantage point over the sprawling Burbank Union Airport, where a constant hive of progress played out below. From this height, the unpaved dirt and grass runways formed a crisscross pattern, stretching out like veins that fed the heart of the aviation industry.

Across the field, the sleek art deco passenger terminal stood as a beacon of modernity, its geometric design catching and reflecting the sunlight. Nearby, the sturdy control tower loomed tall, symbolizing the growing sophistication and ambition of aviation.

The airfield below was alive with activity. Aircraft and passenger planes of all sizes lined the edges of the runways, their metallic surfaces gleaming in the sunlight. Enormous steel hangers clustered on one side of the field. Their massive doors stood open, widely accommodating, revealing the enormity of the work inside—mechanics bent over engines, aircraft being wheeled out and in through the sharp scent of oil that carried on the breeze.

Beyond the airfield's boundaries, the landscape softened into tranquil farmland and open fields, a pastoral contrast to the hum of engines and frenetic activity below. Yet even in this quiet countryside, the visionaries at the window could sense the transformative power of the airfield, radiating outward.

'The future, Charles—you never get tired of it, do you?' Robert said with sentiment, breaking the silence between them.

Charles didn't speak at once, absorbing and admiring the scene before him.

'I need a plane, Robert,' Charles replied at last, his extended silence bolstering the seriousness of his request.

'A fast one?' Robert asked. His voice carried a knowing tone, the weight of Charles's request hung in the air.

Charles said nothing, his face unreadable.

Robert paused, exhaling slowly as he took in the gravity of the moment. 'Well, we don't build them any other way,' he said finally, moving to the side bar. He poured a single glass of bourbon, the amber liquid catching the sunlight.

'When are you going to fly for us here at Lockheed, Charles?' Robert asked, his tone genuine as he crossed to his desk.

Charles loosened his tie, but his eyes didn't leave the view.

'Claire, could you step in, please?' Robert called.

The door opened promptly, and Claire entered with an air of polished efficiency. Her dark brown hair was styled in soft waves, and her bright hazel eyes complemented her warm smile. She wore a modest yet stylish dress with a fitted waist, a scalloped collar, and a subtle floral pattern. A string of pearls and low-heeled shoes completed her look, underscoring her poised professionalism.

'Yes, Mr. Gross?'

'Could you get Victor Fleming on the line for me?' he asked.

'Of course,' she replied with a nod before stepping out.

'Thank you, Claire.'

As she left, Robert turned back to Charles. 'You'll like Victor. He's a motion picture man—working on a pirate film, buried treasure on an island, as I understand it. Mad keen on aviation. Quite the pilot himself. A good customer. I think he has what you need.'

MGM Studios
Culver City, California, United States of America. 1934.

Approaching the edge of the set quietly, the young woman waited carefully for the right moment to interrupt. She cut a sharp silhouette amid the sea of costumed chaos—poised and precise, unwavering in the storm of activity.

'Crane up! More light—it's an island for crying out loud, not a cave. More light!' Victor Fleming bellowed into his bullhorn, his tall frame unmistakable even seated in the director's chair. His sun-burnished skin glowed under the harsh stage lights, his piercing blue eyes missing nothing.

'Can we get *wardrobe* on stage? Now!' he barked again, eyes never leaving the unfolding action.

The *Treasure Island* set loomed large behind him—towering masts, rope-lashed rigging, and a full-scale pirate ship that looked plucked from the high seas. The air was thick with heat and the smell of fresh paint, sawdust, and sweat. Stage lights blazed down, casting dramatic shadows across the deck.

Technicians shouted over the thrum of machinery as they repositioned massive cameras. Cables coiled across the floor like tangled seaweed. Extras in tricorn hats and sailor coats lounged near the wings, awaiting their cue, while actors sparred with swords, the *clack-clack* of steel punctuated by swells of the off-stage orchestra.

'Excuse me, Mr. Fleming, sir,' the young woman said, stepping forward between orders.

'Yes? What is it?' Victor replied, still watching the set.

'There's an urgent phone call for you, sir.'

'Take a message.'

'It's from the President of the Lockheed Aircraft Company—Mr. Robert Gross. He has Sir Charles Kingsford Smith on the line with him.'

Victor's head snapped around, the name catching him like a wire trap.

'Charles?' he repeated, rising from his chair in a flash. He brought the bullhorn to his lips.

'That's a wrap for today!' he announced.

Groans rose from the crew, but no one questioned him.

Turning to her, he added sharply, 'Gracie, have them bring my car around—and tell Robert I'm on my way.'

She gave a crisp nod, already turning on her heel.

'Yes, Mr. Fleming.'

Burbank Airport
Los Angeles, California, United States of America. 1934.

Bathed in the golden light of the setting Californian sun, Robert and Charles stood outside the hangar, the rolling hills behind them painted in amber hues. A sleek black Rolls-Royce sedan glided toward them, its polished body reflecting the last glints of daylight.

The driver stepped from the vehicle and briskly rushed to open the back door, and from it stepped two Hollywood starlets—Lillian Rivers and Evelyn Hayes.

Lillian's auburn curls framed piercing green eyes, her silk gown catching the breeze like a whisper. Beside her, Evelyn was elegant, with her sleek black bob and crimson lips giving her a bold, magnetic presence. Their heels clicked smartly on the tarmac as they moved with graceful ease.

Trailing behind them, Victor emerged—sharp as ever, perfectly tailored, with the energy of a man who could command a studio or a storm.

Robert raised an eyebrow toward Charles. 'Yes. That's Victor,' he murmured, smiling at the flamboyant arrival.

Charles smirked. 'Oh, we know each other.'

Victor approached with warmth and gusto.

'Victor, hello,' Robert greeted, extending a hand.

Victor shook it briskly. 'I believe you know—'

'Kingsford Smith!' Victor beamed. 'Had I known you were in town, I would have called earlier.'

'Victor,' Charles grinned, gripping his hand with equal enthusiasm.

'It's been years,' Victor said, stepping back to take him in. 'Last time must've been the Paramount lot—early twenties—just after the war. During your stunt flying days.'

'Good times,' Charles agreed. His grin widened as he reminisced.

Victor turned to his companions. 'Miss Rivers, Miss Hayes—this is Sir Charles Kingsford Smith, one of the greatest fliers the world has ever known.' The ladies nodded politely, their opera-length cigarette holders poised elegantly between their fingers, exhaling tendrils of smoke like actresses caught between takes.

'I believe we share a friend—Captain Allan Hancock,' Victor added. 'Splendid fellow. We must do lunch. Swing by the studio sometime, you'd love it.'

Then, his mood shifted abruptly.

'Now—where is she?' he asked, scanning the hangar with sudden urgency.

Silence reigned. Toward the back of the hangar, cloaked in stillness and a soft coat of dust, she sat—forgotten, waiting.

'Ah, there she is,' Victor said with pride. '*Virginia*.'

They approached.

'Victor's had her on the market for a while now,' Robert added, tone measured.

'I can see why,' Charles replied, his eyes narrowing as he took in the plane for the first time.

The Lockheed Sirius—single engine, open cockpit—rested with quiet grace. She was sleek. Her metallic light blue skin shimmered beneath the film of time. A sweeping white tail offset her name: RICHMOND VIRGINIA, boldly slanted down her sides. She exuded speed and daring. But she was tired. In the race for the skies, time had overtaken her.

Charles walked slowly around her, one hand trailing gently over her fuselage. The wear was obvious—scratches, dents, long-faded polish. Still, something about her lingered.

'She's been through a lot,' he said softly.

'Douglas and I were flying her down in Mexico,' Victor explained. 'Fairbanks, the actor. Came down rough. Real rough. Nearly broke the poor girl's back.'

'I can see that,' Charles replied, his hand resting on the fracture line along the cowling.

Victor chuckled. 'Scared the hell out of both of us. These days, we stick to yachts. Far more gentlemanly. Robert has assured me she can be salvaged.'

Charles glanced at Robert, and Robert nodded, confirming his thoughts, 'She is all we have available,' Robert conceded.

Victor stepped back and adjusted his fedora, eyes shining with fondness. 'Broken, but you won't find a better ship. She's got spirit!'

'Meets your price,' Robert added.

Charles circled back, carefully eyeing her sharp clean line from the nose to the tail once more. She wasn't just a machine. She had a soul.

'Spirit, you say,' Charles echoed, glancing at Victor.

'Spirit,' Victor affirmed.

Charles nodded, slowly. He knew.

'I'll take her.'

Chapter 16

Lympne Aerodrome
Kent, England. 1934.

Eerie was the calm that clung to the aerodrome as Grosvenor House was rolled from her hangar into the crisp veil of early morning fog. The hush was heavy, sacred. Dozens of mechanics, engineers, and ground crew swarmed over her bright red frame—checking, measuring, tightening, then checking again.

The Comet punched through the muted dreary mist that drifted low across the deep green field. She was a beacon—glowing, fiery, alive. She wasn't just ready. She was *waiting*.

Scott and Black approached at a determined stride, their pace deliberate, purposeful. Their arms swung less, hands working tight into leather gloves. No chatter. No nerves. Their fear had been set down somewhere far behind them. This was war. And they were walking straight into it.

'She's ready,' the chief engineer said simply, stepping aside as they arrived.

Without a word, they climbed onto the wing and dropped into the cockpit—tight, narrow, mechanical. Scott glanced into a small mirror mounted to his right side to Black peering back at him over his shoulder behind.

Their eyes locked in the reflection.

No words needed.

They were ready.

'Clear!' Scott shouted.

He reached down. The starboard engine roared to life—then the port. Together they warmed harmoniously, balanced and tempered in perfect mechanical synchrony.

Scott whispered, almost to himself, 'Let's do this.'

His hand found the throttle.

He eased it forward, feeling the power surge through his flesh and bone, rumbling within, as they became one.

Burbank Airport
Los Angeles, California, United States of America. 1934.

Robert leaned heavily over the sprawling blueprints, his brow furrowed, concern etched deep into his features. The bench was a sea of paper—measurements, schematics, and scribbled notations. He flipped pages back and forth, checking dimensions against work orders, biting his lip.

Charles stood nearby, arms folded, head tilted, watching. Waiting.

'I don't know, Charles,' Robert finally said, breaking the silence. He exhaled hard, scratching his head as he studied the plans again. 'What you're asking for . . . it's never been done.'

Charles didn't flinch. 'It works.'

All around them, *Virginia* lay in pieces—gutted from nose to tail. The wing had been removed and was resting separately. Her fuselage was open, exposed, vulnerable. The cavernous hangar buzzed with purpose—mechanics, engineers, and craftsmen moving with relentless urgency. Sparks flew, hammers clanged, sawdust spun into the air.

The facility was state-of-the-art. Timber work. Sheet metal. Paint bays. Precision instruments. Every inch of the workshop beat like a heart under pressure.

'This is more than a refit,' Robert said, scanning the checklist. 'Dual controls—sticks, rudder pedals, throttles, mixture regulators, stabilizers . . . new panels, new forward cockpit, landing lights, tail wheel, fuel gauges for each wing tank, repairs from the crack-up, new right aileron, new fin, new rudder . . .'

He shook his head, overwhelmed, before continuing.

'New ribs in the wing, fresh plywood, fuselage shell work, new cowling, gas tanks, repaint, retractable undercarriage, batteries, heaters, flares, electric start, variable-pitch propeller, torque bracing in the nose . . .'

Robert looked up, stunned. 'You're not fixing an aircraft, Charles. You're building a new one.'

Charles didn't blink. 'We have time.'

Robert frowned. 'It's not time that worries me—it's the budget.'

'I will get the money,' Charles replied, unfazed.

Robert stared at the pages again. His cheeks ballooned as he exhaled, lips tight, the weight of risk pressing down on him.

'She will want to be the best,' he said finally, his voice low, reluctant—his reputation now on the line.

Charles smiled.

'She will be the best,' he said. 'Better than anything you have ever seen.'

'Just don't forget whose name is on it,' Robert reminded Charles.

'As long as you do not forget whose name is *in* it,' Charles replied, his wit quick.

They looked at each other, both nodding in agreement; they were in this together.

Lympne Aerodrome
Kent, England. 1934.

The Comet roared, a red streak against the darkened sky, slicing through the air like a weapon unleashed. She wasn't flying—she was hunting, predatory like a dragon.

'Power ninety percent. Speed one-eight-five miles!' Black called over the rush of noise. 'Holding!'

'Let us see what she has got,' Scott replied, voice tight with focus.

He pulled her into a sweeping arc, slicing the air with mechanical precision. As the wings leveled, he feathered the controls—light, delicate—guiding her like a fencer's blade.

'Powering up!' he shouted. 'Come on, girl,' he muttered to himself.

Black leaned forward, eyes locked on the speed gauge.

'One ninety . . . one ninety-five . . . two hundred.'

Scott eased the throttle forward, the vibration growing, the cockpit trembling with potential.

'Two twenty . . . two thirty!' Black yelled, excitement rising.

'Power at one hundred percent,' Scott called, pushing her to the edge.

'Two thirty-seven! Holding! Two thirty-seven!' Black's voice cracked with exhilaration. 'Yes!'

The Comet shuddered at her limit, air screaming past her frame. Scott held steady, letting her sing at full stretch before easing gently back, guiding her away from the brink.

A new record.

Black slammed his fist against the canopy with pure joy. 'Yes!'

Scott's unfamiliar grin stretched wide across his face.

'For King and country,' he said, his proud smile earned.

Chapter 17

Burbank Airport
Los Angeles, California, United States of America. 1934.

His shadow stretched long across the hangar floor, reaching for the light while he remained still.

Charles sat alone on a crate, a makeshift stool in the emptiness. The echo of distant tools had long faded; now, only silence remained. His head was low, his thoughts deeper still, though his breathing was slow, steady. The final inches of a cigarette glowed between his fingers, its smoke curling up into a shroud around his face. He took one last drag, then flicked the butt to the concrete and crushed it beneath his boot.

He was ready.

As he stood, he pulled the zipper on his flying suit up to his chest, took a long, grounding breath, and turned toward the open doors. The hangar yawned wide, sunlight pouring in like a divine spotlight, framing him in white as he stepped into the brightness beyond.

And there she was.

No longer *Virginia*, no longer the battered remains of a memory. The Lockheed Sirius 8D Special had become something else entirely. Now, she stood proudly—a new model, reborn, refined, unapologetically modern. Her sleek lines caught the light just right, her new skin glistening with promise. Every curve spoke of speed. Every angle of precision. She was no longer trying to prove herself. She simply was.

The men whose skilled hands and bright minds had borne her stood in quiet ranks along his path—engineers, mechanics, machinists—solemn in their shared pride, watching him like a congregation as he walked toward the altar.

'Good luck, sir.'

'Luck, Smithy.'

'Luck Sir.'

'Luck.'

Their voices came softly, earnestly.

Charles gave only small nods in return. No speeches. No sentiment. Just the quiet presence of a man walking toward destiny.

He climbed onto the wing and dropped into the cockpit, the controls greeting him like old friends dressed anew. It was tighter now. Cleaner. Sleeker. The machine hugged him.

An engineer stepped up beside the cockpit, leaning in close.

'We've scheduled you to land in an hour,' he said, his tone clipped but respectful. 'She's got enough for two. Give her a good run—but watch your speed.'

Another appeared behind him, arms folded, voice more relaxed. 'Smithy . . . this is a test flight.'

Charles didn't respond right away. He ran his hands across the panel—flicking switches, testing tension, touching her like a man reunited with someone he never stopped loving. The gauges were new, but they spoke the same language.

He finally glanced up, gave the man a crooked grin.

'Do us a favor, take it easy.' The engineer repeated.

Charles rested his hand on the throttle. The silence before ignition was almost sacred.

'Godspeed,' the man whispered.

Charles looked forward through the glass.

'Godspeed,' he replied.

Then the engine roared to life. The Altair breathed.

On the wall, the clock in Robert's office labored, conveying an uneasy sense of time slowing down. Robert sat attentively in his chair, watching the hands move with a concerned stare. Claire stood idly and silently by, her chin resting in her folded arms as she directed her gaze to the floor.

Outside, nervously, they watched the fading light in the sky above. The large group of Lockheed engineers stood gathered, all eyes turned skyward, assembled in a flock-like formation, their matching gray overalls, bearing the company logo, mirrored the darkening sky. Expressions of concern etched their faces, each man and woman holding silent prayers within.

With every passing moment, the sun dipped lower, casting long, blurred shadows across the tarmac. A cool breeze stirred, carrying the faint scent of oil and fuel. It rustled through the engineers' clothing and lifted the edges of their flat caps, but it did little to alleviate the unease creeping through the crowd.

'He should've been back by now,' one engineer muttered, his voice edged with worry.

'There must be a problem,' another replied.

The words rippled outward, passed from mouth to mouth. The crowd thickened as shift workers emerged—secretaries, support staff, maintenance crews—all drawn together by a shared fixation on the sky. Their murmurs grew, a hushed chorus of growing tension. Time stretched. Eyes darted between the horizon and each other, searching for reassurance, finding only mirrored dread.

A lead engineer—tall, with a stern, weathered face—stood slightly apart. His arms were crossed tightly, fingers drumming an anxious rhythm against his sleeve. He'd overseen countless flights, but this one was different. And with each silent minute, the knot in his stomach twisted tighter as he hovered near the hangar entrance.

Behind him, with Claire in tow, Robert approached, alarmed by the gathering.

'How long has he been out?' he asked.

'If he's still flying, his fuel ran out five minutes ago,' the engineer replied, his tone flat.

Robert paled. His expression contorted—vulgar worry etched across his face without a single word. Then a sharp ring split the air, the telephone mounted beside them shattering the silence. Both men startled, eyes wide, lungs catching on hope. The engineer leapt for it.

'Yes? Put him through. *It's him!*' he exclaimed, releasing the breath he'd been holding. He handed Robert the receiver and called out to the crowd. 'It's him!'

They surged forward, racing to gather around for word. Robert pressed the phone to his ear.

'Where are you?' he asked down the line.

* * *

On the other end, Charles gripped the receiver tightly to his ear, trying to muffle the roar of the crowd behind him.

'San Francisco!' Charles shouted back, turning to glance over his shoulder. The Altair sat proudly behind him, gleaming amid a sea of stunned onlookers.

* * *

'Where?' Robert barked. 'Oakland?' he tried again, struggling to hear. An eager engineer pressed closer.

'Where is he?'

Robert batted down the question, motioning for quiet. '*Where?*' he asked again, louder, more urgent.

* * *

'Fisherman's Wharf. The Bay,' Charles replied, a wide, proud grin spreading across his face. Behind him, the Golden Gate Bridge loomed majestically, framing the surreal scene. The docks, usually humming with the sounds of the sea, had fallen into a stunned hush as the crowd swarmed around the aircraft.

* * *

'He's in the Bay—Fisherman's Wharf!' Robert called out. One of the engineers began scribbling rapidly into a notepad.

'We'll get some people down there!' Robert shouted into the receiver before slamming it down. He turned, dazed. 'What the hell is he doing in San Francisco?' he muttered aloud.

'Boss. Boss.' The note-taking engineer looked up, his voice almost reverent. 'By my calculations, boss . . . he just set a new airspeed record.' His voice rose as he handed the calculations to Robert. As Robert examined the calculations, the excitement grew. The engineer paused, eyes gleaming with pride. 'I make that a top speed of *two twenty-five miles per hour*. Gentlemen—' he turned to the crowd '—we just built the fastest single-engine aircraft in the world.'

A roar erupted. Hats flew. Engineers embraced. Applause broke out from the onlookers as shouts echoed through the gathering. 'Did you hear that? A new record!'

One engineer threw his arms around Robert, only to pull back in alarm at the grease smearing Robert's suit. Robert laughed, unbothered. 'We did it, boss! We really did it!' the man bellowed, nearly overcome.

'This is going down in history!' The engineer decreed as Robert's smile widened, unable to further contain his relief.

'He had you worried, didn't he,' Claire whispered, as she smiled gracefully.

'He did Claire,' Robert chuckled subtly. 'He did.'

The low-hanging fog clung to the moist night air as Charles approached the hangar. The doors, left slightly ajar, spilled a sliver of light across the ground—a golden path that led him forward. He paused between them, a silhouette in the doorway.

His eyes landed on her.

Bathed in an angelic glow by the floodlights surrounding her, the Altair stood radiant, defiant in the stillness. The cavernous hangar embraced her like a shrine. Charles took in the sight, eyes crinkling with pride, his chest heavy with emotion. She was everything he had dreamed of.

She was sleek, sophisticated. Her low-wing design was a study in grace, the lighting catching each subtle curve. Her wings stretched outward, tapering to rounded tips, angled slightly upward as if poised to leap back into the sky. Her fuselage was long, her nose muscular and commanding, tapering into a delicate, swallow-like tail.

From the finest Canadian spruce, she had been born—streamlined for speed, strength, and elegance. This was no mere machine. This was an artist's vision, forged into the language of flight. Every contour told a story of knowledge, of craft, of unmatched precision.

She wore a deep, dark blue—Consolidated Blue—accented with a silver stripe edged in red. It ran the length of her side, harmonizing with the blue and silver wings. Together, they whispered of red, white, and blue—two nations, one vision, ocean-spanning ambition.

A quiet rustle behind the aircraft broke the silence. A man stood on a ladder, a few open paint tins at his feet. Long-bristled brushes poked from the back pocket of his splattered overalls, beside a worn rag. He worked with care, pausing to glance over the top of his glasses, perched low on his nose.

'Plenty of good writers down in Burbank,' he said casually, spotting Charles. 'Not that I don't appreciate the work.' He looked back at the fuselage. 'What brings you to Oakland?'

'Quick business trip,' Charles replied with a smile. 'I appreciate you coming in this late.'

The signwriter carefully cleaned his brush with the rag. 'Well, that's this side done.' He exhaled, admiring the name freshly painted. 'Interesting name,' he inquired with an air of curiosity, having no knowledge of the significance it held, as Charles slowly stepped around the aircraft to join him, smiling knowingly, nodding a pleased nod.

'You do good work,' Charles acknowledged.

'Thank you. I am proud of this one!' The signwriter replied.

Charles momentarily paused in thought. 'So am I. So am I.'

Chapter 18

Steamship Mariposa
Pacific Ocean. 1934.

Piercing the surly crests of each wave, the liner's sharp bow cruises above the depths of the never-ending Pacific it traverses, en route through the darkness of the night that has fallen, its destination Sydney.

Through the lavish passageway, Captain Jonathan Reynolds makes his way toward the dining room, meticulously attired in his tailored white uniform, his double-breasted jacket shimmering with gold buttons, the insignia on his shoulders polished to perfection, marking his esteemed rank, and his epaulettes adding an air of authority to his broad shoulders. His peaked cap, adorned with the maritime emblem, sat squarely on his head, a symbol of his command. The sharpness of his appearance contrasted with the weathering of his skin by time and the harsh ocean winds; his face bore the marks of experience and wisdom.

As he entered, the crew paused to his attention as guests greeted his entrance. Shimmering light danced in the reflection of the ornate chandeliers adorning the first class dining room, gently swaying at the behest of the ocean's rolling swell. The soft golden glow danced across geometric wall panels and mirrored columns. The air was perfumed with aged wine, polished silver, and the aroma of buttered lobster and truffled consommé.

Among the most prominent people gracing the room, at a round table dressed in pristine linen, two couples sat basking in the easy charm of good company and better champagne. Richard and Eleanor Montgomery, travelling abroad and the very embodiment of transatlantic sophistication. Richard, tall and commanding, wore a midnight tuxedo that accentuated his lean frame and silver temples. His eyes, thoughtful and observant, rarely missed a detail—a banker's mind behind a gentleman's polish. Eleanor, elegant in a gown of deep sapphire with beaded sleeves, was luminous in the chandelier light. Her golden-blonde hair was styled in soft, structured waves, and a diamond-studded comb adorned the side, catching sparks of light as she moved. A long string of pearls draped gracefully along her collarbone, matching the refinement of her manner.

Across from them, Edward and Lillian Whitmore added a spirited energy to the group. Edward, a sun-bronzed Australian with a squared jaw and easy smile, exuded rugged charm in his ivory dinner jacket. Lillian, his wife, had a vivacious warmth about her. Clad in a silken gown of burnt sienna with a scooped neckline and feathered shawl, her green eyes glittered with curiosity and playful wit. She leaned forward with interest, raising her glass.

'I am sorry I am late, duty on the bridge,' the Captain interrupted as he sat to join his guests. 'What did I miss?'

'Ah, Captain we are so glad you can finally join us, we were in the throes of discussing the name the very fine name Sir Charles has chosen for his aircraft,' Richard boldly replied, bringing the captain up to date on the conversation.

'And a fabulous name it is, I think it is *fabulous*, Sir Charles,' Lillian said with an unmistakable lilt. 'So strong. So bold.'

'I agree,' said the Captain, lifting his glass. 'It is a defiant name.'

'Victorious,' Edward added, nodding with pride.

'A toast,' the Captain declared, his baritone calm but resonant. 'To Sir Charles—and to victory!'

The crystal glasses chimed like delicate bells.

'How does one go about choosing a name for an airship?' Lillian asked, tilting her head.

'I have no idea what it means,' Richard muttered, half-smiling.

'It is almost like a guessing game,' added Eleanor, her voice silken with amusement.

Captain Reynolds sipped, then set down his glass with care. 'It is a name that represents courage, sacrifice, and an endurance that will never own defeat.'

'How *wonderful*,' Eleanor breathed.

'It also represents a disdain for authority,' the Captain added, eyes narrowing ever so slightly, 'something I will not tolerate aboard my ship . . . Sir Charles?' The Captain laughed at the pointed suggestion, as the guests acknowledged his quip.

Edward chuckled. 'If I'm not mistaken, the grand tradition of American pilots is to name their aircraft after their hometown. A tribute to their roots.'

Charles, quiet until now, finally interjected. 'And a fine tradition it is.'

'So it is not the name of your hometown?' Eleanor asked, intrigued.

'No,' Charles said, with a flicker of mystery. 'But it is where our Australian spirit lies.'

'Another clue,' Eleanor said with delight.

'Like the Southern Cross we were born under,' Lillian added, casting a wink toward Edward.

'Where our heart lies,' Charles affirmed.

'I still have no idea,' Edward replied, laughing.

Just then, a young cabin boy in a pristine white uniform appeared at Charles's side with a discreet bow, holding a telegram. Charles accepted it, his fingers tightening slightly as he read. His expression held for a beat too long.

The Captain leaned in, voice low but pointed. 'Is there a problem, Sir Charles?'

Charles folded the telegram crisply, his jaw clenched just so. 'Excuse me.'

He rose, dabbing his mouth with his napkin, and exited with quiet haste. The guests resumed their banter, though a flicker of curiosity lingered. Lillian reached out, resting her hand lightly on the Captain's arm. 'My only complaint, Captain, is that none of us have had the chance to enjoy tennis.'

'Yes,' Edward chimed in, 'Surely Sir Charles could have found a more suitable place to park.' They laughed in unison.

Outside, the wind was soft and perfumed with salt and varnish. The sea shimmered under moonlight, stretching endlessly into the dark. Charles stood at the edge of the promenade deck, eyes fixed on the shadowed bulk of the Altair—the sleek airship that now sat, tethered and looming, atop the ship's tennis court.

He placed a gloved hand on the railing, his other clutching the telegram like a secret too heavy for words. The quiet thrum of engines pulsed beneath his feet, but his thoughts were adrift, pulled back to another chapter of his life . . . one marked by choices that could not be undone, choices made by the young man he once was.

Charles clambered down the webbing slung over the rail of a troop ship and stepped into the landing boat beneath him. The human cargo of newly arriving reinforcements, packed in together, shoulder to shoulder as they launched, rowed toward the distant military establishment nestled precariously low against the vast hills of the Gallipoli Peninsula.

Amid the slapping oars and heavy breaths, grunts, and groans of the oarsmen, the faint sound of a German Taube aircraft could be heard approaching, the trepidation felt. The Taube was state-of-the-art, imposing, its design resembling that of an eagle, a bird of prey, and equally as lethal in the sky.

The landing boat was heavy, and the steel girth of the hull was wide as the sailors rowed their fellow soldiers to shore. Charles stared with a nervous, excited anticipation as the boat lurched with each demanded stroke of human authority propelling them. The oarsman to his front was not new to his calling; rugged, hardened, his imposing force carving out a contrast to the fresh faces of the youth they transported like fodder. As he rowed, he scanned Charles's character with his heavy eyes, wondering if this one would make it, if he had it in him to survive the hell that awaited his arrival, the same question he had asked in his mind of the many fresh faces that had sat before him.

'Oi!' he yelled, gaining Charles's attention. 'Light that for us will ya?' he asked, pulling a cigarette from behind his ear with one hand whilst continuing to row with the other. Taking the cigarette, Charles reached for his matches in his breast pocket.

'You might want to make it quick,' the oarsman said, directing Charles's attention skyward to the aircraft approaching in the distance. Charles hurried, lighting and returning the cigarette to him, before looking toward the sight.

'Ever see a plane before Cobber?' the oarsman asked. Charles, mesmerized by the spectacle, shook his head.

'I hope you can swim,' the oarsman laughed as a tin whistle screeched loud in the silence. A Sergeant yelled, 'Row!'

Slicing through the water, the wake from the landing boats' bow grew, the oarsmen's knuckles turned white as their grip tightened, and their breathing became heavy. With every stroke, they dug the oars deeper into the water, rowing hard in the race to shallow water and the safety of cover onshore, as the aircraft loomed.

The Taube began its dive, narrowing in on its easy prey, well within sights, unleashing a barrage of machine gun fire, the bullets tracing through the water and exploding on a direct path toward the target.

'Jump!' The Sergeant ordered. The men scrambled, launching themselves over the gunnels to hapless safety as lead shredded through steel. Overboard they piled, the hiss of rounds piercing the water's depth. Charles dove deep, struggling under the weight of gear and rifle, as bullets plugged the water around him in slow motion. He stayed down, his breath holding until they were clear, before bursting back to the surface.

The oarsman's head bobbed before him, the wet cigarette still clamped between his lips as Charles took a deep gasping breath.

'Welcome to the war,' the oarsman exclaimed with a sarcastic grin.

'I was fourteen when I enlisted,' the Captain interrupted with the flash of a match as he joined Charles on the rail, striking up the conversation along with his pipe.

'The sea still calls,' the Captain continued, 'I saw a lot in those years of war. The name you have chosen for this ship, Charles, serves as a great honor to the memory of the men who served.'

Charles remained silent, as he glanced down, his eyes perusing the telegram in dismay, as they together reflected.

The Captain drew a deep puff of his pipe. 'One of the crew informed me. I will have them cover it before we arrive.'

The Captain consolingly placed a firm hand on Charles's shoulder with a squeeze before returning to his engagements.

Anderson Park
Sydney, New South Wales, Australia. 1934.

Men clad in gray coveralls strained against weight and water as they rolled the Altair from the harbor barge onto the foreshore. Long timber planks, spanning the gap between water's edge and grassy flat, flexed beneath her weight, groaning under the burden. The task proved difficult, but amid the struggle—and under the watchful eyes of dozens upon dozens of onlookers—the team succeeded.

A wave of applause broke out. Cheers rippled through the crowd as the aircraft made landfall. The Altair came to rest gracefully after her long journey. She sat boldly, yet where her name had once been stenciled along the fuselage, it now lay hidden, concealed beneath brown paper taped to her flanks; the pride she had once borne with dignity now banned from display, hidden from the world.

The natural amphitheater of the park in the bay had swelled with bodies. The spectacle of a takeoff from such an unsophisticated location was a first. A tree-lined patch of grass sloped gently into hilled sides, running flat toward the harbor's edge—a strange choice for a runway, but the only one that would serve.

The crowd was alive with energy, a living thing. Excited murmurs drifted like mist over a sea of shifting bodies. Men in neatly pressed suits and fedoras mingled with women in cloche hats and fine summer dresses, parasols tilted against the sun. Children darted and tumbled in the grass, their laughter high and bright. All had gathered in the name of progress, drawn by the promise of aviation's marvel and the hope of glimpsing their hero in the flesh.

The Altair, now grounded, moved slowly forward under man power. Charles walked just behind her, hands tucked into the pockets of his jacket, steps measured. Close behind him, a customs official stalked with relentless purpose, clipboard in hand, eyes scanning the field like a hawk. His stern face was set in a permanent scowl beneath a clipped mustache—his bearing rigid, precise, every inch the bureaucrat.

Rifling through paperwork, he spoke over the rustle of the crowd.

'You understand that this flight has been permitted for the purpose of transportation directly to Mascot only,' he stated, voice firm, each word carrying authority.

Charles nodded silently, eyes forward, his calm unbroken.

Tommy joined them, falling into step beside him.

'How long?' Charles asked, eyes sweeping the grassy stretch ahead.

'Seven hundred and fifty yards,' Tommy replied with quiet certainty.

Charles took in the field again, lips tightening slightly.

'It is short,' Tommy added. 'We could do with another two hundred, at least.' His voice held a flicker of concern.

Charles turned to him, a wry smile blooming across his face. He reached out and tousled Tommy's hair with a lighthearted chuckle.

'For you maybe,' he teased, his laugh easing the tension.

Tommy grinned wide, his earlier worry fading in the warmth of Charles's confidence. They walked on, the sound of the crowd swelling behind them as the Altair crept forward—toward the edge of history.

Stationed on the hillside above, overlooking the orchestrated pandemonium below, Frank and his wife Dawn sat comfortably on a tartan blanket, enjoying cucumber sandwiches from a well-prepared picnic basket. The hum of anticipation drifted upward, mingling with the faint salt on the breeze.

Frank, ever dignified, did his best to comfort himself against the stubborn discomfort of old bones and unforgiving ground. His thinning combover whisked hopelessly in the wrong direction, the wind making a quiet mockery of his grooming. He wore a double-breasted suit of fine navy wool, its sharp lines contrasting against his crisp white shirt. A burgundy silk tie added a touch of regal color, though it sat slightly askew. It was an ensemble more suited to a club luncheon than a picnic on a hillside, but Frank would argue it was appropriate for any outing of merit.

Beside him, Dawn exuded a grandmotherly elegance, her face softened by gentle curls of silver and warmed by a rosy glow, the subtle rouge on her cheeks catching the light just so. Her style, an endearing blend of refinement and idiosyncrasy, was mismatched in the most charming way. Over her floral dress, she wore a fox fur coat—sable and lush, a testament to their quiet affluence. Around her neck hung a delicate string of pearls, understated and classic, while gold-rimmed spectacles perched on her nose as she peered keenly through a pair of opera glasses.

Down below, the park had grown denser with activity. Reporters in trench coats darted between tripods and cables, scribbling in notebooks, shouting questions to no one in particular. Flashbulbs popped in bursts of magnesium light. The rumble of newsreel cameras filled the air—a mechanical chorus of whirring reels and clicking gears capturing every moment for the cinemas of the Empire.

Tall, boxy camera rigs stood like sentinels above the crowd, their operators hunched beside them, heads beneath hoods, adjusting dials and focus. A small scaffold had even been erected for better vantage, crowded with broadcasters, their microphones held aloft like relics of some ceremonial rite.

A thick cordon of rope and uniformed constables did little to contain the growing tide of bodies pressing forward for a better view. The scent of grass, salt air, and machine oil mingled with the electric sense of occasion.

'I cannot spot him . . . Oh! There he is, on the flying machine!' Dawn exclaimed, her voice rising with delight as she patted Frank's knee and pointed toward the aircraft now poised like a predator at rest.

'Let me see,' Frank requested, lifting a hand.

'In a minute, Frank,' Dawn replied, eyes locked through her opera glasses, unwilling to miss even a breath of history in the making.

Charles stood on the wing beside the cockpit, his hands moving with practiced ease as he performed his preflight checks. The crowd swelled around the aircraft, pressing in with curiosity and reverence. Camera shutters clicked. Voices murmured. Yet within the commotion, his focus remained steady—until a voice called his name.

'Smithy!'

A man stepped forward—working class by the look of him, his trousers worn at the knees, sleeves rolled to the forearm. In his arms, he held a young boy, cradled close, eyes alight with wonder.

'Would ya mind if me boy had a quick look?' the man asked, voice tentative but hopeful.

Charles glanced down, a smile easing across his face.

'What is his name?'

'Billy,' the father replied.

'Hello there, little man,' Charles said warmly, crouching and extending his arms. 'How old are you, Billy?'

'I am five,' came the reply, soft and earnest.

'Five! Well now, that's a fine age,' Charles said, scooping him up with care. 'Do you want to be a pilot one day?'

'Yes,' Billy said, barely above a whisper.

Charles grinned. 'Let us get you in the captain's seat then.'

He lifted the boy gently, setting him down in the cockpit. Billy stared ahead, jaw slack, breath caught. He said nothing—his wide eyes taking in the sweep of dials and toggles, chrome-edged instruments gleaming against dark panels, each one a mystery, a marvel. The world of flight stretched out before him, silent and infinite.

Charles glanced back at the father, who stood beaming with pride, hands trembling slightly with emotion. *Thank you*, the man mouthed, bowing his head in quiet gratitude.

Charles nodded in return, the moment unspoken but understood.

'Alright, Billy,' he said gently, reaching back into the cockpit, 'unless you're planning to take off without me, we'd better get you down.'

He lifted the boy into his arms once more.

'Did you like that?'

Billy nodded, still speechless, his small face radiant.

'Good on ya, Smithy,' the father said, accepting his son once more.

Charles held his gaze a moment longer, then said, 'I have one myself. A little younger.'

The two men exchanged a proud smile—one of shared understanding—and shook hands. No more needed to be said. The father turned back into the crowd, disappearing among the sea of hats and shoulders. Charles watched him go, the boy still clinging to his neck, both of them carrying something quietly unforgettable.

For a brief moment, Charles lingered there alone—on the wing, above it all—savoring the quiet within his thoughts.

'Boss.'

Tommy's voice cut through the din as he appeared at the side of the aircraft, his face half-shadowed beneath his cap.

'Nice day for a fly, Tommy,' Charles said, his tone light but laced with gravity.

'She is all set. You are good to go,' Tommy replied, a subtle tension in his voice—professionally calm, but edged with something more personal, his smile a subtle give away..

'Thanks, Tommy.' Charles winked.

'I'll see you back at base,' Tommy said, then paused. 'Don't be late.' Tommy laughed knowingly.

Charles chuckled. 'Me? Never.'

The two men locked eyes for a second longer, the weight of the moment suspended between banter and history. Then Tommy stepped back, giving Charles room.

With measured ease, Charles climbed into the cockpit, his movements fluid, unhurried. He settled into the seat, the familiar cockpit wrapping around his body like an old coat. For a moment, he sat still, taking in the world beyond the glass—the crowd now quiet, the harbor gleaming in the sun, the wind shifting gently through the trees.

He inhaled once, deeply—steadying breath, centering calm.

'Here we go again, just you, me and the sky,' he whispered. He looked out the port side to Tommy on the ground.

'Clear!' he called, his voice sharp and certain.

'Clear!' Tommy replied.

The engine cracked like a gunshot as he fired her up. A thunderclap shattered the echoes through the surrounds, the propeller spun, and with a sudden roar, the engine surged to life. The crowd flinched as one, a ripple of stunned silence folding over them. Dust kicked up from the grass. People scattered backward holding their hats to their heads. Children shielded themselves behind their parents. The Altair had awakened.

And she was hungry for the sky.

Charles, stoic at the controls, wound the blades up to speed under full brake. The force of the thrust surged down the length of the aircraft, peeling back the paper that hid her name—first a flutter, then a rip. As Charles pushed the throttle further forward, the paper surrendered completely, tore more.

Below, the customs official erupted into a panic.

'Stop!' he bellowed, breaking into a sprint, feet pounding the grass, arms flailing like broken wings as he charged toward the aircraft.

But his shouts were swallowed by the engine's roar.

Up on the hillside, Dawn's opera glasses snapped into focus.

'What is that chap doing, Frank?' she asked, clutching his arm, her voice tinged with equal parts alarm and delight.

'What chap?' Frank replied, still waiting for his turn with the glasses.

'It appears—oh dear—it appears he is trying to stop him, Frank! Oh, this is terribly exciting.' She clutched her pearls with both hands.

In the cockpit, Charles advanced the throttle. The engine howled, the propeller a blur. With calm precision, he released the brakes.

The Altair lurched forward.

'Oh! Here he goes, Frank,' Dawn exclaimed, leaning forward, her excitement mounting. The mechanical thunder drowned out the official's frantic screams.

'Stop! You are not cleared—STOP!' the man shrieked, arms waving helplessly, a puppet against the storm.

'There is some sort of kerfuffle, Frank,' Dawn remarked, not without glee.

'Let me see!' Frank insisted.

'In a minute, Frank,' she replied, eyes locked on the unfolding drama.

The crowd, sensing the moment, erupted. A wave of noise surged forward—cheers, whistles, applause. Newsreel cameras cranked furiously. Hats flew into the air. The Altair charged down the runway, paper shreds trailing from her fuselage as the paper blew free from her sides.

Fully revealed, her name—*ANZAC*, bold and defiant against the sun.

She tore forward, parting the honor guard of people lining the runway, their fists raised in celebration. The roar of her engine became the voice of a nation.

Tommy stood near the edge of the field, urging her on.

'Come on, girl . . .' he murmured, excitement giving way to a creeping edge of concern as the end of the field neared.

'Pull up. Pull up . . .' he whispered, the words half prayer.

A hush fell over the crowd as the *ANZAC* dipped—dangerously low—disappearing below the embankment.

Gasps.

A beat of silence.

Then—triumph.

The *ANZAC* rose from beneath, straining but victorious, climbing fast and strong into the sky. A collective roar erupted below. Cheers burst like fireworks. Hats soared again. Strangers embraced. Children shouted and ran. The crowd danced with wild joy, their voices blurring into one mighty cheer.

Tommy exhaled at last.

High above, silhouetted against the blue, the *ANZAC* banked gracefully to port, turning east toward the coast.

'Oh, hooray! Frank, he made it!' Dawn clapped her hands with delight. 'Quick now, you'll miss it—here!' She handed over the opera glasses at last.

Frank, moved by something deeper than he could articulate, brought the glasses to his eyes just in time to catch the aircraft wheeling out over the harbor, its thunder fading.

But the official was not done.

'Mascot is the other way! He's gone the wrong way!' he shouted, spinning toward Tommy in dismay.

Tommy barely missed a beat.

'Ah, yeah . . .' he replied, lips quivering into a grin, his mind turning for an any excuse. 'He has to turn into the wind.'

The official threw his hands into the air before slamming his clipboard to the ground in frustration. Tommy simply looked skyward, his smile widening as the *ANZAC* climbed higher, free.

Behind the controls, Charles was home.

The *ANZAC* soared gracefully low over the harbor, her silver wings spread out like those of an angel against the bright blue sky. Below him, the swell rolled gently across the harbor, the deep brilliant blue only broken by the ferry traffic traversing her sides. The headlands shimmered, cliffs of gold topped with lush green bushland lapped by the crisp white waves breaking against their rocky shores. The sun made every bit of the world beneath bright.

Up here, everything was clarity—pure, vast, and utterly his.

In this moment, he knew the eyes of a nation were upon him, and he relished it. Not with arrogance, but with the quiet pride of a man who had *earned* the right to linger in the sky a little longer.

The extended joy flight was not indulgence.

It was a tribute.

Chapter 19

Wyndham, Western Australia, Australia. 1934.

The baked ground shimmered in the heat, dancing with mirage-like waves rising from its scorched surface. A dust devil flirted by in lazy circles, kicked up by the dry wind as the temperature crept steadily higher. Humidity clung to everything, thick as syrup.

Inside, it was darker and a little cooler, but the tension hung heavy—like the air, thick and close, pressing in with the weight of something about to boil over.

A fly crawled slowly across the sticky countertop, its legs dragging through the amber rings of dried beer—the sweet, fermented residue left behind by glass after glass.

SMACK.

A newspaper slapped down hard, flattening the insect beneath a bold, black headline:

NAME BANNED

'Have you seen this bloody nonsense, Bill?'

Bev—sharp-eyed, short-fused—stood behind the bar, still gripping the newspaper as if it were a live grenade. The page trembled faintly in her hand.

'Seen what?' Bill asked, not looking up, still drying a glass with methodical care.

'What they're doing to Smithy, that's-what's-what!' she snapped. 'They've banned him from using the name *ANZAC*. ANZAC, Bill! Can you bloody believe it? *Look!*'

She shoved the paper across the bar.

Bill took it, leaned in, and squinted at the type. He read slowly.

Carefully. Said nothing.

'Un-bloody-believable, this lot,' Bev muttered, pacing. 'The whole country's in an uproar. Some bloody thanks, eh? That's gratitude for you.'

In the corner, Reg sat with his elbows on the table, nursing his schooner with both hands like it might spill history if he let go. He looked up, brow drawn.

'Smithy in a spot again?' he asked, voice dry but soft with concern.

'He's not in a spot, Reg. He's being bloody done in,' Bev fired back. 'He fought for that name—same as the rest of the boys around here—and now they won't even let him use it.'

Bill adjusted his glasses and flipped the page. 'Says here the Act was passed in 1921. Bans commercial use of 'ANZAC' unless approved by the minister.'

He paused. 'Seems from this as though half the country agrees.'

Bev leaned in, eyes sharp as flint.

'Well that's bloody garbage. Which half? The half that weren't there?'

She gestured fiercely. 'They think he's slapping it on a tin of condensed milk? He named a plane, Bill. A bloody flying tribute!'

'It hardly seems fair,' Bill murmured, flattening the paper. 'That name wouldn't even exist if it weren't for all those blokes like Smithy.'

'No one could argue that,' Reg added, raising his glass slowly in salute.

'I've half a mind to write to those bastards myself,' Bev muttered, crossing her arms tight.

'Give 'em hell, Bev!' Reg called out, fired up at last.

'Too right, right I bloody will,' she snapped, silencing the room. And for a moment, the voices of those lost found flame again.

Kingsford Smith Air Services
Mascot, Sydney, New South Wales, Australia. 1934.

Within her new home, the Altair stood gleaming beneath the harsh glare of the hangar's overhead lights. Charles, Tommy, and Stannage admired her, their presence dwarfed by the aircraft's sleek, silver form.

Tommy, wholly absorbed in the mechanics, ran his hands lovingly over the engine. 'Five hundred forty horsepower, nine-cylinder Pratt and Whitney radial. Twelve-times supercharger. Variable-pitch propeller. . .' His voice was reverent as he traced his finger over the enamel Pratt and Whitney logo embedded in the face of the cast iron.

The engine was a marvel, each component meticulously engineered for peak performance. His eyes sparkled as he traced the intricate connections, mind racing with the machine's possibilities.

Stannage, drawn more to beauty than engineering, grinned as he circled the aircraft. 'I like the color,' he said, his fingers trailing along the elegant lines of the fuselage. The deep blue paint shimmered under the lights, giving the Altair an almost ethereal presence. He admired the craftsmanship—the seamless joints, the flawless finish.

Charles stood with arms crossed, nodding in approval. 'She's bloody fast,' he said, watching Tommy's eager inspection. The Altair radiated power and speed, a machine built to conquer the skies.

Leaning against a nearby tool chest, John raised an eyebrow. 'Fast enough to win, Charles?'

Before Charles could answer, the hangar doors groaned open. Heavy boots echoed across the concrete as a team of customs officials strode in, their presence slicing through the moment like a blade. The hum of the hangar dimmed. Tools stilled mid-motion. Workers paused, turning toward the sound.

'Mr. Kingsford Smith,' the lead official called, his voice sharp and clipped.

Charles turned to John with a dry smile. 'This is the problem with having your name on the building,' he muttered, just loud enough to carry.

'And the problem you have when you fail to comply with directives of the government,' the official shot back. 'Mr. Stannage. Mr. Kingsford Smith was warned.'

A grim-faced worker approached the Altair and ignited a blowtorch. The sudden flare cast jagged shadows across the walls. Its hiss cut through the silence. Acrid smoke curled into the air.

Tommy lunged forward, voice urgent. 'Wait! You can't—'

Charles grabbed his arm, holding him back. 'Tommy. We don't need more trouble.'

The official stepped closer, his eyes steely. 'You've contravened legislation restricting the use of the word 'ANZAC' for promotional purposes. This permit allows us to forcibly remove it.'

Charles drew a steady breath, struggling to contain his anger. 'Gentlemen, surely there's a more reasonable solution.'

The official remained unmoved. 'Under Proclamation 109, which bans the importation of US-built aircraft into Australia, we are also authorized to seize and impound this aircraft until it can be returned to its country of origin.'

Charles's fists clenched, knuckles white. Around him, the team stood silent, waiting.

The official extended a clipboard toward John. 'Sign here. And here.'

John scanned the paperwork, then glanced at Charles with a shrug that said *there's nothing we can do*. He signed.

'There is your copy.' The official tipped his hat, his smile smug and victorious. 'Have a nice day, Mr. Kingsford Smith. Gentlemen.'

'Men!' he barked to the workers behind him, gesturing toward the Altair.

The boots of the departing officials echoed once more in the now-silent hangar.

Charles didn't move. He stood rigid, fury burning beneath the surface as the name *ANZAC* blistered under the torch's flame.

Darkness had descended over the day. The hangar lay quiet, save for the soft scuff of tools and the occasional sigh from Tommy. He worked meticulously, his face bathed in the glow of a solitary work lamp as he repaired the damage. The air still held the acrid scent of scorched timber and burnt paint. The steady rasp of sandpaper echoed faintly in the space as he assessed and reassessed the harm done.

'Tommy, I am heading off.' Jack, a fellow engineer softly mentioned as he approached to leave.

'Thanks Jack, I appreciate the help.' Tommy replied.

Quietly, Jess stepped in, her footsteps light on the concrete as she approached, drawing both Jack's and Tommy's attention. Jack simply turned back to Tommy and smiled.

'I will leave you to it.'

'Thanks again Jack.' Tommy replied before turning his eyes back to Jess.

She wore a pale blue blouse tucked into a high-waisted skirt that fell just below the knee—simple, but carefully chosen. Her hair was pinned back in soft waves, and a delicate hint of perfume followed her, just enough to be noticed over the lingering scent of grease and paint. She didn't look like she'd come from work; she looked like she'd dressed *intentionally*—to be seen.

'Working late?' she asked, her voice soft—almost a whisper—careful not to startle him. In her hands, she held a thermos and a sandwich wrapped neatly in paper. 'I thought I would bring you something.' She hesitated, uncertain. 'Is it bad?'

Tommy looked up, wiping sweat and grime from his forehead.

'Right back to the timber,' he said, tired but resolute. 'They nearly put a hole straight through her.'

His eyes lingered on her—just a second longer than they should have. He took the sandwich with a grateful nod, his stomach growling. The food was a welcome pause from the frustration.

As he looked around, suddenly aware of the mess, he fumbled to make space.

'Uh—hang on,' he said quickly. He shuffled over a pair of crates, dragging them closer to the lamp. Then, catching sight of the dust, he hastily pulled a rag from his pocket and began wiping one down, more vigorously than was strictly necessary.

'I, uh—sorry,' he mumbled, not quite meeting her eye.

Jess smiled, amused but touched. 'Thank you.'

Tommy gave a sheepish shrug and motioned for her to sit. They settled in together, Jess's fiery red hair alive under the soft, intimate light, the crates serving as a makeshift table and chairs.

Jess watched him as he unwrapped the sandwich, her expression gentle with concern.

'Thank you, Jess,' Tommy said after a moment, offering a tired but warm smile.

Jess frowned, her voice uncertain. 'Do you think everything is going to be alright? I mean . . . around here?'

Tommy paused mid-bite, then reached out and gently took her hands. His were calloused, stained from grease and grit—but his touch was careful, almost reverent. He met her gaze.

'Everything is going to be fine, Jess,' he said, his voice quiet but firm.

She smiled faintly, a small breath of relief escaping her.

'Besides, if there is one thing I know about Smithy—it is that he does not give up. I have never seen him in a situation he could not get out of.' He gave her hands a gentle squeeze. 'We will be alright.'

Jess nodded, comforted. They both glanced down at their joined hands, his fingers still resting over hers.

Then Tommy seemed to realize. 'Sorry,' he muttered, blinking as if coming out of a trance.

Jess looked up again, their eyes locking—there was something unmistakable in the silence between them.

'I should probably let you finish eating,' she said, her voice soft and a little nervous. 'And let you get back to work.'

'Yeah,' Tommy said, his smile returning as he scratched the back of his neck. 'Unless, uh . . . unless you do not have anywhere else to be. You are welcome to stay, if you would like.'

Jess hesitated, cheeks turning a shade pinker.

'I can stay for a little while,' she said softly.

Chapter 20

Flemington Racecourse
Melbourne, Australia. 1934.

The fog hung thick with the scent of wet grass and horse manure, draping the impressive stables in a dense, almost tangible curtain. The early morning buzz of race day preparations stirred around them. Stable hands moved with purpose, tending to the myriad tasks that readied the horses for their impending races. The clink of metal, the murmur of voices, and the occasional whinny created an excitement that drifted seamlessly into the mist.

The weather deepened the atmosphere—picturesque, yet faintly foreboding. A heavy mist clung to the ground, swirling with every movement, making the world feel smaller, more intimate. The air was cool and damp, heavy with the scent of wet soil, horse and hay. Dew clung to everything—from the blades of grass to the wooden beams of the stables—sparkling faintly in the early light. Overhead, a blanket of thick darkening skies hid the sun, promising an overcast day. Moisture dropped steadily from the eaves, a quiet reminder of the night's rain.

Mac and Charles walked side by side through the fog, their footsteps muffled by the damp earth. Mac paused beside a stall and reached out to rub a horse's muzzle with a touch that spoke of deep affection and familiarity.

'Sultan,' he murmured.

The horse responded with a soft nicker, nudging into Mac's hand.

'One of my favorites,' Mac said, his voice warm with pride. 'Stallion. Fine breeder. Excellent racer, once.' He pulled a sliver of carrot from his pocket. Sultan accepted it eagerly.

As the horse chewed, Mac turned to Charles. 'Fourth Light Horse Regiment during the war, were you not?'

'I was,' Charles replied evenly, as they resumed their walk.

'Egypt?'

'Before the front,' Charles said, eyes distant, lost in memory.

Mac nodded thoughtfully. 'Then you understand horses, Charles. And if you understand horses, you know you pick a winner from its bloodline. It's breeding.'

They stopped again to admire another stallion, its sleek coat gleaming even in the dim light. 'You give a horse everything—best stable, trainer, feed, jockey. But in the end, there's only one thing that makes a winner.'

He looked Charles in the eye. 'Spirit. What's in their heart. A true thoroughbred has spirit.'

Charles opened his mouth, but Mac's voice rose, firm.

'But they break down, Charles. You push them too far, too often, they shatter. Some are put down. Most work the rest of their days. But the great ones—they carry on. They pass on that spirit. They build the next generation of champions. And what holds it all together?'

'Mac—' Charles interrupted.

'Rules, Charles.' Mac's voice cut in, louder now. 'We may not always agree with them. But they are there for a reason.'

He softened, seeing Charles's expression change.

'In racing, like in life, when you break the rules, you pay the price. And while I feel the injustice of your situation, as a businessman, I can no longer support you. My decision is final.'

Charles stood still, the weight of Mac's words settling heavily.

'Thank you, Mac,' he said quietly.

'They are stacking the odds against you, Charles,' Mac added. A touch of empathy, uncommon in his demeanor, crept in. 'Look at it like a handicap, Charles, you are carrying a lot of weight; it reminds me of the great Phar Lap—they handicapped him heavily, yet, all the weight in the world could not break his spirit. Surely, you don't think they can break yours Charles.'

The last words lingered in the heavy fog that rolled in, consuming the pair.

Kingsford Smith Air Services
Mascot, Sydney, New South Wales, Australia. 1934.

Bright yellow, the Tiger Moth gleamed under the crisp sunlight of the cool day as Nancy stood cradling Charles Jr. in her arms. His blonde curls fluttered gently in the breeze as he tugged at the flying scarf loosely draped around her neck.

'The whole idea terrifies me,' Nancy admitted, eyes soft as she traced his tiny fingers, trying to keep his restless curiosity engaged.

Mary reached out, squeezing Nancy's arm with quiet reassurance.

'You have got a few years before you need to worry about motherhood. You are only seventeen—and well on your path to a wonderful career.'

Nancy adjusted her grip on Charles Jr., who was now tugging at her with growing impatience.

'I would have to find a husband first,' she said with a half smile.

Mary chuckled, letting her hand fall to her side. 'You're certainly in the right place for that. No shortage of men around here—all slightly mad, of course.' She nodded toward a nearby group of pilots, laughing and joking near the hangar.

Nancy laughed, shifting her weight. 'True. But it would be nice to find someone more interested in me than in these airplanes. Oh—I didn't mean—' She bit her lip, glancing at Mary.

Mary waved a hand, smiling. 'It is perfectly alright. I often wonder to myself what the attraction is.' She adjusted her hat, the brim casting a thoughtful shadow across her face.

'You have not flown?' Nancy asked, surprised.

Mary looked down at her hands, clasped together. 'No. Oddly, no.'

Nancy's voice dropped with concern. 'Oh my. Do you worry about Charles?'

Mary shook her head, a small smile forming. 'No,' she said, her voice tinged with something held back. 'Charles and I have a deal.' She reached out and touched the wing of the Moth, her fingers brushing the smooth metal.

Nancy leaned in, intrigued. 'A deal?'

'Yes,' Mary said, eyes drifting to the horizon. 'Flying is Charles's passion. His life. I have accepted that. We have a special deal.' She tucked a loose strand of hair behind her ear, smiling distantly.

'That is beautiful,' Nancy whispered.

'It is,' Mary said softly. 'It took time. But I understand now. His heart is in the sky—but he always lands with us.'

Nancy sighed, stroking Charles Jr.'s hair as he reached again toward the Tiger Moth. 'Maybe I need someone with both feet on the ground.'

'You will find him,' Mary said. 'Plenty of men would happily ground themselves for you.' She shaded her eyes, glancing toward the hangar where mechanics worked and more planes lined up for flight.

An engine roared to life, startling them both. They turned as a plane lifted from the runway, wheels rising cleanly into the sky. Charles Jr. pointed excitedly, his eyes wide.

Nancy turned back to Mary. 'Do you think you will ever fly?'

Mary considered the question, folding her arms against a sudden gust of wind. 'Maybe someday. But for now, I am happy here. Supporting Charles. Looking after this little one.'

Nancy nodded, kissing the boy's head. 'It is brave, what you do.'

Mary laughed gently. 'It is just life, Nancy. We all have our paths. Yours will be an adventure, I am sure.'

They stood in quiet reflection until Mary spotted a familiar figure near a plane.

'Speak of the devil,' she said, nodding toward Charles—aviator jacket and goggles on, animated in conversation.

Nancy watched him for a moment. 'He really does love it, does he not?'

Mary nodded. 'It is like a second home up there.'

'Dada!' Charles Jr. called, wriggling in Nancy's arms.

She set him down, and he waddled, legs wobbling and arms flailing, across the grass toward his father.

'Charles always makes time for him,' Mary said. 'No matter how busy.'

They watched as Charles scooped up his son, laughter ringing out. With the boy on his shoulders, Charles walked toward them, still mid-conversation with another pilot.

'I hope I find someone like that,' Nancy said softly.

'You will,' Mary replied, giving her a gentle elbow. 'Just keep being you.'

Charles arrived with a grin. 'Ladies. Everything all right over here?'

'Just fine,' Mary said. 'Nancy was telling me about her future plans.'

Charles looked at Nancy with a grin. 'Well, if you are husband-hunting, I am sure we can find a decent one among this mad lot.'

Nancy laughed. 'Thanks, Charles. I'll keep that in mind.'

'Mama!' Charles Jr. called, reaching down.

Mary took him gently. 'I think someone's had enough excitement for one day.' She kissed his forehead.

Nancy watched the small family, a smile touching her lips.

'I will be in the office if you need me,' Charles said, kissing Mary. 'See you, Nance.' He turned and headed inside.

'It never ends, Nancy,' Mary said with a knowing smile as they continued their conversation.

The carved light of a bright blue day sliced through the office air, the banding of light highlighted in the cigarette smoke as it cast long shadows across the floor. Charles paced back and forth, his arms folded, his chin lowered, resting in his hand. The floorboards creaked under the tap of his heavy soles with each step.

'There must be another way,' he muttered, his thoughts churning.

John stood by the bay window, light glinting off his glasses as he rubbed his jaw.

'Temporary importation was the best I could do. I have tried everything.' He exhaled, frustration showing in the slow deflation of his shoulders. Outside, the world moved on, oblivious.

Charles stopped, shoes scuffing the floor. He sighed.

'I cannot see another option.'

He looked up. 'Thanks, John. You have done well.'

'That's all we have got.'

Charles leaned over the papers strewn across his desk. The scent of old paper and polish filled the room. He ran a finger along the page edges.

'We will use Taylor.'

'Not Tommy?' John blinked. 'Why not?'

'I need Tommy on the ground,' Charles said firmly. The ticking clock grew louder, breaking the silence.

'How do you want to play it?'

'I'll need every cent we have got—for the tests, the race, the entry fee.'

John's brow furrowed. 'How much?'

'Five thousand.'

John paled. 'That's everything in the business.'

'Mortgage the house.'

'Charles?' John's voice cracked, caught between loyalty and disbelief.

Charles met his eyes. 'I will see what I can do.'

'Thanks, John. Run it by Tommy. I will cover Mac and repay him out of the prize money.'

John hesitated. 'If these flights do not prove she's airworthy, there *won't* be any prize money.'

'She is a good plane John, and I am a good pilot.'

John gave a slow nod. 'I know. It is just . . .' He trailed off. 'I know that look in your eye.'

Charles softened.

'Have you thought about a name?' John asked.

'I have,' Charles said, walking to the window.

He gently parted the venetian blinds. Mary stood outside, bathed in sunlight, her white dress glowing softly, her laughter carried on the breeze as she moved gracefully across the grass. Her joy painted the moment with fragile beauty.

'I have something very special in mind,' he said, a warm smile blossoming across his face.

The wings of the Altair bent the air, her spirit rose over a new dawn, powerful, strong, blistering through the heavenly skies, untamed, now named *Lady Southern Cross.*

Charles flew on the wings of an angel, possessed.

Chapter 21

Royal Aero Club
London, England. 1934.

A. O. Edwards, the distinguished businessman and owner of Grosvenor House, possessed a commanding presence that reflected both his wealth and refined tastes. Standing at an imposing six feet, he carried himself with the assurance of a man long accustomed to deference. Despite the passage of time, only a few strands of gray had threaded through his thick, dark hair—a testament to his vitality and vigorous lifestyle.

His voice, a deep and resonant baritone, conveyed both authority and cultivated sophistication. A man of few words, he preferred to let his actions and achievements speak for him. Yet when he did engage in conversation, it was with a sharp intellect and a wit that left a lasting impression. Tonight, seated comfortably within the hallowed halls of the Royal Aero Club, the company of his guests was both welcomed and purposeful.

The club itself was a seamless blend of traditional British elegance and the daring spirit of aviation. Every detail—from the dark mahogany furnishings to the gleaming brass instruments and framed flight charts—had been meticulously selected to evoke both luxury and inspiration. It was a fitting tribute to the pioneers and patrons of flight.

'Gentlemen, I am nervous,' Edwards began, handing them each a piece of paper. 'Kingsford Smith has conducted seven intercity flights in under a month—each of them record-breaking: Sydney to Melbourne, two hours and twenty-five minutes, Melbourne to Sydney in . . . two hours and eleven minutes, Melbourne to Perth in ten hours, nineteen minutes' He paused, looking heavily at both men.

Then continued:

'Perth, Adelaide six hours, Adelaide, Sydney three hours thirty two.' His voice remained steady, though tinged with unease, as he slowly swirled the brandy in his glass. Around them, the soft clinking of cutlery and low murmur of conversation lent the room a dignified ambiance.

Scott leaned forward, a confident gleam in his eye. He was dressed impeccably in a double-breasted navy suit, its wide lapels framing a patterned silk tie. A neatly folded white pocket square peeked from his breast pocket, and his polished brown brogues gleamed beneath the table—understated, but flawless.

'Sydney to Brisbane, two hours and thirty-five minutes and Brisbane to Sydney two hours and sixteen minutes, gentlemen.' He paused.

'His ship is certainly proving itself worthy competition,' Scott said, his tone a careful blend of respect and resolve.

Edwards paused, ignoring his comment.

A burst of laughter erupted from a nearby table, where aviators swapped tales of near misses and mechanical triumphs, added a ripple of energy to the atmosphere.

'As is he,' Black added, puffing thoughtfully on a cigar. He wore a rich brown herringbone tweed suit, paired with a cream shirt and dark green tie. His leather shoes, while polished, bore subtle scuffs—evidence of a man who balanced form with function. The embers of his cigar glowed as he inhaled, exhaling a thick plume of smoke that curled lazily upward into the haze.

'One can certainly appreciate how Kingsford Smith earned his title,' Scott continued. 'It would be a mistake to underestimate his abilities, Mr. Edwards.' The soft rustling of newspaper pages punctuated his words.

'Or his character,' Black noted, tapping ash into a crystal tray. 'He has lost the backing of Sir Macpherson Robertson, I understand?'

'So it seems,' Edwards said, seizing the moment. 'What of his copilot—Taylor?' he asked, curiosity piqued, as he took a measured sip of brandy, savoring its warmth.

'He is regarded as a gentleman, and held in high esteem by all who have flown with him. 'Steely' was the word one pilot used. Over a map, he is unmatched,' Scott attested, his tone marked by clear respect.

'Kingsford Smith is not one to fly with anything less,' Black added. 'His reputation for surrounding himself with only the best is well established in aviation circles.' From across the room, a quiet debate over the latest airframe innovations drifted toward them.

Edwards leaned back, his expression darkening, a cigar now resting between his fingers. His tailored three-piece suit fit flawlessly; the vest was fastened over a crisp white shirt and a deep blue silk tie. His shoes, polished to a mirror shine, caught the flickering light of the hearth. He took a deliberate draw, exhaled, and watched the smoke curl upward into the lamplight.

'My name—and the reputation of my business—are emblazoned on the very side of your ship, gentlemen. Not to mention the modest fortune I have invested,' he said coolly. 'Your admiration of your adversary does little to inspire my confidence. While we sit here in the comfort of these hallowed walls, I would caution you against allowing my trust in you to become . . . an afterthought.'

The fire crackled softly behind them, casting a warm glow that did little to temper the gravity of his words.

Scott straightened, his voice firm with resolve. 'Our advantage still lies in speed, sir. We remain faster than the Altair.'

He took a short puff from his cigar; the tip glowed briefly in the dimness.

Black nodded. 'Experience is not always recorded in ink, sir. It is proven in the moment. I would wager that Kingsford Smith's greatest flaw, under these conditions, may well be in his choice of aircraft.'

Edwards's gaze narrowed as he held his cigar aloft. 'I certainly hope so, gentlemen. This is no longer just a race of man against man—but of machine against machine.'

'Rather sporting, one would say? One great nation against another,' Black replied.

'A small fortune,' Edwards rebuked. 'I trust I shall not need to remind you of that again.'

'No, sir,' both Scott and Black replied in unison, their determination renewed.

Edwards leaned forward slightly, extinguishing his cigar with deliberate weight.

House of Lords
London, England. 1934.

Scott and Black stood side by side beneath the vaulted ceiling of the ancient chamber, staring down the semicircular arrangement of solemn faces. At the center of the oversight committee sat Lord Liard, a stern figure whose powdered wig seemed less decorative than ceremonial—a reminder of centuries of unbroken authority.

Lord Liard adjusted his spectacles as he peered over a sheaf of briefing papers.

'Mr. Scott, it is the understanding of Parliament that the speed of both aircraft is very similar. Are you not concerned by this fact?'

Scott straightened, his expression composed but resolute.

'My Lords,' he began, 'the Comet remains a superior aircraft. Sir Charles's decision to enter a single-engine design allows no margin for error. It is, quite frankly, a risky choice for any man serious about winning.'

A low murmur rippled through the panel. Lord Liard lifted a hand, silencing the room.

'Questionable reliability of his aircraft does not ensure your success, Mr. Scott. We need not remind you of the government's investment in this venture.'

Scott's jaw tightened slightly, though he remained measured in his reply.

'My Lords, it has come to our attention that the fuel capacity of the American aircraft is substantially lower than that of the Comet. This single fact will cost Sir Charles valuable time. For every three refueling stops made by our craft, his will require a fourth. When combined with the maintained cruise speed, I am afforded a practical advantage of over five hundred miles.'

Lord Liard exchanged a glance with one of his colleagues, then turned back.

'Advantage or not, Mr. Scott, our concerns are well justified. Which is precisely why we've authorized three British entries.'

Scott offered a thin smile.

'With or without advantage, I can beat Sir Charles.'

A pause hung in the air. Then:

'Thank you, Mr. Scott. That will be all.'

Scott gave a shallow bow and turned to leave. His polished brogues echoed faintly on the stone floor as the committee sat in still silence.

Once the door closed behind him, one of the peers leaned toward Lord Liard, voice dry with aristocratic amusement.

'You must admire these adventurer types. For them, victory is a matter of sportsmanship.'

Liard's expression remained stone cold, expressionless he tapped his papers into a neat alignment.

'Personally,' he said, 'I prefer a more bankable guarantee.'

Parliament House
Canberra, Australian Capital Territory, Australia. 1934.

The skies had darkened over the Capital. Rain tapped rhythmically against the tall windows, trailing down the glass in silvery veins, casting warped reflections across the faces of the officials seated neatly around the baize-covered table. The fire crackled in the hearth, its warmth doing little to lift the chill that hung in the room, still thick with smoke and unspoken agendas.

Shephard moved with quiet precision, placing a slim report before each man as he circled the room.

'As you will see outlined in the report,' he began carefully, 'public support for Sir Charles has only grown, sir. There is a growing perception that the government is not doing all it can to support his entry. The press has begun suggesting that bureaucracy is stifling his efforts.'

Sir Duddevin gave a curt sniff, tapping his gold-nibbed pen absently against the folder before him, his eyes scanning the text at a glacial pace.

'We did issue a temporary importation,' he said coolly.

'We did, sir,' Shephard replied.

'That, surely, is sufficient. Public sentiment does not negate the fact that he has failed to obtain certification.'

'The aircraft has proven itself airworthy, sir,' Shephard countered, his voice tightening. 'Given the recent flights, the press is celebrating his success. There is a growing public impression that we are obstructing—not regulating.'

Duddevin exhaled slowly through his nose.

'I—we—are growing rather tiresome of this situation, Shephard,' he said, voice clipped. 'We are here to *govern*. Or have you forgotten?'

A pointed silence followed.

Shephard stood his ground. 'An oversight in the supply paperwork is hardly justification for barring his entry. If that is seen as the sole reason for denying certification, the public will view it as bureaucratic sabotage. The optics would be . . . damaging.'

Sir Duddevin leaned back in his chair. His fingers steepled beneath his chin, expression unreadable.

'Then find something, Shephard.'

'We could perform further inspections, sir.'

'Yes, yes—further inspections,' Duddevin muttered. 'Though I suspect those will not favor us either. Carry them out regardless.'

'Yes, sir.'

The fire snapped. Rain ticked louder against the glass. The silence returned—heavier than before.

Then, a voice from the far end of the table.

'If I may, Sir Duddevin.'

Duddevin gave a slight nod.

'Perhaps we might arrange a test—conducted under our own authority. A formal performance evaluation. Controlled conditions. A measure by *our* standards.'

Duddevin raised an eyebrow. 'A test?'

'Yes, sir,' the man continued. 'A demonstration, staged to highlight the aircraft's inadequacies. It would validate our concerns—establish the current decisions as grounded in aviation safety rather than politics.'

Sir Duddevin turned to Collins.

'Shephard?'

'It could be arranged,' Collins replied smoothly.

'Then see to it. Immediately. And Collins—'

'Yes, sir?'

'Encourage the press to attend.'

A pause. Then, 'yes, sir.'

The room stilled once more, the weight of the order settling across the table like dust. In the corner, the grandfather clock ticked steadily on—its rhythm a quiet reminder that time, and politics, waited for no man.

Chapter 22

Mascot Aerodrome
Sydney, New South Wales, Australia. 1934.

Rolling off a large wooden spool, a line of twine stretched taut from the nose of the *Lady Southern Cross* into the waiting hands of two crewmen. Step by step, they walked slowly down the length of the runway toward a towering canvas screen—twenty feet high, strung tight between two steel poles. It stood in the aircraft's path like a judgment.

It was a good day to fly—clear skies, not a breath of wind. The air was still, but the field around the aircraft held a doubtful, curious, restless energy.

A semicircle of spectators pressed in—a mix of engineers, flight officers, Royal Air Force observers, and a small flock of reporters scribbling rapidly, notepads twitching in anticipation. Whispers passed from mouth to mouth like wind through grass. Doubt. Admiration.

Charles and Tommy stood shoulder to shoulder beside the aircraft, hands in pockets, boots planted firm. Waiting.

At the far end of the runway, the crew halted. One called out, voice loud and clear.

'That is five hundred!'

The murmur rippled through the crowd. Five hundred yards. Not much runway at all.

The screen loomed—unforgiving and final.

Tommy shifted, energy crackling beneath his skin.

'By the way. . .' he muttered, low. 'When were you gonna tell me those two extra tanks were not part of the original spec?'

Charles didn't look at him. 'Probably about the time these blokes figured it out.'

'Well—they did,' Tommy replied.

Charles chuckled softly. 'So much for leveling the playing field.'

'Five hundred yards is short.'

'For you maybe,' Charles replied, finally glancing sideways with a smirk.

He reached out, tousled Tommy's hair with easy affection. Tommy rolled his eyes, lips curling into an unwilling grin.

'I *hate* when you do that,' he said, laughing despite himself.

'It is nothing for an old barnstormer like me, Tommy.'

'It is two fifty shorter than Anderson's run,' Tommy added, tone now serious. 'And you are hauling two hundred pounds more fuel.'

'You get the weight down?'

'The best I could.'

Charles gave a short nod, calm and final.

'I will get her up.'

The words hung between them like a promise—or a dare.

From the crowd, a uniformed figure pushed forward, parting bodies with stiff courtesy.

'Excuse me. Excuse me.'

The Air Marshal emerged, cap low over cold eyes, clipboard tucked tightly under one arm. Behind him, a trail of observers and flight officers followed, scribbling notes and muttering quietly.

He came to a stop just short of Charles and Tommy, and sniffed once.

'Do you still wish to proceed, Mr. Kingsford Smith?' he asked, his voice dry, clipped, and clearly hoping the sight of the canvas wall might inject second thoughts.

'Do I have a choice?' Charles replied, eyebrows raised. Tommy smirked beside him.

The Air Marshal pursed his lips and lifted a page from his clipboard.

'Right then, now. Mr. Kingsford Smith. As per directive, you are afforded *one attempt*—from a standing start. You must achieve takeoff within five hundred yards and clear the top of the screen directly ahead. If *any* part of the aircraft contacts the screen, the aircraft will not be certified for flight. Do you have any questions?'

Charles took a breath, as if truly considering the question. Then he grinned.

'Yeah. How many *British* aircraft have passed this test?'

A flicker of irritation moved across the Marshal's face—but he said nothing.

'You may proceed when ready, Mr. Kingsford Smith.'

Charles turned toward the aircraft.

Tommy caught his arm.

'I gave her a bit of a kick,' he said quietly. 'Listen—once she is up . . . take it easy.'

Charles gave him a crooked grin. 'Always do.'

He climbed into the *Lady Southern Cross* like a man slipping into an old suit. He moved with the certainty of ritual—settling into the seat, tightening straps, hands brushing across switches and dials like a pianist finding his keys. The cockpit closed. The world hushed.

On the ground, Tommy stepped back, sliding into position near the Air Marshal and his grim retinue.

The engine roared to life—spitting fire, screaming with restrained fury.

Tommy turned to the Marshal. 'Five quid says he makes it.'

The Marshal blinked, considering. He extended his gloved hand. 'You are on.'

The crowd stirred. Bets exchanged hands. Coins flashed in sunlight. One could almost hear the tension tighten like the drum of a snare.

Charles throttled up under full brake.

The engine howled, straining against its leash. The aircraft trembled, twitching at the reins. Its propeller blurred to silver, and the ground quaked beneath her.

Tommy's lips moved. A prayer. A command.

'Hold… hold…'

He watched.

'*Now!* Release.'

The brakes let go.

The *Lady Southern Cross* launched forward like a cannon shot. Dust and grit exploded behind her. The fuselage tore down the runway, nose low, tires screaming almost faster than the Marshal could get the words out.

'Fifty!' the Air Marshal shouted.

'One hundred!'

Tommy stepped with her unconsciously, his breath caught, hands clenched.

'One fifty!'

The screen towered, rushing forward. The distance was bleeding away, the wall filling the windscreen.

'Two hundred. . .'

The Marshal's voice cracked. 'Two hundred and—'

Before the words could finish, the nose lifted—hard and clean.

The *Lady Southern Cross* rose as if launched from a ramp, her shadow shrinking beneath her.

'—fifty,' the Marshal breathed, barely audible as the final word leaked from his lips.

She cleared the screen by yards—sunlight flashing across her body like a crown. The crowd froze for a heartbeat.

Then erupted.

Cheers broke like thunder. Reporters shouted into microphones. Hats flew. Whistles. Applause. Shouts of joy.

Charles grinned wide inside the cockpit, the force pushing him deep into the headrest. The sky stretched ahead—blue, boundless, his.

Tommy turned to the Air Marshal and extended his hand.

Still stunned, the Marshal reached into his coat, pulled out a folded note, and slapped it into Tommy's palm.

'God bless America,' Tommy muttered, eyes skyward.

Above, the Lady Southern Cross banked gracefully, wheeled, and then—without warning—rolled. A full, elegant barrel roll, slow and deliberate.

Gasps. A collective intake of breath. Silence.

Even the Marshal blinked.

Tommy's grin collapsed into horror. 'Oh, you son of a—' He held his head in both hands as the aircraft leveled out, wings steady, and climbed into the fading afternoon light. Tommy, furious, backed away and briskly left.

Dust kicked up as Tommy blasted in on his motorcycle and brought it to a screeching halt. The engine cut hard under the darkness of night. Silence fell. Charles turned from the *Lady Southern Cross*, gently wiping his hands with a rag to greet him.

'I was wondering where you were,' Charles said, voice cool.

Tommy swung off the bike, helmet under one arm, eyes blazing.

'Why? Another plane need fixing?'

'No, I just wanted to thank the bloody little genius who saved the day today.'

Charles stepped forward, reaching to ruffle Tommy's hair. Tommy shrugged him off with a growl of frustration.

'This is not a joke, Charles.'

'You and Jess again?'

'No. You and me. I have had it, Charles.' Tommy's voice cracked with exhaustion. 'Every goddamn night, I'm working my arse off just to keep you in the bloody air.'

'Tommy—'

'We just had to clear the screen.'

'And we *did*.'

Tommy stepped in close now, eyes sharp. 'The last thing I told you was—*when she's up, take it easy*. Does this look like a bloody stunt plane to you? You are not back in *Hollywood*, Charles.'

'Tommy.'

'Do not *Tommy* me!' he barked. 'My job is to keep you alive. To get the weight down, I stripped every non-essential nut, bolt, and bracket those inspectors wouldn't see. Fine for a straight-line launch. But when you *inverted*—when you rolled—Christ, Charles. You could have sheared the stabilizer clean off the rudder assembly.'

Charles didn't flinch, but the silence between them was heavy.

'I do not want to explain to *Mary* how I killed you,' Tommy said, softer now. 'We are not here for stunts. We are here to *win*. You want to be the best? Then bloody well remember—we are the ones making you the best.'

Charles looked down. Tommy continued.

'There are other people involved in this, Charles. I'm a shareholder. A partner. Your *chief engineer*. And if none of that matters—then at least listen to me as your friend.'

A long pause. Charles finally met his eyes.

'I do listen to you, Tommy.'

'Do you?' Tommy shot back. 'Certificate or no certificate, if you keep pushing her like this, she will not make the start line. And even if she does—you can't win. The Comet's still got you on speed.'

Charles straightened. His tone sharpened.

'Tommy. Do not underestimate me. And for Christ's sake, don't start questioning why you're here.'

Tommy stepped forward, face inches from his. 'Then why *am* I here, Charles? Answer me that.'

Charles turned away, rifled through the cluttered workbench until he found a folded map under a set of oil-streaked engine notes. He slapped it open, spinning it around.

'Because you are the best bloody engineer in the Commonwealth,' he said. 'Because you are the only man stubborn enough to keep up with me.'

He jabbed his finger at the map.

'Look.'

The route was underlined in red grease pencil. Numbers scribbled in the margins. Fuel stops. Elevation. Temperatures.

'The Comet has a twelve mile per hour advantage on the Lady. At top speed, over the full course—how far ahead of me will Scott be when he hits Darwin?'

Tommy squinted, running the math aloud.

'Eight thousand miles . . . twelve mile an hour differential . . . fifty-four hours to Darwin . . . six one-hour fuel stops. . .' He paused. 'He will have six hundred and forty-eight miles on you.'

Charles nodded.

'And what happens when the Comet hits the coast?'

Tommy blinked. 'He will . . . overheat.'

Charles looked at him, steady and certain.

'That is right. Those Pommy engines will fry like farm fresh eggs. Too much pressure, too little cooling. They built it for speed—not for *Australia*. Just like the Gull.'

Tommy exhaled, shoulders sagging.

'That is why you are here, Tommy,' Charles enforced.

A beat.

'I am sorry.'

Charles turned, brow furrowed.

'What are you sorry for? For figuring out how to beat him?'

'For thinking you were not listening.'

Charles softened.

'Tommy . . . my life *depends* on you. On *that brain* and those two bloody hands of yours. You think I don't listen? I *hear everything.* Every wrench turn. Every hesitation in your voice.'

He stepped closer now, voice quieter.

'And Tommy . . . that barrel roll at two hundred feet?'

He grinned.

'Come on.' Charles paused. 'That *was* me taking it easy.' Charles laughed.

Chapter 23

Lympne Aerodrome
Kent, England. 1934.

The hangar had been transformed into a cathedral of British engineering. It shone under the dazzling flood of spotlights—steel and rivets bathed in ceremonial glow. Tonight, it was no mere hangar. It was a

showroom, a stage, a sanctum to celebrate the might and mastery of British aviation. Giant beams of light swept the sky, carving white arcs into the low clouds like celestial fanfare. Below, a red carpet stretched elegantly from the main entrance, welcoming the nation's elite—aristocrats, dignitaries, MPs, foreign correspondents, and excitable reporters, all eager to witness the birth of victory.

Inside, the three Comets stood in silent splendor.

Gleaming. Perfect. Poised for greatness.

At the center, commanding the eye like a jewel beneath a crown, stood *Grosvenor House.*

She glowed under the white-hot lights—a brilliant, burning red. Her flawless crimson skin shimmered, polished to the finest sheen. Bold white lettering stood in sharp contrast, catching every flash and flicker. Her lines—sleek, aggressive, elegant—drew audible gasps from the crowd. She looked fast even at rest.

Before her, standing with the stillness of soldiers and the tension of men born to compete, stood Charles William Anderson Scott and Tom Campbell Black. Their uniforms were precise, their posture controlled. War heroes, record-setters, legends in the making. The favorites. Unquestionably.

To her right, *Black Magic* stood like an empress at court—dark and commanding.

Her fuselage was a rich, absorbing black, kissed by soft reflections of gold leaf that traced her contours with aristocratic confidence. She exuded mystery and menace in equal measure, a stark contrast to her scarlet sister. Amy and Jim Mollison posed easily before her—husband and wife, twin spirits of the sky. Their chemistry was effortless, their ambition razor-sharp behind the practiced charm of their public smiles.

To the left, quieter in presence but no less potent, stood the third Comet—unnamed, but no longer unseen.

She bore the simple registry G-ACSR, her British racing green-gray catching the light with a subtle, steely gleam. She was a whisper of power, understated and deadly. Her pilots, Owen Cathcart Jones and Ken Waller, stood together, calm and composed, betraying no nerves, no doubt—only the cold discipline of men who intended to fly, not perform.

Then the crowd fell into reverent hush.

A. O. Edwards ascended the dais, the Union Jack draped behind him like a banner over a battlefield. His presence commanded the room.

'Ladies and gentlemen,' he declared, his voice ringing with imperial pride, 'what you see before you is not just aviation—it is *evolution*.'

He turned, arms outstretched toward the trio of Comets.

'The de Havilland DH.88 Comets represent the very pinnacle of British craftsmanship—speed, precision, endurance. Every rivet, every bolt, has been engineered to command the skies.'

A pause.

'And now, with these machines—and the finest airmen,' he added, glancing with showmanship toward the Mollisons, 'and air*woman*, of course—Britain shall lead the world into the next age of flight.'

Applause rolled through the hangar like thunder. Flashbulbs ignited, immortalizing the moment. The crowd leaned forward as one, drawn into the orbit of power, glory, and engineering divinity.

Off to the side, Lord Liard observed it all, glass of scotch in hand. He sipped slowly, eyes narrowed—not with suspicion, but pride. His lips curved into a tight, satisfied smile.

Beside him, Collins stood straight, the gold trim on his lapel gleaming beneath the lights.

'Three against one,' Lord Liard murmured, voice low with pleased vindication. 'Well done, Collins.'

'Thank you, my lord,' Collins replied simply, his chest swelling ever so slightly.

The spectacle glowed on—bright, bold, and British.

Kingsford Smith Air Services
Mascot, Sydney, New South Wales, Australia. 1934.

The clock ticked relentlessly toward 4:52 p.m. in the cramped office. The room had grown dim as the sun lowered outside, casting long shadows across the cluttered desk. John and Tommy fidgeted with growing impatience; the tension between them all was thick enough to touch. Charles and Taylor, already suited in their flight gear, sat with quiet resolve. Though composed, their stillness betrayed an underlying impatience.

A knock on the door cut through the silence.

'John, I have finished for the day,' Jess announced, stepping in with a tired smile. 'Is there anything more I can do?'

'No. Thank you, Jess,' John replied with a terse nod, the strain carved clearly into the lines of his face.

Jess glanced warmly toward Tommy, offering a brief, endearing smile—something private and tender that lingered for only a moment before being swallowed by the tension in the room.

John snapped, breaking the silence as he began pacing. 'Two bloody weeks to issue a goddamn permit. Five to five on the day you have to leave, and still nothing. It's no bloody wonder nothing gets done in this country.'

Tommy shook his head, arms folded tight. 'How the hell do they expect you to get to England in a week? You'll have to break every bloody record from here to Mildenhall just to make the *start*. It's a twenty-four-thousand-mile round trip. They're already lined up over there, and you haven't even left. If anything goes wrong, I'm not there to fix it. This is beyond stupid.'

'We might as well fly around the world,' Taylor said with a wry smile, his arms crossed, voice laced with dry sarcasm.

'It is the same bloody distance,' Tommy muttered under his breath, shaking his head in disbelief.

'This is ridiculous.' John spun on his heel and grabbed the telephone. 'I'm calling them.'

He dialed swiftly, fingers tapping against the desk while the others watched in tense silence.

No answer. He hung up and shook his head. The clock ticked over to 4:59.

'Is that clock right?' Charles asked.

In unison, they all checked their watches.

Then—*the phone rang*, its sharp tone slicing through the room like a knife. John lunged for it.

'Hello. Yes,' he said, tension coiling in his voice.

Stannage leaned in, scribbling notes furiously as he caught snippets of the exchange.

John paused. 'Okay.' He hung up slowly, turning to the group. His face was unreadable.

'We got it,' he said. But his tone was cautious—measured, like a man waiting for the second half of a sentence.

'Yes!' Tommy burst out, a flicker of hope igniting in his expression.

But John remained still. 'Do not get too excited,' he said grimly. 'They've imposed a seven-hundred-and-fifty-pound limit on fuel.'

'What?' Tommy blinked. 'She passed well within the safety margins!'

'That is a quarter less than the Comet,' Taylor added, calculating aloud. 'They are cutting our range before we have even taken off.'

'You are back to a thousand miles behind before you begin,' John muttered, frustration seeping into every word. 'You may as well have taken the Comet they offered you.' He sighed, the weight of the moment sagging in his shoulders. 'Even if you make the start, their advantage is too great.'

The room fell silent.

Then Charles leaned forward, voice low but steady. 'I do not know . . . I still think we can beat them—handicap or no handicap.'

He waited, the silence stretching.

'What do you think, Tommy?' Charles asked.

Tommy didn't answer right away. His gaze drifted toward the window, mind racing—mental math, fuel stops, margins of error.

Then, slowly, he nodded.

'I think I should start warming her up,' he said, that familiar glint returning to his eyes. 'We have come this far—what is another twenty-four thousand miles?'

Charles smiled, looking at each of them individually. 'Let us go break some records.'

The room stirred to life. The air shifted—no longer thick with dread, but charged with focus. Jess lingered for a moment, watching Tommy move with purpose. Her eyes held a mix of pride and quiet worry.

John resumed barking orders, his voice clear, direct. Every word had urgency. Every task, meaning.

Outside, the evening air was crisp against their faces. The aircraft loomed ahead, silver and silent beneath the darkening sky—a creature of ambition, daring, and defiance.

Charles and Tommy approached with reverence, their steps firm, their purpose clear. This was no longer just a race. It was a test of every lesson, every mile, every sacrifice.

Tommy climbed into the cockpit, his hands steady as they swept across familiar controls. The switches and gauges welcomed him like old comrades. Charles joined him, slipping into position wordlessly—years of partnership needing no narration. The engine fired. Loud.

From a distance, John watched them. Eyes narrowed, thoughts ticking through last-minute checklists and what-ifs. He knew the odds. But he knew his team even better.

Taylor stepped up beside him and gave his shoulder a firm pat.

'See you in a few weeks,' Taylor said, the words light, but steady.

John cracked a smile. A knowing one.

Behind his desk, John hunched over the ledger, pencil moving in swift, frustrated strokes. The late afternoon heat pressed in through the windows, and the fan overhead did little to fight it. Beads of sweat dotted his brow. Numbers weren't adding up, he shook his head in frustration, looking over them again, hoping.

The phone rang, sharp and sudden. He grabbed the receiver.

'Hello? Yes? …Where?'

His voice shifted—sharp, alert. The room stilled.

'Is everyone alright? What happened? Oh no. . .'

He stood slowly, the chair groaning behind him as he listened. His eyes tracked across the wall map, fixing on a point in the north.

'I will get Tommy on it,' he said, and slammed the receiver down with finality.

'Tommy!' he shouted.

Tommy appeared a moment later, wiping grease from his hands with a rag, brow furrowed. 'Yeah, John?'

'They are down.'

'Down? Where?'

'Cloncurry.'

'Are they okay?' Tommy's expression changed instantly—serious now.

'They are all fine,' John replied.

'What happened?' Tommy asked urgently.

'The engine cowl cracked. It is bad.'

'Damn it!' Tommy swore under his breath. 'I told him he was pushing her too hard.'

John nodded grimly. 'Well, she cracked. They're limping back here.'

Tommy ran a hand through his hair, the rag now forgotten in his fist. 'What about the race?'

'There might still be time. They are going to need a new one.'

Tommy didn't wait for more. 'That is not an easy fix. I will get on it,' he said, already turning on his heel.

Chapter 24

Mildenhall Aerodrome
Suffolk, England, 1934.

The heightened activity surrounding the final preparations of *Grosvenor House* was no surprise; the entry favored to win and rival the *Lady Southern Cross* was heralded with worthy attention. Engineers, mechanics, and officials attended to her every need, swarming over the Comet in a hive of motion and muttered urgency. Tools clanked, voices clipped and sharp, nerves stretched taut. Scott stood at the nose, watching, his jaw clenched.

'Check it again,' he ordered, not taking his eyes off the undercarriage. 'I want everything triple-checked. Thank you chaps.'

Black hovered nearby, eyes darting between the team and Scott.

'She is looking grand,' Black commented.

That is when Allcot approached, cutting through the bustle timidly, a white envelope in hand.

'Mr. Scott,' he said, holding it out. 'This just arrived. I thought you should see it right away. I think you will appreciate the content.'

Scott took it, distracted, still tracking the work being done. But as his eyes scanned the typed message, his breath caught. He read it again.

And again.

Then his fingers clenched, crumpling the page in his hand.

'What is it?' Black asked, alarmed.

Scott didn't answer right away. His expression was stone—only the fire in his eyes gave him away.

'He is out,' Scott finally muttered.

'Who?' Black asked urgently.

'Kingsford Smith. The *Lady Southern Cross* has been forced to withdraw.'

Black stared. 'That cannot be,' he replied, catching the disappointment like a contagion.

Scott looked away, his throat tight. Angry.

'It would appear, Mr. Scott,' Allcot said quietly, 'This one will be all yours.' He smiled happily.

Scott turned sharply, fury flashing behind his gaze. Not the triumph of winning—this was something colder. Sharper. He handed Allcot the crumpled mess. Stared him down and left him wondering what he had missed.

'I am just the messenger,' Allcot yelled, as Scott walked away, his footsteps felt like an earthquake.

MacRobertson Steam Confectionery Works
Melbourne, Victoria, Australia. 1934.

The boardroom was cloaked in shadow. Heavy rain lashed the tall windows, the distant rumble of thunder echoing through the building. Electric light flickered against the oak-paneled walls, casting elongated silhouettes across the long, polished table.

The air was dense with the scent of damp carpet and old smoke. Conversations collided in a hushed frenzy, murmurs turning to pointed declarations.

'We are unanimous,' one voice finally cut through. 'His Majesty's government has made its position clear.'

Sir Macpherson stood at the head of the table, framed by the storm beyond the glass. His expression was carved in stone.

'I understand that, gentlemen,' he said slowly, voice cold. 'But an air race without Sir Charles Kingsford Smith can hardly be called a race at all.'

'That Sir Charles will no longer be participating,' another member countered, 'does not disqualify the event from legitimacy. There are twenty-seven other competitors readied on the start line as we speak.'

Mac's fingers curled into the table's edge.

'It is my race,' he growled.

'The objection from the British government to postponement,' one board member said, his voice clipped and precise, 'could be construed as tampering—intervention that favors one man over others.'

'It would be perceived as a tipping of the scale. Sir Macpherson. If you were to postpone and if Sir Charles were to win, it would be perceived as a hollow victory at best.'

'Such favoritism,' another added, 'would only amplify the whispers already surrounding this controversy.'

Outside, the wind howled. Lightning flashed, illuminating Mac's face in a fleeting burst—his eyes sharp, his jaw clenched.

'Scales, you say,' Mac muttered darkly. 'They preach fairness while drowning in it. And yet, as luck would have it, the weight has tipped toward their favor.'

A long silence stretched, broken only by the tick of the grandfather clock in the corner and the drip of rain sliding down the glass.

'The race must proceed,' one said finally.

'As scheduled,' came the confirmation.

Mac's gaze drifted across the table—each face, composed, compliant, distant. He nodded once, slowly.

'It pains me, gentlemen,' he said, voice low, controlled. 'For what they now crown as success . . . is, in truth, a failure profound and irreversible.'

He turned toward the window, watching as the rain blurred the city lights beyond—distorting the future that might have been.

Sydney, New South Wales, Australia, 1934.

The red glow of the On Air sign snapped to life above the recording booth, casting a faint blush across the otherwise dim room. Inside, Charles sat alone before the radio microphone, the brushed steel cool beneath his fingertips. He leaned in slightly, shoulders tense, hands folded just out of view. The room was still—dead still. So quiet, one could hear the subtle *crack* of his dry lips parting, the faint *gulp* of his swallow breaking the silence like a pin dropping in a cathedral.

Beyond the glass, the announcer sat poised, voice calm, rehearsed. He introduced the 'important announcement,' then lifted a hand and pointed gently—cueing Charles.

Charles leaned in.

His voice, when it came, was low, measured, and resolute.

'As it happens in the challenging endeavor of pioneering aviation, my aircraft, the *Lady Southern Cross*, has experienced a mechanical problem.'

He paused. The silence pressed in tighter. Even the faint hum of the microphone seemed to recoil, as if holding its breath.

'Despite every effort, the problem cannot be rectified in time to make the start line in Mildenhall, for the Centenary Air Race. I, therefore—and with great regret—inform you today of my withdrawal.'

Another pause. He took a breath, eyes fixed not on the mic but on some distant point beyond the glass.

'I wish all the competitors a safe and fortunate journey.'

He leaned back slowly, the finality of the words hanging in the charged silence.

From the speaker beyond the glass, the announcer returned, voice a shade more somber.

'That was a special announcement from Air Commodore Sir Charles Kingsford Smith on his retirement from the Centennial Air Race, due to a mechanical failure of his aircraft, the *Lady Southern Cross*.'

Then, the scratch of a phonograph needle. A soft hiss. And the gentle swell of a slow, wistful band number began to play—low brass and strings, bittersweet and cinematic, washing through the room like fading light.

Charles opened the door and stepped from the booth.

The soft *thud* of the door closing behind him echoed faintly down the corridor, as if sealing something away. He stood there for a moment—shoulders slightly hunched, head bowed, the fire gone from his posture.

Mary was waiting. Silent. Still.

She stepped toward him, her heels muted on the linoleum floor. Her hand came to rest lightly on his shoulder, fingers firm, grounding.

'I am proud of you,' she said softly, her voice warm and unwavering. No pity. No platitude. Just pride.

Her eyes met his—clear and certain, full of a deeper knowing. In her gaze was the flight he'd never take, the nights he hadn't slept, and the truth that no announcement, however public, could measure the private weight of all he'd carried.

Charles looked at her. For a moment, the exhaustion in his eyes flickered, replaced by something gentler.

A quiet smile tugged at one corner of his mouth.

'Well . . . I guess that is that,' he said.

His voice was tired, but not bitter.

Just . . . accepting.

Dinner was on the table, and the room was filled with the warm, savory aroma of roasted chicken and fresh vegetables. Steam curled lazily upward from the serving dishes, catching the soft light above. At the stove, Mary stirred the gravy in slow, practiced circles, the quiet *clink* of metal against enamel echoing softly in the stillness.

In the entry hall, just outside the dining room, Charles stood with the telephone pressed to his ear. His posture was both rigid and resigned. On the other end, Tommy's voice murmured faintly, half-heard through the woodwork.

Charles listened in silence, eyes fixed on nothing in particular.

'I know,' he said at last, voice low. 'You got it done as quickly as you could. Just . . . not quick enough.'

A pause.

'No, I understand. Thank the boys for me. Thanks, Tommy.'

He hung up gently, the *click* quiet, but final.

At the table, Charles Jr. gurgled in his high chair, joyfully smearing mashed carrot across his tray. Mary watched him fondly, then glanced up as Charles returned to the room. Their eyes met.

'Eat something,' she said softly, her voice warm, a gentle tether.

Charles gave a wan smile. 'My pride?'

'No,' Mary replied, her tone light with affection. 'I think you have swallowed enough of that for one day, any more and you might get fat.'

It drew a small, reluctant chuckle from him.

'What would I do without you?' he asked, stepping closer, the weight of the day still visible in the slump of his shoulders.

'Laundry,' she said with a mock sigh, her smile teasing. 'A lot of laundry.'

Charles let the silence settle between them for a moment, then dropped into the chair across from her with a sigh. 'I should have listened.'

Mary reached across and placed her hand over his. Steady. Warm.

'Listening,' she said, 'has never exactly been one of your strong points. It is both a blessing and a curse.'

She paused, watching him closely.

'Everything you have done, Charles—you did it because you did not listen. Not to the odds, not to the doubters. That's how you got as far as you did. Given what you were up against, I am amazed you got off the ground at all. And no one—not the press, not the officials, not even yourself—can take that from you.'

He nodded slowly, his gaze drifting toward the food. The plate in front of him remained untouched. After a moment, he looked back at her.

'I think I might take a walk.'

Mary hesitated. 'Your tea?'

'I will eat it later.' He offered a small smile, stood, and reached for his coat.

The door closed softly behind him. The latch clicked—a sound Mary had heard a thousand times, yet tonight, it echoed just a little longer.

The room was quiet again.

Charles Jr. cooed contentedly, smearing gravy with his fists like an artist with finger paint. Mary sighed, reached for a cloth, and leaned in close to him.

'Oh, Charles,' she murmured.

Then, with a smile tugging at the edge of her mouth, she added gently, 'You're a mess . . . just like your father.'

She wiped his tiny hands, her touch tender, the moment small, but filled with love.

Under the cool hush of night, the air hung thick with damp moisture, clinging to the collar of Charles's coat and cooling the heat of his thoughts. He strolled slowly beneath the glow of the streetlamps, their dense amber light cutting long shadows beneath his feet. His hands were pressed deep into his pockets, collar turned up, shoulders hunched against more than just the chill.

Each footfall echoed softly, a measured rhythm that matched the weight of his mind.

He turned down a quieter row, and ahead, the warm murmur and bright lights of a public house spilled into the street. The familiar scent of beer, tobacco, and conversation lingered faintly in the misted air.

The hum of voices grew louder as he approached—laughter, the clink of glasses, the comforting din of the ordinary. There was always a kind of peace to be found in the bottom of a pint glass, surrounded by the uncomplicated company of like-minded men. For a moment, that grounding pull tempted him.

Charles paused at the door, resting his hand on the wood. He took a slow breath. Inside, he could hear the crowd—jovial, casual, alive.

But the mood wasn't what he expected.

A voice, slightly muffled, carried through the glass.

'He knew he was never going to bloody win. Everyone knows he threw it.'

Another chimed in, a gruffer tone.

'Fair crack of the whip. They were *never* going to let him win.'

Then the first voice, louder now, more cutting.

'Oh, come *on!* The Great Smithy? Hands down, he threw in the towel. Engine trouble? My ass.'

Laughter followed. The sound of a pint glass slamming on the bar. The debate raged on, drunk and self-certain.

Charles stood motionless. His hand slid from the door.

He'd heard enough.

He turned away slowly, the weight of it not quite anger—more a familiar ache. A private hurt worn thin with time.

From his coat, he pulled a cigarette, struck a match against the wall, and lit it with steady hands. He took a long drag, the tip flaring briefly in the dark.

Then he walked on, back into the night.

No rebuttal. No fanfare. Just smoke, silence, and the long road home. Behind him, the voices continued—still debating a man who was already gone.

The house was silent.

Only the porch light remained on, casting a muted yellow halo across the front step. Charles moved quietly up the path, the night's cold following him like a shadow. His breath drifted in pale clouds, vanishing in the still air.

He reached the door and stopped.

There, lying askew on the welcome mat, was an envelope—unmarked, slightly curled at the edges, the paper damp from the air. No name. No stamp. No address.

Charles looked around him with a suspicious curiosity before bending down to retrieve it. The street was empty. The night was still. He bent down slowly, picking up the envelope with a hesitant hand. It was unsealed. Light, but not empty.

He opened it.

Inside was a single slip of paper, on it written thick.

One word—angry, uneven, trembling with judgment.

Coward.

Charles stared at it. His stomach turned cold. The paper felt heavier than it was.

Then, drifting from the envelope's edge—silent as snow—three white feathers slipped out and fell to the ground, the sound of them silently awakening his past.

A blast ripped the earth apart.

No warning. Just a gut-punching thud—and then dirt, blood, and bodies raining down.

Charles hit the trench floor hard, filth filling his mouth, the stink of rotting flesh thick enough to choke on. Around him, men screamed, some pleading, some already too broken to make a sound.

He shoved upright, boots sinking into mud mixed with blood. His hands shook on the rifle but his eyes—his eyes moved, scanned, hunted.

Another shell landed nearby. The trench wall caved in, swallowing men like a beast.

Charles stumbled forward. Bodies littered the flooded pathways—faces slack, eyes staring at nothing, mouths frozen mid-begging, mid-scream. One arm still clutched a helmet. Another gripped a letter now soaked crimson.

Gallipoli.

The name whispered in the smoke.

And then—The ground shifted under him.

The golden desert of Egypt swallowed the mud.

He roared forward now on a battered motorcycle, rattling across cracked, blistering sand. The sun hammered down. His throat cracked with thirst. Sandstorms clawed at his goggles, grit slicing at his face like razors.

The shells didn't stop.

Explosions punched craters into the earth ahead, geysers of dust and bodies.

Wire flashed past, twisted and rusted. Mines pocked the ground. Aircraft wheeled overhead, circling, waiting for the kill.

Gunfire raked the air. Bullets stitched the sand in murderous patterns. Charles weaved, cursed, gunned the engine harder, desperate to outrun death.

But it followed.

The sand dissolved into mud again, thicker, blacker.

He was on the Western Front now—France.

Rain fell in sheets. Trenches flooded, swallowing gear, swallowing men. The dead floated alongside the living. The very ground writhed under shellfire, a landscape of endless, heaving rot.

He slipped, skidded, clutched the bike upright.

Artillery lit the sky. Flashes of white seared against endless black. Trees stood like splintered fingers, broken and burning.

Another shift.

The ground fell away entirely.

He was in the cockpit now, thrown into the screaming sky.

The stick jerked in his hands, leather gloves squealing against it. Sweat streamed into his eyes. His heart hammered so hard he thought it would break his ribs.

Enemy in his sights.

He squeezed the trigger. The guns roared. The recoil nearly tore his arms out of their sockets. Black smoke burst from the enemy fuselage. The plane dipped, spiraled, died.

One kill.

Then another.

Another.

The sky littered with the falling dead.

Each kill added weight to his chest, pressing harder, tighter.

Gunfire stitched across his wings. Bullets screamed past, ripping through canvas, tearing the world apart.

The shockwave punched through the cockpit.

Then—

His boot exploded. Leather. Blood. Flesh torn apart. He fought on.

Chapter 25

St. Mary's Cathedral
Sydney, New South Wales, Australia. 1934.

Harmonious were the voices of the boys' choir as they echoed through the grand arches of St. Mary's Cathedral in Sydney, their angelic sound reverberating off the stained glass windows and intricate stone carvings. The golden light of the setting sun streamed through the windows, casting a kaleidoscope of color onto the marble floor. Charles sat in one of the pews, his gaze unfocused, absorbing the ambient sound, seeking solace in the familiar surroundings.

The cathedral had always been a place of grandeur, but now, it felt different—smaller, yet more distant, as though time had stretched it beyond his reach. The vaulted ceilings soared overhead, their ribs intersecting like an intricate web. Stained glass windows lined the walls, their biblical scenes illuminated by the dying sunlight. The air smelled of burning wax and soot, the same scent he remembered from childhood.

His fingers grazed the polished wooden pew, tracing the name 'Chilla' crudely carved into the timber by a restless boy who had once sat here before him. Charles chuckled softly, a quiet remembrance of youth—wide-eyed, full of promise. Before the war. Before everything.

In neat rows before the altar, a sea of youthful, uncorrupted innocent faces, their expressions serene yet focused. Dressed in traditional choir robes—crisp white surplices draped over deep red cassocks—they looked almost ethereal in the fading light. The fabric shifted as they moved, the red swaying gently as they breathed, hands clasped in quiet reverence. A few younger boys fidgeted, adjusting stiff collars or smoothing the folds of their robes, but their discipline held firm as they followed the lead of their choirmaster.

Their voices wove together in perfect harmony, rising and falling in an ethereal cadence. The altos' smooth steadiness, the sopranos' soaring clarity, the warmth of the tenors, and the deep resonance of the basses blended into something transcendent. The organ's deep notes rumbled beneath them, a steady foundation. Charles closed his eyes, letting the music fill the empty spaces inside him.

Then, footsteps. Steady. Measured. A slight creak of the wooden pew.

Charles opened his eyes as an elderly priest settled beside him. He was a man of nearly seventy, Irish, with sharp blue eyes that had lost none of their clarity over the years. His presence commanded respect, but there was kindness in his worn features.

'It feels like a lifetime ago since you were singing in that very first row,' the priest said, his Irish lilt adding a lyrical softness to his words. 'Your mother still comes in every week. She prays for you, still calls you Chilla. Your exploits still give her chills, Charles.'

Charles exhaled a quiet breath, a faint smile tugging at the corner of his lips as he subtly covered the old carving with his hat. The nickname carried a warmth he hadn't felt in a long time.

'Been a long time, Father.'

'Aye, that it has.' The priest's gaze held both understanding and scrutiny. 'I recall you arriving late for one rehearsal, your face bruised, your nose dripping blood.'

Charles smirked slightly, the memory resurfacing like an old scar. 'I did not start that, Father,' he stated emphatically.

'No, but as I recall, you did finish it.' The priest's eyes twinkled with a mix of pride and admonition. 'Mind you, you did much prefer our boxing lessons over choir practice.' He chuckled softly.

Charles chuckled too, the sound foreign to his own ears.

'I have followed your adventures with great interest,' the priest continued, his voice shifting to something more measured. 'That intrepidness with which you fly—or, as many now refer to it, the ANZAC

Spirit. Courage, camaraderie, irreverence, recklessness, disdain for authority, and an endurance that will never own defeat. All good qualities, Charles. Qualities that have served you well. That helped you survive the war. That made you the man you are today.'

Charles listened quietly, reflecting on his words.

'But the very same spirit that carried you to great heights,' the priest continued, his voice softer now, 'can just as easily carry you to your fall. It is a double-edged sword.'

Charles considered his words carefully. 'It's hard to see where it went wrong, Father.'

The priest held his gaze. 'You climbed to the top of the ladder, Charles. And when you got there, you found you had nothing to hold on to. Simply, it happens to many great men.'

Silence stretched between them. The choir's voices drifted through the vast cathedral, reverberating in the sacred stillness.

Then, after a long moment—

'Call on your mother, Charles.'

Charles exhaled slowly, nodding in agreement. His eyes drifted toward the altar, where golden candlesticks gleamed in the fading light. The brocade cloth shimmered, embroidered with gold thread, its intricate patterns almost hypnotic.

He thought of his mother—her quiet prayers, her unwavering faith. She had written to him during the war, every week without fail. Even when he hadn't written back. Even when the silence had stretched for months.

The priest placed a firm, reassuring hand on his shoulder. 'She has never stopped believing in you.'

Charles swallowed, his throat tight. He gave a slow nod. 'I will call her.'

The priest smiled, as though he had expected no less.

The choir's voices swelled, filling the cathedral, rising to meet the grandeur of the space. For the first time in a long while, Charles let the music move through him—not just as sound, but as something deeper. A memory. A promise. A prayer.

As the last rays of sunlight bathed the cathedral in gold, he stood. 'Thank you Father.' Charles acknowledged his guidance. The weight of the past was still there, but it no longer felt insurmountable. He turned toward the exit, the path ahead uncertain—but no longer unbearable.

The priest turned over his shoulder, pausing Charles at the doors. 'Charles! You must ask yourself what you are going to do,' he said.

Charles hesitated. A thought surfaced—unexpected, unbidden. He glanced back at the priest, who studied him with quiet expectation. Charles smiled. Tipped his head in thanks. And then, as his grin grew, he answered.

'Find a bigger ladder.' Charles smiled and laughed, and with that, he stepped into the light.

Kingsford Smith Air Services
Mascot, Sydney, New South Wales, Australia. 1934.

Taylor leaned in, running a hand over the smooth engine cowling, inspecting the fresh repairs. The afternoon light caught the sheen of new metalwork, the scent of oil and hot steel still sharp in the air.

'The boys really got that sorted,' Taylor said, stepping back with a nod of approval.

Tommy wandered over, wiping his hands on a rag.

'They reinforced the mounts,' he said. 'I do not think we will see that problem again.'

He hesitated, his smile fading a little.

'Still sorry we could not get her done in time,' he added, voice low.

Taylor shrugged, glancing sideways at him.

'It was not a little job,' he said.

'No,' Tommy agreed quietly.

Before they could say more, Charles strode into the hangar, his steps quick, purposeful.

'She ready?' he called, cutting straight to the point.

'She is ready,' Tommy replied, squaring his shoulders.

Charles grinned, clapping a hand onto Taylor's back.

'Do not unpack your things, Bill. We have got some business.'

Taylor raised an eyebrow. 'Where?'

Charles's grin widened.

'America!'

Chapter 26

Mildenhall Aerodrome
Suffolk, England, 1934.

The field was a sea of humanity.

Thousands upon thousands of spectators pressed against the roped boundaries, spilling across the grassy expanse in a rippling wave of excitement. Bright banners snapped in the stiff breeze. Tents and vendor stalls dotted the edges, and the air buzzed with raw, crackling energy—an entire nation holding its breath.

It was a festival of aviation—engines sputtering, flags whipping, the mingled scents of oil, wet grass, and hot food thickening into a dizzying, intoxicating fog.

From the raised platform near the starting line, announcers barked names and numbers over blaring loudspeakers, their voices booming across the grounds. In the grand box bleachers, dignitaries, sponsors, Air Marshals, and notables like A. O. Edwards and Lord Liard sipped champagne breakfasts, the clink of crystal punctuating the low rumble of engines.

News cameras cranked furiously, capturing the moments for posterity. Press photographers lined the railings, their flashbulbs popping like distant gunfire, catching faces in frozen white bursts—pilots, spectators, children perched on shoulders, women waving handkerchiefs.

One by one, aircraft lined up at the start—engines coughing, wheels bumping over the uneven turf—before surging forward into the blanketed gray morning sky.

Each name rang out over the loudspeakers—veterans, rookies, national heroes—hailed like gladiators stepping into legend.

The excitement built, stacking higher, tighter, a living wall of sound and expectation.

From the loudspeaker:

'Next to take off—Flight Lieutenant Jameson and Navigator Harris in the Bristol Blenheim!'

The crowd erupted in a wave, the ground almost vibrating with cheers as the Blenheim gathered speed, lifted from the grass, and soared into the heavens.

The final moments approached.

Only two remained.

The favorites.

The ones everyone had been waiting for.

At the far end of the field, *Black Magic* sat gleaming like a predator—sleek, raven-dark against the pale grass. Behind her, C. W. A. Scott and Tom Campbell Black sat poised, eyes narrowed against the wind, bodies taut with purpose. The Comet perched like a striking hawk, engines rumbling low and hungry.

Across the field, the sea of people thickened. Children were hoisted higher on the shoulders of those taller. Hats flew into the air. A frenzy of cameras captured every second.

'Jim is off the ground,' Scott said, glancing at the empty stretch ahead.

'First to leave—let's hope he's not the first to finish,' Black quipped, his hand steady on the controls.

'Second to none, Tom.'

'Second to none.'

The loudspeaker crackled again:

'Ladies and gentlemen, our final entry—*Grosvenor House*—Captain C. W. A. Scott and Captain Tom Campbell Black!'

The roar that followed was deafening—a living, breathing roar that shook the air, rattled the bleachers, and made the banners snap harder against the poles.

Scott gave a small nod to Black. No words needed.

In the cockpit, Scott leaned forward, hand firm on the throttle.

The Comet's engines snarled to life, a feral growl that vibrated through the bones of every man, woman, and child watching.

The crowd pressed even closer, breathless.

Scott throttled up.

Released the brake.

The *Grosvenor House* shuddered—then bolted forward, sleek and savage, carving a brutal path across the grass with stunning speed.

A sea of hats and handkerchiefs flew into the air as the Comet hurtled past the roaring crowd, a blur of polished red and white.

Scott leaned into the controls, shouting over the deafening roar:

'Tom, let us go win this!'

Royal Aero Club
London, England. 1934.

Within the hallowed walls, the massive race board loomed. The giant map of the world commanded the space, oceans and continents unfurling in muted shades. Tiny model aircraft, one for each of the twenty-seven competitors in miniature, clung magnetically to its surface, their progress nudged forward one by one by attentive clerks, every movement a fresh heartbeat of the race.

Beside the map, tall ledgers bore neat columns—start times, elapsed times, positions—painstakingly updated from radio transmissions relayed through aerodromes scattered across the Empire of the British Commonwealth.

The atmosphere crackled with a heavy, expectant tension.

Gentlemen in fine suits and polished shoes clustered near the great windows, cigars smoldering between their fingers, the sweet, pungent smoke curling lazily toward the high, ornate ceilings.

Pilots, former and current, leaned in, their crisp uniforms marked with polished wings and service bars. Conversations were low and urgent, punctuated by the occasional clink of cut glass as stewards circulated with trays of the finest whiskey and brandy.

Messengers darted back and forth, passing updates to the race officials stationed at long oak tables. At the front of the room, the senior stewards of the club stood in a tight knot, hands clasped behind their backs, watching the board with hawk-like focus.

As the tiny models edged forward, mile by mile, the gentlemen of London's elite watched history unfolding, drinks in hand, breath held.

The race was on.

Kingsford Smith Air Services
Mascot, Sydney, New South Wales, Australia. 1934.

The *Lady Southern Cross* sat poised on the tarmac, its polished frame gleaming under the early light. Taylor was already in the rear cockpit, checking instruments with a practiced hand. Nearby, Mary stood with Charles Jr. in her arms, her expression composed but tender, there was no fanfare, only family.

Charles turned to her.

'Are you going to be okay?' he asked gently.

'Yes,' Mary replied, steady.

'I will be back soon,' Charles said, offering the words like a promise.

Mary nodded. 'We have a deal, remember? I'm proud of you. You are doing the right thing.'

Charles kissed her softly, then leaned down and kissed his son's forehead.

Without another word, he turned and jogged toward the aircraft. He climbed swiftly into the cockpit, buckled in, and adjusted his headset.

'First time to America, Taylor?' he called over his shoulder.

'Yes,' Taylor replied, eyes on the gauges.

Charles smiled. The engine turned over, its rumble growing as the Altair prepared to rise.

A knock.

'Shephard, enter,' Duddevin said without looking up.

The aide stepped in, precise and calm.

'All the entries have departed Mildenhall, sir. The official start times are confirmed, should you wish to follow their progress.'

'Thank you, Shephard,' Duddevin replied coolly, still reading.

Shephard hesitated, then added, 'Also, sir—Kingsford Smith has departed for America.'

Duddevin looked up, faintly amused. 'That is nice. Thank you, Shephard.'

'In the *Lady Southern Cross*, sir,' Shephard continued.

There was a pause.

'What?' Duddevin said, lowering the paper. 'Don't be absurd. That's impossible. No one has dared attempt the Pacific since—'

'Since Sir Charles, sir,' Shephard interrupted, quietly.

Duddevin stared, incredulous.

'I did not authorize this flight.'

'We were not informed of his plans, sir.'

Duddevin stood, pushing back his chair with slow deliberation. He moved to the window, scotch in hand, jaw clenched.

'A *single-engine* aircraft cannot cross the Pacific. It's lunacy. It's tantamount to suicide, Shephard.'

'Yes, sir.'

'We didn't support his first crossing, and we will *certainly* not be supporting this one,' Duddevin snapped. 'Keep our awareness to an absolute minimum. I want no correspondence. No involvement. *Plausible deniability* will be our strongest position when the inevitable occurs.'

He turned back toward his desk, muttering darkly as he sat.

Shephard lowered his head slightly. 'Yes, sir.'

House of Lords
London, England. 1934.

Collins entered the office sharply, moving without hesitation. Papers clutched neatly in hand, he approached.

'My lord,' he said quietly, bowing slightly as he stopped at a respectful distance from where Lord Liard stood, drink in hand.

Lord Liard did not turn. His gaze remained fixed on the rain-slicked view beyond the tall windows.

'Jones and Waller are experiencing engine trouble,' Collins continued, voice low but clear. 'They have returned to Baghdad, my lord.'

For a long moment, only the hiss and crackle of the wireless sets filled the heavy air.

Lord Liard exhaled sharply, a sound somewhere between a growl and a sigh. His grip tightened imperceptibly around the crystal tumbler.

He flicked a glance toward Collins—brief, cool, dismissive.

'Keep me informed. No interruptions unless it is vital.'

'Of course, my lord,' Collins replied smoothly, bowing again before retreating into the shadows.

Lord Liard turned back to the window, drink untouched, as the gray skies deepened outside.

The race was already taking its toll.

Royal Aero Club
London, England. 1934.

A quell and a grumble befell the room.

Wagers quietly changed hands as gentlemanly bets were settled with murmured curses and tight smiles. Clerks moved swiftly, heads down, updating entries with chalk and magnets as fresh radio reports crackled in from across the Commonwealth.

The times and positions were meticulously noted, the information rippling across the thick carpets like a silent current.

Then—a fresh murmur.

Eyes turned toward the towering leaderboard.

The Comet G-ASCR—*Black Magic* herself—was marked as stopped.

Gentlemen leaned in closer, cigars momentarily forgotten, whiskey glasses frozen halfway to their lips.

The faint scent of burning tobacco and aged leather hung heavier now, as if the very air thickened with suspense.

No one spoke above a whisper.

In a race where minutes meant survival, a stopped aircraft could mean only two things.

The murmurs spread quickly—speculation, rumor, dread—rippling through the room like a gathering storm.

Allahabad, India. 1934.

The dry, dusty airstrip swelled under the brutal midday sun, the heat rising in shimmering waves off the parched earth.

Black Magic sat idle at the edge of the strip, her once-proud frame baking under the merciless glare. Steam coiled from the engine cowl, rising in lazy clouds only adding to the temperature.

Around her, the attraction was inescapable, and a crowd had gathered—local Indians in traditional flowing robes and bright turbans, their faces a mixture of awe and curiosity. Goats and skinny cattle wandered freely among them, kicking up dust, while barefoot children darted about, laughing and pointing in amazement at the grounded machine from another world.

At the heart of the chaos, Jim Mollison and his wife Amy worked feverishly. Their sleeves were rolled up, hands blackened with oil and grime, sweat pouring down their faces.

Mollison cursed under his breath, tools clattering to the ground. Every second lost under this pitiless sun drove them closer to defeat.

The race was slipping through their fingers—and the *Black Magic*, so full of promise, now lay helpless under a foreign sky.

Royal Aero Club
London, England. 1934.

Inside the Royal Aero Club, the tension was a living thing. The heavy murmur of conversation faltered as a fresh update clattered onto the race board. Clerks moved briskly, chalk dust swirling as they stepped back from the towering map. On the leaderboard, under the harsh light of the chandeliers, a new mark was drawn beside the Comet: *Black Magic—Retired.*

For a moment, the room held its breath.

Then, like a slow rolling storm, an unfortunate groan rumbled through the crowd—an eruption of disappointment, shock, and pity.

House of Lords
London, England. 1934.

Collins entered briskly, papers tucked under one arm.

'Scott has passed *Black Magic* at Allahabad, my lord,' he reported crisply.

Lord Liard drew hard on his fat cigar, the crackle of the burn audible as the smoke billowed from his mouth.

'Is Scott in a position to beat Sir Charles Kingsford Smith's record?' he asked, voice measured, almost detached.

Collins consulted his notes quickly, head lowered in deference.

'It would appear so, my lord,' he replied.

Liard drew back hard again.

South East Asia. 1934.

The storm hammered them.

Dark, swollen clouds rolled overhead, the sky flashing intermittently with distant lightning. Rain lashed against the canopy, *Grosvenor House* bucked and jolted like a wild thing beneath them.

Inside the cockpit, Scott wrestled the controls, muscles straining with every sharp jolt.

Behind him, Black braced himself, trying to make sense of the instruments as they were bounced and rattled by the turbulence. The weather was relentless, sending turbulence rattling through the frame.

Scott yelled back over the roar of the engines and the howling wind.

'I thought you said the reports out of India were good!'

Black shook his head, gripping the edges of the panel to steady himself.

'I have no idea where this came from!' he shouted back.

Another heavy jolt slammed them sideways. The Comet dipped as they fought their way through.

Scott grimaced, scanning the bulging skies ahead, not one to doubt the machine's wooden structure and its resilience, but the question of how far and how long could it sustain this punishment had entered his mind.

'This is going to cost us. Pull back. Power sixty-five percent,' he yelled sharply, easing off the throttle, frustration clear in his voice.

Black gave a curt nod.

Royal Aero Club
London, England. 1934.

With careful, practiced hands, one of the clerks reached up and shifted the small model of *Grosvenor House* forward—nudging it across the map to its new position.

The Gulf of Martaban.

A murmur spread among the gentlemen gathered beneath the map. Cigars glowed faintly through the wafting smoke and dimness. Glasses clinked. Wagers adjusted. Eyes narrowed.

Grosvenor House battled on—but the margin was shrinking.

Pacific Ocean. 1934.

At cruising speed above the vastness of the never-ending ocean beneath it, the *Lady Southern Cross* roared steadily through thinning light. Ahead, the world darkened.

'You see that?' Charles asked, calling back to Taylor.

'That came out of nowhere,' Taylor replied, his eyes fixed forward.

What had started as distant streaks of cloud had now formed into a towering black wall—an immense, roiling storm front rising from the ocean like a living mountain. Lightning flickered within its depths, illuminating turbulent curls of vapor and rain that spiraled like smoke from an unseen fire. The clouds were thick, bruised with violet and steel , stretching across the entire horizon like a closing curtain.

The calm of the open sky was gone. This was something else—something ancient, powerful, unforgiving.

Taylor didn't take his eyes off the approaching storm. 'Too wide to go around!' he yelled back. The storm spanned from horizon to horizon—a monstrous, unbroken front.

'Too high to get over,' Charles called out, checking his altimeter. The wall of clouds towered beyond fifteen thousand feet, higher than they could safely climb.

He paused, eyes scanning the instruments. 'Hawaii?'

'Four hundred miles out,' Taylor replied. His voice was tight, controlled—but edged with tension.

'We are in for a ride,' Charles muttered grimly.

'Ceiling is fifteen thousand!' Taylor warned.

Charles gritted his teeth, hands steady on the yoke.

Ahead, the sky churned. Rain sliced down in ghostly sheets, streaking the windscreen. Thunder rumbled—long, low, and endless, like the growl of something immense just waking up.

The aircraft did not flinch.

It surged forward—into the heart of the storm.

And disappeared.

Parliament House
Canberra, Australian Capital Territory, Australia. 1934.

The interior of the parliamentary car was lined with dark leather and mahogany trim. Thick cigar smoke curled lazily through the afternoon light slanting in from the window. Sir Duddevin sat reclined, his legs crossed, the motion of the car gentle beneath him as it approached the steps of Parliament House.

A glass of scotch rested in one hand, half empty. The other held a folded newspaper, creased neatly, his thumb holding place on a modest headline buried deep within the pages.

SMITHY DEPARTS SUVA ON PACIFIC FLIGHT

Duddevin exhaled a long stream of smoke, letting the article settle in.

No comment. No expression. Just the slow shift of his eyes as the government vehicle rolled to a halt outside the sandstone colossus of Parliament.

He folded the paper once more and set it beside him.

Then he took another sip of scotch.

Royal Aero Club
London, England. 1934.

A clerk stepped forward, reaching up with steady hands to slide the small model of *Grosvenor House* further across the great map.

The tiny aircraft clicked cleanly into its new position. Keen eyes across the room followed every movement, watching with taut anticipation.

Singapore.

Pacific Ocean. 1934.

Within, lightning lit the interior in savage flashes, illuminating the chaos. The aircraft bounced violently, the storm battering it with brutal force.

Visibility was gone. Darkness consumed them. They were tossed and thrown like driftwood in a maelstrom.

'Fuel consumption is high!' Taylor yelled over the roar, eyeing the rapidly falling gauge.

Charles glanced at his own panel—same story.

'Headwind?' he called.

'No!' Taylor scanned the instruments, eyes darting.

'Are we losing fuel?' Charles yelled, urgency mounting.

'We are losing speed,' Taylor shouted, confused.

CRACK.

The aircraft jolted violently. A lightning strike—or worse. The engine groaned under strain.

'What have we lost?' Charles shouted, gripping the yoke.

'Air speed: one eighty,' Taylor reported, tapping the gauge. 'We are still dropping.'

'Have you got it?' Taylor called again.

'No!' Charles fought the controls, muscles straining.

'Air speed: one twenty! Approaching stall! Got it?'

'No!'

'Forty!' Taylor yelled. 'I cannot see anything!'

'I cannot hold it!' Charles cried.

The aircraft stalled—nose high, speed gone. She dropped, slipping into a flat spin. The altimeter plummeted as they spiralled out of control.

'Anything?' Charles demanded.

'No! Altitude: fourteen thousand . . . thirteen . . . twelve—Got it?'

'I have no control! Take it!' Charles shouted, releasing the stick.

Taylor grabbed it from the rear position, battling to steady her. Charles scanned desperately—gauges, levers, anything. The cockpit spun, the compass a blur, the altimeter falling.

'Six thousand! Charles!'

Then—he spotted it. A control lever, jolted loose in the storm's violence. The elevator trim was jammed forward in the down position. He threw it back.

'Two thousand!' Taylor yelled.

'Got it!' Charles snapped. 'Mine!'

He yanked back control, slammed the throttle forward, and roared the engine back to life.

'Fifteen hundred! Charles! One thousand!'

Charles wrestled with the stick, fighting to level her. To pull her back from nowhere.

'One thousand . . . seven-fifty . . . five hundred!'

Within, the storm front continued its thunderous demolition over the intense blue of the ocean beneath, masking their fate. Its thick black underbelly, capped with white peaks of heavenly height, brilliantly struck by the light spoke in a colossus form.

In a trailing wisp of turbulent vapor, the *Lady Southern Cross* burst from the storm, exploding into the dry, cool, calm clear air. The cockpit filled with blinding light burning their dilating pupils; level, controlled, Charles had brought her back from the brink.

They screamed—wordless, primal, exultant.

Laughter, praise, prayer—all tangled into a single, deafening release.

'That was bloody close, Charles!' Taylor whooped.

'*Too* close,' Charles replied, chest heaving. 'Holy hell!'

'I think you just played your last Jesus card!'

Taylor burst out laughing with relief.

'Yours,' Charles called out, handing him the controls.

Taylor took the stick. Charles unlatched the canopy and slid it open, he stood, arms outstretched wide, against the backdrop of the lingering clouds behind them—defiant, immortal. Sunlight broke over his shoulders like divine fire, painting the storm behind him in gold. He closed his eyes and lived in that moment.

'Charles!' Taylor yelled. To his left hand side, an aircraft slowly rose up beneath them, cruising beside. Then another on his right.

'Charles!' Taylor yelled again. The pilot waved a salute. 'Charles!' Taylor yelled, finally getting Charles's attention. Charles opened his eyes and dropped back down into the cockpit.

'We have got company,' Taylor yelled, and as Charles looked to his left and right, more aircraft emerged off their port and starboard wings, and an entire squadron, the United States Army Air Corp, finalized their position in formation around beside them. Like angels sent by heaven. Taylor and Charles were no longer alone.

Timor Sea
Northern Territory, Australia. 1934.

Approaching the coastline, Scott and Black flew low over the picturesque Australian desert. The Comet roared through the cloudless, bright blue sky, slicing through the stark silence of the outback. Below, the hot red earth stretched endlessly—a vast tapestry of ochre and rust shimmering under the relentless sun.

From the cockpit, Scott and Black peered down as the ocean vanished behind them. His eyes traced the faint scars of old stock routes and dry riverbeds etched into the ancient land.

Dust devils twisted and danced in the distance. Sparse tufts of spinifex cast feeble shadows on the cracked ground. Scott adjusted his goggles, squinting against the glare. The compass wavered slightly—a reminder of the desert's vast, featureless expanse.

The plane's shadow skimmed the surface, racing fleetingly across the barren land. Black checked his watch.

'Not far now,' he called, confident. 'We'll be in Melbourne before sundown.'

A sudden jolt of turbulence snapped Scott back to the present. He tightened his grip on the controls, steadying the aircraft. The desert below remained indifferent, a timeless expanse where survival was a constant battle.

'We are certainly not in England anymore,' Scott muttered. 'Quite the contrast to green fields and gray skies.'

'Are you seeing the engine temps?' Black shouted over the comms, eyes locked on the rising needle.

Scott scanned the control panel. 'I see it,' he replied. 'Take her up—see if there's cooler air.'

He pulled back on the controls. The altimeter climbed, but so did the temperature.

'No change,' Black yelled.

'Climbing to eight thousand,' Scott called.

'Must be scorching down there,' Black replied, as the oil temperature gauges climbed steadily through the green arc and well into the caution range; it would not be long before they reached the redline. 'You have got to find cooler air,' Black added.

'Ceiling is twelve thousand,' Scott said. 'We do not have the altitude. They are not coming down.'

'Then we need to reduce speed,' Black snapped.

'Drop speed?'

'Drop it.'

'Dropping speed,' Scott echoed, slamming a fist against the console. 'Damn it! Looks like we'll be limping into Melbourne.'

Disappointment etched itself into Scott's face.

'Damn it,' he repeated quietly. 'Recalculate.'

Chapter 27

Honolulu, Hawaii, United States of America. 1934.

Charles sat heavily on the edge of the bed, his shoulders sagging under the weight of exhaustion. Dark circles framed his eyes—bruised and hollow—a testament to sleepless nights haunted by memories he couldn't escape. His breath came in shallow, uneven gasps, each one a struggle against the lingering grip of fear from his recent brush with death.

Dim light cast long shadows across the room, echoing the unrest within him. The hotel suite, once a haven, now felt distant and unreal. Wicker furniture—delicate yet sturdy—stood in quiet arrangement. A large, inviting armchair waited by the window, untouched. In the corner, a writing desk sat abandoned. The bed beneath him creaked softly, its ornate wooden headboard carved with Hawaiian motifs, weathered by time but still intricate.

Above, a ceiling fan turned slowly, its palm-leaf blades stirring the humid air. Sepia-toned photographs adorned the walls: tranquil beaches, lush green valleys, serene mountain ridges—snapshots of paradise that mocked the chaos inside him. Heavy floral drapes framed the windows, slightly parted, offering a distant view of the ocean where waves rolled in, gentle and constant.

Charles stared, unable to escape his reflection in the mirror that sat on the dresser as he ran a trembling hand through his disheveled hair, fingers pausing at his throbbing temples. The dull ache pulsed with each heartbeat, veins rising beneath the skin. His dry, cracked lips pressed into a tight line, trying to hold together the strain that threatened to unravel him. In the silence, the ticking of a nearby clock sounded thunderous. Each second a sharp reminder of time slipping by, indifferent.

The clock—a brass-finished art deco piece on the mantel above a small fireplace—seemed to watch him, relentless and unmoved.

Outside, Hawaii offered its surreal contrast. The air was warm and thick with humidity, perfumed by salt and blooming hibiscus. Waves kissed the shore with rhythmic indifference, and birds called lazily in the distance. Palm fronds rustled in the breeze, whispering serenity—a cruel counterpoint to the storm inside his chest.

The heat, once comforting, now clung like a shroud. Sweat pooled at his brow and slid down his temples, merging with tears that welled, unbidden. The world outside gleamed in lush greens and ocean blues, blazing with the fiery hues of a setting sun. But to Charles, it all felt foreign—distant, an unreachable brightness.

His mind replayed the moments—those terrifying seconds when everything hung by a thread. When the ocean called his name, the decisions. The panic. The silence that followed. He squeezed his eyes shut, chasing peace in the darkness, but the images only sharpened. The echoes of fear surged louder, relentless.

He was drained—emotionally hollowed. Every nerve felt stripped raw. The adrenaline was gone, leaving behind an ache deep in his core. Vulnerability crept in, slow and smothering. A guilt he couldn't name twisted in his gut, pressing against his chest like a stone.

Even brief moments of stillness brought no relief. Closing his eyes unleashed a tide of flashes—sounds, sensations, glimpses of the edge. His heart thudded in phantom panic. Mortality pressed close, a shadow that wouldn't leave.

The walls seemed to close in. Solitude turned suffocating. He longed for a hand to hold, a voice to pull him back from the brink—but there was only silence. Only the oppressive stillness and the sound of his own shallow breath.

He raised his hand to his face, gripping tightly, as though to keep the pieces from falling apart. A sob escaped—raw, unfiltered, slicing through the quiet as he forced it back deep inside himself. The sob deepened through the thoughts of what could have been. His once-unshakable mind now trembled under pressure, fragile as cracked glass.

Quickly he drew a deep sharp breath, wiping his face back to a reality where these thoughts, emotions, and feelings were banned from a man. He looked hard in the mirror as he shook from him the weakness that had been allowed to lean in on him. The dread stayed, a shadow stitched into his soul; he refused it, breathed heavily, and looked into his own eyes.

'You will never own defeat,' he said to his reflection.

Wheeler Army Airfield
Honolulu, Hawaii, United States of America. 1934.

Stepping from the taxi, Charles and Taylor were immediately met by a cluster of military police stationed at the main gate. The guards moved quickly, rifles checked and ready, their expressions sharp and unreadable.

'Smith. Taylor. You are to be detained here,' one of them stated crisply, already striding toward the guard box to place a call.

Charles and Taylor shared a glance, a flicker of concern passing between them.

Charles leaned sideways, muttering under his breath, 'Did you go out last night?'

'If anything is wrong, sure enough it will be your doing,' Taylor murmured back, barely moving his lips.

Before they could say more, the sound of a fast-approaching vehicle grabbed their attention.

An open-top military vehicle tore toward the gate, its tires kicking up a fine mist of dust. Seated rigidly in the rear was a high-ranking American officer. His tailored olive drab uniform was immaculate—brass buttons gleaming, insignia polished to mirror shine. His peaked cap sat crisp and unshaken, polished leather boots catching the morning sun.

The vehicle raced to a halt.

The officer stepped out with fluid authority, his posture straight and commanding.

'Major General Howard Calhoun Davidson, Commanding Officer,' he barked. 'Follow me.'

Charles and Taylor fell into step behind him, and were escorted swiftly to a waiting staff car. An aide opened the door. Without a word, they slid into the back seat.

As the vehicle rumbled toward the hangars, Davidson spoke over his shoulder, his voice clipped and formal.

'I regret to inform you we cannot release your aircraft,' he said. 'As the first foreign-registered plane to land in the Territory of Hawaii, we cannot permit your continuation to the mainland in the condition your aircraft arrived in.'

Charles stiffened. His heart sank. Taylor tensed beside him as they approached one of the massive hangars. The car slowed, then stopped.

Davidson handed Charles a clipboard stacked with official documents.

'You'll need to sign these,' he instructed curtly.

Without protest, Charles scribbled his signature, his mind spinning through worst-case scenarios.

As they stepped from the car, the massive hangar doors began to roll open with a slow, mechanical groan.

And there she was.

The *Lady Southern Cross*, gleaming under the Hawaiian sun. Her once battered body now sparkled, every scar of her crossing erased. Fresh polish gleamed along her sleek frame. Her surfaces—meticulously restored—shone like a jewel.

An honor guard lined the hangar apron, standing at crisp attention, their uniforms razor-sharp against the blue sky. All around them, a crowd of mechanics, engineers, airmen, and naval personnel stood proudly gathered, faces lit with pride.

Davidson allowed a rare smile to break his stern face.

'You didn't think we'd let you show up on the mainland in one of the finest American aircraft ever built looking the way she came in, did you, son?' he said.

Charles swallowed hard, a lump rising unexpectedly in his throat.

'Courtesy of Uncle Sam,' Davidson added proudly.

The entire hangar erupted in cheers and applause.

Slowly, men and officers stepped forward, offering handshakes, congratulations, and words of admiration. The thanks and well-wishes seemed endless, a steady stream of honor from those who understood what it meant to defy the sky.

Taylor leaned over to Charles, grinning.

'I thought you played your last Jesus card,' he teased.

Charles allowed himself a breathless laugh.

'I should have checked my other sleeve,' he replied simply.

Oakland Airfield
Oakland, California, United States of America. 1934.

The *Lady Southern Cross* dipped low over the grassy field, her engines humming with quiet triumph. She bounced once, then again, before settling gently along the landing strip. A low cheer rippled across the perimeter where spectators had gathered in anticipation. Journalists clutched notepads, photographers jostled for position. Children perched on shoulders, faces bright with awe. The air thrummed with anticipation—electric with reverence and disbelief.

From a tower speaker, a rich, accented voice crackled to life over the noise.

'It was in 1928 that Sir Charles Kingsford Smith took off from this very field to begin his epic flight to Honolulu, Suva, and Brisbane, Australia . . . and now, here he is once more, roaring over Oakland Airport to complete the last leg of his return—two thousand four hundred and eight miles, over open water. Ahead of schedule, no less. A remarkable achievement by Sir Charles and his navigator, Captain Taylor.'

The *Lady Southern Cross* taxied to a stop, engines hissing, the crowd swarming to greet her. With his signature modest grin, Charles leaned from the cockpit and raised his hand.

'Sorry we are a little late,' he called dryly.

Robert pushed through the crowd, beaming. 'There are a lot of folks here who are frankly in disbelief.'

Taylor joined Charles, both waving, both looking remarkably fresh for men who had just crossed the Pacific.

'And to prove their freshness,' the newsreel narrator continued, 'the two men leap from their cockpits and turn first to their ship. Ordinary mechanics now, inspecting every rivet, every line. With this flight, Sir Charles Kingsford Smith becomes the only man in history to fly the Pacific Ocean in both directions—securing his place among the immortals of aviation.'

The newsreel trumpet fanfare blared triumphantly.

The White House
Washington, DC United States of America. 1934.

The room was dark, save for the soft flicker of the newsreel projector casting black-and-white light across the velvet walls of the White House screening room. Dust floated silently through the beam, a quiet reminder of the stillness in the shifting world.

On-screen, the title card blazed boldly in stylized lettering, the opening music blared: British Paramount News, Smithy – Breaks Record!

Then, motion.

The image of the *Lady Southern Cross* filled the screen, wheels kissing the tarmac at Oakland to the cheers of an awaiting crowd. The newsreel's narrator cut in, his clipped British accent brimming with restrained enthusiasm.

'Another record-breaking flight is in the making,' he said, 'as Sir Charles Kingsford Smith and his navigator, Captain Taylor, fly from Australia to California. They left Brisbane for the Fiji Islands, then tackled a three thousand, one hundred and fifty-mile stretch to Honolulu. Now, the final lap—completed in a blaze of glory as the *Lady Southern Cross* touches down on American soil.'

The audience in the room remained still.

On-screen, Smithy and Taylor grinned from the cockpit, cameras flashing wildly around them. Smithy leaned across the fuselage, shaking hands with Robert. 'I am very glad to see you,' Smithy said, his voice clear over the grainy footage.

The narrator continued, voice dipping slightly.

'The world hails the flyers as pioneers of a new transpacific air service. Yet rumor has it Sir Charles may be forced to sell his aircraft to defray the cost of the flight. Such is the reward for blazing the trail.'

Cut to a brief interview. Smithy, dressed in his thick bearskin flight suit, stood before the microphone with the same modesty that made him beloved across oceans.

'There's not much to tell, really,' he said with a soft smile. 'We arrived via Suva and Hawaii, touched down in Oakland about three o'clock. No real trouble with the trip. Captain Taylor did a magnificent job navigating. That's all I care to say. Cheerio.'

The reel clicked to a stop. Lights rose. Curtains were drawn. Silence hung heavy.

President Franklin D. Roosevelt sat forward slowly, elbows on his knees, brow furrowed in thought. Around him, a cluster of military advisors sat in stillness, each man acutely aware of what had just played across the screen.

General Whitaker was the first to speak, his voice quiet but firm.

'The implications of this flight, Mr. President, are wide-reaching. In Europe. And in the Pacific.'

Roosevelt turned to him, his eyes steady. 'You're suggesting an aircraft of that design could place our enemies within striking distance of the mainland.'

Another general nodded. 'We are, Mr. President. The range. The speed. The ability to operate with minimal infrastructure. This is a fast long-range aircraft with significant payload potential Mr. President.'

FDR's jaw tightened, his gaze returning to the blank screen.

'We must consider this emphatically as a threat to the security of the nation Mr. President. This will not go unnoticed.'

Reich Chancellery Building
Berlin, Germany. 1934.

Under the flickering staccato of projected light, Adolf Hitler sat in rigid silence.

The private screening chamber within the Reich chancellery was austere—concrete walls, a low ceiling, and a stale chill that clung to the skin. The only illumination came from the projector at the rear, its rhythmic clatter echoing softly in the enclosed space. Before him, the newsreel danced and juddered across the screen in black and white.

He did not blink.

Surrounding him were the most senior members of his High Command—Göring, Himmler, Keitel, and others—seated upright, their faces a mixture of curiosity and calculation. Not a single breath dared rise too loudly.

' . . . the first and only man to have flown the vast expanse of the Pacific in both directions,' the British narrator intoned from the screen. Grainy footage showed Sir Charles Kingsford Smith, beaming modestly beneath his bearskin flight suit, waving to crowds in California, then shaking hands with American officials.

The *Lady Southern Cross* rested behind him—small, elegant, and unyielding.

The room remained still.

Hitler's fingertips tapped the armrest once. A small, sharp sound.

'In both directions . . .' he repeated quietly, under his breath. His German accent lent the English words a weight they had not carried in the narrator's mouth.

Göring shifted, sensing the pulse of interest. 'He used a modified Lockheed, my führer. Civilian. Nothing extraordinary in the machine itself.'

'Not the machine,' Hitler said, his voice cold and precise. 'The mind that flies it.'

Keitel cleared his throat cautiously. 'With the proper resources, our engineers could—'

'No,' Hitler interrupted.

The reel continued, showing the aircraft on approach, then a cheering American crowd erupting as the wheels touched down. Hitler leaned slightly forward.

'He has proven the impossible possible,' he murmured.

The film whirred to an end. The screen went white.

Silence.

Then, slowly, Hitler stood.

'He shows the world that oceans are no longer walls,' he said. 'Soon, there will be no more distances. Only targets.'

No one dared reply.

He turned to Göring.

'I want every scrap of information you can gather on that aircraft. The design. The pilot. His engineers. Everything.'

Göring bowed his head. 'Jawohl, mein führer.'

Hitler paused one final moment, staring at the screen as if trying to conjure the pilot through it.

'Men like him are dangerous . . . not because they build weapons—but because they become one.'

He turned, and without another word, exited the room.

The door shut softly behind him.

The projector clicked to a halt.

And the shadows sat a little deeper than before.

Royal Palace
Tokyo, Japan. 1934.

The light dimmed to black, and the whir of the newsreel projector slowed to a gentle, final click. The white screen at the front of the chamber vanished into darkness.

No one moved.

Not yet.

Across the vast tatami-floored room, beneath the ornate coffered ceiling and gilded screen walls, the emperor of Japan sat still as stone. His face, once softly illuminated by the flickering light of Sir Charles Kingsford Smith's transpacific triumph, had now retreated fully into shadow.

He did not speak.

He did not need to.

His advisors shifted ever so slightly in their seated positions, kneeling in traditional seiza. The mood was dense, the silence not uncomfortable, but *deliberate*. Every eye remained fixed on the emperor, awaiting the next move.

What he had just witnessed was not merely a feat of aviation—it was a demonstration of reach, of range, of potential dominance in the vast skies that stretched from one empire to another.

And it had not come from Japan.

A quiet breath was drawn somewhere across the chamber.

The emperor's gaze had not wavered. Though his features were now cloaked in shadow, his intent was crystalline.

Finally, from the far end of the chamber, a single voice spoke—low, respectful, carefully measured.

'We must begin . . . immediately.'

There was no disagreement. Only a silent, collective bow.

The White House
Washington, DC United States of America. 1934.

The silence returned—deeper this time. Weightier. Beyond the tall windows of the White House screening room, the Potomac shimmered in the pale afternoon sun, its slow current blissfully unaware that the course of history had just shifted—on the wings of a battered blue aircraft from a far-off land.

President Franklin D. Roosevelt remained still for a moment longer, his hands clasped before him, his gaze distant.

Then, softly—without turning—he spoke.

'Send Mr. Kingsford Smith a letter of congratulations,' he said. His voice was calm, but laced with a rare reverence. 'I'd like to meet him.'

He paused, considering the quiet outside, the peaceful surface of the river, the deceptive ease of it all.

'And get me the president of Lockheed on the phone.'

No one questioned the order. No one needed to.

The room stirred back to life, the silence retreating like the tide.

Roosevelt kept watching the river.

He knew what the world had just witnessed.

Chapter 28

MGM Studios
Culver City, California, United States of America. 1934.

The sun hung high over the sprawling studio lot, casting sharp, geometric shadows on the maze of soundstages bustling with activity. The air was thick with the scent of fresh paint and sawdust, mingled with a flurry of extras moving about their calls.

In a shaded corner, tucked away from the frenzy, a small garden oasis offered respite. Beneath the wide branches of an oak tree, a wrought-iron table stood dressed with a crisp white cloth, the gentle clink of cutlery against china resonated over the fine meal before them. The breeze carried with it the soft gurgle of a nearby fountain, bees buzzing by roses, and birds whispering songs.

Victor Fleming lounged with the ease of a man used to chaos. His panama hat tilted against the sun, a cigar burning idly in one hand, his eyes roving the lot like a general surveying a battlefield, Charles ate, hungrily, thrilled to be a part of the commotion and to have been invited by his friend.

The contrast was stark—one a craftsman of dreams, the other a maker of history.

Victor, ever the showman, leaned forward, a stack of letters in hand, his excitement rising with every name he read aloud as he flicked through the pile.

'Invitations Charles. Adolf Hitler . . . Benito Mussolini . . . an invitation from the White House . . . *the emperor of Japan* . . . New Zealand. Charles! My God, these aren't fan letters—this is diplomacy in ink!'

He shuffled through them again, almost reverently. 'World leaders, Charles. Extraordinary. This is more than a flight—it's a motion picture.'

Charles smiled politely, but his eyes drifted. He sipped his drink. The silence between them stretched.

Victor caught it.

'What about home?' he asked, looking up. 'Anything from Australia?'

Charles shook his head slowly. 'Nothing on that front, Victor.'

His voice was quiet, but the weight behind it pressed the tablecloth flat. A kind of sadness crept into the moment, quiet and uninvited.

Victor, sensing the shift, clapped a hand on his friend's shoulder.

'Ah, the greatest flight since Orville and Wilbur! There's a picture here. What about James Cagney? He's your height. Or no—wait! Errol Flynn! Bit more your look, and just the right kind of rogue.'

Charles chuckled, the edge of his melancholy softening.

'Cagney might be closer to the mark,' he said with a grin.

'I *can see it*, Charles. I'll set up the meeting. The studio won't pass this up. And the title—listen, we're close. Something with peril, grandeur . . . *The Wings of the Trepid* . . . no, too stiff. *On a Wing and a Prayer*—eh, a little Sunday sermon . . . wait—wait!' He threw his hands up theatrically. "Trepid Were Their Wings!' You see it, Charles? *Marquees! Headlines!* I promise, we'll have half the globe queuing up for a ticket!'

Before Charles could reply, Victor's assistant approached quietly.

'Mr. Fleming, urgent telegram for you sir.'

'Thank you,' Victor said, taking the envelope. 'Pardon me, Charles.'

He opened it with the practiced hand of a man who had seen countless scripts, contracts, and last-minute rewrites.

But the moment he read the message, the color drained from his face.

His breath stopped.

'Victor?' Charles leaned forward. 'Everything all right?'

Victor didn't answer at first. He read the telegram again, slower this time, as though he hoped the words would change.

Finally, he looked up.

'They have asked me to inform you. Your friend, Charles Ulm, is missing. They lost radio contact. He . . . he never reached Hawaii.'

For a moment, the sounds of the studio evaporated. There was only the wind in the trees.

Charles froze. 'Oh no, not Charlie . . . no—no, not Charlie.'

The words came out as a whisper, hollowed by disbelief. His fingers gripped the edge of the table, as though anchoring himself to the earth.

'I need to get to my plane,' he said suddenly, rising. 'I have to get out there. Now.'

Victor stood with him, steadying him with a firm hand on the shoulder.

'Charles—wait. Just a moment.'

But Charles's eyes were wild, already somewhere above the Pacific.

'My God, Victor. *My God.*'

Charles's fingers gently traced the navigational markings left by Taylor on the map he held, retracing the memory of the route left behind, the wide expanse of the Pacific. He stood silently over the wing that had carried them so far, to the ocean that had claimed his friend.

The pictures behind his eyes told the story as they followed the route—now behind him, behind aviation. There was an emptiness in knowing how little was left to conquer. The time was fast approaching when even distant memories would run out.

'You look like you are cleaning out your office,' Robert said, breaking the silence.

'It feels that way,' Charles replied, a reminiscent smile crossing his lips.

'They mentioned you were out here.' Robert approached, his footsteps echoing through the emptiness of the hangar.

Charles barely looked up. His movements were slow, deliberate. The rustle of paper punctuated the quiet as he folded the map. He gathered the small items he'd removed from the cockpit and placed them neatly in his briefcase. With practiced precision, he closed the case and snapped each lock shut.

'Any word?' he asked, voice tight—a thin thread of hope still clinging.

‘They’ve called off the search,’ Robert said gently. The words hung between them. ‘There’s a lot of ocean out there, as you know.’

Charles nodded—he knew all too well. He placed the briefcase on the ground beside him and stepped back, laying a hand on the aircraft’s side, absorbing her energy one final time.

‘You two flew a lot of miles together,’ Robert said quietly. His hands were tucked in his pockets.

‘We had a rule, Robert. He broke it,’ Charles said.

Robert said nothing. In a moment like this, there was little that could be said.

‘In ’28, before Charlie and I flew the Pacific, the Australian government pulled their funding. We were broke, living in a tin shed on the Oakland airfield,’ Charles recalled. ‘They used to lock us in at night.’ He smiled faintly, shaking off the memory.

‘The story goes, the sheriff seized your plane,’ Robert said, half-smiling, trying to lighten the mood.

‘They did. Seized it for unpaid debts,’ Charles nodded. ‘We had nothing. Just two one-way tickets home.’ He paused. ‘It was Charlie’s idea to sell them. To buy us some time. We were not ready to give up on the dream—being first to cross the Pacific.’

He looked out across the hangar, lost for a moment.

‘Two days later, we met Hancock. He bought the *Southern Cross*, paid off our debts, and funded the flight. Charlie, Jim, Harry, and I—together, we conquered the Pacific.’

Robert listened.

‘If it were not for you Yanks, we never would have done it,’ Charles furthered as they shared in the acknowledgment.

‘After that, we made a rule: never separate the crew from the pilots,’ Charles continued, then stopped. His voice cracked. ‘He broke that rule, Robert. And now he is gone.’

‘One could say the greater the reward, the greater the risk,’ Robert offered gently. ‘It’s a dangerous business, Charles.’

'The only reward is knowing you beat the risk,' Charles replied. 'Then you are just left asking why you took it in the first place.' He paused again, his voice softening.

'The last time I saw Charlie, he said he didn't want his son growing up without a father—chasing records,' he said. His breath hitched in his throat. He inhaled sharply, the sound sharp in the quiet. 'Said it was all business now.'

He shook his head, a sad smile flickering across his lips.

'Robert, it does not matter which path we take. The stakes are the same.'

'The luck of the game,' Robert replied, resignation in his voice.

'Luck of the game,' Charles echoed. 'A game really not worth playing anymore.'

He reached down, picked up the case, and extended his hand to Robert.

'I am tired, Robert.'

'You're always welcome here, Charles. Please, consider our offer.' Robert extended his hand—a gesture of business, and friendship.

'It is never easy letting go Robert! Get what you can for her,' Charles said, his grip strong but his eyes resolute. He let go, walked past Robert, and left his footsteps to fade into the silence behind them.

Chapter 29

MacRobertson Steam Confectionery Works
Melbourne, Victoria, Australia. 1935.

Charles and Mac strolled through the vibrant never-ending backdrop of manufacture. The air was thick—heavy with the scent of sugar, cocoa, and the sharper tang of machinery oil. Warm currents swirled through the space, the result of countless boilers hissing and groaning under pressure. Steam hissed from valves and pipes overhead, curling into the rafters like ghostly tendrils. Somewhere nearby, a release valve let out a shrill, staccato whistle, like a kettle brought to full boil.

Workers moved with practiced urgency, their voices blending into the symphony of clattering tools, squeaking wheels, and the low, pulsing thrum of conveyor belts. The machines breathed, churned, and snapped with mechanical precision—confections tumbling down the line in a blur of color and shape. Beneath the polished surface of it all was a constant heartbeat of pressure and motion.

'It is a hard game, business,' Mac said, his voice cutting just above the swell of confectionery being printed like money—it *was* money to Mac's ears—as they navigated the labyrinthine plant. His words rode the undercurrent of hissing pipes and stamping gears. 'It takes more than passion and determination. Even belief in one's ability to deliver is often not enough these days, Charles.'

As they moved through the factory floor, the ambient heat intensified. Sweat beaded on Charles's brow, and he wiped it with a handkerchief from his pocket. The thud of mechanical arms provided a steady backdrop to Mac's words. A worker, his face flowered with caked on ingredients and the sheen of perspiration on his temples, tipped his hat in passing.

'Mr. Robertson,' he greeted respectfully.

Another nodded with a smile, maneuvering a cart stacked high with molded candy. Steam rose from cooling racks along the walls, momentarily clouding their path in fleeting clouds of vapor before dissolving into the rafters.

'You had great favor among the people, Charles,' Mac continued, his sharp eyes scanning every motion on the floor. 'Which in itself is a powerful tool. Public opinion can sway governments—but it's not enough. It is a delicate balance, and a dangerous one.'

'Mac—' Charles began, but his voice was almost lost in a loud *clang* as a machine nearby slammed shut a row of caramel molds.

'On one side of the scale, you have the people,' Mac continued. 'On the other, the government. Tip too far to one side and the balance is lost. You don't win favor by proving the government wrong. You win it by proving them right—even when they are not.'

Steam hissed again—this time from a long pipe just beside them, the burst startling in its suddenness. Mac didn't flinch.

'Generally speaking, they're a bunch of bumbling idiots who couldn't run a school fair,' he muttered. 'And yet they hold all the cards. While we Australians speak with pride, our government still thinks like loyal subjects. We are still British, Charles. In voice, in fear, in instinct.'

The noise swelled around them—workers shouting orders, valves screeching, chocolate cooling under long sheets of metal conveyor. Every movement was heat, steam, momentum. Mac's voice remained measured, clinical, slicing through it all.

'Take your views on American aircraft. Everyone knows you are right. Who would doubt Sir Charles Kingsford Smith? Your experience in this would save lives. It is noble, and it is visionary.'

'Mac,' Charles tried again, louder, as another boiler let off a sharp, hissing exhale.

'But the more you expose their incompetence, the more they will work to perturb you,' Mac pressed. 'Not just in policy—but in public perception. They can't afford to let you be right. If they do, they will look like the fools they are, so they'll do what fools do—endeavor to destroy you. Where does that leave you Charles?'

Charles remained silent.

'Beating your head against a wall? In ruin? Correct?' Mac answered himself. 'They will never admit their failings, they are politicians Charles. They will have to erase your credit from the record—while smiling and shaking your hand. Parasites, clinging to your popularity, draining it dry.'

'Sir,' a passing worker greeted, hands full of trays laden with freshly wrapped chocolates.

Mac nodded slightly. 'Businessmen who understand this play the game. They tip the scale to the side that counts. Contracts, influence, favor—it all leans toward those who toe the line. Not those who attempt to defy it.'

'Mac?' Charles's voice was quiet again, like someone speaking in a storm.

'Now then,' Mac snapped, halting near a vat of molten caramel, the golden liquid swirling under a sheen of rising vapor. 'For me, it is about maintaining balance. Not losing it. Balance.'

'Mac?'

'Charles,' Mac turned, his tone softening. 'I admire you. But you are placing too much weight on your side of the scale. You are a true gentleman. That I would no longer support you financially does not mean I expect the money to be repaid.'

'I know,' Charles said, drawing an envelope from his coat. 'However, it was clear that the responsibility was mine, and mine alone.'

He handed it over—an envelope heavy with finality. Mac took it, slipping it into his jacket without a word.

They shook hands—firm, final—among the blur of moving belts and the ghostly veil of steam.

'They will defeat you Charles,' Mac said at last, the words rising above the mechanical noise and hanging in the air.

House of Lords
London, England. 1935.

Ah, Collins. Unfashionably tardy, let us not make it a habit.'

The words landed with clipped precision as Lord Liard rose smoothly from behind his grand oak desk.

Collins, ever proper, offered a short bow as he stepped forward. 'No my lord. I apologize, my lord.'

Lord Liard didn't sit. He paced, the excitement in his voice unmistakable beneath the practiced formality.

'To form part of the activities surrounding His Majesty's Jubilee celebrations,' he began, 'The king has requested that his personal mail be sent to the furthest colony in the Commonwealth—New Zealand—by air.'

He turned sharply to Collins, relishing the weight of the news.

'The Ministry of Air,' he said, pausing with emphasis, 'has been specifically delegated this operation.'

'Yes, my lord,' Collins replied, his tone perfectly neutral.

Lord Liard stepped closer, eyes gleaming behind the thin rims of his spectacles.

'His Majesty,' he said, holding out a cream-colored directive bound with ribbon, 'has personally requested that 'his friend,' Sir Charles Kingsford Smith, undertake this leg of the journey.' His smile deepened with satisfaction. 'In honor of his first crossing of the Tasman, Sir Charles will deliver the Royal Mail from Australia to New Zealand.'

He handed the lettered request and directives to Collins, who received it with a respectful nod.

'To be working directly under the instruction of His Royal Highness,' Lord Liard mused aloud, resuming his slow, delighted orbit of the room, 'is quite the honor, Collins.'

'It is, my lord,' Collins affirmed.

'A grand opportunity to demonstrate the successes we have driven in aviation,' Lord Liard continued, bouncing lightly on his heels. 'A showcase of British influence and Commonwealth unity. You understand the significance, yes?'

'Absolutely, my lord.'

'I need not underline how committed and excited we will be to work with Sir Charles, do I, Collins?'

'Not at all, my lord.'

'Good!' Liard snapped, clapping his hands softly once. 'I'll let you take care of the formalities.'

'Yes, my lord.' Collins sifted through the documents. 'There is no mention of a fee for the services to be provided by Sir Charles, my lord.'

'That is correct Collins, the services are to be provided as an honorific, complimentary, demonstrating the great strength and pride of the Commonwealth.' He paused. 'The king will take great favor upon his loyalty and generosity, Collins.' Lord Liard paused again, fixing Collins with a weighty look over the rim of his glasses.

'We do not want to disappoint His Majesty.'

Collins inclined his head with the barest flicker of a smile. 'We do not, my lord.'

Sydney, New South Wales, Australia. 1935.

Mary took Charles's hand, squeezing it tightly as she rested hers on his thigh. The back seat of the taxi offered the perfect intimacy for a quiet exchange. City lights flickered past the windows, casting fleeting shadows across their faces. Glancing at him, Mary gently prodded his silence.

'If one could guess,' she whispered, her voice barely rising above the chug and rumble of the engine.

Charles turned to her with a soft, almost distracted smile. 'Guess?'

'You are a thousand miles away, Charles. If someone could guess what foreign land or far-off adventure holds your thoughts, I am sure it would be me, the love of your life.'

His smile faded, the warmth draining from it. He looked away, out the window, watching the night slip by. 'Guess,' he echoed, more to himself than her—almost as if issuing a challenge.

Mary laughed softly, trying to break the weight in the air. 'I cannot guess, Charles. There are too many. I would have better luck throwing a dart at a map.'

Charles remained silent. The distant look in his eyes made Mary's heart ache. She squeezed his hand again, more firmly.

'Did everything go well in Melbourne?' she asked.

He nodded slightly, a motion more out of obligation than reassurance. His eyes never met hers.

'I have an idea, should we stop by the theater?' Mary offered, her voice lighter, hopeful. 'We have not been out together alone in forever.' Mary paused, 'We can sit in the back row, just the two of us,' Mary intimated suggestively.

Charles turned to her then, taking her other hand in his. 'You know . . . I would like that,' he said warmly, though a flicker of unease still lingered in his expression.

The taxi pulled up to the theater, and they stepped out into the cool night air, invigorated by its crispness. Arm in arm they rushed to the ticket booth.

'Two, please,' Charles said at the booth, reaching into his wallet.

'Door two,' the attendant replied, handing over the stubs.

They hurried inside like young lovers sneaking away from the world. The dim interior welcomed them as they slipped into the back row, hidden from view. Popcorn in hand, they nestled into each other as the house lights lowered to the prelude.

'See? This is nice,' Mary said, resting her head on Charles's shoulder, trying to coax him into the moment.

'Did you catch what's showing?' Charles asked, glancing toward the screen as it flickered to life.

'No, did you?'

'No.'

The silver screen lit up, bathing the room in its soft glow. The audience hushed as a crackling orchestral theme signaled the beginning. Mary smiled, nostalgia tugging gently at her.

Then the Movietone newsreel began:

> 'Great Scott! England to Australia in fifty-four hours! C. W. A. Scott and Campbell Black touched down in Melbourne after smashing the England to Australia flight record once held by Sir Charles Kingsford Smith.
> 'We are very tired; it was a demanding flight, and we are very proud to have captured this victory for Great Britain."

Scott's voice resonated throughout the theater.

Charles's jaw clenched. His hand tightened around Mary's with such force it made her wince.

She looked at him, alarmed. 'Charles . . . do you want to leave? We can go.'

He didn't respond.

She scanned the dark room—other patrons were beginning to take notice. Their whispers grow over their shoulder glances.

'Just leave it alone, Mary,' Charles growled, standing suddenly. The seats squeaked beneath him. Without looking back, he stormed out, his footsteps echoing down the aisle.

Mary remained, stunned. The eyes of the audience were now fully on her. Her cheeks flushed with heat as she shrank back in her seat, torn between chasing after him and staying seated to avoid further spectacle.

The evening only further soured. Later, the way Mary folded the clothing made her displeasure unmistakable—each sharp crease, each aggressive snap of fabric a quiet accusation. The silence between them was dense, filled with unspoken words and unresolved tension.

'I am sorry,' Charles offered—simple, tentative. He stood in the doorway, shoulders slumped, hands buried in his pockets.

'I do not want to talk about it,' Mary replied sharply, her voice tight with emotion.

'Mary, please—'

'I do not want to talk about it.' She paused, then threw the garment in her hands onto the bed. Her voice rose. 'Actually . . . I do want to talk about it. You embarrassed me. You left me there in front of all those people—all because you didn't win that . . . that *damn race!*'

Her voice cracked, and tears slipped down her cheeks. Charles moved in, reaching for her shoulders, a silent plea for forgiveness in his touch.

'Why, Charles? Why do you care so much? Why is it more important to you than *us*? Than me? Than your son?' Her voice trembled, heavy with hurt and disbelief.

Charles held her close, silent, the air thick with all he couldn't say. The weight of his unspoken regret pressed against her grief.

Mary gently pulled away, wiping her face. 'I just want to understand,' she whispered.

Charles looked down, struggling for words, trying to untangle the knot inside him.

'It is not about the race,' he finally said, voice low and strained. 'It is about feeling like I have failed. Like I have failed you. Failed everyone.'

Mary's expression softened, but the ache in her eyes remained. 'You did not fail, Charles. You haven't failed us. I just need you here—with us. Not lost in some past glory . . . or haunted by some imagined failure.'

She reached up and touched his cheek, her palm warm against his skin. The edge in her voice softened, her love trying to bridge the distance.

Charles met her gaze for the first time that night. 'I know, Mary. I am trying,' he said. 'It is just . . . hard. It is hard to let go.'

Mary stepped closer, taking his hand in both of hers. 'We can do it together, Charles. Just . . . do not shut me out. Promise me that.'

He nodded, pulling her into a tight embrace. 'I promise,' he whispered into her hair, clinging to the hope that this time, he could keep his word, the simmering defeat still crawling beneath his skin.

Chapter 30

Offices of Sir Charles Kingsford Smith
Sydney, New South Wales, Australia. 1935.

John breathed heavily beneath his sweaty brow as he lowered a large box to the floor in the chaos of the move. Jess, flushed from the climb to the fifth floor, set down another box atop an empty desk with a relieved exhale.

'Are you keeping up?' Jess teased, playing on his age as she brushed a stray strand of hair from her face.

'Thank God,' John replied, wiping his forehead and glancing around the new space. 'I think that's the last of them.'

The office was bright and spacious, with wide windows welcoming in the city light—a stark contrast to the cramped quarters they'd left behind.

'You would think Charles could have chosen a lower floor. But no,' John added with a laugh. 'He has to be up in the sky.'

Jess hauled a heavy box of files toward a cabinet. 'Oh, to be youthful again,' she said, grinning as she surveyed the room. 'I love it. It is bright. And being in the city . . . it's going to be exciting.'

She closed one of the windows, muting the distant hum of traffic and horns below.

'I love the overall look, Jess. Very becoming,' John said, eyeing her outfit with amusement.

'Oh, this?' Jess glanced down, wiping her hands on the gray coveralls. 'Borrowed them from Tommy,' she said with a laugh.

'I hope you are not thinking of switching departments,' John asked, stirring her.

Jess chuckled. 'That depends on how close my desk is to yours. I *think* this one belongs to Tommy.'

'That one?' John asked.

'No, that one over there,' Jess said, pointing toward a desk by the window where sunlight streamed across the polished surface.

'By the window?' John raised an eyebrow. 'Did we give Tommy a promotion?'

Charles entered just then, his timing perfect.

'Who did I give a promotion to?' he asked, walking in with casual ease.

John followed him into his new office, knocking lightly on the door frame.

'You got a moment?'

'Is it about Tommy's promotion?' Charles grinned, leaning back in his chair.

'I wanted you to hear it from me,' John said, voice quieter now. 'The government just announced the tenders for the England–Australia run.'

Charles's eyes narrowed slightly. 'Let me guess.'

'They're calling it the 'All-Red Route.'' John hesitated. 'I'm sorry, Charles. Thought it best you heard it from me.'

Charles exhaled deeply, shaking his head as if the outcome had been inevitable.

'Well. Good thing we didn't sign the lease on the bigger office, ay?' He gave a bitter laugh. 'Disappointing, John.'

'Charles, you know as well as I do . . . there is more to this,' John replied gently.

Charles stood and turned toward the window, the city skyline reflected in his eyes.

'I pioneered that route, John,' he said quietly. 'The whole damn way. All ten thousand damn miles of it.'

'We all know what this is about, Charles.'

Charles was silent for a moment, jaw tight. 'Yeah. Balance.'

Mary entered just then. Charles didn't turn.

'I have got more boxes to move,' he said, excusing himself. He left without another word, the weight of the news trailing in his posture.

Silence lingered between John and Mary.

'Did I miss something?' Mary asked, her tone casual but her eyes searching.

'Oh, it's just the move, selling the business and all, all the changes. It's nothing to worry about I am sure,' John said quickly, but the reassurance in his voice rang hollow.

'No, John. He is obsessing again. That *damn race*—I'm tired of it. It is absurd.'

'Mary . . . it is not the race.'

She stared at him. 'No? Then what is it, John? And do not shut me out like he does, I want to know.'

John hesitated, then spoke reluctantly.

'Charles received white feathers through the mail Mary.'

Mary froze. 'White feathers? From who? I do not understand John.'

John nodded grimly. 'White feathers are the mark of a coward Mary. Someone sent them to him after he withdrew from the race. They have labelled him a coward.'

Her face went pale, Mary lifted her hand to her mouth in disgust and without another word, she backed away slowly, before turning and rushing out after Charles, her heart pounding in her chest as she raced as best she could down the flights of stairs to find him.

Mary burst onto the bustling Sydney street, her heart pounding. The sun beat down heavily on the pavement, bright as her eyes adjusted. People walked busily, cars moved by filling the streets amid the city's hustling and bustling noise. Through it, Mary's eyes darted frantically, she looked hard through the all-around movement, searching.

Then—she saw him. Charles. A determined silhouette moving away.

Without hesitation, she kicked off her heels, left them where they lay and broke into a run, the rough pavement burning beneath her bare feet, as she stopped traffic moving through the street.

'Charles!' she yelled, gaining on him. 'Charles Kingsford Smith!' she called out, her voice straining under her breath. 'Sir, have you forgotten—' She stalled behind him.

Charles stopped but did not turn. 'Not now,' he said curtly, frustration tightening his tone. His shoulders were tense, his body already halfway gone.

But Mary wouldn't be pushed aside. She surged forward and grabbed his arm, spinning him to face her. '—who you are,' she finished breathlessly.

Their eyes locked. Hers, full of pain and fire. His, haunted.

'Who are you, Charles? Or have you forgotten?' Her voice trembled, but she stood her ground. She saw it—the war behind his eyes. The need to protect her clashing with the instinct to push her away.

He tried to pull back, but her grip held firm.

'I have not stood by you idealistically,' she said. 'And I will not stand by you idealistically now. How *dare* you. How dare you think, even for a second, that I—your wife, your friend, your lover—would take the judgments of others and make them my own.'

Her voice was steady now, sharp with truth. The city faded around them.

'I know you do not talk. I know you hold it in—to protect me from the horrors you've seen. But that's not strength, Charles. *Strength* is believing in me. It's knowing that I am not just behind you—but I am the one who is standing firmly beside you.'

She stepped closer, pounding her fist into his chest hard, her words rising like a battle cry.

'You are *not* a coward. Cowards run. Cowards hide. Cowards send anonymous letters filled with feathers, symbols of shame, while they hide behind their own failures. They are faceless pretenders. In their wildest dreams, they could not achieve a fraction of what you have.'

She was shaking now—not from fear, but conviction.

'And the more you carry their lies, Charles, the heavier they get. Their judgment is a weight that will *crush* you if you let it. Let it go. Let *them* go. Let them scream from the shadows. But *do not* forget who you are.'

Tears glistened in her eyes, but her voice remained strong.

'I am beside you. And I will stand here until the last breath leaves me. You *will* fight. You *will* rise. And you *will not* bow to the cries of lesser men.' Mary leaned in, the final blow landed gently, firmly, her fist turning to a palm placed over his heart. Her voice softened—but her conviction burned even brighter.

'I am beside you, and albeit my sacrifices may not be celebrated in headlines, but they are *equal* to yours.'

Charles's eyes shimmered. Something broke inside him—and something else, something vital, returned. He pulled her into a desperate embrace. His kiss was fierce, filled with apology and need and love. Around them, the world blurred. The crowd melted. The noise vanished. There was only Mary. Only this.

She held him tightly, grounding him with the strength he had forgotten.

She looked up, her gaze unwavering. 'Let me remind you who you are.' He nodded slowly, her words sinking deep, anchoring him.

'Mary,' he murmured, 'I could not do this without you.'

'You do not have to,' she replied softly, smiling through her tears.

Chapter 31

Sydney, New South Wales, Australia. 1935.

Mary helped Jess with the final touches to her wedding veil in the vestibule as they prepared to enter. John stood quietly, careful not to impose on the moment.

'You look wonderful Jess,' Mary whispered softly. The soft white fabric shimmered gently under the sunlight spilling in from the entrance. Her gown was modest, with a delicate lace and understated sophistication, a perfect blend of refinement and simplicity.

'Oh Mary, I am so nervous,' Jess whispered through the veil, her voice trembling slightly. 'Do you really think I am doing the right thing?'

Mary smiled warmly, her hands steady as she adjusted the veil. 'You are going to be very happy. You are just having some pre-wedding jitters, that is very normal,' Mary replied gently, her tone calm and reassuring.

Jess fidgeted with her fingers, her gaze bouncing anxiously.

'Let me straighten this.' Mary carefully folded the fabric of the gown, straightening it. 'I think you are ready.' Mary smiled.

'Mary, I . . . I . . . tonight, I—' She faltered, her cheeks flushing with a mix of nerves and anticipation, her heart thudding in her chest.

Mary paused, and she took Jess's hands and gave them a steady squeeze. 'Oh, Jess. You'll be just fine. Focus on your vows—the rest will all come naturally,' she said, her voice like a calming breeze. 'This day is about love. Everything else is decoration.'

Jess inhaled slowly, trying to calm the fluttering in her chest. She looked at Mary with watery eyes, overwhelmed with gratitude. 'Thank you. I do not know what I would do without you.'

'Ready?' Mary asked.

'Ready,' Jess replied.

John opened the church door, just enough to cue the proceedings. And with that, the organ began the slow march of music that would accompany them down the aisle. Charles stood proudly beside Tommy, their tuxedos fine, their posture proud as Jess, the picture of every bit of beauty a man could desire, walked slowly toward them.

As all eyes focused on Jess making her way, the sighs of awe reverberated softly off the sandstone walls.

'Do you remember your lines?' John whispered as he walked beside her.

'I do,' she replied under her breath.

'Well you have that one right,' he whispered in reply.

The comment raised Jess's smile, and she stood taller with confidence.

Charles gave Tommy a gentle nudge.

'I got a plane waiting out back if you change your mind,' Charles whispered with a playful glint in eye; the offer, however sounded somewhat serious. Mary noticed and looked sternly toward Charles with an evil eye. He straightened up immediately as John and Jess reached the altar and he gave her away.

She faced Tommy with held breath and hands that still trembled slightly. His warm, steady smile met hers and melted her nerves, if only just.

'Breathe,' Tommy whispered softly.

The light of the morning filtered through the church's tall stained glass, coloring the scene as the organ slowly came to a rest, leaving them silent in each other's gaze.

When it came time to speak, Jess's voice rang out, surprisingly steady, though a quiver still danced beneath the surface.

'I, Jess, take you, Tom, to be my lawfully wedded husband,' she began, eyes locked with his. 'To have and to hold, from this day forward, for better, for worse, for richer, for poorer, in sickness and in health, to love, honor and obey, until death do us part.'

Tom's eyes glistened as he returned the vow, his voice carrying both pride and tenderness.

'I, Tom, take you, Jessica Emily Lockett, to be my lawfully wedded wife. To have and to hold, from this day forward, for better, for worse, for richer, for poorer, in sickness and in health, to love and honor, until death do us part.'

Tommy slid the ring gently into place, adorning her fragile finger with this symbol of love and commitment—simple, elegant, eternal. It was just the two of them, bound together in the choices, the challenges, and every quiet hope they had ever shared. As their lips met, it wasn't just a kiss—it was a promise, sealed in front of family and friends, a quiet vow to face whatever might come, together.

Applause erupted around them—cheers, laughter, clinking glasses. A joyous symphony of celebration filled the air. Charles shook Tommy's hand vigorously. Jess caught Mary's gaze through the crowd, her eyes bright with happiness. A smile passed between them—pure, wordless gratitude.

Mary smiled back, her heart full. Watching Jess and Tommy step into their future, she felt the undeniable truth that some love stories were simply meant to be.

Seated among the stunning gardens of the reception, guests basked in birdsong and the warmth of spring, wine flowing freely, filling already content stomachs. Laughter and chatter rippled through the floral-scented air, while the sun cast a golden glow across elegantly adorned tables. Floral arrangements graced the white linen, their sweet aroma mingling with the rich scent of the feast laid before them.

Charles stood, tapping his glass with a knife. The gentle clinking echoed through the garden, gradually drawing the guests' attention. All eyes turned toward Tommy and Jess—she glowing in a simple, elegant gown that caught the light, he sharp and handsome in his suit, the perfect counterpart. The atmosphere brimmed with love and joy, an idyllic setting for a heartfelt speech.

'If I could have your attention, please. Ladies, gentlemen . . .' Charles called, attempting to calm the cheerful chatter. Slowly, conversations faded to a murmur. 'Please.' He smiled, waiting until silence settled. 'Thank you.'

A deep breath. 'Dearly beloved . . .'

The crowd responded with mock solemnity, echoing the tone of a church congregation. Tommy nudged him playfully, prompting a ripple of laughter that rolled warmly through the garden.

'Not my line, obviously,' Charles grinned. 'It is a great pleasure to stand before you today as the best man.' Another gentle jab from Tommy made him chuckle. 'But today is not about me. It is, of course, about Jess and Tommy. I think we can all agree Jess looks like a picture of beauty. And Tommy . . .'

Laughter stirred again.

'Grease under your nails, mate? Understandable—he is the finest engineer in the business. Which is, naturally, why I hired him. I first met Tommy at Richmond Airdrome in nineteen twenty-eight. Handsome young lad, back then. As many of you know, he was enlisted, and we became fast friends. What you may not know is . . .'

A few mock gasps and whispers of 'uh-oh' rippled through the crowd.

'. . . upon recognizing his mechanical genius,' Charles continued, nodding solemnly, 'I bought him out of his military contract so he could work for me. Which, by my calculations, means I still own Tommy for another two years, three weeks, and four days.'

The guests erupted with laughter, some raising glasses mid-toast.

'However,' Charles added with a twinkle in his eye, 'I am willing to sell him to Jess for the modest sum of one pound fifty . . .'

Laughter echoed through the garden again, richer this time.

'What? That is only slightly more than I paid. A man has to make a profit.' He raised his glass high. 'To my dear friend, business partner, and the engineer who kept me in the skies—John Thompson Pethybridge, affectionately known to us all as Tommy—and to his beautiful bride, Jessica. We wish you a long, joyful life together. It's my great honor to offer this toast to the bride and one of the best pilots I have ever known.'

'To the bride and groom!' the crowd roared in unison. Cheers, whistles, and popping corks rang out as glasses clinked, joy spreading like sunlight through the garden.

Charles found a quiet moment, standing apart from the crowd beneath the branches of a flowering tree. The background hum of music, laughter, and clinking glasses faded as he lit a cigarette, enjoying the solitude.

'Beer?' John approached, two bottles in hand.

'Yeah, thanks, John.' Charles accepted the bottle with a nod.

'It's a good thing you are a pilot, Smithy—because your speeches are bloody awful.' They laughed together, loud and easy.

'You alright?' John asked after a pause, his tone shifting.

'Just getting some air. It is a big day.'

'A good day,' John agreed. 'The government wants you to fly to New Zealand.'

'Why don't they ask Empire?' Charles asked, shoulders tightening.

'You know Empire cannot do it.'

'I am not interested, John. I am tired of paving the way for everyone else.'

'The king requested you personally, Charles.'

'George?'

'You have got friends in high places.'

'I have only met the bloke twice,' Charles dismissively replied.

'And both times, he pinned a medal on you.'

His reply earned a reluctant smile. 'When?' Charles asked.

'Next month. You will be delivering his personal mail. Looks like he is pinning this one on you, too. You cannot say no.'

'I will need the Altair.'

'They won't issue a certificate.'

'You checked?' Desperation crept into Charles's voice.

'I did.'

'You cannot be serious. The Old Bus? She is not fit for the Tasman.' Charles raised concern.

'She is all we have got. And she has done it before.'

'Tommy will be out for a while. It will be tough. Just the three of us—me, you, and Taylor. What do you think?' John raised an eye to the question.

'I think you still own the Tasman.'

'I do.' Charles's eyes lit with the spark of realization. 'I bloody do!' He clapped John on the shoulder and strode back toward the party.

'What do you want me to do?' John called after him.

'Set it up!' Charles called back, weaving through the tables until he reached Mary, seated with friends.

'Hello, darling,' she said, surprised but delighted.

'Excuse us for a moment?' he asked politely. Taking her hand, he guided her onto the dance floor and into his arms.

'Lady Mary,' he murmured softly.

'Sir Charles. What do I owe the honor?'

'Can a man not dance with his beautiful wife, simply because he wishes to?'

'You do not dance,' Mary smiled. 'We have not danced since our wedding night.'

'Seven wonderful years, three beautiful months, and twenty-three perfect days,' he replied, sweeping her into a slow dance as the music swelled around them.

'You are up to something,' she whispered. 'But I will not ask. I'm just going to enjoy this moment.'

'Good plan,' Charles said, dipping her with unexpected grace. He kissed her gently—slow, full of meaning—as the world around them faded to nothing.

Chapter 32

Canberra, Australian Capital Territory, Australia. 1935.

High above the heart of Canberra, the *Southern Cross* dipped low, held aloft by the rush of air beneath them moving effortlessly through a sea of brilliant white clouds. Below, the land gleamed under a crystal-blue sky—sunlight dancing off rolling fields of green that stretched like a velvet carpet across the landscape. In the distance, Parliament House stood dignified and solid, its bright white facade reflecting back the bright morning light, stately and unmoved.

Sheep scattered lazily across the surrounding lawns, lifting their heads as the drone of engines grew louder. The sound churned the stillness into motion, sending flocks scrambling, mustering in all directions beneath the ship's shadow.

In the cockpit, Charles and Taylor sat steady at the controls, their eyes sweeping the horizon. Behind them, Beau and John leaned forward, taking in the breathtaking view.

'Where do you want to set her down?' Taylor shouted over the engine's hum, his voice clipped by wind and altitude.

Charles squinted at the scene below, tracing the gentle curve of the land with practiced eyes. A clear stretch opened just beyond the front lawn, framed by Parliament's grandeur and a modest ring of hedgerows.

'I think right there will be good,' he called back, pointing.

Taylor nodded, already adjusting the trim. Charles took the yoke with confident ease, the aircraft banking gently, beginning her descent in a wide, deliberate arc.

The *Southern Cross* circled once more—graceful and commanding—before angling in, ready to land upon the political soil that had so often debated his legacy.

A secretary walked Charles, John, Beau, and Taylor into Shephard's small office.

'It is very nice to meet you Sir Charles.' Shephard extended his hand, greeting him warmly.

'I trust you know John Stannage and Patrick Gordon Taylor, or Bill, and Beau Sheil,' Charles replied, introducing them.

'Welcome, welcome to Canberra, please take a seat. Tea? Biscuits?'

'Where fine thank you,' Taylor replied on their behalf.

'Well I must say, congratulations on the flight crossing the mighty Pacific. It certainly was an extraordinary achievement for the country, for the Commonwealth,' Shephard said.

Charles sneaked a look sideways to John and Bill.

'Thank you, it was,' Charles replied.

'We are very grateful for your time, as you are aware the Jubilee Mail Flight is fast approaching. The minister unfortunately had other obligations. He has expressed his apologies for not attending our meeting today, he also expressed his excitement toward your involvement in this historic event celebrating the completion of the All-Red Route.'

Moments later, the four of them sat on the steps of Parliament House like a group of schoolboys, fresh from the office headmaster, caught between mischief and memory. They soaked in patches of sunlight that drifted over them.

Elbows on knees, jackets unbuttoned, they gazed out over the rolling lawn where the *Southern Cross* stood parked with casual perfection. The giant silver wing atop her body glinted, engines silent now, casting a long shadow across the green.

Around her, sheep grazed contentedly—wandering between wheel struts, oblivious to her purpose, other than the shade she offered. The whole scene was absurdly serene.

'The way that bloke carried on,' Charles muttered, a grin breaking across his face, 'you'd swear *they* flew the Pacific.'

The others laughed.

'You did not throw any fists,' Beau teased. 'You getting soft in your old age?'

'Thirty-eight ain't old,' Charles shot back, mock defensive.

'Christ, you look like crap, Smithy. I thought you were sixty,' Taylor added, deadpan.

The laughter came harder now, full-bellied and unrestrained.

Silence settled for a beat, the kind born from shared air and long friendships.

Charles looked around, letting his eyes sweep across the quiet countryside that stretched beyond the city's core.

'This really is in the middle of nowhere,' he said. 'You have gotta wonder why they stuck the bloody capital here.'

'Safer,' Stannage offered, smirking. 'The people can't get to 'em.'

Another round of chuckles.

But then Charles's gaze drifted back to the *Southern Cross*, and the humor faded from his face.

'The Tasman flight is a hard flight,' he said, voice lower now—weighted.

Taylor turned to him, more serious. 'Worried?'

'No more than you blokes should be,' Charles said, his eyes never leaving the plane. 'You are coming with me, remember.'

The four of them sat in stillness then, watching the sheep roam under the shadow of history. The wind rustled through the grass, and somewhere in the distance, the soft sound of a bell rang out.

And for a moment, nothing moved—except time.

Sir Duddevin stood motionless, half-shadowed by the heavy curtain, watching from the tall window with a careful eye. He did not lean forward, nor draw attention to himself—caution shaped his posture. The distortion of the old glass warped the scene slightly, but there was no mistaking the figure outside.

Charles moved with purpose across the lawn, making final preparations. From the distance, even his gestures seemed imbued with certainty.

Shephard stood beside Duddevin, his hands neatly folded behind his back, his eyes also fixed on the man below.

'He was surprisingly pleasant,' Shephard offered, voice neutral but tinged with thought. 'Even went as far as to compliment you on your plans, sir. I can certainly appreciate the sentiments of the people in their support for his greatness.'

Duddevin's jaw twitched, his eyes still locked on the figure beyond the glass.

'The Australian government does not support *greatness*, Shephard,' he said coldly. 'It supports the *Commonwealth*.'

There was no room for misunderstanding.

'Yes, sir,' Shephard replied quickly, his attempt at lightness shut down with precision.

A long pause followed.

'And Shephard,' Duddevin added, voice low but sharp, 'next time . . . ensure that you instruct Kingsford Smith not to park on the lawn. It is manicured.'

Shephard nodded, biting back a smile that would never see daylight.

'Yes, sir.'

Chapter 33

Sydney, New South Wales, Australia. 1935.

Mary stood in the kitchen, gently spoon-feeding Charles Jr., smiling as she concentrated on the task of maintaining his attention on eating.

'Here comes Daddy. . . delivering the mail . . . all the way over the ocean . . .' she cooed, playfully drawing out her words whilst swooping the spoon through the air like a miniature aircraft. Charles Jr. giggled, reaching for the spoon with chubby fingers.

The telephone rang.

Mary paused. She reached for it, tucking the receiver tightly between her shoulder and ear.

She listened.

Her smile vanished instantly.

The handset slipped from her shoulder, clattering against the countertop as she rushed to the wireless.

She turned the dial sharply, static giving way to the crackling voice of the radio announcer.

'*We repeat. Urgent distress calls have been received from the Southern Cross, being flown by Sir Charles Kingsford Smith and Captain P. G. Taylor, en route to New Zealand carrying the Jubilee Mail . . .*'

The words hit like a slap. The walls closed in, shrinking the room.

At that moment, the front door burst open.

'Surprise, we are back!' Tommy and Jess chimed together, laughing as they stepped inside, still glowing from their honeymoon.

'Tommy!' Mary called, urgency cracking her voice. The ghostly look on her face said it all. Tommy immediately dropped his case and rushed toward her. Jess followed as Mary covered the quiver of her lip. Jess froze, the voice from the speaker bellowed.

'*The signal, transmitted by radioman John Stannage onboard, reports the aircraft in grave peril, heading toward the sea. One engine has been lost. Their fate, at this time, is unknown . . .*'

Tommy sprang off his heels, making for the door.

'I have to go.'

'Where?' Jess asked, stunned, fear now blooming over her demeanor.

'I need a plane,' he yelled as the door slammed behind him.

Low over the angry ocean, the swell heaved beneath the *Southern Cross* in its battle to stay aloft.

The starboard engine was dead—its propeller blade snapped clean away—leaving the center engine and port engine to work hard against the increased drag.

John leaned desperately over the radio, sending frantic transmissions into the void, his hands shaking with the force of urgency, frantically navigating between messages in order to secure their position for anyone listening to their cry.

'Still losing altitude!' Taylor yelled across to Charles, his voice barely cutting through the exhausting roar and wind.

Wrestling the controls, Charles could feel the aircraft sagging under the strain.

'We need to lose weight!' he barked back, his hands heavy and brutal on the yoke.

Then—another cry.

'We have smoke!' Taylor yelled, pointing across the cockpit.

The port motor was overheating, and a stream of blue smoke trailed through the air into the distance behind them.

Rapidly, his eyes dancing from gauge to gauge across the instrument panel, Charles continually assessed status. The oil pressure gauge was falling—steadily, remorselessly.

The *Southern Cross* shuddered and groaned against the sky, fighting a battle she could not win.

'We are too heavy!' Charles yelled. 'Dump the fuel and anything we don't need.'

Sir Duddevin stood motionless at the window of his office, his eyes fixed on the horizon beyond the sandstone colonnades of Parliament House. The late afternoon light filtered in, casting long shadows across the polished floor and the rows of parliamentary papers spread on his desk.

Behind him, Shephard hovered near the wireless set, adjusting the dial with careful precision. The familiar crackle of static gave way to a low, solemn voice that filled the room like a creeping fog.

'*Still no further word has been received,*' the announcer intoned, his voice tight with emotion, '*as the entire nation waits breathlessly for news from the ill-fated Southern Cross. . .*'

The words lingered, heavy in the air.

Neither man spoke.

The wireless hummed softly, a haunting undertone to the tension that now gripped the country—and the silence in that room.

Shephard glanced at Duddevin's back, uncertain if he should speak, uncertain if he dared.

But Sir Duddevin remained still, his shoulders squared, his face unreadable in the reflection of the glass. He didn't turn. He didn't move.

He simply stared outward—into a sky that, for all his power and planning, held no answers.

Away from the radio, John made his way forward, bracing himself heavily against the trembling airframe between Charles and Taylor in the cockpit.

'That is everything except the radio!' he shouted over the deafening roar.

'We are still too heavy!' Charles yelled back, fighting the stick with brutal focus.

'There's nothing left!' John replied, desperate.

Charles didn't hesitate.

'Ditch the mail!' he barked.

John spun on his heel and raced back into the cabin.

One by one, he grabbed the heavy canvas satchels—precious cargo, hundreds of letters and messages destined for loved ones—and hurled them out the open hatch.

The satchels tumbled end over end into the raging sea, disappearing with a final splash into the endless ocean.

The bar had fallen still.

Beer glasses hovered halfway to mouths, card games froze mid-hand, and cigarette smoke seemed to hang motionless in the air. All eyes were fixed on the battered radio perched on the shelf behind the bar, its glowing dial the only light in the room.

Someone had turned up the volume, and the static gave way to a breathless voice:

'*This! Just in! Ladies and gentlemen . . . the Southern Cross is still in the air.*'

A gasp rippled through the crowd.

The bartender leaned in closer, his hands still gripping the tap. A man at the end of the bar crossed himself. A woman in the corner clutched her scarf to her mouth.

'*They have turned back ladies and gentlemen, they have turned back toward Australia, the crew of the Southern Cross are reporting their position at four hundred miles from the Australian mainland . . . with one engine out—*'

Murmurs rose around the room.

'*—and now, ladies and gentlemen a second engine is failing.*'

Gasps turned to stunned silence.

The voice continued, faltering only slightly.

'*. . . forcing the crew to dump the Jubilee Mail overboard into the sea.*'

There was no reaction at first. Just stunned stillness. Then, a glass clinked softly on a table. Someone exhaled sharply. A man whispered, 'God help them.'

'Come on, Smithy!' another murmured as the bar remained frozen, a room full of strangers united by a single fragile signal from the sky.

The smoke streaming from the failing port engine thickened, billowing behind them.

'We are not going to make it!' Charles yelled, his voice ragged from the strain. 'We are losing too much pressure!'

At the rear of the cabin, John hurled the final satchel, the gauges dipped lower, and the frame of the *Southern Cross* shuddered under the failing thrust.

Then—Taylor leaned forward, his eyes flashing with sudden, desperate inspiration.

'I have an idea!' he shouted, ripping his briefcase from the compartment beside him.

Charles shot him a look—part disbelief, part last-ditch hope—as the aircraft continued to sink lower.

The house was quiet, the kind of silence that swells when everyone is listening at once.

A family—mother, father, children—stood huddled in the living room, their neighbors gathered close behind them. The radio crackled from its place atop the sideboard, its single green eye glowing as if it too were straining to catch every word.

'*Three hundred miles out,*' the announcer said, his voice urgent, barely above a whisper. '*The Southern Cross is still in the air, as it limps toward the mainland . . .*'

The father gripped his beer bottle tightly. One of the children clung to her mother's hand. The air was thick with tension, as if breathing too loud might break the signal.

'My dear Lord,' the announcer continued, audibly moved. *'Ladies and gentlemen . . . we have a report just in.'*

The crowd leaned closer.

'John Stannage radioing from aboard the ill-fated aircraft is reporting Captain P. G. Taylor has climbed out on the wing.'

Gasps.

The mother covered her mouth. The boy nearest the set blinked, unsure he heard right.

'*Yes, ladies and gentlemen,*' the announcer repeated, slower this time, reverent, '*Captain Taylor has climbed out onto the wing . . .*'

The room fell into stunned silence.

The image was unthinkable—and yet, perfectly real. Out there, somewhere over the sea, a man clung to a flying aircraft in the midst of a storm and failing engines, defying death with nothing but resolve and instinct.

The children looked to the adults, eyes wide, waiting for reassurance no one could give.

And the voice on the radio went on, weaving history into the air.

Gripping the strut above him with one arm, Taylor braced himself against the fuselage, his soles pressed firmly on the narrow two-inch-wide metal support below. He looked down—the caps, dips, and peaks of the ocean surged beneath him, rippling past in a blur of violent motion.

'Steady now,' John called, leaning out to hand him a spanner.

Taylor took it, loosened the drain plug, then passed the tool back. In return, John handed him a coffee thermos. They repeated the process over and over, slowly filling Taylor's briefcase with the precious oil.

Taylor's hands were slick, the metal slippery under his grip. Beneath the white-knuckled tightness of fate, he clambered back into the cockpit.

Inside, John—pale and sweating—emptied the oil from the briefcase into the thermos, slow and steady.

No time for words.

No time for fear.

Taylor climbed out again, this time toward the starboard engine. Smoke still streamed from it, trailing the force it barely sustained. As he reached for the cowling, the slipstream struck him hard, flinging him sideways. His shoes skidded. His body twisted.

For a heart-stopping second, he dangled—arms flailing, fingers scraping for purchase—nothing between him and the roaring sea below.

With a wild grunt, he found the strut again, hauled himself back, chest heaving, lungs burning.

'There's too much force!' he bellowed.

Without hesitation, Charles pushed the nose up, grinding the *Southern Cross* higher into thinner air. He threw a hand signal back and throttled the dying starboard engine to idle.

The pressure dropped instantly. The aircraft sagged. The ocean began to rise.

Taylor didn't wait.

Out again—muscles burning—he fought his way along the strut, wedging himself against the cowling. The wind ripped at him. Heat seared through his clothes as he removed the fill cap.

John leaned out, stretching with the thermos. Taylor reached back, took it, and poured, gripping the strut with everything he had.

Inside, Charles fought alone, nerves taut, hands fused to the controls. The *Southern Cross* bucked and groaned, bleeding speed and life.

The altimeter spun downward.

The ocean rose.

Gravity clawed at his gut.

'Come on, Bill,' Charles muttered through gritted teeth. 'Come on!'

Taylor slammed the empty thermos shut and crawled back, battered, burned, and barely hanging on.

As he grabbed the strut, Charles roared the throttle forward. The engines screamed. The old girl climbed, inch by tortured inch.

John, soaked in sweat, refilled the thermos.

Without a word, the cycle began again.

Mary sat stiffly in the armchair, her hands clasped in her lap, eyes fixed on the radio across the room. The soft hum of static crackled between spoken words, and her breath caught as the announcer returned.

'*There have been no reports on the fate of the Southern Cross,*' the voice said, solemn and clear.

'*We can only fear for the worst and hope for the best, as we wait for further word . . .*'

The radio transitioned into soft music—'Cheek to Cheek' by Fred Astaire. A popular ballad, but in that moment, it sounded like a lullaby for the lost.

'*Heaven, I'm in heaven,*
And my heart beats so that I can hardly speak,
And I seem to find the happiness I seek,
When we're out together dancing, cheek to cheek . . .'

Mary stared ahead, blinking slowly. Her foot tapped the floor unconsciously. Every tick of the clock was a throb of helplessness.

The front door opened gently.

'Nancy,' Jess called softly as the woman stepped in, already removing her gloves.

'I came straight over,' Nancy said, crossing to them.

She paused as she noticed the telephone, still dangling off the hook. Silently, she replaced it.

It rang almost immediately.

Everyone jumped.

Nancy picked it up without hesitation.

'Hello . . . yes . . . thank you, Tommy.'

She turned to Mary, eyes bright with urgency.

'Mary—Tommy wants you there.'

Mary nodded, already rising. Her face was pale but focused. She didn't ask where. She didn't need to.

'*That was the sound of Fred Astaire with his new song 'Cheek to Cheek,''* the radio continued, his voice returning.

'*As we wait in hope for an update on the fate of the Southern Cross...*'

The music faded behind them as they gathered their coats and stepped into the unknown.

Taylor, slick with oil and trembling from exhaustion, clawed his way back into the cockpit, collapsing hard into his seat.

His suit was soaked, blackened from head to toe, his face smeared black.

Charles shot him a glance—quick, fierce, grateful—but said nothing. No words were needed.

With steady hands, Charles reached for the throttle.

He eased the port motor back up to full throttle.

For a moment, the engine sputtered, coughing black smoke, threatening to die.

They held their breath.

The oil pressure needle, trembling on the gauge, began to rise—slowly, painfully—creeping back toward the green.

Taylor and Charles locked eyes.

They watched it climb.

The Old Bus wasn't dead yet.

The pub was packed, it was standing room only but no one was speaking.

Every patron stood or sat with their eyes fixed on the radio set mounted above the bar. The bartender had turned it up full. Even the clink of glassware had stilled. Smoke curled lazily in the air, forgotten.

Then, through the fuzz of static, the announcer's voice cracked to life once more.

'Ladies and gentlemen . . . we have just received another urgent transmission from the Southern Cross . . .'

A beat. Every soul leaned in.

'The Southern Cross is within sight of the mainland . . . with some twenty miles to go.'

For half a heartbeat, the silence held—fragile, suspended.

Then the room erupted.

Cheers burst like a dam breaking. Men slammed their hands on the bar. Women wept and laughed at once. Hats flew, drinks spilled, and strangers embraced like family. A song started—half-formed and joyous—before dissolving into a roar of relief and jubilation.

The impossible was suddenly, gloriously within reach.

The *Southern Cross* limped low over the churning ocean, barely clinging to the wounded air.

Her engines coughed and sputtered, the battered frame sagging relentlessly.

Ahead—the coastline.

Thin at first, a wavering line between water and sky.

Then clearer.

The crowds had already gathered.

Lining the foreshore, thousands stood shoulder to shoulder, straining their eyes toward the horizon. Men, women, and children—hats clutched in their hands, flags drooping in the damp sea wind.

Waiting.

Hoping.

Praying.

As the aircraft staggered closer, a tremor ran through the masses—a wave of sound, half cheer, half gasp—as the battered *Southern Cross* crept into view, defying the odds, refusing to fall.

Then the roar lifted as she made it, passing overhead. The old bus was home.

The radio studio was alive with electric tension.

Technicians hovered over consoles, and reporters leaned forward into their microphones, scripts clutched tight in their sweating hands.

A sudden flurry of movement—the announcer pressed his finger to his earpiece, listening intently.

Then he spoke, voice trembling with emotion.

'This just in—

'A pause, a breath.

The Southern Cross has passed the coastline, headed for Mascot!'

Another heartbeat.

'Ladies and gentlemen—they are home. Charles Kingsford Smith and the Southern Cross are home!'

Cheers erupted in the background—wild, irrepressible. The sound of feet stamping, hands clapping, hats thrown into the air.

Across Sydney, radios blared the news into the streets, into homes, into hearts.

But not everywhere was the sound of celebration.

At the other end of the city, within the cold, oak-paneled chambers of government, Sir Duddevin stood rigid by his desk, his face a mask of thunder.

He slammed a palm onto the polished wood with a sharp crack that echoed through the marble halls.

His mouth tightened into a thin, furious line.

The wheels of the *Southern Cross* kissed the earth at Mascot, bouncing once, twice, before settling heavy and sure onto the runway.

The battered aircraft taxied to a rough stop, engines sputtering to silence.

For a moment, there was nothing but stunned stillness.

Then—the crowd surged.

A tidal wave of humanity broke across the field, roaring, cheering, weeping.

Before they could even climb down, hands were reaching for them.

John Stannage and Bill Taylor were swept up onto the shoulders of the crowd, carried aloft like conquering heroes. Their laughter and protests were lost in the deafening celebration.

Charles fought his way through the pressing throng, ducking hands, pushing past well-wishers and wide-eyed children, heart hammering in his chest.

He wasn't looking for adoration.

He was looking for her.

Frantic, his eyes scanned the sea of faces, blurred with sweat and exhaustion and raw emotion.

And then—there she was.

Mary.

Tears streaked her face, her arms reaching for him even before he could reach her.

Charles surged forward, grabbing her up into a fierce, crushing embrace.

Neither spoke.

There was no need.

In that moment, with the world roaring around them, they were the only two people alive.

Leaning against the perimeter fence, Taylor stared out across the field. The activity beyond was steady—mechanics moving between planes, the hum of engines starting, tools clinking. But Taylor wasn't seeing any of it. He stood quiet, thoughts drifting, eyes distant.

'You never get tired of it, do you?' Charles said, approaching softly and taking his place beside him.

'We are getting too old for this,' Taylor replied, his voice low and contemplative.

Charles smiled, a hint of sarcasm warming the words. 'I do not know, Bill. A couple of young lads like us? I reckon we have got a few more oceans left in us.'

Taylor chuckled faintly, but his eyes didn't leave the horizon. 'If I was not working with you, I would have been on Charlie's flight.'

Charles nodded. No need for words. He understood.

'That . . . the Pacific . . . now this,' Taylor continued. 'Makes a man think.'

'You are not quitting on me, are you, Bill?' Charles asked, with a sidelong glance.

'No,' Taylor said, smiling now, softer. 'Men like you and me, Smithy—we do not know the meaning of the word. I am just taking a break. It has been an honor flying with you, Charles. I will see you in the skies again.'

Charles clapped him on the shoulder. 'Come on then. You can buy me a beer—for saving your life.'

'Saving my life?' Taylor raised an eyebrow, half-amused, half-challenging.

'Again,' Charles added with a grin as they started walking toward the hangar.

The conversation trailed after them like contrails in a clear sky.

'I think *you* should be buying *me* a beer?' Taylor asked.

'No, see, the way I figure it—' Charles began.

'Oh, the way *you* figure it,' Taylor interrupted. 'Do me a favor—next time you need an oil change, don't call me.'

Chapter 34

Parliament House
Canberra, Australian Capital Territory, Australia. 1935.

The chamber of the House of Representatives buzzed with debate. Papers rustled, voices rose and fell in a steady rumble of democracy at work. Then, the room quieted as Sir Duddevin rose to speak.

Composed, his voice carried practiced authority.

'Mr. Speaker,' he began, 'as a result of the failure by Sir Charles Kingsford Smith to complete the Jubilee Mail Flight—and the fact that it very nearly cost him his own life, and also that of the lives of the crew—the public has voiced considerable concern.'

Murmurs echoed faintly across the chamber.

'The people have called upon the government to retire Sir Charles Kingsford Smith's aircraft, the *Southern Cross*,' Duddevin continued. 'It is now perceived not merely as a machine, but as a national icon. A vessel worthy of preservation. A symbol of courage, yes—but also of caution. And as such, it should be placed in the trust of the Commonwealth for permanent display, it should stand as a memorial and as a testament to the achievements of this great nation.'

He paused, allowing the words to settle.

'At the request of the Australian people,' he declared, 'I hereby move a motion to purchase the aircraft at a cost of three thousand pounds—a sum more than fair, and wholly reasonable.'

A moment of stillness followed.

The Speaker rose.

'All in favor, say 'Aye."

A resounding chorus echoed from the benches:

'Aye!'
Unanimous.
The motion passed.

Sir Duddevin strode briskly through the marbled corridors of Parliament House, the echo of his polished shoes bouncing off the stone walls. Shephard followed close behind, notebook in hand, matching his pace but saying nothing.

Duddevin's jaw was set, his eyes ahead, unmoved by the murmurs of nearby staffers or the ceremonial portraits lining the hall.

He muttered, just loud enough for Shephard to hear—

'It is hard to fly without wings.'

The corners of his mouth twitched—not quite a smile.

And they walked on.

Kingsford Smith Air Services
Mascot, Sydney, Australia. 1935.

Charles stood beside the *Southern Cross*, sleeves rolled up, swapping out the old timber propeller blades for new aluminum ones. The heavy scent of oil, sweat, and metal filled the hangar. His hands worked in practiced silence, each motion measured, deliberate. Outside, the light dimmed slightly as clouds rolled in—just enough to make the steel gleam beneath his grip.

John stepped into the hangar, hesitation in his stride.

'What is the number?' Charles asked.

'The offer is three thousand,' he said cautiously.

Charles didn't glance up. 'I could get three times that from Eastern Air,' he replied, voice edged with frustration. 'Without her, we are not earning.'

He gave the wrench a final tug. The metal rang out—a sharp punctuation to his point.

'Look, with everything that has happened—' John started, but the words faded as footsteps echoed behind him.

Taylor entered, followed by a tall man in his early forties. Beau Sheil carried himself like a man used to decision-making—broad-shouldered, impeccably dressed for the hangar in a tailored jacket and crisp shirt rolled at the sleeves. His presence was that of a man who now dealt in flight paths and risk ledgers more than wrenches. He was handsome, clean-shaven, with sharp blue eyes and a quiet, confident smile.

'I thought you could use a good man,' Taylor said, clapping Beau on the back. 'Beau was working with Charlie.'

Charles finally looked up, wiping his hands on a rag.

He extended his hand without pause.

'Welcome aboard, Beau.'

Beau shook it firmly. 'Glad to be here,' he said, completely unfazed by the grease left behind.

In the middle of a wide, grassy field, hidden from the world, the afternoon sun poured molten gold across the landscape. Wildflowers bent in the breeze. The Tiger Moth cast a broad wing of shade where a worn picnic blanket lay strewn with the remnants of a half-forgotten meal.

Wrapped together in a thick blanket, Tommy and Jess lay tangled in each other's arms. Jess's hair brushed Tommy's chest, her fingers tracing slow, dreamy patterns over his skin.

It was the kind of perfect day every girl dreamed of—sun-warmed skin, blue skies, nothing but love between them.

'I wish we could just keep flying forever,' Jess whispered, her breath stirring against his skin.

Tommy stirred slightly.

'I am leaving tomorrow for America with Charles,' he said—flatly, almost casually, like announcing the weather.

Jess stiffened.

She sat bolt upright, clutching the blanket around herself, her face taut with disbelief.

'What?' she demanded, her voice sharp.

Tommy barely looked rattled. He leaned back lazily on one elbow.

'We are taking the *Lady Southern Cross* from America to England. Under the treaty between the US and the UK, Charles can get her listed on the British register, and then force recognition here. I think he wants me to fly her back with him.'

Jess blinked at him, stunned.

'We just got married,' she said, her voice tight with hurt.

Tommy shrugged, reaching up to tug playfully at the blanket around her shoulders.

'That is why you're coming with me,' he said, grinning wide. 'I thought we could meet in London. Second honeymoon!'

For a beat, Jess just stared at him, her heart thudding painfully.

Then realization dawned. Her face softened. Her lips parted in a slow, incredulous smile.

'You mean it?' she breathed.

'Of course I mean it. London, Jess. Paris if you want. Hell, we will fly the whole continent if you like.'

Jess laughed—an astonished, bubbling laugh—and dove back into his arms, peppering his face with kisses.

'You absolute devil,' she said, still half laughing, half crying. 'You could have *led* with that!'

Tommy caught her, laughing too, the blanket slipping away as they tumbled back into the sun-warmed grass.

'I like watching you get riled up,' he teased, nuzzling against her hair.

Jess thumped him lightly on the chest.

'You are lucky I love you,' she said, mock-stern, before slowly leaning back in to kiss Tommy deeply.

Chapter 35

Mascot Aerodrome
Sydney, New South Wales, Australia. 1935.

Charles moved with practiced ease, guiding the small group of passengers aboard the *Southern Cross*. The aircraft, dignified with age, gleamed faintly in the morning light. Among the passengers was a young boy—John Ulm—Charlie's son, dressed in an oversized military uniform that hung from his slight frame like a borrowed memory.

As Charles turned from helping a passenger aboard, Beau stepped toward him, a small item cradled in his palm.

'These were among Charlie's things,' Beau said quietly, holding out the pair of aviation wings. 'I know he would've wanted you to have them. Thought you might like to fly with them one last time.'

Charles looked down at the wings—worn but polished, still proud. He grasped them firmly, nodding once to Beau, a silent bond passing between them.

He jogged across the tarmac toward the hangar where Mary stood, her hands folded neatly before her, nerves hidden behind a calm smile.

'Are you sure you want to do this?' Charles asked as he reached her, his brow furrowed with concern.

Mary stepped forward, her posture straightening. 'I am going to have to face my fear sometime,' she said. 'Might as well be today.'

Charles smiled, pride warming his face. 'We'll be fine. It's only a short hop.'

'I am proud of you,' he added, his voice low, reassuring. His hand found hers, their fingers locking for a moment.

'Well,' Mary said with a smirk, 'maybe if I like it, you can fly me around the world. To all those exotic places you always talk about.'

He leaned in, and she kissed him softly on the lips—just a peck, but full of promise.

'I would like that,' Charles replied.

Mary straightened her shoulders theatrically, putting on a voice like a genteel old woman. 'Now, just no loopy loops while we are up there, Mr. Kingsford Smith,' she said, winking as she stepped aboard.

Charles laughed. 'Yes, ma'am.'

The engines roared to life, and the *Southern Cross* began her run.

She lifted into the sky with grace and familiarity, her form still commanding, still elegant in flight. Charles sat at the controls, the wind through the vents cool and familiar, his hands steady on the yoke.

A moment later, a soft voice behind him.

'Can I come in?'

It was John Ulm.

Charles turned and smiled. 'Come on. Take a seat.'

John settled into the copilot's chair, his eyes wide, hands tentative.

Charles gestured to the controls. 'Go on.'

The boy's hands reached for the yoke.

'You are going to make a great pilot someday, John.'

Below them, the countryside unrolled in slow, green waves. Hills and rivers and tiny townships passed beneath their wings as the *Southern Cross* glided forward—carrying with her the past, the present, and the promise of all that was still to come.

Richmond Airforce Base
Sydney, New South Wales, Australia. 1935.

The *Southern Cross* sat proudly on the open field, she gleamed.

Around her, a fanfare of activity unfolded. A military band played with measured pomp, its brass tones ringing out over the crowd. Press cameras clicked in staccato bursts, and the murmur of gathered spectators filled the air like a rising tide. A large podium had been erected near the aircraft, its red carpet flanked by uniformed officials and rows of chairs already half filled.

She had landed her final landing, flown her final flight, and drawn her last crowd.

A burst of feedback cracked through the loudspeakers, followed by the clipped, familiar voice of Sir Duddevin.

'So it is with great pride that the Australian government acquires the *Southern Cross* for the people of Australia, as a permanent memorial for future generations to gaze upon—as a symbol of the achievements in aviation by this great nation.'

Applause followed, polite but strong. Flashbulbs popped.

Charles stepped forward, accepting the microphone with a nod. His jacket was pressed, his medals gleaming—but his expression bore the weight of a goodbye decades in the making.

'It is with shared sadness and happiness that I hand over the *Southern Cross*,' he said, voice steady despite the pull of memory. 'Sadness in the fact that Charlie is not here with us. And happiness that his memory will live on . . . in hers.'

He paused, clearing his throat. 'I am not one for speeches, as most of you know. But I wrote a few words I'd like to share.'

He unfolded a small slip of paper from his pocket and began to read.

> 'Old faithful friend, a fond adieu—These are poor words with which to tellOf all my pride, my joy in you.True to the end, you've served me well.
> I pity those who cannot seeThat heart and soul are housed within—This thing of steel and wood, to me,You live in every bolt and pin.
> And so, my staunch and steadfast steed,Your deep and mighty voice must cease.Faithful till death—if God will heed,My prayer, dear pal . . . you'll rest in peace.'

His voice cracked at the final line. He paused, lowered the paper, and stepped back from the microphone, letting silence take the space he could no longer fill.

Applause rose slowly, like a respectful wave. This was not the thunder of celebration—it was the hush of remembrance, the farewell of a nation to a vessel that had once carried its dreams across oceans.

As the final notes of the band's recessional played out, the doors of a great hangar began to open. The crowd parted.

Charles and Mary stood together, hand in hand, as the *Southern Cross* was wheeled slowly toward the shadows.

The aircraft moved with grace, as if she too understood the gravity of the moment. Her wheels turned gently over the field. Her propellers stood still.

And then she was gone—into the dark depths of the hangar.

Sydney, New South Wales, Australia. 1935.

Mary clasped Charles's hands as they sat together in the back seat of the taxi, the city rolling past them like an old filmstrip.

Outside the window, the glow of Sydney Harbour flickered in and out of view—gold and silver reflections dancing on the water. The steel girders of the great bridge whipped past in rhythmic intervals, momentarily obscuring the skyline as if the city itself couldn't decide whether to show them its face.

Mary watched, admiring, then turned toward Charles.

'Sad?' she asked gently.

Charles's gaze didn't shift, but his expression softened. 'A little, yes,' he said. 'A lot of memories, Mare.'

A faint smile touched his lips, though his eyes held something deeper. Not grief exactly—more a quiet ache, as if he were watching part of himself disappear in the rearview mirror.

'It is a good thing,' Mary said, her thumb brushing over his hand. 'They will take good care of her.'

'I know.' He nodded slowly. 'I just . . . I have this strange feeling.'

His voice dropped a register.

'It feels like I'm never going to see her again.'

Mary didn't answer right away. She leaned closer, resting her head gently against his shoulder, her hand still holding his, like an anchor.

Circular Quay
Sydney, New South Wales, Australia. 1935.

The scene at the passenger terminal was a blend of sounds, each one adding to the vibrant, pulsing atmosphere of the docks. As the steamship *Aorangi* prepared for its voyage, the air was alive with falling crepe paper streamers and ticker tape, as if the very harbor held its breath in anticipation.

The distant cries of seagulls arced sharply across the sky, weaving through the steady hum of conversation from the crowds gathered at the edge of the sea. Passengers, dockworkers, and tearful well-wishers formed a sea of voices—some brisk with purpose, others heavy with goodbye. The rise and fall of chatter mimicked the rhythm of the waves lapping against the pier, creating a living soundscape that seemed to stretch to the horizon.

Dockworkers barked commands, their voices rough and urgent over the grind of gears and the scrape of wooden pallets being dragged into place. Crates thudded heavily against the ground, the groan of straining timbers underscoring the muscle of the work. Metal chains clinked and clattered as they were hoisted and hooked, forming a metallic percussion that kept time with the industry of departure.

Above the chaos, the *Aorangi's* horn bellowed—a deep, resonant moan that rippled across the harbor like the call of some ancient leviathan. It cut through the din like a blade, a sound that was both a command and a lament, a voice that spoke of partings and distances and the ache of what must be left behind.

Aboard the ship, the crew moved with purpose. Bells clanged from deep within the vessel, each chime a signal, each note a call to action. The faint, steady hiss of steam escaping from valves whispered of the raw power that would soon drive the liner through vast, unforgiving waters.

Children's laughter pealed through the air, bright and piercing, a joyful contrast to the tension-laced murmurs of adults embracing for the last time. A few dogs barked with excited confusion, their energy adding a touch of chaotic warmth to the bittersweet tableau.

Near the gangway, Charles and Mary stood close, almost impervious to the world around them. Their hands were linked tightly, as though sheer grip could halt time. Charles leaned in, voice low and threaded with reverence. 'Remember this one?'

Mary smiled, her eyes already glassy with memory. 'This is the ship we met on. We had our first kiss right up there.' She pointed to the upper deck, where a pennant fluttered lazily in the breeze.

Their voices were nearly lost in the ocean of sound, but their connection carved a quiet space of its own—fragile, suspended, sacred. As if the very noise of the docks dared not intrude for too long.

A shrill whistle pierced the air as a stevedore directed his team, jolting the moment. The trill faded, but its interruption lingered like a ripple on still water.

The engines, not yet fully alive, issued a low, steady rumble—an audible heartbeat of steel and steam. The sound resonated through the soles of their shoes, vibrating in their bones, a deep note of inevitability.

Charles suddenly swept Mary off the ground, spinning her gently. Her laugh rang out—pure, crystalline—soaring above the clamor like a bell. Passersby glanced over, momentarily caught in the brightness of their joy.

'Exactly seven years, five months, and forty-three days ago today,' he announced proudly.

Mary chuckled, brushing his cheek with her fingertips. 'Two days,' she corrected, amusement twinkling in her eyes.

'Oh no, we hadn't crossed the international date line yet,' he replied with mock seriousness, a grin tugging at his lips. She laughed again, and in that sound was the echo of shared lives, of countless private jokes and endless understanding.

The clank of a nearby crane added rhythm to the moment, the metallic screech of pulleys offering its own commentary. The harbor was alive with sound, but Charles and Mary stood in the eye of it, sheltered in memory and love.

'A picture, Sir Charles?' A young press photographer appeared suddenly, camera raised. The whirr of the shutter captured them in a candid embrace, the click echoing like the ticking of a clock counting down to departure.

The ship's horn blared once more, longer now, more insistent. This time, it seemed to pull the breath from the crowd, the sound hanging like a fog in the air. In its wake came a hush, a pause in the cacophony, as if the world held still for one final heartbeat.

In that quiet, Mary looked up, her voice steady but soft, lined with emotion. 'Do we still have a deal?'

Charles met her gaze, his eyes shining with unspoken promises. 'We still have a deal.'

They leaned in, their foreheads touching in a final moment of closeness. The kiss that followed was gentle, unhurried—a seal upon a vow spoken long ago.

Then he stepped back.

'Got to go.' His voice cracked ever so slightly as he turned and jogged toward the gangway.

Mary stood frozen as he reached the top, pausing to look back with a wave and that familiar, boyish smile.

She waved in return, holding it as long as she could. Around her, the world resumed its roar—shouts, waves, laughter, sobs. The swell of goodbye.

She turned in a slow circle, surrounded by strangers hugging and crying, hands clutching kerchiefs, arms stretched in farewell. The air smelled of salt and smoke and emotion too heavy to name.

Her eyes searched the deck again, hoping—irrationally, desperately—for one last glimpse. But he was gone.

Mary bowed her head, her hands still curled in the shape of his. The swell of sound rose once more around her, but in her heart, there was only the hush of parting, the silence that falls when a piece of your soul sails away.

Parliament House
Wellington, New Zealand. 1935.

Charles stood before the New Zealand Parliament.

The chamber was alive with murmurs and shifting gazes, a space where formality wrestled with fire. The parliamentarians, seated on deep red leather benches, had been immersed in heated debates all morning—each voice layered with the strain of navigating a nation through the economic grip.

The legislative chamber itself bore the weight of empire; it was ornate, commanding, and steeped in history. High vaulted ceilings crowned with intricate plasterwork soared above polished wood panels, carved with motifs of New Zealand's legacy.

At the front, the Speaker's chair loomed—an imposing throne of dark, carved timber, elevated above the rest. Behind it, the coat of arms glinted beneath the lights, a steadfast symbol of sovereignty. The gavel came down once—sharp, final. Order was called.

Charles stepped forward.

He wore his uniform neatly pressed, the shine of medals glinting faintly in the subdued light. His bearing was calm, his voice composed—but there was steel behind it. He had seen the world from above. And he knew what was coming.

'Mr. Prime Minister. Ministers,' he began. 'As a practical flying man, I feel I know what constitutes modern aircraft—and particularly, what sort of aircraft are needed in a region such as ours.'

The room settled.

'The distance between Sydney and New Zealand is thirteen hundred and thirty miles. I would not undertake to run a regular trans-ocean service over that distance with machines such as those of the British, with yesterday's speeds.'

A wave of murmuring swept the benches. The mention of British machines ruffled feathers—Empire loyalists straightened in their seats, eyes narrowing.

Charles pressed on.

'With distance, with strong headwinds, and daylight hours against us, we would be forced to arrive at night. To fly over eight hours on this route, day in and day out, would strain even the most able of pilots.'

Now the silence thickened.

He had touched something real—something they hadn't considered. The practical, the impossible, spoken by a man who had *done* it.

'I believe I am as patriotic as any man in the Empire,' he said, steady and true. 'But I fail to see any patriotism in the present ban on the importation of American aircraft.'

That was the spark.

A low murmur turned to a chorus of protest. Voices rose. Chairs shifted. A few MPs stood outright, faces flushed with outrage.

Charles raised his voice to meet the storm.

'This principle of *parish-pump nationalism* is retarding the development of aviation—and it is as far removed from genuine Empire patriotism as it is from the office bureaucrats winding red tape around their fingers, far from the field, far from flight, and far from the future.'

The chamber erupted.

Jeers. Taunts. The pounding of fists on desks. The high ceiling caught every sound and sent it careening across the chamber. Cries of indignation clashed with shouts for order. The Speaker called for calm.

Charles stood his ground. Unflinching. Unmoved.

He had expected this. Anticipated every backlash.

But he spoke on.

He painted a vision of progress: of faster, safer aircraft, of seamless connections between nations, of New Zealand stepping boldly into the modern world. He argued for American machines—not as a betrayal, but as a necessity. As the next logical step for a country with its eyes on the horizon.

And slowly, beneath the bluster, the fury began to crack.

Some MPs, even those who had shouted the loudest, leaned back in their seats, listening now. Others exchanged glances. The confrontation had not tilted the scale toward his favor.

Charles and Beau sat side by side on the stone steps outside Parliament House.

'Well,' Beau muttered with a dry chuckle, '*that* went well.'

The wind curled around them, cold and persistent, tugging at coat collars and stinging cheeks. It swept through the streets of Wellington and circled the marble facade behind them—imposing and unmoved.

Above, the sky was thick with cloud, a pale gray canopy that smothered any hint of sun. The light was diffused and dull, softening every shadow and lending the moment a quiet, somber tone.

Before them, on the manicured lawn, a flock of sheep grazed contentedly. They moved without hurry, oblivious to the chambered echoes of debate behind them. Their woolly backs bobbed through the grass, heads down, focused only on the next patch of green.

Charles lit a cigarette, the flame sputtering briefly in the wind. He took a long drag, then exhaled slowly. His eyes were fixed on the sheep, but his mind was still in the chamber.

'It was a good speech,' he said, his voice quiet but firm.

'To deaf ears,' Beau replied. His gaze followed the slow, grazing motion of the animals.

'Maybe I should get into politics,' Charles said with a laugh as he looked out over the herd.

'God help us if you were running the country, Smithy.' Beau laughed, then paused perhaps pondering the possibility.

'What is it with bloody politicians and sheep?' Charles said, then laughed again. Beau joined him in the joke, both knowing there was something sharper beneath it.

Cargo Ship
Monterey, Pacific Ocean. 1935.

At full steam, the vessel churned across the vast Pacific, her four screws driving relentlessly through the deep. Foam burst from beneath her stern, a broad swath of white froth marking her wake as she left her past behind. The engines hummed with a deep, rhythmic cadence, the vibration rising through the steel hull into the bones of the vessel itself. Each revolution of the screws was a quiet declaration of forward motion—of escape, of endurance.

The air on the afterdeck was crisp, heavy with salt and the smoke of spent steam. It drifted over Charles, ruffling his hair, sharp in his lungs.

He leaned heavily on the taffrail, shoulders set, eyes fixed on the far-off line where sky met sea. The ocean stretched endlessly ahead—glinting blue under the noonday sun, each ripple a glimmer of light dancing on the swell.

His fingers curled around the cold iron railing, calloused and sure, as if seeking grounding in the face of his own drifting thoughts. He absently stroked the metal, letting the motion anchor him while his mind spun with memories.

The ship sang her mechanical symphony—steam hissed, pressure released in deep, guttural bursts, and pistons thudded in concert. Somewhere overhead, gulls cried. Waves slapped the hull in slow, steady rhythm. The noise was constant and comforting—like a heart still beating after grief.

Charles closed his eyes.

In the darkness behind his lids, the past surged up.

The chamber came to him in brutal clarity—Sir Ethelbert Ransom's voice rising over the seated members, their faces a blur of arrogance and disdain.

'Despite Sir Charles so kindly reminding us that he was the first man to fly to New Zealand, that he has flown here more times than any other, established airfields throughout the country and selected their sites—his enterprise and intrepidity in blazing what might be termed the 'Tasman Sea Trail' do not afford him any prescriptive right to an air service between New Zealand and Australia . . .'

Ransom's words had dripped with venomous politeness, each syllable designed to diminish, to dismiss. The laughter that followed, the jeers echoing through the high walls, had done what bullets never could—pierced his pride.

Charles opened his eyes, the light harsh against the sting of memory.

His gaze dropped to the pair of aviator wings held tightly in his palm. The metal glinted in the sunlight, warm and familiar. He traced each ridge with his thumb—the weight of them heavy with history, with meaning.

He raised them slowly, his arm trembling not with weakness, but with restraint.

'Bye, Charlie,' he whispered.

He threw them with strength.

The wings twirled through the air, catching the light one final time before vanishing beneath the waves. The ocean swallowed them whole.

A long silence followed.

He felt something inside him ease—like a muscle finally unclenched. The ache didn't leave, but it softened. The burden lifted, if only slightly.

Charles stepped back from the rail, the horizon still vast before him, but no longer distant. The *Monterey* surged forward beneath his feet, steady and unwavering.

He inhaled the sea air deeply, tasting salt and steel and something more—*possibility*.

The sun lowered slowly toward the rim of the world, casting molten gold across the water. Sky and sea became a painter's palette of pink and violet and flame. The light reflected in Charles's eyes as he watched, motionless, feeling the world turn quietly on.

Twilight came.

One by one, stars blinked into being above. Ancient, constant. Guiding lights for sailors, for seekers, for those still finding their way.

He remained at the taffrail, alone with the night, with the endless ocean, and with the quiet, dawning certainty that this was not an ending.

Chapter 36

Burbank Airport
Los Angeles, California, United States of America. 1935.

Charles and Robert were seated in the new office, a spacious and modern room with floor-to-ceiling windows overlooking the bustling expansion of the aerodrome. The scent of polished wood and new leather filled the air.

'New office?' Charles commented politely, glancing around appreciatively. The sleek lines of the furniture and the state-of-the-art equipment hinted at the prosperity and forward-thinking mindset of the company.

'We are expanding very quickly, Charles. Development in aviation is moving rapidly, as you know,' Robert replied, leaning back in his chair with a satisfied smile, his eyes sparkling with ambition as he smoked a cigar.

'Cigar?' Robert spun the humidor across the boardroom table toward Charles, offering the fine Cuban cigars. The humidor itself was an exquisite piece, made of rich mahogany with intricate carvings. Charles hesitated briefly before selecting one, appreciating the craftsmanship.

'Claire no longer with you?' Charles asked.

'Married. Starting a family,' Robert replied as a matter of course.

'Wonderful,' Charles conceded.

'I am hoping our conversation today may be cause for celebration.'

Robert slowly slid a newspaper across the table. 'I saved this for you.'

Charles removed a cigarette from his pocket, lighting it slowly as he cautiously read the bold headline:

Lindbergh Says Kingsford Smith Greatest Flyer Of All Time

The print was crisp, and the photograph of him was striking, capturing the intensity of his achievement. Reading into the first paragraph briefly, Charles laid the paper down, gently distancing himself from the praise.

'From Lindbergh . . . that is . . . um,' Charles said, his mind shifting instantly away from the sentiment. He felt a mix of pride and humility, knowing the weight of such praise.

'How is he doing? Since the . . . situation with his son?' he asked, his voice tinged with an empathetic concern.

'As well as can be expected. That entire episode was an absolute tragedy.' Robert's tone grew sober. He shook his head softly. 'Poor little boy.'

'The rumors are, ah . . . well, pretty abhorrent, to say the least,' Charles added, furthering his concern.

'They are indeed. The whole thing is very unfortunate. Yet, sadly, it is the price one pays for fame—as you may be well aware, Charles. It comes with a hefty cost,' Robert replied, savoring the flavorful smoke rolling delicately in his mouth. 'Matters such as these are not resolved quickly. Lindbergh certainly has a difficult road ahead of him.'

Charles nodded thoughtfully, exhaling a thin stream of smoke as Robert steered the conversation to the purpose of their meeting, both men relaxed into their seats.

'Are you certain we cannot tempt you into joining us?' Robert asked, leaning forward, his eyes gleaming with ambition.

'I cannot leave Australia, Robert,' Charles replied firmly. 'They would hang, draw, and quarter me.'

'Well, what if we brought Lockheed to you? We are, after all, looking to expand. Your achievements over the Pacific have advanced aviation by ten years at least. Within the next two years, passenger services will be an absolute reality. Flights to New Zealand and Australia will be a regular occurrence.'

'It is still a very difficult passage, Robert.'

'One proven to now be possible—thanks to you, Sir Charles.'

'Manufacturing rights?' Charles inquired, his interest piqued.

'Yes, and maintenance. Exclusively.' Robert's voice brimmed with promise and opportunity.

'There is still the issue of the ban,' Charles said, aware of the legal restrictions in place.

'Well, you wouldn't be importing, Charles. You'd be manufacturing,' Robert replied with a clever smile, a glint of cunning in his eyes. Charles leaned back, considering the proposition. The potential for growth—and for advancing aviation in Australia—was enormous.

'I can see you have thought this through well,' he admitted, a slow smile spreading across his face.

Robert's eyes sparkled with satisfaction. 'Excellent. We'll make all the necessary arrangements. Your contributions to aviation have been invaluable Charles; together, I do believe we advance aviation into the future.'

Charles nodded, a sense of excitement stirring within him. He leaned forward, extending his hand. Robert rose and shook it firmly, sealing the deal.

The *Lady Southern Cross* stood gleaming on the runway under the morning sun, its frame shimmering like a blade ready to cut through the sky. Charles and Tommy stood beside her, dressed in flight suits, their goggles slung loosely around their necks. The California air was crisp, the horizon blushing with the first light of day.

Beau stood with them, still in business attire—polished shoes, jacket neatly pressed—a figure of steady professionalism amid the charged anticipation.

Tommy adjusted the zippers of his flight suit, then turned to Beau with an easy grin.

'There is a cargo ship leaving New York for London on Tuesday,' he said. 'I have got her booked on it.'

Beau smiled, catching the light mood. 'First class?' he asked, arching an eyebrow.

'All the way,' Tommy replied with a chuckle. 'See you, Beau.'

Charles turned, his expression tightening slightly, more serious.

'Beau, I'm going to need you back here once we leave London,' he said, voice steady, the tone of command unmistakable.

Beau frowned, reading something unspoken in the brief pause that followed.

'Everything okay?' he asked carefully.

Charles offered a small, unreadable smile.

'Very,' he said simply. 'See you in New York.'

He left it at that, his eyes betraying nothing.

Beau nodded, understanding that—for now—questions would have to wait.

They shook hands firmly. A brief clasp, the kind exchanged between men who trusted each other enough not to need words.

The sun hovered low on the horizon, casting a golden blaze across the endless sky. Below, the *Lady Southern Cross* soared low and smooth over the vast, yawning majesty of the Grand Canyon, its towering cliffs and shadowed valleys painted in fire and deepening violet.

Wind buffeted the fuselage, the rhythmic hum of the engine steady and sure.

Charles leaned forward slightly, glancing back toward the rear cockpit.

'Tommy! Know much about racehorses?' he yelled over the roar of the slipstream.

Tommy cupped a hand to his ear, grinning.

'No!' he shouted back.

Charles laughed, the sound whipped away by the rushing air.

'She is all yours!' he called.

Tommy's face lit up, beaming with pride. He tightened his grip on the controls.

'I have got her!' he hollered back, his voice full of excitement and wonder.

Charles smiled to himself and, with deliberate care, slowly released his hand from the stick, relinquishing control.

The *Lady Southern Cross* dipped gently, then righted herself under Tommy's steady touch—flying free over the canyon, two men chasing the falling sun.

Chapter 37

House of Lords
London, England. 1935.

Collins rushed into the grand office, the heavy oak door swinging back with a thud. Without hesitation, he crossed the richly carpeted floor and seized the velvet drapes, yanking them open with a vigorous pull.

Harsh sunlight poured into the room, setting the polished wood and leather-bound books aglow.

'Collins!' Lord Liard barked from behind his imposing mahogany desk, recoiling from the glare. 'I am *resting*, for the love of God! Have you forgotten what it is to be a gentleman?'

Collins, unfazed, approached briskly, a crisp document folder tucked under his arm.

'You may wish to see this, my lord,' he said, his voice taut with urgency. 'We have just received an application to have the *Lady Southern Cross* listed on the British register.'

Lord Liard grunted, adjusting his spectacles with a weary hand. 'That's all very well, Collins. But the aircraft would need to be *in the country* for that nonsense.'

Collins drew the curtains even wider, flooding the office with afternoon light. Beyond the tall windows, the Thames shimmered silver under the sun, and Parliament's towers cast long shadows across the embankment.

'It *is*, my lord,' Collins said, voice clipped and cool.

He gestured toward the window.

'Here, my lord.'

Lord Liard rose stiffly from his chair, annoyance sharpening his movements. He strode to the window and looked out. Through the rain, falling in a steady mist and veiling the city in a damp, metallic gloom, he saw a barge bumping gently against the muddy bank of the Thames, the *Lady Southern Cross* strapped down atop it, gleaming even under the colorless sky.

Then Lord Liard's voice thundered through the stone halls.

'Why was I not *informed* of this?'

The pigeons scattered into the dull rain-slicked skies, seemingly startled by Lord Liard's disgruntled roar.

Charles, Tommy, and Beau worked quickly, unloading the aircraft with practiced efficiency, boots slipping in the wet grass along the riverbank.

Suddenly—cutting through the drizzle and clatter—came a familiar voice.

'Tommy!'

Jess's cry rang out, bright and uncontainable.

Tommy turned just as she broke into a sprint across the wharf, her coat flaring behind her, her cheeks flushed with excitement.

'You made it,' Tommy called, grinning wide as she threw herself into his arms.

'I missed you,' Jess squealed, laughing and half crying as she clung to him.

Across the barge, Charles turned to Beau with a chuckle.

'Young love,' he said, shaking his head.

Beau smiled back. 'Probably the last we will see of him for a while!' he replied, a glint in his eye.

Charles sat in contemplative silence on a weathered park bench, its green paint peeling under the weight of countless seasons. The late afternoon sun cast long shadows through the trees, dappling the ground in a quiet dance of light and shade. Around his feet, a flock of pigeons cooed softly, pecking eagerly at the breadcrumbs he scattered. Overhead, the rustling leaves offered a soothing backdrop, mingling with the distant murmur of the city, muted by the park's gentle sprawl.

He fed the pigeons methodically, almost ritualistically, as if the simple act could help him digest the monotony of the hours they were stranded in. The soft crunch of the bread beneath his fingers was punctuated by the occasional flutter of wings as the birds jostled for position.

Beau, his old friend and confidant, sat beside him. The usual energy that animated Beau's movements was subdued now, replaced by a thoughtful stillness. The park offered rare peace—a quiet reprieve from the eyes that trailed them everywhere, eager for a glimpse of the man who had become something of a legend.

'They are intentionally delaying the registration,' Beau said, his voice low, barely rising above the ambient sounds. A distant child's laughter mingled with the steady rhythm of a jogger's footsteps on the path.

'Let us hope they do not find it,' Charles replied, eyes never leaving the birds. He tore off another piece of bread, tossing it evenly among the flock. The pigeons clambered over one another, their beady eyes catching glints of gold from the setting sun. The tap of their beaks on stone and soil formed a soft, repetitive clatter—like rain on a windowpane.

'You know, Beau,' Charles said, a note of nostalgia threading through his voice, 'I remember a time when flight was free. When the spirit of man, untrammeled by earthly things, could chase the horizon without restraint.'

Beau chuckled, the sound deep and warm, resonating with the park's stillness. 'Philosophy, now? Really, Charles?'

Charles smiled, wistful. 'Look,' he said, pointing. Beau followed his gaze to the birds' ankles—each one banded with a small blue aluminum tag, numbers stamped into the metal. A stark reminder of their tethered existence. 'Even the bloody pigeons here are registered.'

He threw the rest of the bread, watching the birds descend on it with fervor. Their frenzy was almost comical—a flurry of wings and excited coos—a mirror of the greater world's scramble for control.

Beau laughed, unable to resist the irony. 'They think you're after the record.'

Charles's gaze sharpened, his expression hardening with the quiet resolve that had carried him through every trial. 'Who says I am not?'

The park seemed to breathe with them, ancient trees standing as silent witnesses to their conversation. The air hung thick with the scent of earth and greenery, stirred now and then by a breeze that carried the city's distant hum. Sparrows chirped in the underbrush, and a lone crow called out from somewhere overhead. Charles leaned back, the bench creaking under his weight, and closed his eyes, letting the sounds and scents wash over him.

'What if they do find it?' Beau asked, barely above a whisper—his voice nearly lost in the wind.

Charles opened his eyes, meeting Beau's with calm determination. 'As someone once told me, it is not a problem until it is a problem.'

Beau nodded, comforted by his friend's quiet certainty. They had faced worse before—and survived. Yet something about this felt different, like a shadow lingering just beyond the edge of understanding.

'Do you ever think about giving it all up?' Beau asked suddenly, the question escaping before he could stop it.

Charles turned to him, a slow smile playing on his lips. 'And do what? Feed pigeons all day?'

Beau laughed, lighter this time. 'There are worse ways to spend your time.'

'True,' Charles said, and for a moment, that simple truth was enough.

They sat in companionable silence as twilight crept in. The soundscape shifted—day birds giving way to owls, insects humming in the gathering dusk, the distant croak of frogs rising from hidden corners. The pigeons, their hunger sated, fluttered off one by one, their coos fading with the light. The sun dipped low, casting the park in a warm, golden hush.

As dusk settled over Hyde Park, the two men rose from the bench. Their conversation lingered in the air like the fading light. They walked slowly, gravel crunching beneath their feet, each step bringing them closer to the world beyond the park's fragile peace. The hum of traffic grew louder, folding into the rustle of leaves and a dog's distant bark.

'We will figure it out, Beau,' Charles said, his voice steady.

'You always do,' Beau replied.

The gates loomed ahead, marking the boundary between sanctuary and storm. Charles paused, casting one last look back at the quiet expanse. It was a fleeting symphony of peace, and he committed it to memory.

'There is a discrepancy, my lord,' Collins said, his voice hushed but precise as he laid the documents out with meticulous care. The soft rustle of papers echoed faintly through the high-ceilinged chamber, broken only by the muffled ticking of a clock on the mantel.

'The all-up—or total weight limit—listed in the application does not align with the Department of Commerce's Certificate of Airworthiness. If you'll note here . . . and here, my lord.' He tapped twice with a silver-tipped pen.

Lord Liard leaned forward, the light from the tall windows catching on the sharp edge of his profile. Outside, the gray ribbon of the Thames glimmered under a pale autumn sun.

'And again, here and here,' Collins continued, fingers moving like a surgeon's. 'This is the same irregularity raised prior to the air race. The excess load pertains directly to fuel capacity. Technically, the certificate does not bar the aircraft from British registration. However, it does render it unfit for takeoff when fully fueled.'

Liard gave a slow, mirthless chuckle, folding his hands behind his back.

'Fascinating, Collins. The audacity to imagine this would slip by . . . it reveals much about Kingsford Smith's character. Arrogance, certainly. And a gross underestimation of our diligence.'

Collins allowed himself a thin smile, licking his lips with the satisfaction of a lizard that had just swallowed a fly. 'Quite so, my lord. Under normal review standards, it may have been overlooked. But we've taken the liberty of examining his submission more thoroughly than most.'

Liard turned from the desk and paced toward the window, boots echoing faintly on the polished stone floor. He stopped at the edge, gaze fixed on the misted cityscape beyond. The light was cool, almost clinical, casting long shadows across the room.

'Approve the flight,' he said after a beat. 'Set it for the twenty-third. I will be returning from the country that day.'

Collins bowed slightly. 'Yes, my lord.'

Liard did not turn from the window.

'I would like to watch him leave.'

Chapter 38

London, England. 1935.

Gentle snowflakes dotted the cool air—not quite a winter snowfall, but an early whisper of the colder weather to come. A bell jingled brightly as the door opened.

'Top of the morning to you, sir,' the shopkeeper said with a smile, greeting Charles as he entered the quaint toy store.

'Good morning,' Charles replied, brushing the cold from his sleeves and removing his gloves. His eyes slowly wandered over the myriad of colorful offerings, each one carefully arranged to catch the eye.

'Is there anything in particular one might assist you with, sir?' the shopkeeper inquired.

'I might take a moment and look, if you do not mind.'

'Not at all, sir.'

'Thank you,' Charles said, beginning his quiet exploration, eyes scanning for something that will be well received.

Behind the counter, the shopkeeper shifted his attention to the front page of the *Daily Herald*, its bold headline proclaiming: SMITHY OUT TO BEAT SCOTT, accompanied by a photograph of Charles himself.

Recognizing the unmistakable figure before him, the shopkeeper ventured, 'Is it for a boy or a girl, sir?'

'A young boy, a very, very special young boy,' Charles replied.

'If I may suggest, sir, toy airplanes have been quite popular this year.'

'I am not surprised,' Charles said with a knowing smile, sensing his identity may have been discovered.

'Especially among the boys,' the shopkeeper added, aware his recommendation might lead toward an easy sale.

'That I can understand,' Charles said, continuing to browse, his eyes now more purposeful—seeking something small, yet something very special.

'And not just the boys,' the shopkeeper continued. 'Quite many young girls have taken a shine to the pastime of flight. Not the traditional request, perhaps, but I suspect it has stirred a little adventure in the younger generation.'

Charles paused before a display of miniature toy cars on a nearby shelf. He studied them intently—he'd never seen anything quite like them.

'They are the Dinky Toys die-cast miniature range,' the shopkeeper said, noticing his interest.

'I have never seen them before,' Charles murmured.

'They are quite new—just released this year. All manufactured right here in Liverpool. That blue one there is the MG Magnette. Very popular.'

'They are heavy,' Charles said, picking up the long, sleek, almost rocket-like racing car. Deep blue, with a silver racing stripe running over its bonnet, and a bold number circled in red—it carried a striking, futuristic appeal with coloring similar to his own machine.

He approached the counter. 'I will take this one.'

'Oh, a very fine choice, sir. Would you like that wrapped?'

'Please.'

Outside, Beau warmed himself as he waited patiently for Charles.

'How did you go?' he asked as Charles stepped from the store.

'Really well,' Charles replied, and the pair began walking down the street.

'What do you want to do?' Beau asked.

'I have not seen Mary in months, Beau. And with Charles's birthday approaching, I have to get back.'

'Have you seen Tommy?' Beau asked.

'No. If you do, tell him the honeymoon is over.'

River Thames
London, England. 1935.

The gloom of the city had softened. A pale sun peeked through the stubborn cloud cover, casting a watery light across the stone and steel. The drudge of London took on a shimmer, just briefly, as morning broke over the Thames.

On the riverbank, the aircraft stood proud—a mechanical marvel against the skyline. It had drawn an enormous crowd. Onlookers clustered together, craning their necks, wide-eyed in wonder. Children pointed. Elders recalled stories. A soft hum of awe hung in the air like static.

The press was out in full force—reporters elbowing for position, photographers jostling for the clearest frame, newsreel men shouting over one another for just a few seconds of footage. Flashbulbs sparked in quick bursts, capturing the moment for posterity.

Charles stood before the microphones, unbothered by the noise. His voice was steady, composed beneath the hum of anticipation.

'On my eighth trip between England and Australia, I am awfully glad indeed to have the opportunity to say cheerio—and express my appreciation for the innumerable messages of goodwill I have received from so many friends on this side of the world.'

A flicker of charm passed across his face, though his eyes seemed already skyward.

'Naturally, I am very anxious to get home. I am sorry, in a way, to leave these very hospitable shores—but with a wife waiting for me, and a very small and very important child . . . I will not be sorry to get underway.'

He offered a brief nod, then stepped away without lingering over the applause, moving with quiet intent back toward the aircraft. The crowd roared in his wake, but he paid it little mind.

'Fill the two extra tanks for me, boys,' Charles called out, rolling up his sleeves. One of the mechanics nodded, already moving.

Away from the flurry of spectacle, tucked behind the commotion, Tommy and Jess stood alone in their own corner of the world. The river breeze tugged gently at Jess's hair.

'So—you are okay to get to the ship?' Tommy asked, holding her hand, thumb brushing softly across her knuckles.

'I will be fine. I promise.' Jess smiled, bouncing on her heels, her eyes lit with the thrill of the journey ahead, but also a lingering sadness.

'I will see you when you get home,' he said, a wide grin spreading across his face as he locked eyes with her.

'I do not want to leave,' Jess replied softly. 'I miss you already.'

'I do not want you to leave either,' he admitted, a wistful note in his voice. 'But . . . we cannot stay here forever, can we?'

She shook her head, barely.

'No. We cannot.'

There was a pause—long enough to mean something.

'I love you,' Tommy whispered.

'I love you too,' Jess said, and stepped into his arms.

They kissed—tenderly, fully, as if trying to make the moment stretch out, to leave a mark on time itself. A goodbye kiss that lasted until the noise of the crowd became distant, like waves.

Lord Liard stood at the tall window, his gaze fixed hauntingly across the river. The glass reflected only faint traces of him—shoulders square, posture statuesque, his hands clasped loosely behind his back. His face was unreadable. Below, the city stirred with the excitement of departure, but in this office high above the Thames, the air felt still. Watchful.

The door opened softly behind him.

'Good morning, my lord. You are in early today,' Collins offered as he entered, his voice warm with habitual politeness.

'Morning, Collins,' Liard replied without turning. 'Yes. It is a fine day.'

Collins moved with practiced efficiency, heading to the tea service.

'And how was your time in the country, my lord?' he asked, as he prepared the morning ritual.

'Cold,' Liard said flatly. Nothing more.

Collins offered a faint smile, unfazed. 'With the imposed fuel limit, there is no possibility of reducing Scott's time—seventy-one hours. Remarkable, really. To cover such a distance in three days.'

'Rather,' Liard murmured, still watching the chaos of the riverbank with the same calm detachment.

From this height, the people below were small—busy, insignificant.

'Customs have a good handle on things, my lord,' Collins added, approaching with the tea, careful to place the cup just so on the table beside Liard.

Liard did not move. His eyes tracked a flash of silver—the glint of the aircraft's frame as it caught the rising sun.

'We shall see,' he said at last, so softly it might have been to himself.

Charles moved with purpose, weaving through the chaos on the tarmac. His boots struck hard against the pavement, each step firm, decisive. Voices barked orders. The scent of fuel hung thick in the air.

He joined Beau near the aircraft's wing.

'How are we looking?' he asked, without slowing.

'Almost there,' Beau replied, his tone tight with focus.

Then, just beyond the cordon, a sleek black vehicle rolled to a silent stop. Its presence was too deliberate to be casual. The doors opened one by one, and three men stepped out—dark coats, sharp movements, eyes sweeping the crowd like hounds scenting blood.

'Smithy,' Beau muttered, nodding toward them.

Charles turned. Their gaze was already fixed on him.

'I think they are looking for you,' Beau added under his breath.

Charles didn't hesitate. He spun on his heel and strode back toward the fueling crew.

'Stop!' one of the men shouted, clipboard raised like a weapon. 'Stop what you're doing!'

His voice, authoritative, carried over the crowd.

'Keep going!' Charles called back the men refueling, louder.

The crew hesitated only a heartbeat—then resumed, hose still hissing into the fuel tank.

'Keep going!' Charles called back, louder.

One of the officials stepped forward now, a British customs officer. He held up a thick sheaf of paperwork, stiff-backed with authority.

'We have orders,' he announced, clipped and cold. 'We are to inspect and measure your fuel loading—immediately.' He looked to the men, 'Stop fueling now.'

'Keep going,' Charles shot back.

The men, fueling, simply shrugged and kept loading fuel.

Charles squared up to him. Shoulders drawn back, jaw locked, eyes hard.

'You can't do this now,' he said low, but fierce.

'I assure you, we can,' the officer replied. He didn't blink.

Neither man moved at first. Then Charles stepped forward, toe to toe. The officer held his ground, and their shoulders clashed, sharp and unyielding. A brief, restrained struggle—more posture than violence, but volatile nonetheless.

Beau shoved himself between them.

'Easy, mate,' he said, hand pressed against Charles's chest. 'This is not the place.'

The moment only escalated. The other officials surged forward, sensing tension. No punches flew, but the jostling turned rough, heated, attention from across the crowd now drawn to the fray.

Tommy, halfway through a goodbye kiss with Jess, caught the commotion from the corner of his eye. He smiled through it, kissed her one last time.

'Gotta go!' he grinned, and darted off.

He barreled into the commotion a moment later, already elbowing someone out of the way. He didn't know who they were—just that they weren't one of his.

'What the hell is going on?' he shouted, eyes wild, fists half-raised, as the scrap widened.

From the height of the government offices across the river, the scuffle was no more than a ripple of motion against the chaos of the launch.

Lord Liard stood by the window, tea in hand, his expression unchanged. Beside him, Collins adjusted his spectacles, peering down over the bustling scene below.

'There appears to be some sort of scuffle, my lord,' Collins observed, gesturing discreetly with his teacup.

Liard didn't look away. He sipped, slowly. 'It does not surprise me, Collins.'

He placed the cup gently onto its saucer, the porcelain clinking softly.

'They are Australians, after all.' A pause. 'Riff raff.'

His tone was not cruel—just tired, like a man stating an obvious, unfortunate truth.

Collins said nothing, though his eyes flicked momentarily toward Liard. Then back to the melee, where movement continued—messy, unrefined.

The scuffle didn't break clean—it unraveled, messily, as arms pulled and voices barked over one another. Beau had an arm around Charles's chest, dragging him back with quiet force, while Tommy shoved the last of the officials out of their space, teeth clenched.

Charles threw his hands in the air, exasperated. 'To hell with it,' he muttered, turning and storming off toward the riverbank, shoulders heaving with fury.

'You will be hearing more about this!' the customs officer shouted after him, his voice shrill above the retreating noise.

'Let it go, Charles,' Beau said, still beside him.

Tommy jogged up, brushing off his jacket. 'You alright, boss?'

Charles exhaled sharply through his nose. 'Bastards,' he muttered, then gave Tommy a quick nod. 'Thanks. Get her ready.'

'On it, boss,' Tommy said, already pivoting toward the plane.

Charles paused at the river's edge. The breeze curled around them, cool and damp, carrying the distant hum of the crowd behind them. A moment of quiet, at last.

'Christ, Smithy,' Beau said, catching his breath. 'These clowns will not let up.'

'If they restrict the fuel,' Charles said, eyes still on the horizon, 'I might as well push her back home.'

Beau gave a short, incredulous laugh. 'Christ, Charles. You were not seriously going to go for it . . . were you?'

Charles didn't answer.

'Oh Christ, you were.'

Beau raked a hand through his hair. 'What do you want to do? Delay?'

'There is nothing we can do,' Charles replied calmly. His voice had shifted—measured now, decisive. 'Get on the first ship back to the States. Contact me when you get there. I need you on the Lockheed deal. I will get her home.'

Beau blinked. 'You are sure?'

Charles nodded, already mapping it out in his mind. 'I will manage.'

For a moment, he stood there in silence, staring across the river.

His eyes locked on the House of Lords.

It loomed beyond the water, its ancient facade staring back at him through the lifting fog. Behind its glass, somewhere high above, he could feel them watching. He didn't need to see their faces. He saw enough.

The glass couldn't hide them.

Not from him.

'More tea, my lord?' Collins asked, already reaching for the pot.

'Thank you, Collins,' Lord Liard replied, his voice absent. His eyes never left the window.

The river glinted faintly beneath the morning light, and beyond it, the commotion around the aircraft continued to mount.

'I assume it will not be too much longer, my lord.'

Liard's expression did not shift.

'One would assume this will be the last we are seeing of Sir Charles for quite some time, would you not agree, Collins?'

'I am certain that would be a fair assumption, my lord,' Collins answered, smooth and unfaltering.

He refilled the cup with practised grace, the delicate clink of porcelain the only sound between them. Then, after a pause, he stepped closer to the window, joining Liard in the quiet vigil.

Below, the crowd that had gathered around the *Lady Southern Cross* began to shift—drawn back as ground crew cleared her path. The aircraft gleamed, defiant under the morning sun.

'It would appear they are making progress, my lord,' Collins observed softly.

'Yes,' Liard murmured. 'I would like the reports on my desk before lunch.'

'Of course, my lord,' Collins replied.

'I must admit I am rather enthused,' Lord Liard said, the small amount of emotion that rarely entered his soul exposing itself in the moment as from the overhead vantage point, they watched on as the engine fired.

Charles vaulted into the cockpit with a quick, practiced motion, his hands already moving across switches and gauges. Behind him, Tommy ran through final checks with speed and precision.

'Set!' Tommy yelled over the rumble of the engine.

Charles didn't answer. His eyes weren't on the controls—they were fixed ahead, staring through the windshield, past the spinning blades toward the towering silhouette of Big Ben. The great clock stood tall above the rooftops, unmoving in its stone stillness, but its hands . . . they ticked.

'Set!' Tommy called again, louder this time. 'What are you waiting for?'

6:59 a.m.

Charles held.

The massive hand clocked forward, striking twelve.

The bells tolled. Once.

Charles slammed the throttle forward.

The engine roared as he released the brake. The *Lady Southern Cross* surged ahead, tearing down the makeshift runway, skimming the riverbank like a dare. The wheels screamed against the earth.

The bell tolled. Twice.

He pulled hard on the stick.

The aircraft responded instantly, nose lifting, the propeller taking bigger and bigger bites of the early air. She climbed fast, punching upward with righteous defiance.

'Finally, Collins,' Lord Liard murmured, turning slowly from the window, having seen enough. He stood calmly, stonelike.

Charles slammed the stick, he banked the aircraft hard, left, the aircraft diving sharply toward the river, then arcing high again in a powerful, sweeping climb.

The bell tolled. Three.

'Are we good?' Tommy shouted, wide-eyed, clutching his harness.

Charles didn't respond—he only grinned.

He turned the aircraft again, harder this time—one hundred and eighty degrees in a single sweeping motion—diving quickly, roaring back over the Thames in a breathtaking aerobatic sweep.

Tommy's eyes widened. 'Oh shit,' he muttered, grabbing the control panel with both hands.

The bell tolled. Four.

Lord Liard lifted his teacup, a self-satisfied smile just beginning to tug at the corners of his mouth.

The bell tolled. Five.

Then it hit.

A deafening blast of wind and engine thunder shattered the stillness.

The *Lady Southern Cross* screamed past the government offices like a bullet, engines howling in righteous fury. The windows shuddered violently. Tea cups shattered. Collins dove instinctively, knocking the service tray to the floor with a crash of china.

The entire building seemed to rock.

Lord Liard staggered back, a hand flying to his chest. His complexion drained to a ghostly white.

'For the love of God!' he bellowed.

In the sky above, Charles pulled back hard on the stick. The aircraft surged upward, carving a brilliant line through the cloud-slashed morning.

'Woohoo!' Tommy hollered, eyes wide, face flushed with adrenaline.

Charles banked left again, this time sweeping wide around Big Ben. The tower turned slowly below them like a monument to the conquered.

'Let's go home, Tommy,' Charles said, nodding with grim pride.

The bell tolled. Six.

He leveled the wings, leaving London behind.

Chapter 39

Lympne Aerodrome
Kent, England. 1935.

Through the thick London fog, a pair of yellow headlights cut a narrow path, wailing to a halt outside the hangar. The cab door burst open, and Beau leapt out into the chill of the night, breath fogging as he sprinted across the damp tarmac.

His footsteps echoed off concrete. The urgency in his stride was unmistakable.

Inside, the *Lady Southern Cross* sat like a ghost in the shadows—silent and beaten. Her once-proud silhouette now wilted beside the glowing inferno radiating from Scott's Comet, still smoldering in the reverence of its glorious victory over them. The contrast was brutal.

Beau's eyes scanned the scene.

The Altair was wrecked—wings bowed, panels split, the fuselage battered and dirtied by the storm.

Charles stood in front of her, unmoving. Shoulders slumped, arms folded tightly across his chest. His head hung low. Nearby, Tommy paced in slow, silent circles, eyes downcast.

'Smithy,' Beau called out as he stepped inside.

Charles looked up slowly, weariness dragging on his expression.

'I came as soon as I got the message—what the bloody hell happened?' Beau asked, still catching his breath.

'We got hit hard over Italy,' Charles replied, his voice dull and gravelly.

'Christ, Smithy.' Beau turned, taking in the mangled state of the aircraft.

'Tommy—you alright?' he asked, glancing toward him.

Tommy nodded, but it was an empty gesture. 'Yeah,' he said softly. 'Just . . . pissed off.'

'I have never seen anything like it,' Charles said, eyes still locked on the battered Altair. 'The worst conditions I have ever seen Beau.'

'Snowstorm,' Tommy added, voice flat. Just one word, but it carried the weight of everything they'd endured.

'There was no choice, Beau,' Charles said finally, his breath fogging in the cold air. 'We had to turn back.'

He said it like it hurt to speak—like every word admitted a defeat that clung to his bones.

Beau didn't answer right away. The silence hung between them, Beau walked slowly around the Altair. His expression said it, he shook his head almost speechless to the condition.

'What do you think Tommy?' Beau asked.

'Have you got a match?' Tommy replied, shaking his head in despair. 'I don't know Beau, if I work on her day and night, maybe a month, maybe more.'

'Christ, you are lucky you are both alive.' Beau shook his head still in disbelief. 'I have got a car outside.' He paused. 'I organized a couple rooms.'

'I will stay here,' Tommy replied.

'Charles?' Beau asked.

'Yeah,' Charles replied.

The hotel room was quiet, untouched by morning. Outside, London's streets whispered beneath the weight of night, the sky still a heavy blue-black. The clock read just after four, the early hours of the morning had come about quickly under the pressure of time.

Charles stepped inside, his movements slow and deliberate. His hands were black with grease, streaked up his forearms, caked into the creases of his knuckles. His face was no better—oil smudged across his cheek like war paint, his eyes hollowed by the long night. He said nothing as he closed the door behind him with a muted click, sealing the world out.

In his hand, the birthday present.

He placed it gently on the small writing desk, as if it were something fragile. Maybe sacred. The paper was worn now, creased from travel, soft at the corners. It had endured the flight in the same manner he had, rough.

Charles stood there for a while, staring at it. Then, without urgency, he sat down. The lamp cast a pool of yellow light across the wood, dull against the darkness pressing at the window.

He picked up the small package again, turning it over in his hands. His fingers trembled, just slightly, but he steadied them. The silence stretched, filling every corner of the room, until it wasn't silence anymore—it was a desire, a desire to be somewhere he was not.

He opened the attached card, slowly, as if only to glance.

He didn't need to read it. He already knew the words. Had carried them in his chest like a pocket charm. But still, he read it again, the words a simple reminder.

> To my dearest son, Charles Arthur,
> As you turn three—I only wish to see— you grow into a fine man one day.
> Happy Birthday.
> From your loving father.

The words reflected in his eyes, echoing in his bones. He stared at the card for a long moment, then carefully closed it.

He didn't move.

A deep breath shuddered through him. His chest rose and fell once, and then again, slower. He rested his forearms on the desk, his fingers interlaced, oily palms pressed together like a prayer. The mirror before did not let him escape himself, not for a moment.

What now?

The question arrived not as thought but as presence—dull and heavy. It sat across from him in the silence, waiting.

He closed his eyes. Not to rest. Just to shut the world out for one more moment.

Charles signed an autograph for a young couple as he sat with Beau in the small, dimly lit London restaurant. The place had an old-world charm—vintage posters lined the walls, and a soft jazz tune drifted through the air. The gentle murmur of conversations and the occasional clink of silverware created a warm, cozy atmosphere. Charles's hand lingered on the piece of paper, a faint smile on his lips as he returned it to the couple, who thanked him profusely before slipping away.

'You look like crap, Smithy,' Beau said, taking a sip of his coffee. His eyes lingered on Charles's tired face, noting the dark circles and the stubble that hinted at several sleepless nights.

Charles sighed, rubbing his temples. 'She's nearly done,' he murmured, voice raspy with exhaustion. He leaned back in his chair, the weight of the past few weeks pulling his shoulders down. He coughed.

'You getting sick?' Beau asked.

'No, just the cold over here, you know.'

'How is Tommy holding up?' Beau asked, leaning forward, concern etched into his features. He knew how much this meant—to Charles, and by extension, to all of them.

'He has been sleeping in the hangar,' Charles said, worried, threading through his words. 'I do not know where we would be without him. He has been working nonstop, like the rest of us.'

'This is crazy, Charles. We should just ship her home?' Beau's voice rose slightly, frustration creeping in. He couldn't understand why Charles kept pushing himself—and everyone else—to the edge.

'Ship her home with what, Beau?' Charles snapped, the frustration and helplessness in his voice colliding. He raked a trembling hand through his disheveled hair. 'We have poured everything into this. Every last penny. All I have got left is the money they owe me for the *Southern Cross*.'

'Then use it, Charles. You are in no condition to fly—neither is Tommy,' Beau replied, his tone softening, nudging him gently toward reason.

'Maybe you are right,' Charles said, finally, lowering his head into his hands in reluctant surrender.

'I think it is the best solution, given the circumstances.'

'Contact John. Have him organize the money,' Charles said quietly.

'You want to ship her?' Beau asked, surprised, his brow lifting.

'I do not think there is any other choice?' Charles's voice was barely a whisper, his eyes heavy as they met Beau's.

'I'll take care of it,' Beau said after a beat. 'You are doing the right thing, Charles.'

Charles gave a slow nod, his jaw tight with reluctant agreement. 'Yeah,' he said, the word hollow but grateful.

The door clicked shut behind Tommy as he stepped into the small recording booth. It was cramped, barely enough room to shift his weight, but it held a certain magic. He looked around, eyes wide, curiosity lighting up his face.

The instructions were printed on a small placard above the machine. He read them carefully, tracing the words with his eyes as if decoding a secret. The technology fascinated him—equal parts strange and thrilling, as he investigated it, attempting to understand its inner workings. He grinned, shaking his head. 'Bloody hell,' he murmured. His fingers hovered over the knobs and levers, marveling at the contraption like it might spring to life.

After another glance at the instructions, he dug into his pocket and dropped a coin into the slot. With a soft metallic clink, the machine whirred to life. A thin aluminum disk lowered onto a spinning turntable, gathering speed until it hummed steadily beneath the booth's soft lighting.

Tommy's grin widened. His hand reached for the receiver, hesitating just a second before lifting it to his mouth. A small red light blinked on.

He looked around nervously, half expecting someone to peek in.

'Hi Jess,' he said into the receiver, his voice slightly too loud at first. He adjusted, lowering it with a sheepish smile. 'I think this is on . . . hi . . .'

Wretched over the toilet bowl, Charles's body convulsed with another violent heave. The sickness tore through him like fire, relentless and cruel. He coughed hard, spitting bile.

The bathroom tiles were mercilessly cold against his skin, a cruel contrast to the fever burning beneath. Sweat clung to him, chilling fast, turning every inch of flesh to aching.

With a groan, he rolled onto his side, elbow hugging the porcelain. His forehead pressed briefly to the rim—not out of need for comfort, but from the sheer lack of strength to lift it any longer.

Light came from the comfort of the bed, casting thin shadows across the tiled walls. But around him, it was mostly darkness.

He sat, alone.

'Mary,' he whispered.

Offices of Sir Charles Kingsford Smith
Sydney, New South Wales, Australia. 1935.

A gentle knock on the office door broke the stillness.

John looked up just as it creaked open and Mary stepped in, Charles Jr. squirming in her arms. She struggled slightly with the weight of the child on one arm and a few shopping bags on the other.

'Hi John,' she said with a warm, polite smile, her voice light despite the wriggling toddler. 'We were just in the city doing a little shopping, and thought we would stop by—to see if there is any further news.'

John stood slowly, the weight of the day heavy in his spine. His eyes dropped to the letter on his desk, hands bracing either side of it.

'Not good news, I am afraid, Mary,' he said, tiredness bleeding through his tone.

Mary shifted Charles Jr. in her arms and gently lowered the bags to the floor.

'What is it?' she asked, concerned; it could be felt in her voice.

Wordlessly, John handed her the letter. She read it quickly, eyes scanning line after line, her brow furrowing.

'I . . . I do not understand, John.'

'They are refusing to pay for the *Southern Cross*,' he said quietly.

'But they already have it,' she said, bewildered.

John nodded grimly. 'The government's claiming they never agreed to purchase it—only that they *might*, someday.'

Mary blinked, disbelieving. 'John, that aircraft was the most precious thing Charles owned. *They* were the ones who wanted it preserved, memorialized. Charles didn't even want to sell it.'

'I know,' John said gently.

'Oh, John . . .' she exhaled, shaking her head. Charles Jr. began to fuss more in her arms, but she held him tighter, gently rocking.

'This is absurd. They *promised* us that money. We *need* that money. Charles is stranded in London without it—how is he supposed to get home?'

Her voice cracked near the end, not out of anger—but a helpless kind of indignation.

'Mary, I know,' John said again, the sorrow in his voice rising. 'I'm trying everything. I swear I am.' His hands lifted and fell in a defeated gesture. 'I do not know what else to do.'

Mary's eyes welled as she looked down, then back up, her jaw tightening.

'It has been months, John. I will sell the bloody house if I have to,' she snapped, more to herself than to him.

The words hung in the air.

She gasped, a hand flying to her mouth as she realized what she'd said. Her eyes flashed with guilt.

John looked at her, stricken—not because of the outburst, but because he knew she meant it.

The hotel room was quiet, dimmed by heavy curtains drawn against the London gray. Charles lay in bed, stripped to his undershirt, fever sheen glistening on his brow. A doctor moved methodically beside him, checking vitals. Charles didn't flinch. Despite the illness, it was business as usual.

Beau stood near the foot of the bed, arms crossed, tension wound tight in his shoulders as he paced back and forth.

'Word from John is . . . there is no money,' Beau said loud.

Charles turned his head, the weight of it slow. 'What do you mean there is no money?'

'The government is refusing to pay for the *Southern Cross*.'

'The three thousand?' Charles said.

Charles stared at him, the disbelief not born of surprise, but of wearied expectation.

'They are arguing you were never the rightful owner,' Beau continued. 'That Hancock never officially transferred the title. They are claiming he still owns her.'

Charles gave a low, bitter laugh. 'He gifted me the *Southern Cross*, Beau. You know that. *They* know that.'

'Everyone knows it, Charles.'

'Bastards.'

The doctor pressed a stethoscope to Charles's chest, nodding to himself as he listened. Charles winced but didn't complain.

'John is working on it,' Beau said. 'He is doing what he can.'

A beat passed.

'What time do you leave?' Charles asked.

'First light. I can stay, if you need—'

'No.' Charles shook his head. 'Get the Lockheed deal done.'

'I will contact you from the States,' Beau replied.

The doctor adjusted the covers, leaned in again with the small light, peering into Charles's eyes with clinical detachment.

Beau watched him. Then turned back to Charles.

'Are you sure you are alright?'

There was no answer. Charles simply looked him in the eyes, there was no more that needed to be said. Beau knew that look.

A soft knock landed on the door.

Footsteps echoed faintly from within, and a moment later the door swung open to reveal Tommy, his eyes lighting up the second he saw Charles.

'You are up!' he exclaimed, his face breaking into a grin. 'You have *got* to see this.'

Without waiting, he darted over to the small table inside, picking up the thin aluminum disk—the voice recording—and holding it up like a trophy.

But Charles didn't care.

'We are changing the route,' he said flatly, already stepping into the room. 'Get your gear together.'

Tommy froze, blinking. 'We are flying?' He placed the disk back down on the table.

Charles didn't answer. He moved to the desk with purpose, pushing aside a stack of papers and dropping a folded map on top of Tommy's voice recording. He spread the map wide.

'We refuel here, in Allahabad,' Charles began, jabbing his finger at the point. 'Then overfly Calcutta, Akyab, and Mingaladon. Instead of turning toward Singapore, we hold a straight course through Burma, all the way to the coast—here.'

Tommy leaned in, following the trace of Charles's finger. 'It is longer.'

'Only by seven minutes,' Charles said. 'But it saves us a stop.'

He paused, tapping once more.

'By flying the coastline, we are only over water for a hundred and fifteen miles. The direct route? Five sixty.'

Tommy nodded slowly, realization dawning. 'Safer.'

'You got it.' Charles looked up at him, the fire returning to his eyes. 'The most dangerous leg . . . ain't so dangerous anymore Tommy.'

There was no smile—only steel.

But Tommy didn't need one to know.

They were back in the air.

Down the hall, a firm knock echoed.

'Mr. Kingsford Smith?' a voice called, distant but direct. 'Mr. Kingsford Smith.'

Charles stepped out of the room, his footsteps slow. A young messenger stood at attention, crisp uniform, cap slightly tilted. The messenger approached as Charles stood at the door.

'Telegram for you, sir.'

Charles took the envelope, nodding in thanks, and returned quietly inside. He broke the seal with a steady thumb.

The paper crackled softly as he unfolded it.

"URGE YOU NOT TO FLY STOP HAVE A BAD FEELING STOP PLEASE RETURN BY SEA WILL SEND MONEY STOP LOVE MARY STOP"

He stared at the words, his breath caught somewhere behind his ribs.

A long silence.

Charles took a deep breath, folded the telegram in half, then again, tighter. He clenched it in his hand like something he could physically hold back.

'Everything all right?' Tommy asked from across the room.

Charles nodded once. 'Yeah. Everything will be fine.'

He walked past, his footsteps steady, but his eyes shadowed.

Tommy watched him go. The door clicked shut behind Charles.

He turned back to the map, smoothing it across the desk. He studied the new route, his fingers tracing the planned path once more. Then, quietly, he lifted the map and glanced down to the disk still lying there.

A half smile tugged at his lips, but it didn't reach his eyes.

'Guess I am gonna get there before you,' he murmured to himself. His hand caressed over it, as if caressing Jess herself.

Chapter 40

Lympne Aerodrome
Kent, England. 1935.

Tommy leaned over the edge of the rear cockpit, already suited up, goggles resting on his cap. The crowd pressed close around the *Lady Southern Cross*, a sea of warm farewells and reaching hands. One by one, Tommy shook them—grinning, laughing, receiving their wishes with good humor.

To one well-dressed gentleman, he pressed a small aluminum disk into his palm.

'Drop that for me, will you?' he said with a nod, gesturing toward a waiting postal crate.

The man returned the nod with assurance.

The *Lady Southern Cross* purred beneath him, her engine warming. She basked in the morning light, cloaked in admiration and history, surrounded by those who revered her legacy and the man she carried.

Elsewhere, inside the quiet and still of the hangar, Charles stood silently within the shadowed space. The atmosphere was cool, still. Dust drifted lazily through the shafts of heavenly light streaming down from above him. Alone, he pulled on his flight suit—each movement slow, deliberate. Ritual.

Within the dark shadows, a figure appeared, looming in his presence.

At first, little more than a silhouette. Hidden, his form wrapped in a long dark coat, unnoticed by Charles, he watched, waiting.

'Let me guess . . .' a voice echoed out, smooth, flat, polished. 'You are not going after my record.' The voice carried the quiet weight of someone who hadn't come to be seen.

Charles looked up.

The figure stepped forward into the light.

Scott.

A smile tugged at Charles's mouth. 'Me?' he said, grinning. 'Never.'

They stood toe to toe—adversaries, face-to-face, the smoke from Scott's cigar coiling between them like a veil.

No words were needed.

They clasped hands firmly. The grip was strong, mutual, and heavy with all that remained unsaid.

Charles gave a single nod. Patted Scott on the shoulder, then walked by him into the light.

Scott didn't follow him with his gaze. He stayed in the shadows, drawing once more from his cigar. The ember flared.

'Godspeed, my friend,' he whispered. Smoke trailed behind his words.

Charles launched himself into the cockpit.

There was no ceremony. No lingering farewell. Only purpose.

He moved with the precision of a man who had nothing left to prove—only something left to finish.

'Let's go home, Tommy!' he shouted over the engine's rising roar.

His hand gripped the throttle, and with a single surge, the *Lady Southern Cross* began her run. The propeller blurred into fury. The aircraft lifted. The airstrip fell away behind them as Charles raised his fist into the air, triumphant, defiant.

The crowd behind them erupted in cheers, hands waving, voices rising, but the sound was already lost to the sky.

The *Lady Southern Cross* was gone.

The *Lady Southern Cross* sat gracefully in a lush green field, surrounded by the rolling hills of an olive grove stretching as far as the eye could see. The leaves of the olive trees shimmered under the morning sun, and the air was filled with the faint scent of fresh olives and wildflowers. The crisp, cool breeze beneath the bright blue sky brought a refreshing chill, contrasting with the warmth of the rising sun cresting the hills.

The aircraft's engine was idle—a rare moment of stillness for the usually bustling machine.

Charles leaned back against the fuselage, heavy with the stillness of the moment, and spat an olive pip from his mouth. Nearby, Tommy paced in slow, restless circles, shuffling his boots through the grass, hands in his pockets, head lowered with impatience.

'Want one?' Charles asked, offering an olive from the pile in his palm.

Tommy remained silent.

Charles, unfazed, popped another olive into his mouth. 'They are good,' he insisted.

Tommy continued wearing down the same strip of grass he'd already walked flat before finally breaking the silence.

'Any idea why we are stuck here in an olive grove in Greece?' he asked, his frustration barely restrained.

Charles didn't respond. He simply spat another pip to the ground, his expression unreadable, though a knowing glint sparkled in his eye—a quiet appreciation for the impatience he himself, in youth, had once known.

'We are burning time we do not have,' Tommy muttered, trying again to provoke a response. 'Christ, Charles.' He threw his arms up in exasperation.

The grin on Charles's face only widened.

'This ain't funny, Charles,' Tommy snapped, angrily unzipping the front of his flying suit and yanking the sleeves down from his arms and shoulders, trying to relieve the discomfort and heat of the moment.

Charles slowly savored another olive as he watched Tommy tie the sleeves around his waist. The tight white undershirt clung to Tommy's youthful, toned frame.

'You putting on a little weight, Tommy?' Charles teased.

'Jesus, Charles.' Tommy looked down at his body, twisting in place. 'No!'

Charles laughed, then turned his attention toward a faint dust trail rising beyond the hilltop.

Tommy followed his gaze. 'Is that . . . is that *Vacuum Oil*?' he asked as the shape of a fuel truck began to take form.

'They would not let us fill up in England,' Charles said, his grin growing. 'But no one said we could not fill her up *here*.'

'We are going for the record?' Tommy's eyes lit up, flickering between disbelief and excitement.

'Oh, you bet we are.'

'We are going for the record! Woo!' Tommy whooped, rushing over and grabbing Charles's cheeks, planting an excited kiss on them.

Charles chuckled. 'Tommy, the only time a plane carries too much fuel is when it's on fire.'

'We're going for the record!' Tommy sang, spinning in place with a ridiculous, joyous shuffle. His rhythm was hopeless, but the enthusiasm was electric. Charles watched on, bemused, as he popped the final olive into his mouth and dusted his hands off. His grin lingered.

'Right on time,' he murmured, glancing at his watch. 'Right on time.'

The dirt road came alive as the Standard Oil tanker rumbled into view—large and imposing against the tranquil olive grove. The company's iconic logo gleamed on its sides as it pulled up alongside the *Lady Southern Cross*.

'Geiá sou,' the driver greeted warmly, stepping down from the cab alongside his offsider. Both men tipped their caps with easy smiles.

'Geiá sou, geiá sou,' Charles replied, shaking their hands. 'Thank you, thank you.' The driver nodded again, repeating, 'Geiá sou,' as he rubbed his brow and admired the *Lady Southern Cross*, cap in hand. His offsider moved to attach the fuel line to the intake.

Tommy bounced with enthusiasm, climbing atop the nose of the aircraft to access the fuel hatch.

The driver, clearly in awe, let out a laugh. 'Se! Se! Eísai trelós,' he exclaimed, making a wild hand gesture mimicking a plane swooping through the air.

Charles nodded, smiling. The driver shook his head in amused disbelief, slapping his cap against his thigh as he turned to start the pump.

The *Lady Southern Cross* drank deep—full to the brim.

'You could have just told me,' Tommy called down.

'Where would be the fun in that?' Charles replied.

'We will easily make up this time,' Tommy shouted.

'Get everything you can in there, Tommy. We are gonna need it.'

Charles turned to join the driver and sign the delivery papers. The driver grinned and repeated the hand gesture once more, laughing as he said again, 'Eísai trelós.' His body language said it all: He thought they were completely mad.

Mary sat quietly, gazing into space, her eyes fixed but her thoughts far away. In her mind, she wandered through memories and worries, all while gently nursing Charles Jr. through his restless sleep. The dim kitchen held a hush, the soft ticking of the clock and hum of the refrigerator her only companions. Evening had closed in fully now, desaturating the room of color. The stillness was soothing, but the long hours—stretched thin with silence and solitude—ate at her.

The phone rang.

The sudden sound tore through the calm like a snapped thread. Mary flinched, startled, then quickly shifted into motion. She cradled Charles Jr. closer, covering his ears with a protective hand, and rose from her chair to reach the phone.

'Hello,' she whispered, her voice barely audible.

A familiar voice responded—John. He apologized for calling so late.

'No, no, it's fine,' Mary said softly, eyes still on her son. Her tone was calm, but her chest tightened. She listened intently.

'When?' she asked, her voice rising slightly with surprise. 'I thought he was still sick. I thought he was not going to fly.'

She paced a slow step, her fingers curling more securely around the receiver.

'He has already left?' she echoed, the disbelief creeping in.

'When?' she asked again, breath caught. 'That soon?'

There was a long pause as she listened. Her free hand gently stroked Charles Jr.'s hair, calming him—and herself.

'No, no, it is good news, John. Really good news,' she said, her voice more certain now. 'Thank you.'

'I will. Thank you,' she repeated, softer this time, as she slowly returned the receiver to its cradle.

Mary stood there for a moment, suspended between shock and wonder, as if the air had changed but her body hadn't caught up. She looked down at Charles Jr., his little face nestled peacefully against her, and something inside her cracked open. A warmth. A lightness.

She hugged him closer, kissed the top of his head, and exhaled a breath she hadn't realized she'd been holding for days.

'Well,' she said softly, a tremble of joy in her voice.

Mary moved her little boy away, slightly, back just enough to look at him, her lips parting in a smile that bloomed like spring after a long winter.

'Guess what,' she whispered, her voice lifting into a hush of joy. 'Daddy will be home for your birthday.'

The smile stayed, radiant and tender, spreading across her face as she pressed her cheek to her son's soft, thick, golden curls. The emptiness that had haunted the quiet hours had loosened its grip, replaced by the fulfillment of promise.

Chapter 41

Rangoon, Burma. 1935.

'Tea,Oliver?'

'That would be lovely, yes sir.'

The two air traffic controllers sat tucked inside the modest tower at the edge of the field. Outside, darkness clung to the landscape. The hour had slipped well past midnight. Dim, amber lighting cast long, soft shadows across the room, doing little to rouse either man from their drowsy vigil.

Emmit stood and stepped away from the chessboard they had been quietly circling for hours.

The moon hung low and full, bathing the fields in a silvery stillness. The air was calm—motionless save for the occasional wisp of breeze rustling the rice paddies that surrounded the aerodrome like a quiet sea. Somewhere in the distance, a night bird called once and fell silent.

The kettle whistled softly. The radio crackled with faint static, rising and falling like an unseen breath. A row of clocks lined the wall above the radio, each marked for a different city—London. Rangoon. Singapore. Their ticking was steady, solemn.

'Thank you, sir,' Oliver said as Emmit poured.

They sat again, resumed their tea, and leaned in over the board.

Hard into the night, the *Lady Southern Cross* roared through the velvet sky. The hours had passed in shadows and static. Now, Burma's midnight air pressed close around them, the blackness lit only by moonlight and memory.

Tommy checked his clock, then leaned forward.

'Time: zero one hundred hours,' he called.

Charles responded with a silent thumbs-up from the front cockpit.

'Tower in minus thirty minutes,' Tommy added.

'Dropping to five hundred,' Charles called out.

'Seven thousand—dropping to five hundred,' Tommy echoed, watching the altimeter needle fall as Charles gently brought them lower.

'Altitude: five hundred,' Tommy confirmed, eyes on the instruments as the jungle below gave way to the quiet sprawl of Rangoon, tucked along the riverside like a secret whispered into the earth.

'Starboard,' Charles called.

Tommy glanced right—and gasped.

Just below the wing, the Shwedagon Pagoda rose like something imagined. Its golden spire pierced the night, illuminated in full moonlight, its sacred crown gleaming like a beacon from another world. The city bowed low around it, dwarfed by its splendor.

Tommy simply stared, gazing in awe, momentarily lost by the sight seen only by a small few from the air.

'Dropping to one hundred,' Charles said.

Tommy snapped back to the cockpit.

'One hundred?' he repeated, incredulous.

'One hundred,' Charles confirmed, eyes fixed ahead.

'Time: zero one twenty-four. Tower in minus six minutes. Altitude one hundred,' Tommy reported.

Then—alarmed—'We're *low!*' The bamboo houses and rice fields whipped by beneath them.

Charles didn't answer. He just grinned.

On the chessboard, nothing had moved. The same play still lingered, suspended in half-thought.

Then, ever so subtly, each piece began to tremble. Pawns quivered. Knights shifted. The delicate china teacups followed suit, heavier, their porcelain bodies rattling on saucers. The window panes vibrated as a low rumble crept into the room—distant at first, like thunder rolling in on dry wind.

'Earthquake?' Oliver whispered.

The vibration deepened. The pieces fell, clattering across the board as the table shuddered. The teacups skittered. The entire tower groaned. The sound was no longer distant—it filled the room, climbing up through the floorboards and into their bones.

They exchanged a look—eyes wide.

Then it hit.

BOOM.

The *Lady Southern Cross* screamed past the control tower, just feet from the glass. The whole structure shook. Maps flapped on the walls. Paper flew. The controllers ducked instinctively as the shockwave rolled through them like cannon fire.

They scrambled to the window.

The aircraft pulled sharply upward, its silhouette cutting into the moonlit sky—rising.

'*Time!*' one controller barked as he reached fast for the binoculars.

'Zero one thirty!' the other shouted, breathless, catching the aircraft through magnified lenses.

'Log it!' he yelled.

'G-ADUS,' he read as he peered.

'G-ADUS, that's Kingsford Smith,' Oliver exclaimed in awe.

Silence returned to their watch.

'Whoo!' Tommy yelled, his voice punching through the cockpit roar. 'That woke 'em up!'

He laughed, heart pounding, adrenaline still singing in his veins.

Charles grinned, glancing back over his shoulder.

'Time?' he called.

Tommy checked his logbook, flipping the page with a quick, practiced hand.

'Thirty-six thirty-two,' he replied, scribbling it down.

The *Lady Southern Cross* climbed steadily, the ground falling away beneath them. Higher and higher they rose, the lights of the earth shrinking to pinpricks against the vast black ocean of night.

Within moments, they vanished into the darkness—just a faint echo in the sky.

Sydney
New South Wales, Australia. 1935.

In the darkness of the bathroom, Mary lay motionless beneath the water, submerged in the bathtub. The porcelain was cold against her back, the water icy around her skin. Strands of her hair floated weightlessly around her face, pale and lifeless.

Tiny bubbles slipped from her lips, rising silently to the surface.

Above the waterline, somewhere in the suffocating darkness, a clock ticked—sharp, mechanical, counting the seconds with pitiless precision.

Tick. Tick. Tick.

She strained upward, but the surface felt miles away. Her lungs burned. Her hands clawed at the slick sides of the tub, scrabbling for purchase that wasn't there. Her legs kicked feebly, the heavy water dragging her down.

The blackness pressed tighter around her.

She couldn't breathe.

She couldn't reach the air.

Panic rose inside her like a scream underwater.

She was drowning.

Then—without warning—she burst upward.

'Charles!' Mary screamed, jolted awake, screaming into the silence, gasping, thrashing against the bedsheets that clung to her slick, sweat-soaked body. She sat bolt upright in her bed, chest heaving, clutching the fabric as if it could anchor her to the waking world.

The bedroom was silent—except for the ticking of the clock.

Tick. Tick. Tick.

Mary stared into the darkness, wide-eyed and trembling, every nerve in her body taut with panic.

Gulf of Martaban, Burma. 1935.

The *Lady Southern Cross* roared through the high skies, her engine humming steady and strong.

'We're just under three hours behind Scott!' Tommy yelled, leaning forward from the rear cockpit, his logbook clutched tight as he scribbled frantic calculations.

Charles remained fixed on the controls, jaw set, eyes steady on the endless horizon.

'If we maintain our current speed, we'll cut that gap, we'll drop Scott's time by at least five hours!' Tommy shouted over the engine's deep thrum, excitement sparking in his voice.

'This'll be a flight they'll *never* forget!' he added, unable to hide his grin.

Charles allowed himself a tight smile—small, knowing—his gloved hands never wavering on the stick.

'How's everything back there?' Charles called, his voice sharp and clear over the drone.

'Ninety percent power, two hundred, seven thousand feet,' Tommy called out in reply.

Charles scanned the gauges, his voice calm.

'Ninety percent power, two hundred miles per hour, seven thousand feet—confirm.'

The *Lady Southern Cross* cruised through the night sky, her engine a steady roar of precision—smooth, measured, flawless in her pursuit of performance. She moved like a shadow through the stars, suspended in the stillness of space around her. Under Charles's control, she was nearly flying herself.

In the rear cockpit, a soft amber glow from the navigation lamp cast a warm halo over Tommy's chart. He leaned in, calculating silently, his pencil dancing across the map.

The flight was near mundane. No turbulence above. No threat below. Just the Gulf stretching out smooth and endless beneath them, a mirror to the quiet skies above.

'Estimated time to land—twenty-four minutes. Dead ahead,' Tommy called, checking his figures again, eyes flicking between chart and instruments.

'Reduce speed to fifty percent. One-twenty-five,' he added.

'Reducing speed to fifty. One-twenty-five,' Charles replied, reaching for the throttle with practiced ease. He eased it back, glancing down just once to confirm. 'Power at fifty.'

'Maintain current heading,' Tommy said. Then, after a pause: 'Begin slow descent. Bring her down to five hundred feet.'

'Maintaining heading. Descending to five hundred. Mark.'

'Mark,' Tommy confirmed, starting his stopwatch as he watched the altimeter needle drift downward.

Outside, the moon gleamed across the canopy glass as the ship slowed and descended. The air was warm—a perfect dry season night. The *Lady Southern Cross* dropped lower and lower, the darkness of the ocean rising up to meet her.

There wasn't much to see. Just a few scattered lanterns below, lighting the waters to attract squid to the small fishing vessels, dots on the ink-black surface that offered the only sense of movement. Above them, a million stars spilled across the sky—majestic, magical.

'Five hundred feet,' Charles called out.

'Five hundred,' Tommy confirmed. 'Coastline in four minutes, thirty seconds,' he added, eyes locked on the stopwatch.

Charles leaned forward, improving his forward view. He looked left to port, then right to starboard. The aircraft was nearing its final turn toward Singapore, south.

'Maintain five hundred,' Tommy called again, checking the eight-day clock against his stopwatch.

Without warning a loud backfire from the exhaust, and again, the engine choked, coughing as its smooth steady rhythm became rough.

'We are losing speed,' Tommy yelled. 'Altitude dropping,' he furthered, his eyes fixed on the instrument panel.

'Carb ice,' Charles yelled. 'Carb heater on.'

'Carb heater on,' Tommy replied as he threw the switch. The engine responded, misfiring further as Charles throttled the engine to clear the problem and regain altitude.

'Altitude five hundred,' Tommy called. 'Heading one-five-three in thirty seconds. Mark.'

'Mark,' Charles replied, voice steady, scanning the panel and horizon.

Then Tommy's gaze shifted to his right. He froze.

'Coastline—starboard!' he shouted, voice cracking.

'Where?' Charles shouted.

'Starboard! Starboard! Climb, climb!'

Charles whipped his head right—and saw it.

A dark wall of jungle. Too close.

He slammed the throttle forward. The engine, still rough, misfired, coughed. He pulled back hard on the stick.

BANG.

A volley of explosive impacts hit the ship in rapid-fire succession, each imploding through the windshield—glass erupted inward, debris blasted through the cockpit. The wind screamed. Shards flew. Charles's head snapped back, the force slamming his back into the rest behind him. Blood splattered, thick, coating the cockpit and covering Tommy behind him.

'*Charles!*' Tommy screamed.

The *Lady Southern Cross* shuddered violently. The engine choked, coughed, missed—then sputtered, losing power. The nose dropped into a gut-wrenching dive.

She was falling. Fast.

Tommy lunged, grabbing the controls, pulling back hard.

'Charles!' he yelled again.

Tommy gripped the throttle, pulling it back hard, then rammed it forward, clearing the blockage.

The engine sputtered. Gasped. *Coughed.*

Then caught.

The propeller roared as Tommy fought the dive, muscles straining against the downward pull.

'Come on . . . come on . . .' he gritted through clenched teeth. 'Pull up!' Tommy begged.

The altimeter spun wildly. The airspeed screamed. The ocean was a black wall rushing up to meet them.

And still he pulled harder, gripping tightly with the full force of both hands.

'*Come on! Come on!*' Tommy gritted, the nose responded, as it began to rise as he banked starboard, using the dive's momentum to claw back control. The altimeter bounced on zero.

The tip of the wing strafed the glassy surface of the ocean, carving a fine silver wake before lifting again.

Tommy leveled the wings. '*Come on!*' he growled.

The *Lady Southern Cross* lifted, the needle bouncing upward. He banked hard to starboard again. The engine protested, coughing and rattling as he scanned ahead—then he saw it.

A beach. Flat. Empty. Safe.

He turned sharply toward it.

Gear down. Flaps dropped. Throttle eased back. The aircraft groaned as it held the turn, the beach rushing up to meet them.

'*Thirty!*' Tommy called, eyes flicking between gauge and ground. '*Twenty!*'

The airframe rattled. He eased back.

'*Ten!*'

Wings level. Stick back.

'*Five! Come on!*'

The undercarriage locked. A shrill warning sounded in the cockpit.

Then—

CRASH.

The aircraft slammed down onto the uneven sand. The landing gear compressed hard, but held. She bounced. Jolted. The cockpit rattled as Tommy fought to keep her steady. Sand and grit exploded outward as she slid to a grinding, bone-jarring stop.

Breathing hard, Tommy whipped through the checklist shutting the engine down. Silence drifted over the darkness.

'Charles!' he shouted, as he threw open the canopy. There was no response, Charles sat motionless, his head slumped forward, blood covered his lifeless face.

Tommy scrambled out, boots thudding onto the wing. The forward canopy, latched shut from the inside, Tommy reached through the shattered windscreen, unlatching it and slid the canopy back.

'Charles!' Tommy yelled again, ripping off Charles's goggles and helmet. '*Charles!*'

A faint groan. Movement.

'We down?' Charles murmured, groggy.

'We're down.'

Charles tried to move. He groaned in pain.

'You're hurt.'

'I'm okay,' Charles said, his voice graveled but steady.

'Jesus, I thought you were gone.'

'What the hell happened?' Charles asked as slowly came to.

'I don't know. Where are you hurt?' Tommy examined him quickly, hands moving fast, checking his face.

'You look alright . . .' Tommy exclaimed, confusedly as he wiped the blood from him.

'I think that's from the other chap,' Charles muttered with a faint grin.

'Christ. Can you move?'

'I think so.'

'Sit forward.'

Charles winced. 'Argh . . .'

'You good?'

'I'm good.'

'Let's get you outta there.'

Tommy hauled Charles from the cockpit, pulling him up onto the wing, then helping him to the sand below.

Charles leaned back against the wing, stretching slowly, breath heaving.

'That was definitely a ten count,' he muttered, sucking in air, not his first knockout, but a long time since.

'Stay there.' Tommy jogged toward the nose of the aircraft.

Charles lit a cigarette, the flame flickering against the dark. He exhaled slowly, trying to collect himself.

Tommy returned, slamming something wet and heavy onto the wing. The crushed remains of a massive fruit bat sprawled out grotesquely.

'Chicken, anyone?' Tommy quipped, smirking.

'Jesus.'

'Nope—bats. We must have hit dozens of them, look at the size of this one!' Tommy held up the leftover remains of its mutilated corpse. 'They are plastered all over the front of this thing.'

'At least we won't starve. Is it bad?'

'It ain't good.' Tommy vaulted onto the wing and grabbed the map from the rear cockpit. Charles handed him the lighter.

Tommy spread the map across the wing, lighting it with the flicker of flame.

'There's nothing here.'

'What do you mean?' Charles asked.

'There's nothing on the map. No land. No beach. Nothing. According to this—' Tommy traced a line with his finger '—we should be three miles offshore. We should be swimming.'

Charles looked out across the darkness.

'Are we off course?'

'No. We can't be. Look—there's land to the south. Our heading is east. By this—' he tapped the map again '—the coast should be *dead ahead*.'

'Compass?'

Tommy climbed back up, checked both cockpits.

'Identical!' he called down, jumping back to the sand. 'It doesn't make sense.'

Charles nodded slowly. 'You go that way, I'll go this way.'

They looked at each other—both uneasy, both pretending not to be.

'Right,' Tommy replied, bouncing off his heels and moving forward along the plane's starboard side to its forward direction.

Charles moved to the rear, his steps heavier, slower, limping into the darkness.

The moon bathed the scene in silver. The stars hung motionless above.

The only sound was the faint ticking of cooling metal.

They walked.

Into the unknown.

The hard packed golden sand, firm underfoot, was wet, potholed with pooled patches of water extending well into the distance. Looking back a few hundred feet toward the aircraft almost out of sight, Charles paused then kneeled, placing a palm down firmly. The sand was drenched. Scooping up a fistful, he tightened his grip, wringing the moisture from it.

Looking forward, he saw that the sand extended as far as his eyes could see. To the left, a short distance, fifty or so feet, water lapped still against the shoreline; to the right, the same. Charles stood, brushing the sand from his hand; the realization setting upon his mind, he turned quickly, moving as fast as he could back the way he came.

Tommy, running quickly, came to a halt as he reached the shoreline ahead of them, where the sand quickly tapered off into the water surrounding him. In the distance, a large protruding headland and rocky outcrop sat high in their path. The mountain reached back from high into the air to his south, the sight turning him around, causing confusion in his mind. He could see the rocky cliffs and dense jungle of the coastline ahead of him. It didn't make any sense. He quickly turned back, running hard.

'I cannot work this out. I have got land there to the south. A headland dead ahead and water all around. The coastline is dead ahead,' Tommy, out breath, explained to Charles when he reached the Altair.

'I got sand that way.' Charles pointed back. 'And sand fifty yards either side. This ain't a beach Tommy—we're on a sandspit.'

'What?'

'Show me the map. Maybe here? This island?' Charles pointed.

'It is too far south,' Tommy replied, 'we would be miles off course.'

'Here?' Charles pointed to another island.

'We would be miles out to the north. This just does not make sense. I have not missed a single mark.'

'Yeah. I know Tommy. I am thinking maybe this mark ain't even on here.'

'Uncharted?'

'Uncharted! This island ain't even on the map.'

'Can we make shore?' Tommy asked.

'That current looks like it's running north pretty hard. I don't think we could swim it.'

'Wait 'til light?' Tommy questioned.

'I don't know, if we are on a bar, this puts us at low tide on a full moon. That tide is going to pick up,' Charles shook his head. 'In about thirty minutes we're gonna be underwater.'

'We are gonna lose her?'

'Even if we swim for it, and make it, they will never find us out here Tommy.'

'What do you want to do?'

'Can we get her up?'

'We got her down,' Tommy replied.

'Check for damage,' Charles said, the urgency building in his voice. Tommy rushed to the front of the aircraft. Charles studied the map, making adjustments and calculations.

'We got prop damage,' Tommy yelled.

'Bad?'

'We have no pitch control.'

'What degree?'

'Locked in fine pitch,' Tommy yelled back. 'The intake looks clear, I can't get in there without pulling it out.'

'Can you get her up?'

'I got her down,' Tommy said again, bobbing up from under the wing. Charles folded the map, stuffing it directly into the lining of his heavy bearskin flying suit.

'I had a clear run coming in, do you want to turn her around?'

'Safer,' Charles replied. They moved quickly to the tail.

'Ready? On two,' Charles said. 'One, two.'

They both lifted and pushed, muscling hard, grunting and groaning, but the ship did not budge.

'Go again, on two! One, two.' They lifted again, harder this time, straining hard to get her to turn, their teeth gritted; failing, they dropped the tail.

'The tires are digging in, she ain't moving.'

'The sand is softening. What did you have your way?' Charles asked.

Tommy shook his head. 'I don't know, you got about two hundred feet of sand, and a three hundred foot headland to get over. It's short.'

Charles grins. 'For you maybe!' He laughed, ruffling Tommy's hair.

Tommy shook his head and laughed. 'I hate when you do that.'

'We either fly or float out of here Tommy.'

'Flying is good,' Tommy replied.

'Dump as much oil and fuel as you can, get the weight down,' Charles commanded.

Without hesitation Charles climbed up over the wing and across the front of the fuselage to the forward storage compartment, inaccessible from the ground. Opening it, he began removing every single thing from within it, one by one, dumping them to the ground.

'The tools are down there,' Charles yelled to Tommy, who rushed over for them.

'I got the supercharger clear, the rest of it should burn through,' Tommy yelled, collecting the tools before rushing back to the engine. Charles dumped their luggage, and as he threw everything clear of the aircraft, he removed the final item, the birthday gift. He paused, holding the thoughts in mind momentarily, the chaos of the situation halted as he weighed the gift in his hand. He smiled to himself as the image of his son nestled in his thoughts.

Tommy, under the wing, drained the fuel from one of the auxiliary tanks. 'We are not going to have much fuel, but it should be enough to limp in,' Tommy yelled, breaking Charles's distant thoughts; he quickly shook off his emotion and stuffed the gift inside his flying suit, over his heart.

'We are good up here,' Charles yelled back, making his way over the windshield and into the cockpit. Sliding down into the seat, he leaned forward, pushing the rest of the broken glass out, clearing his forward view.

'How are we looking Tommy?' he yelled.

'Fuels done! I'll dump the oil,' Tommy replied.

Charles checked the gauge, pulled the map from his flying suit and noted his calculations.

With the clip of a pair of pliers, Tommy worked quickly, cutting the safety wire securing the nut on the oil sump; spannering it free, he removed the penny from within it, placing it between his teeth as the oil flowed down into the bottom of the cowl. Maintaining the time, he watched the seconds tick, calculating the flow rate in his mind.

Charles stuffed the map back into his flying suit as he looked left and right checking the wing, tail flaps, and rudder, noticing the increased size of the pools surrounding them. 'Tommy! We got to go,' he yelled.

'I need another minute,' Tommy yelled.

'We don't have it,' Charles yelled urgently. Tommy returned the nut wrenching it tight, removing the penny from his clenched teeth, quickly kissing it for luck, before replacing it back into the center.

'I need a locking wire,' Tommy yelled.

'We don't have it!' Charles yelled back.

Tommy threw the wrench, raced back under the wing, and climbed up into the cockpit.

'She's good.'

'How high is the headland?' Charles yelled as they both recapped their flying helmets and goggles.

'I don't know, two fifty maybe three hundred.'

'Jesus,' Charles muttered under his breath, his eyes doubtful. He hit the button engaging the start motor, and the propeller turned slowly, one blade, two blades. Charles turned on the mags and then hit the booster. *Bang*. Nothing, the blades stopped.

'It didn't prime,' he yelled.

'Prime it again,' Tommy yelled back.

He engaged the starter motor again, re-primed the engine, closing after a few more pumps, turned on the mags and hit the booster again. As the engine slowly turned, the penny began to slowly vibrate loose.

'Tommy?'

'Keep cranking.'

BANG.

The engine fired and revved, and the force worked the penny free from the locking nut.

Charles and Tommy burst ecstatically into a victorious cheer.

'Yes!' Charles screamed.

'Yes!' Tommy yelled, as the penny slowly fell, spinning to the ground as if it had been tossed in a wager.

Charles wound up the throttle, but the aircraft didn't move.

'She's not breaking,' Charles yelled, as the wet sand slowly tightened its grip.

'Give it more,' Tommy yelled.

Charles pushed the throttle forward.

'Nothing.'

'Come on.'

'She's not breaking free.'

'I got it,' Tommy yelled, jumping from the cockpit.

'Tommy!' Charles yelled, his feet splashing wet into the sand. He fell to his knees as he scrambled to the tire. Digging deep and hard in front of the wheel as the spit slowly filled with the incoming tide, Charles held the revs hard, the force working in Tommy's favor.

Slowly the wheel started to lurch forward, lifting slightly as the aircraft rocked, wanting to move. It lifted up and over as Tommy jumped to the other wheel, digging to assist in its escape. The force of the aircraft pulling around worked the wheel free as it started to move, the wing passing slowly over Tommy's head. He stood, turning to run, as he chased down the aircraft quickly gaining speed.

'Tommy!' Charles yelled.

He lunged, diving onto the wing, catching a grip on the foothold. He struggled hard, desperately pulling his body weight forward onto the wing.

'Hit it,' Tommy yelled.

Charles throttled up the power. Their speed built as the tail wheel lifted, the tires pounding through pooled water on the wet sand.

'Go! Go! Go!' Tommy yelled as he climbed aboard and in.

'I can't get speed.'

'Hit her harder.'

'It's too early.'

'Hit it!' Tommy yelled.

Charles throttled to maximum power, the wheels lifted, then dropped, then slammed, then skimmed over the pools of puddles. The sand disappeared and the puddles turned to water as the wheels skimmed over the surface. The *Lady Southern Cross* lifted, and Charles pulled back hard on the stick.

'Yes,' Tommy yelled, punching the control panel with the palm of his hand in excitement.

'Come on. Come on!' Charles willed the ship into the air.

'Gear up!' he yelled.

Tommy hit the hydraulics. 'One hundred, climbing!'

Charles held the stick hard back.

'One fifty!'

The undercarriage slowly retracted, the alarm screamed in their ears.

'Two hundred,' Tommy yelled.

The headland loomed large before them as they climbed.

'Two fifty.'

'Trees!' Tommy yelled.

BANG.

The starboard undercarriage buckled hard in the collision, jamming the hydraulics; the force dropped the nose.

'Losing power,' Charles yelled.

The claxon, silenced, the alarm switching off as the port wheel locked into the wing.

'We're going down!' Charles screamed, skillfully finessing and feathering the controls for a water-based landing.

'Gear is up!' Tommy braced, steadfastly yelling to Charles

'Twenty feet!' he fearlessly called the descent with the assured knowledge he was in the hands of a god.

'Ten!' he called, as Charles leveled the ship, guiding her gracefully with measured authority; his face, bloodied and beaten, was consumed with a sheer defiant determination, a confidence in his strength and an ability that could only be weighed in the volume of a man who has met death many times, shaken his hand, and walked away.

'Five!' Charles breathed in a relaxing breath.

'Four!' He pulled back easy on the controls.

'Three!' His eyes were stagnant, the ship glided gracefully, within feet of the surface.

'Easy,' Charles willed quietly to himself. 'Nice and easy.'

Unaware, Charles gently eased off on the stick, The wheel caught, biting hard into the ocean, the aircraft spun sideways, the port wing dipped, digging deep into the water, cartwheeling the ship, flipping her upside down instantly, violently hurling water skyward in an explosive impact.

Chapter 42

Sydney, New South Wales, Australia. 1935.

The newly built kitchen in the Kingsford Smith residence gleamed in the soft afternoon light. The scent of fresh paint and polished wood lingered in the air, mingling with the warm aroma of steeping tea. It was a room of fresh beginnings—modern appliances, pristine countertops, and the quiet satisfaction of a home finally settling into itself.

Mary gestured around with a bright smile. 'This is the kitchen.'

Jess's eyes widened. 'Oh, Mary. It's stunning. You must be thrilled.'

'I am,' Mary said, cheeks flushed with pride. 'Thank you, Jess. Tea?'

'Please.'

Mary reached for the teapot, pouring hot water over the loose leaves. Fragrant steam curled into the air.

'So, tell me everything,' she said, smiling. 'How was the trip?'

Jess leaned in, her face alight. 'It was amazing. London is incredible, it's so big and the fashion Mary—oh my the fashion—'

A sudden, urgent knock, bashing hard at the front door, sliced through the stillness, Mary paused with concerned curiosity as her smile faltered. She wiped her hands instinctively on a towel, tension stiffening her frame as she straightened her dress.

The kettle began to whistle softly behind her.

'Hold that thought, Jess,' she said, her voice tight. She disappeared down the hall.

She opened the front door.

John stood there. Pale. Still. His eyes were heavy with the kind of dread that arrives wordlessly.

Mary's breath caught. Her grip tightened on the edge of the door.

'John. Oh God . . .' Her voice broke into a whisper. 'No. No,' Mary whispered, knowing the impromptu call could only mean something was not right.

Jess appeared behind her, sensing the shift. The kettle's whistle grew louder, shrill and rising.

'What is it, Mary?' Jess asked, the sense of alarm flickering in her voice.

John swallowed hard. 'Charles and Tommy . . . have failed to arrive in Singapore. They are missing Mary.'

Jess froze. 'Missing?' Her voice cracked. 'What do you mean missing?'

Mary leaned against the doorframe, suddenly cold. 'I don't understand. Missing—how? What do you mean they have failed to arrive?'

'They were meant to arrive in Singapore this morning, they haven't made their scheduled landing,' John said quietly. There's been no contact. No sightings. Nothing.'

'No John, it'll be fine,' Mary said quickly, too quickly. Her voice trembled. 'It's probably just a delay. I am sure it is nothing.'

Jess stared at her. 'But how do you know that? Mary, how can you say that?'

John stepped forward, calm but firm. 'Jess, listen—aircraft and ships have been dispatched out, they are searching already. I am certain they will be found.'

Jess's panic grew. 'How many planes? What do you mean searching? I don't understand—how? I don't understand.'

'Smithy's been through worse,' John said, trying to steady her. 'He's survived storms, engine failures, God knows what else. And Tommy—he could fix a motor with gum and wire. If anyone can survive this, they can. They have probably just set down on a beach somewhere, we don't know. But every effort is being made right now.'

'But they're so far . . .' Mary whispered, her voice cracking. 'John, they are so far away.'

'I know,' he said gently. 'But that doesn't mean that we need to worry. It could be anything. A forced landing. We've seen it before.'

Jess began to cry, her hands trembling. 'So they could be . . . somewhere? Still alive?'

Mary wrapped her arms around her. Jess collapsed into her shoulder, sobbing, clutching the front of Mary's blouse.

'I know, Jess,' Mary whispered through her tears. 'We just have to stay calm and wait.'

'Exactly,' John said, holding still. 'It's going to take time. But we will hear something. We will.'

The kettle screamed in the background, shrill and insistent. No one moved to silence it.

The tea sat untouched.

The kitchen—so full of life just moments before—now stood quiet, the warmth replaced with something colder, something hollow. A fragile shelter from a storm they hadn't yet seen, but could already feel coming.

Offices of Sir Charles Kingsford Smith
Sydney, New South Wales, Australia. 1935.

John stood rigid behind his desk, fury simmering just beneath his skin. His hands gripped the edge like it was the only thing anchoring him to the ground, knuckles white with pressure. From where he stood, he could see Charles's desk—and Tommy's too—both untouched, still, hauntingly empty.

The telephone was pressed tight to his ear.

'It's only been nine goddamn days,' he barked, voice taut with disbelief and rage. Before a reply could even form on the other end, he slammed the receiver down. The sharp *clack* echoed through the office like a gunshot.

In the doorway, Mary stood frozen.

Her face was pale. Her lip quivered. In her trembling hands, she held the morning paper, folded and creased with disbelief. She had stared at the headline for minutes before she could move, before she could breathe.

Slowly, she stepped forward and handed it to him.

The headline: AUSTRALIA LIFTS BAN ON AMERICAN AIRCRAFT – NEW PACIFIC ROUTE ANNOUNCED.

A smaller subhead, like a blade: NO CHANCE OF FINDING LOST FLYERS.

'John?' she asked, barely more than a breath.

He looked at her slowly, hollow-eyed. 'They're calling off the search, Mary. I'm sorry. I—' The words stumbled out, helpless and heavy.

Her breath caught in her throat. She took a step forward, as if movement alone could change what she'd just heard. 'But John . . . they can't. They *can't* call it off. Tell them to keep looking!' Her voice cracked, trembling with disbelief. 'You know he's out there, John. He's *out there*!'

Her cries burst through the silence—raw, desperate, uncontrollable.

John moved toward her, arms extended, ready to hold her, to say something, anything—

'No.'

She stepped back suddenly, arm flinging out, palm raised to stop him.

Her grief twisted midair, warping into something fierce, sharp, defiant.

'No, *no*, John!' she shouted. The words fractured the room. 'You make them keep looking! I am not giving up hope, John! I will *never* give up hope!'

Tears streamed freely down her cheeks now, blurring her eyes as she turned and ran.

The door slammed behind her—*CRACK*.

The glass panel in the center shattered, a long jagged fracture slicing clean through the name etched in gold leaf. Slivers rained to the floor.

John didn't move. He stood there, stunned, breathless, helpless in the face of grief that mirrored his own.

He raised a trembling hand to his forehead, the weight of everything pressing down.

Then, in one violent motion, he slammed his fist into the headlines.

The desk thudded under his rage.

'Where the hell are you, Smithy?' he growled, voice cracked with anguish.

Like angels, they sang.

Their voices rose softly at first, then gathered strength, growing together as one, they reverberated throughout the cathedral. The harmonies echoed against the vaulted arches, soaring above the ornate imagery of religion, each note a soul-filled prayer, floating, suspended in air.

In a pew, an elderly woman sat alone.

She was dressed with quiet dignity—a dark coat fastened neatly, a small hat veiling her silver hair. A simple handbag rested in her lap, her fingers trembling slightly against its clasp.

She held her head high, though her chin quivered faintly.

Tears rolled slowly down her cheeks. She did not wipe them away.

She watched the boys with eyes full of memory, her gaze fixed, unwavering. She listened—not just to the sound rising toward the heavens, but to what lived beneath it. In her silence, she remembered.

Her little boy, Chilla, who once stood among them. Sang with the same light, her little boy thusly named, whose spirit for adventure and daring so often sent chills down her spine, sang no more.

And now, only his memory sat beside her.

The choir steeped, deeper into song, filling that void of emptiness as she was holding him again. Gently, with a slow understanding the priest approached, sitting down on the pew beside her. He held the Bible firmly in his lap, the words within on hand if needed.

He didn't speak. There was no need.

They were in the comfort of God's presence.

Uneasy and alone, Jess stepped toward the gramophone.

The room was dim, the shadows long. Outside, the wind moved restlessly through the trees as the rain trickled gently down the glass panes but inside, there was only the sound of her breath—and the weight of something unheard, unexpected, unknown.

Her hands trembled as she reached out, fingers brushing the edge of the tonearm. She hesitated. Just for a second.

Her eyes shimmered with pain, but she didn't cry. Instead, her jaw set, her spine straightened—grief wrapped in grace, fear hidden behind the quiet determination to hear his words.

She placed the record gently on the turntable.

The aluminum disk began to spin, slow at first, then faster, until the grooves became a blur. Jess lowered the needle with the care of someone handling something sacred.

A crackle hissed in the air—soft, warm, electric.

Then his voice broke through the silence.

'Hi Jess . . .'

It was him. His voice, unmistakable. Slightly tinny through the speaker, but still full of life. That sheepish smile of his somehow carried through the sound.

'I think this is on . . .' he said, then laughed awkwardly. 'Hi. I hope this recording reaches you before I do, so you're not alone while I'm away . . .'

Jess pressed a hand to her mouth, her knees weakening, but she didn't fall. She closed her eyes, letting his voice wrap around her like he held her once more.

Like he was still here.

Home.

Beau gently slid the paperwork back across the desk to Robert.

Neither man spoke.

The silence between them said enough—they stood slowly, solemnly. No need for formality now. They shook hands, firm but quiet. A gesture of respect, and something deeper. Sadness, even if unspoken.

Beau reached for his hat, which rested on the edge of the desk. He took it carefully, as if it meant more now, his head dipping in reverence. Then, without another word, he turned and walked out.

The door closed softly behind him.

Robert sat back down slowly, the chair creaking under the weight of a moment too heavy to bear standing.

He stared at the papers for a long moment. Then picked them up, turning through the pages—contracts, agreements that could have been. Now, they felt like echoes of a future that would never arrive.

At the final page, he stopped.

Their two names, Robert Elsworth Gross and Charles Edward Kingsford Smith, side by side, in print, in black and white.

Unsigned.

Her lips trembled as she listened.

His voice continued to crackle, further into the past.

' . . . I have great news, but you can't discuss it. Charles has a big deal on the go. Beau is heading to the States soon to get things underway . . .'

Jess pressed the edge of her sleeve to her mouth, forcing herself to hold back the emotion curling behind her ribs.

The house was filled with the sound of laughter.

Children hovered over the candles of the cake Charles Jr. sat before, Mary tight behind him holding his sides in the center of it all—three years old, his cheeks flushed with excitement, curls slightly askew. He beamed as he leaned forward toward three small candles flickering atop the thick frosting.

He blew, he blew with all the breath his lungs could muster until the flames were extinguished, he breathed in deeply again and smiled to all the applause and hoorahs bestowed.

Mary smiled. She smiled, for the children. She smiled for her son.

But it was the kind of smile held together with thread. And yet, beneath her proud gaze, her heart ached. But she stood tall, wiping her eyes discreetly with a napkin.

She would not let her son's birthday be stained by absence.

'We'll be back before the end of the month. We have a great future ahead Jess. I love you, I miss you and I cannot wait to be back in your arms.'

His voice faded. Ended. The repeated crackle of the needle skipped, looped like a heartbeat.

Her hand lowered from her mouth, slowly down over her chest to the bump in her belly, to what of him she still carried within her, to what he never knew. She sobbed, unable, unwilling to hold back anymore.

Alone.

The house was quiet, empty—wrapped in the stillness of Christmas Eve. The kind of silence that felt sacred, and unbearably loud all at once.

Mary knelt beside the Christmas tree, her movements slow, deliberate. She placed a small present beneath the branches—its wrapping crisp and careful, the bow tied just so. The card attached, written in her delicate hand, read only:

To my husband, Charles.

Her fingers lingered on the box longer than necessary. She drew a breath, stood, and smoothed the front of her skirt. Her eyes glistened, but her jaw held firm. There was still hope. Faint, quiet—but alive.

Then—

A sudden, sharp *knock* at the door.

Mary flinched. Her heart lurched.

For a moment, just a moment, a glimmer of something sparked in her chest.

From the hallway, a sleepy voice called out.

'Daddy?'

Charles Jr. stood in the doorway of his bedroom, small fists rubbing his eyes, his hair tousled from sleep. His voice was soft, unsure, but hope bloomed behind it like a fragile flame.

Mary moved quickly, her breath tight as she approached the door. She opened it slowly, her heart in her throat.

A man in uniform stood on the porch.

His cap sat low, his expression unreadable.

'Yes?' she asked, voice barely steady.

The man nodded. 'Mrs. Kingsford Smith?'

'Yes.'

He held out a sealed envelope.

'Telegram. Signed delivery.'

Mary took it with both hands. 'Thank you.'

She closed the door gently behind her, the latch clicking with finality.

The envelope in her hands felt impossibly heavy. She stared at it for a moment, as if it might reveal itself without being opened—then, with trembling fingers, she broke the seal.

She unfolded the contents.

And gasped.

Her hand flew to her mouth.

Tears burst forth before she could stop them. Her knees gave way, her back hitting the door as she slid to the floor, the sob breaking loose from the center of her chest.

It wasn't a letter. Not a message. Not a miracle.

A check.   Three thousand pounds.

A government-issued payment.

Too late.

Too late to bring him home. Too late to save him.

She crumpled around the pain, shaking with sobs.

Then—

Rushed footsteps.

Charles Jr. charged toward her, half tumbling into her arms. She pulled him in close, her hands trembling as they clutched his tiny frame, desperate to hold onto something—*someone*—still here.

The check fell to the floor beside them.

'Don't cry, Mommy,' Charles Jr. whispered softly into her ear.

But the tears came harder.

'We had a deal,' Mary sobbed. 'You would always come home . . . you would *always* come home . . .'

Chapter 43

Montana, United States of America. 2018.

Charles's eyes, darkened slightly toward the inner edges with a deeper red, glistened in the light of the setting sun as they lifted from the weight of his thoughts. A long silence held the moment—an uncomfortable pause that left the air between them bereft of words, as though the memory itself clung to him with a closeness, a warmth, a caring that refused to let go.

'I remember that,' Charles said softly, his voice cracking with a dry, brittle edge. 'I remember that night . . . I remember my mother cried a lot.'

Damien exhaled slowly, his breath barely audible, as Charles's thoughts drifted between now and then.

'She held me so tightly . . . all night. Of course, I didn't understand the pain behind her tears. I couldn't.' Charles swallowed, his voice distant. 'I was only three.'

Long unspoken, the memory settled before Charles drew a deep breath to steady himself.

'Yeah,' he nodded, letting the memory pass.

'Did your mother talk about your father much?' Damien asked gently.

'A little,' Charles replied. 'But I don't think the pain ever really left her. I knew it was hard for her. I guess I didn't ask much. We moved here, to the US, when I was five. But I don't think even this far was far enough to escape the memories. Not knowing . . . that hurt her the most.'

'Hurt you?' Damien asked, a suggestion in his tone.

'More than I would admit,' Charles replied, pulling his shoulders back. Damien nodded, understanding well, as together they sat silently, letting the past breathe without the need to tidy it.

Reaching forward to the table where his cigarettes sat, Damien gently picked up the photograph resting beside them. He looked it over carefully, his eyes studying the image.

'This photo, Charles . . . it was taken the day your father left Australia. The last time he saw you. The last time you saw each other.'

Charles's eyes narrowed slightly, curiosity flickering beneath the surface. 'You know this?'

Damien nodded, pointing. 'Just here, on his uniform—you can see he's wearing two pairs of flight wings.'

Charles leaned in.

'One set is his,' Damien continued. 'The other belonged to Charles Ulm. He wore them the day he flew the *Southern Cross* for the final time—the day he left for America.'

Charles's fingers brushed the edge of the image. His hand trembled faintly, but he steadied it, his eyes focused.

'The last day I saw him?' Charles asked.

'Yes,' Damien replied.

'You know your history well,' Charles said, his voice thick with words unsaid. 'It's impressive.'

He placed the photo back down, gently.

'That said,' Charles added carefully, 'it is a history that has been written.'

'You don't believe that history, do you?' Damien asked quietly, firmly.

Charles didn't answer at once. He looked out into the stillness of the yard—the porch, the old trees, the sun casting a shifting tapestry of shadow and color that shimmered with a strange kind of wonder.

'The history is quite clear, Damien. It's been written. In black and white,' Charles said, voice flat with finality.

'But not in stone,' Damien replied. His words hung in the air like a challenge.

Charles turned to him slowly. 'It's been written. And rewritten. By people of note—experts, authors, people far more notable than you, Damien.'

'That doesn't make it right,' Damien said. There was no venom in his voice—just truth.

'No,' Charles agreed, his tone tightening. 'But it makes it the accepted truth. And that . . . is the truth I've had to accept and live with, my entire life. Despite your efforts—which I must say are commendable—I fail to see how you, or anyone else, given the time that has passed, could undo what *is* now.'

He didn't raise his voice. The quiet weight of his finality was louder than any shout.

Scratching his forehead, his thoughts piled behind his eyes, Charles spoke again.

'Damien, I was a young boy when he left. Just shy of three when my father disappeared. I grew up knowing him only through the books. He was the man every boy wanted to be. I wanted to be. My hero—alive inside me, even though he wasn't there.'

Damien said nothing. He listened.

'But as time passed, with every story, every article, every book, I held on to hope. That he was still alive. That he was living in some distant jungle or stranded on a desolate island living like Robinson Crusoe. I dreamt of finding him. Of the great adventures that would bring him home. But the older I got, the more I learned, the more I saw—he wasn't a hero. Just a drunk. A womanizer. Fame meant more to him than my mother and me.'

Charles's voice thickened.

'He left us. No words. No goodbye. So I stopped reading. Stopped caring. Stopped wanting to know.'

He paused. Let the silence settle.

'He was no hero. Whether he fell asleep, whether he was too old, whether Tommy was at the controls, whether the plane caught fire or the engine failed—I've heard every theory. And that's how he's remembered. That's the father I grew up knowing. That's the man I grew old not wanting to know.'

Charles exhaled.

'All the books, all the history—took him further from me.'

His voice cracked.

'Look, Damien. The way you tell my father's story is heartwarming. Really. But he chose his pursuits over us. He abandoned us. There's nothing heroic in that.'

'Your father died with honor, Charles. Tommy too. They made the ultimate sacrifice. That it wasn't during war doesn't diminish it,' Damien said firmly. 'They've written your father off cheaply.'

'You can't change the past,' Charles said.

'No. But you can change the future,' Damien countered. 'They deny him, in his moment of extremity, the recognition of his skill—a skill that was singular, that was genius.'

'Right there, Damien. You argue *for* them. Not *against.* The history has been written.'

'Yeah,' Damien said quietly, nodding in agreement gently. 'It has been. It has been written by people who never looked for him.'

The conversation stopped cold. A standoff.

Charles stood slowly. Damien sat, cooling. The door creaked as Charles stepped inside. It banged shut behind him like a gavel—history sentencing him.

Charles approached the sink, his hands resting heavily on the thick porcelain edge. He stared into the distant nothing of his mind, drawing in a long, deep breath before exhaling. He turned on the faucet; the water rushed over his fingers, cool and grounding. Collecting a glass, he filled it and took a slow sip—his thoughts still adrift.

Mary sat at the kitchen table, tidying a stack of paperwork, her eyes lifting over the rim of her glasses to study Charles quietly.

'Are you two doing alright out there?' she asked gently.

'Yeah,' Charles replied.

Mary stood slowly, approaching him.

'Charles, you know,' Mary began delicately, 'when your mother remarried, she insisted you keep your father's name. The Kingsford Smith name. There is a reason for that. The Kingsford Smith name is a good name.'

Charles turned toward her, feeling the quiet warmth that always existed between them.

'Though your mother may have needed to escape the past,' Mary continued, 'she never wanted you to forget it—or him. That matters. As hard as this is . . . it's important.'

She ended with a small, kind smile.

Mary's words rang true. Charles nodded, offering a faint, grateful smile in return.

'Thank you, Mary.'

The door creaked open as Charles returned to the porch. He stepped outside slowly. Damien extinguished his cigarette—the ashtray full. Charles sat again, inhaling deeply, steeling himself, then stared at Damien.

'What's it like . . . down there?' he asked.

The question came cold, unexpected. Damien's eyes closed reflexively against the memory. Behind his lids, he was there again—in the dark, cold, unfriendly depths of the ocean.

Only black.

The sound of his own breath, amplified in his ears. Inhale. Exhale. Inhale. Exhale. Each breath bubbling, strained through the regulator. And between them . . . the quiet. The awful, weighted quiet.

Crabs. Thousands of them. Claws click-clacking in the dark. Loud. Endless. Waiting for their next meal—you.

A place he never wanted to be again.

Damien's hand trembled faintly as he rubbed his eyes open.

'Dark,' he said, nodding, his voice soft.

'Quiet.' He looked at Charles.

'Peaceful,' Damien lied. He didn't want to speak the truth.

Charles nodded slightly, building the image in his mind.

'Is there much that still remains?'

'Enough,' Damien replied.

Charles drew in a long, slow breath, contemplative.

'And them?' he asked.

'I think so,' Damien said.

Charles paused, the weight of decades heavy in his lungs.

'Damien . . . you understand this is a lifetime of truth you're asking me to undo,' he said. 'Even if what you say is true Damien . . . no one's going to believe you!'

Damien nodded slowly, sadly.

'I know.'

Together, Charles and Damien sat, they agreed on that, evident in the silence that remained. Damien extended his hand as he stood. Charles looked up and shook it—firmly, respectfully.

'Say thank you to Mary for me.'

'You're welcome to stay,' Charles offered.

'I appreciate that, Charles. But I've got a little girl to get back to,' Damien replied.

He handed Charles the package. 'This is for you. Late birthday present.'

Charles accepted it with a quiet nod as Damien gathered his things.

'Thank you, Charles,' Damien said. He smiled, turned, and walked away.

Behind him, the door creaked open—Mary stepped out, gently placing a hand on Charles's shoulder as Damien faded into the distance.

With Mary by his side, Charles looked down at the package. Slowly, he began untying the string. His fingers worked carefully. The knots were stubborn—like memory.

He peeled back the paper. Lifted the lid.

A single tear welled in the corner of his eye . . . lingered, then fell.

Inside, a small toy car, once lost, corroded by time, now found.

THE END

ACKNOWLEDGMENT

To the families of those long lost—
whose love has carried across oceans and decades,
whose patience has outlasted silence,
whose hope has never dimmed—
I thank you.

To all who, across the years, have walked this path of discovery,
who gave freely of their knowledge, their time, their courage,
who believed that memory is a compass and truth a light—
I thank you.

This journey has never been easy,
but if it were, the meaning would be less.
It is in the trials that we find purpose,
it is in the unknown that we discover wonder,
and it is in the telling of stories that we bring the lost closer to home.

May this book stand as a small offering—
to perseverance, to remembrance, to the spirit that endures.
And may it carry forward the voices of those who can no longer speak,
so that their journey, though unfinished, may never be forgotten.

"Bring 'em home."

www.ingramcontent.com/pod-product-compliance
Lightning Source LLC
Chambersburg PA
CBHW030553310726
48979CB00011B/2136/J

* 9 7 8 1 9 2 3 5 0 1 5 9 1 *